Books by Jane Haseldine

THE LAST TIME SHE SAW HIM

DUPLICITY

WORTH KILLING FOR

YOU FIT THE PATTERN

Published by Kensington Publishing Corporation

WORTH KILLING FOR

A Julia Gooden Mystery

JANE HASELDINE

PINNACLE BOOKS
Kensington Publishing Corp.
www.kensingtonbooks.com

PINNACLE BOOKS are published by

Kensington Publishing Corp.
119 West 40th Street
New York, NY 10018

All Kensington titles, imprints, and distributed lines are available at special quantity discounts for bulk purchases for sales promotions, premiums, fund-raising, educational, or institutional use. Special book excerpts or customized printings can also be created to fit specific needs. For details, write or phone the office of the Kensington sales manager: Kensington Publishing Corp., 119 West 40th Street, New York, NY 10018, attn: Sales Department; phone 1-800-221-2647.

PINNACLE BOOKS and the Pinnacle logo are Reg. U.S. Pat. & TM Off.

ISBN-13: 978-0-7860-4154-1
ISBN-10: 0-7860-4154-4

First Pinnacle mass market paperback printing: March 2019

10 9 8 7 6 5 4 3 2 1

Printed in the United States of America

Electronic edition:

ISBN-13: 978-0-7860-4155-8 (e-book)
ISBN-10: 0-7860-4155-2 (e-book)

To my big brother, Michael Haseldine,
who will always be my first hero.

CHAPTER 1

Angel Perez cursed himself for the stupid-ass Run-DMC T-shirt he was wearing. Angel had ultimately caved to his pregnant girlfriend Sophie's insistence that the shirt would make him stand out in the crowd of the other day laborers, the sorry lot of them hanging around the Dearborn Home Depot like a bunch of male prostitutes in hopes of getting scooped up by a contractor looking to assemble a work crew for the day.

Five forty-five AM. Angel squinted toward the front sliding glass doors of the store to see the first flickers of light come on and prayed he could maybe earn a hundred bucks for eight to twelve hours of sheer unadulterated, dirty grunt work. Hammer, drywall, swig of Mountain Dew, take a piss, repeat.

A small trickle of wet slipped down the center of Angel's back, the first sweat of the morning, making his T-shirt stick to his skin like Velcro. Angel knew this kind of predawn summer heat meant one thing: by ten AM it would be a full-fledged swamp-ass kind of day, a phrase his dad used to use when the two of them were safely out of earshot from Angel's mom, as father and son had worked to replace the worn roof of their house seven years earlier.

Angel scanned the nearly empty parking lot a second time for any possible contractors he could approach and remembered how his dad had taught him the essential home DIY repair skills as a young teen as the two had worked to fix up their own place before his father started drinking and his childhood home was still theirs before the bank took it. The experience had left Angel with shadowy, happy memories of his dad and a pretty decent residual skill of being handy when he had to be.

"Son of a bitch," Angel said as the off-ramp continued to come up empty with cars. Angel closed his eyes and made a silent promise to himself that he wouldn't have to resort to bullshit manual labor jobs much longer.

A low rumble of hunger echoed through his empty belly, and Angel wondered how he and Sophie would make it through the rest of the week if he didn't get work today. The rent on their studio apartment was paid up through the month, and there was still a bottle of milk and some cold cuts and fruit he had left in the fridge for his girl, but they needed the extra money to pay out of pocket for Sophie's twelve-week pregnancy appointment with her doctor. They were close, man, so close. That's what Angel had gently whispered to a half-awake Sophie, who was curled up on their twin-sized mattress that lay on the floor. Angel realized he needed the positive reminder just as much as his girl did. Three more courses at Henry Ford Community College and then he'd have a job with his uncle Edgar in City Hall after he graduated with a degree in website design. His uncle Edgar was a tough man. No degree, no special favors including connecting Angel with a decent job until he earned his diploma.

"Nice shirt, dude."

Angel turned quickly to see the only other chump who had gotten to Home Depot before it opened. Angel took in the guy with the mouth and figured he was probably early thirties, tall and built, not from the gym but by an honest day's work, the kind of guy a contractor would pick first for a job instead of someone who was short and wiry, like himself. Angel turned back around and cursed under his breath as he saw a pickup truck with the name DENNIS COLE CONSTRUCTION, emblazed in red on the driver-side door, the first likely job of the day already lost to Mr. Wiseass. Angel almost felt relieved when the truck didn't approach, but instead parked on the far end of the lot, the driver killing his lights while he waited for the store to open at six.

"The guy's probably already got his team in place. Hey, I was only playing with you about your shirt, bro."

"My girl told me to wear it. She's pregnant. I've got to do what she says."

"I hear that. You were here last Tuesday, right? You were still hanging around when a bunch of us got picked up for a crew—real sweet work, too—Monday through Friday, bro, tearing down ceilings in an old warehouse in the city. All kinds of shit came flying down when we tore it up. Probably asbestos and other crap that will kill you. But we do what we gotta do to make money. You know what I'm sayin'?"

"I got work last week, too," Angel said, not bothering to shield the defensiveness in his voice. Besides, it wasn't a lie. A contractor had finally picked Angel, but he surely wasn't going to share with Mr. Asshole Big-mouth that it was because the only other guy still stand-ing had a gut on him that looked like his diet consisted of a steady intake of Ho Hos and Budweiser.

"Tell you what, bro. It's dead right now. I got a ther-mos of coffee in my car. You want some?"

Angel tried not to look at the off-ramp and tip his hand as he saw a white van coming off the highway and heading in their direction.

"Yeah, sure. That would be great."

"Good. I'm Jose. No hard feelings about the shirt, right?"

"We got no beef. Better go get that coffee before it gets cold," Angel said, and let out a deep exhale as Jose turned his back and headed to a parking area on the other side of the store just as the white van entered the lot. It slowed down for a second in front of the store, and then continued on until the vehicle came to a stop alongside Angel.

The passenger-side window cranked open, and Angel took in the contractor, a giant man with a long, black braid that trailed down his back and the still-angry pink flesh that looked like it never quite healed from a deep scar cut in the shape of a crescent that started at the corner of the contractor's left eye and descended down in a jagged hook until it ended at the man's jawline. The contractor smiled, showing off a set of gleaming white teeth against his olive skin, and Angel figured the man about to hire him must be Native American.

"You looking for work?" the big man asked. "I got a roofing job in downtown Detroit in the Lafayette neigh-borhood. Two days minimum. I just need one more guy for my crew. We start bright and early at seven. I don't tolerate slackers, but you being here before the store even opens, that gives me a real good feeling about you, even though you're a little dude. You up for the job?"

"I'm a hard worker," Angel said, really wanting to tell the contractor to go screw himself for the comment about his size. "What's the pay?"

"One hundred for the full day. We work until five. One half-hour break. It looks like you didn't bring your lunch. Don't be expecting me to feed you. If I like how you work, you can come back tomorrow, and I'll give you one twenty-five."

"Deal," Angel said, and climbed into the passenger seat just as Jose came around the corner with his thermos and two paper cups. The big contractor hit the gas and Angel didn't bother to suppress a smile as Jose shot him the finger as the van passed him.

"Friend of yours?" the man asked. He reached into his worn denim shirt breast pocket and pulled out a cigarette.

"No. The guy seemed like a douche. Hey, your van's empty. You got all your supplies at the work site already?"

The contractor stuck the tan tip of a Camel cigarette between his thick, dry lips and gestured toward the glove compartment. "Yup. Started the job yesterday. Do me a favor. Reach in there and grab my lighter."

Angel bent down far in his seat and worked for a good minute to pop the sticky glove compartment and felt a bead of sweat form on his brow as he realized the contractor was likely judging his shitty performance.

"Got it," Angel cried with a note of triumph in his

voice, which he realized sounded lame as soon as it came out of his mouth. Angel shoved his hand quickly inside the glove compartment to retrieve the lighter, and in his haste to please his temporary boss, accidentally knocked a white envelope to the floor. A half-dozen photographs spilled out, obscene stills of what looked like young men and teenage boys posed against a tree, their eyes fixed with the look of coming death. In each photo, the shaft of an arrow jutted out from the young men's chests in what looked like the precise same spot.

"You saw," the man said.

"No . . . I didn't see anything. I swear," Angel answered, trying as hard as he could to sound like everything was perfectly normal. But Angel's voice cracked on his last word, betraying his realization that he was trapped in a car with a likely monster that kept a cache of macabre souvenirs of his gruesome handiwork. Angel's eyes darted to the passenger-side window where he watched the road underneath him blur as his mind scrambled to come up with an escape plan. Angel could hear the big Indian begin to chant in a strange language and realized his only hope of survival would be to jump out of the moving vehicle. Angel slid his hand toward the right front pocket of his jeans for his keys, his only possible weapon, when the big Indian spoke again, his deep voice sounding like a potent, heavy thundercloud closing in.

"Doesn't matter if you did or you didn't. The outcome would still be the same."

The van picked up speed as it hugged the on-ramp to the highway. Angel swallowed hard and grabbed the door handle just as the locks snapped in place.

"Please, man! My girl is pregnant. You let me go and, I swear, I won't say anything," Angel begged, but the big Indian's mammoth fist came down like a bloody hammer before Angel could say another word.

It was a fever dream, it had to be, one of the really bad ones where his temperature scooted up past 105, when his mom would wake Angel up from the nightmare and hand-feed him spoonfuls of tomato soup and sips of cold water from a straw.

Angel's eyes felt sticky and his left one was swollen shut. He pried his good eye open and was hit with a sickly reality that was worse than the incessant pounding in his head as he recalled the big Indian and the pictures in the van. He quickly took in his surroundings and realized he was on the floor of a small room, wedged in the corner of the tiny space in a fetal position. Angel tried to open his mouth to speak, but his tongue felt lazy and fat as if it was affixed to the sides of his teeth.

"You're up," the big Indian said. "The small ones usually wake up sooner, since the big ones soak up the drugs real slow because of all their body fat."

Angel felt a single tear slide from his right eye and stared straight ahead at a series of tiny, scuffed letters someone had etched like a desperate SOS into the floor border directly in front of him. Angel heard the big man's footsteps thump purposefully in his direction. Before the giant hands pulled him to his feet, Angel silently read the message: *Ben Gooden was here.*

*   *   *

Angel couldn't remember how he got into the middle of the woods, or how long he had been in the little house, but it was night now, pure dark with a blanket of clouds hanging thick and low, shielding any light from the stars that could help him find his way out. Angel looked down at the wide swath of not quite dried blood on his Run-DMC T-shirt. His fuzzy mind was alert just enough to give him one instruction.

Run!

The woods seemed eerily silent as Angel tried to make his escape, but the drugs and the pummeling he took in the van from the Indian slowed him down to an uneven, inebriated gait.

With each step, Angel began to remember the big Indian, who had been dressed in all black with dark smudges of paint that seemed to nearly erase his face, telling Angel he'd give him a five-minute lead before he started the hunt.

"Get it together," Angel panted. He forced his eyes to focus and realized he was in the middle of a clearing, making him an easy target. Angel lumbered awkwardly toward a thicket of trees, his judgment still intact enough to realize if he couldn't run, he could at least hide.

"Chak, chak, chak!" a bird called out its warning.

"Blackbirds aren't red," Angel heard himself say as what appeared to be a large bloodred blackbird swoop down in his direction at breakneck speed. Angel put his hands over his head to protect himself from the oncoming assault, but the bird made a sharp ascent at the last second and was swallowed up into the night sky.

"Shit, man. I'm hallucinating. I've got to get my head straight."

A hum of mosquitoes, a likely new batch ready to feast on Angel's exposed forearms, whined in the near distance. Angel instinctively began swatting at his arms when the sound intensified, not a hum from mosquitoes he realized, but the sound of an object moving at a high rate of speed like it was splitting the air.

Angel felt the steel head of the arrow pierce his chest, and he dropped to his knees. The pain was enormous, like nothing he'd ever felt before, and his heart seemed to quiver in an agonizing, unnatural beat. Angel watched helplessly as the big Indian appeared from behind a tree and pulled a camera out from his waist pack.

"It hurts, I know. The head of the arrow pierced your heart. I'm a perfect shot, but just to be sure, I always lace my arrows with a little something extra."

Angel realized he was being dragged across the clearing. His chest felt like it would explode, and his heart would spring from his body, as the poison the big Indian had added to the arrow was quickly working its way through his system. Angel slumped forward and retched on himself, throwing up his own blood.

The big Indian dragged Angel's body to a giant oak, ready to pose him for his death shot. Angel started to think of his girl, Sophie, but the image of her face seemed to fly away and was replaced by a little boy, maybe nine years old, running through the woods for all he was worth, away from a man who looked like a younger version of the big Indian. Angel could see the boy, bathed in black and white like he was starring in a vintage slasher movie, breathing hard as his lean arms and legs ducked under branches and weaved carefully through the dense woods until he reached a road. An older-model car, which somehow looked brand-new, screeched to a stop as the boy ran in front of its path, and he waved his small hands in the air so the vehicle would be forced to see him.

"Please stop! I've got to get home before they get my sister!" the boy cried out.

Angel felt his torso being propped up against a tree. As the flash from the big Indian's camera lit up a few feet away from him, Angel felt like crying when he saw the image of the car veer to the other lane to avoid the little boy and then speed away.

Not to be defeated, the little boy ran as fast as he could and skimmed the tree line along the side of the road to avoid being seen by the big Indian. The boy followed the bend in the road up ahead of him; and when the child disappeared from sight, Angel let out one last whisper before he died, "I hope the Ben boy made it."

CHAPTER 2

Julia Gooden needed to do the first five-mile loop around Belle Isle Park alone. The unforgiving Detroit morning summer heat made her long, dark ponytail feel slick against her back, but Julia refused to let up on her punishing pace. She pushed herself even harder as she gained ground on two early-thirtysomething male joggers whom she had seen check her and another woman out earlier in the parking lot, the two men snickering like two junior-high-school boys as one obviously said something lewd about Julia to his buddy as they stretched out by their Beemer convertible, a flashy red car with an obnoxious license plate that read *C YABABY*.

Julia felt a screaming burn in her calf muscles, but ignored the pain. The Dossin Great Lakes Museum became a blur as she sprinted past it and edged her way toward the two Beemer guys ahead of her on the path. The men were likely a few years younger than Julia, who was thirty-seven, but she had no plans of letting them win. Being a crime reporter in the city of Detroit for almost fifteen years, Julia knew how to read people in an instant, and she'd bet her life that neither of the two men had to learn the cold, hard lessons she was forced to as a child, that she'd have to fight like hell each and every day just to survive. Julia smiled as she easily outpaced the two men and gave them a victory wave over her shoulder, not bothering to look back as she pounded ahead of them on the trail. Julia had survived several attempts on her life in recent years, and she surely wasn't going to let two prissy guys who thought it was okay to talk smack about women beat her.

Julia looked out at the Detroit River as she looped past the Coast Guard Station and took in the Canadian shoreline in the far distance. Belle Isle was the city's largest public park, and at 983 acres, it was even bigger than Central Park in New York. While the city of Detroit underwent the decline of the automobile industry, a painful bankruptcy, and a scourge of blight as homes and entire neighborhoods on its outskirts were abandoned, leaving many areas of the city looking like a postapocalyptic urban jungle, Belle Isle Park somehow remained untouched. It was far enough away from the city, its only physical point of connection to Detroit being the Douglas MacArthur Bridge, and provided Julia the comfort of anonymity. That was exactly what Julia wanted, a place large enough so that when she met up with her running partner, it would be unlikely that she'd bump into anyone else she knew.

Julia slowed at the meet-up spot, the James Scott Memorial Fountain, and downed half the water from her bottle, shifting her weight from foot to foot in a light jog. As a self-imposed rule, Julia had to keep moving. *Always.* Dr. Alex Bruegger, the psychiatrist she'd seen for the past seven months, and who seemed to have an endless supply of tweed coats, had finally promised he'd stop asking Julia, "How did that make you feel?" Their agreement was made during her second visit after Julia warned the shrink she'd never return otherwise. In one of their early sessions, Dr. Bruegger had asked Julia if her relentless running regimen, up to ten miles a day, six days a week, was a form of punishment for not being able to remember what had happened to her brother, Ben, the night he was abducted, despite the fact that Julia was in the same room when it happened. Julia had discovered Dr. Bruegger routinely circled back to the same theme, and in this case, his belief that much of Julia's residual pain from her childhood tragedy was self-inflicted. Julia denied the doctor's theory, which she really wanted to tell him was bullshit, but kept the real reason to herself. Deep down, in the dark folds of long-ago memories that had never let her go, Julia felt like if she could run fast enough, she could catch the monster that had snatched her nine-year-old brother when they were children. Some thirty years later, Ben's case remained cold but never forgotten, by Julia at least. So being sedentary was never an option that Julia had ever once entertained.

"Wow."

Julia turned around at the familiar voice and grinned widely at her running partner, Detroit police detective Raymond Navarro, who wore loose-fitting black shorts and a sleeveless bright blue compression shirt. The Under Armour tight-fitting top showcased Navarro's barbed wire tattoo on his left bicep and the rest of his well-developed muscles from years of lifting weights in the gym until a bullet to his shoulder recently forced him to put his disciplined workout routine on temporary hiatus until he healed.

Navarro's index finger slowly descended down the length of Julia's throat to her collarbone and wiped away a trickle of sweat before it slid any farther. "You started without me, I see."

"I got here early. Did you know the guy, James Scott, who this fountain is named after, was actually a philandering jerk?"

"Ah, so that's why you wanted to meet here, because it reminded you of another philandering jerk. If you try and vandalize the fountain as payback, you know I'm going to have to arrest you, no matter how much I like you."

"Another Sigmund Freud, just what I need. And for the record, I wasn't thinking about David. Really," Julia answered, and tried to block out an image of her once-estranged husband, David, and the dregs of all that was left of their broken marriage before he was killed.

"I'm not a jealous man, Julia. You know that. But your jogging outfit almost made me hit a tree when I pulled up."

"It's almost ninety-five degrees already. A running bra and shorts is all I can handle."

"You run with me, I don't care what you wear. I just don't want you to get hassled when you're jogging alone."

The Beemer twins, with their matching manicures

and hairless chests, turned the corner and spied Julia, prompting one of them to lean into his friend and say something that likely wasn't the Lord's Prayer. The friend donned a knowing smirk and started to laugh, but his laughter abruptly stopped as Navarro, all six feet three inches and 220 pounds of him, shot off a glance in their direction.

"Have a nice damn day, boys," Julia called out as the two passed.

"You know them?" Navarro asked.

"Just fellow joggers. We're a friendly lot."

"Right," Navarro answered, knowing Julia was feeding him a line of bull.

The Beemer boys picked up their pace as they turned the corner. Navarro then looked over his shoulder to be sure he and Julia were alone. Satisfied, he wrapped one arm around Julia's waist, pulled her body tightly against his, and gave her a deep kiss. Julia felt his hand begin to move down her bare waist and she made herself pull away.

"Hey, we're in public," Julia protested.

"I need to take advantage of the few times when I can get you alone. You know, we did a stakeout here a couple years ago. We busted a drug ring that was doing business at the other end of the park. There's a building by the lighthouse where we did the surveillance. There's not a lot of room in there, but it shouldn't be a problem."

"You can't fool around before you run. You lose your edge," she said.

"My edge, huh? Tell you what, I'm not too worried about my edge right now. You're going to kick my ass out here on these jogging trails anyway. So I'm willing to trade off one performance for another, if you're following my train of thought here."

"We're purely platonic in public. That's the deal we made."

"No one is going to be looking at us going at it inside a building that's supposed to be closed off to the public. Tell you what? If anyone looks in, I'll shoot them."

"Very funny," Julia answered. "I just want to be sure we keep a low profile, right now anyway."

"Come on, Gooden. I was just playing with you," Navarro said. He released Julia from their close embrace, but still hung on to her hand and gave it a squeeze. "I've been thinking, the Woodward Dream Cruise is coming up in a couple of weeks. I bet Logan and Will would love to go. I could take them or we could all go together. What do you say? Thousands of cool cars all cruising down Woodward Avenue. Automotive heaven, Detroit style. Your boys would have a blast."

"I know they would. But let me think about it. I need to make sure I'm not rushing things for them. I hope you understand."

"Of course. It's got to be tough for them, losing their dad."

"It's harder on Logan because he's older, and he knows what his dad did. I'm sorry if you feel like I'm shutting you out, but I need to be sure they're okay before I let them know we're together."

"Nothing to be sorry about. There's no time frame here. You tell your boys about us when you're ready. I waited eleven years to get you back, so I can wait as long as you need. But if I had my way, I'd take out a billboard on I-75 and announce it to the whole world."

"Ray Navarro, the tough cop. If people only knew your soft side, you'd lose that cool macho rep in a heartbeat," Julia said, and brushed her fingers playfully through Navarro's thick shock of dark hair. "Are we running or what?"

"Just be kind. When the shoulder heals, I'll show you up in the gym."

"Sure you will."

Julia began to toss her water bottle back in her waist pack when her cell phone buzzed. "Let me check this. Logan is at camp, and Helen was going to take Will to the zoo, but I want to be sure they're okay."

"Maybe it's your Realtor calling with an offer on your house. That penthouse is still for sale in my building. Just two stories above me and it's got a killer view," Navarro said, and gave Julia a wink. "I so love to bust your chops, Gooden. You should have seen the look on your face just now."

Julia shook her head over Navarro's taunt and reached for her cell phone, just as Navarro's phone and pager sounded in unison.

"It's the chief. I've got to take this," Navarro said. Julia looked down at her phone screen as her city editor's name, Virginia Remi, popped up. Navarro raised his finger for Julia to give him a minute, and she watched as Navarro jogged over to the other side of the fountain, so reporter and cop would be out of earshot from their respected bosses.

"Where are you?" Virginia snapped.

"Taking a run before work."

"You're going to have a heart attack running in this heat. Listen, before you get to the newsroom, can you swing by Gilbo Avenue? Hold on. Let me check my notes. The exact location is Gilbo and Lyford."

"What am I looking for? A residence?"

"A dead body. Sounds like a young guy, possibly Hispanic, male."

"Do you have anything more than that? Could be a drug overdose. There are a lot of abandoned lots down that way. You have a better marker for me?"

"Look for the cop cars. It just came over the scanner. The dead guy could be a druggy or drunk who got rolled, which isn't a story, but from the chatter on the scanner, I think it could be more than that, so check it out. Tom Spiegel is working a story about how the mayor is touting some new report that claims violent crimes are down in the city. Maybe we can tie this in as an example of how Mayor Anderson's new statistics division is manipulating data to come up with yet another bullshit report to try and make him look good."

"Always the cynic."

"That's my job. Call me if it turns out to be anything good."

Julia watched as Navarro rounded the fountain in her direction and hoped she'd never reach the point in her journalism career where she'd wonder if a man's death could hopefully turn into something good.

"Sorry, Gooden, but I have to bail on our run."

"What you got?"

"Dead male, twenty years old. Two neighborhood kids found his body dumped over on Gilbo Avenue. Between us, the vic's name is Angel Perez."

"My editor just called me with the same tip, minus the name. Did he OD?"

"It looks like he was murdered. Blunt force trauma to his head, but the cause of death, depending on what the coroner comes back with, was most likely caused by an injury to his chest."

"A stabbing?"

"The guys at the scene don't think so. Whatever killed Angel Perez was small and precise and went in deep."

"Do we know anything about Angel?"

"College kid. I've got to go down to the scene now, but I'll try and keep the other members of the press away until you get there," Navarro said, and tossed Julia the key to his apartment. "Grab a quick shower at my place and head down to Gilbo Avenue as fast as you can."

"Thanks, I'll take you up on your offer. I have my work clothes in my car. I get the feeling you know more about this guy than you're letting on."

Navarro leaned in and gave Julia a quick kiss on her forehead. "Got to go, beautiful."

"Come on, Navarro. Who is he?"

"Between us. Angel Perez is the nephew of Edgar Sanchez."

"The city councilman?"

"The one and only," Navarro answered. "Sanchez is apparently losing his mind. He's holding a press conference in a couple of hours."

"Okay. Thanks for this. I mean it."

"Keep it under wraps, but this could turn out to be a bigger story than you think. Whoever killed Angel Perez likely did it with a bow and arrow."

"Are you serious? That's got to be a first."

"Not according to the chief. Linderman just told me there have been other victims killed the same way."

"If it's a serial killer, how come I haven't heard anything about it?"

"Linderman just told me the last body was found a long time ago, so the cops figured the killer had died or moved away."

Julia felt a cool shiver run through her. "So the killer is out of hibernation and ready to hunt again."

"Maybe, but why would this guy take such a long break? Doesn't fit the normal profile."

Julia stared vacantly through the swollen sail of a boat that was skimming across the water and felt the familiar grip of desperation and loss squeeze her tight.

"The past is never really over for any of us. I'm betting not even for a killer."

CHAPTER 3

Kirk Fleming slid a cool hundred into the valet's palm as he picked up his car at the Atheneum Hotel.

Fleming would have preferred the presidential suite at the MGM Grand Detroit, the city's most luxurious hotel, but he knew he had to lay low during this trip. The valet, whom Fleming pegged for maybe twenty-five tops, obviously had never received this big of a tip in his entire young life, since he stared down at the bill in his hand as if he took his eyes off it for even a second, it would disappear.

Fleming was dying for one grand showboat move, but unfortunately, being the big tipper at the not even five-star-hotel was going to have to be it. Now that he was back in Michigan, Fleming was savvy enough to realize he'd have to hover way below the radar or he'd be killed. Two shots to the back of his head from a gun with a silencer, execution style. No question, baby.

The people he was up against in Detroit were far different than the garden-variety criminals he had got-

ten used to since he left Michigan. Fleming prided
himself on being exceptional at the razzle-dazzle and
separating people from their cash. But Fleming was
now back on his old home turf, and he'd have to stay
two steps ahead of the big dogs if he was going to live
and cash in on the prize of his life.

"Thank you so much, sir!" the valet said, and pumped
Fleming's hand up and down until Fleming started to
wonder if the kid was ever going to give it up. The hotel
employee opened the driver-side door of Fleming's
rental car, a black Ford Explorer, the only SUV in the
Detroit airport rent-a-car lot Fleming could find with
tinted windows. Fleming had wanted to treat himself
to the BMW convertible or the jet-blue Maserati he had
looked at wistfully in the luxury car section of Enter-
prise. That would have been his reward for making it
through customs, having charmed a female agent in a
putty-colored polyester suit that wasn't doing her any
favors. But Fleming had begrudgingly opted for the
Explorer, since it was pedestrian enough that he'd
blend right in.

The rental car smelled like cinnamon-scented air
freshener as he got in. Fleming blasted the air condi-
tioner to combat the heat and to try and get the cloying
smell out as he carefully drove the Explorer just below
the speed limit for the entirety of three city blocks. He
then took a hard right into an alleyway, pulled out a
new license plate from his briefcase, and did a quick
presto chango with the rental car company's original
plate. Fleming couldn't afford to be traced. He had
paid for his lowly standard queen-sized room in cash
and stole the new license plate from a Prius in the
long-term airport parking lot the evening prior. He had

covered his tracks and replaced the Prius's plate with another stolen one so when the car's owner returned from God knows where, they likely wouldn't notice.

The Explorer cruised onto M-10 and passed the Joe Louis Arena. Fleming self-consciously tugged at the cuff of his soft pink Italian-made long-sleeved shirt as he drove. Late July in Detroit and here he was with every part of his body covered, except his hands, neck, and face. Fleming owned no Polo shirts, no T-shirts, and, God forbid, one of those flimsy tank tops that looked like it came straight from the Walmart rack. If he didn't still have the damn scars from the fire that scorched his arms above the wrist, he wouldn't need to always cover up.

Fleming snapped open a briefcase on the passenger-side floor that held his designer dark glasses inside. He placed them on the bridge of his nose and eased his Smith & Wesson out of his case, placing it on the console next to him. His eye caught the leather binder that held his cache of passports, each with a different name: Brock Valentine, Stanley Sterling, and George Le Troc. He wedged the binder deeper into his three-thousand-dollar leather briefcase. When the passports were safely out of sight, including the one with his latest alias, Kirk Fleming, he closed the case with a quick, one-handed zip.

The I-75 on-ramp sign appeared in the distance just as a series of beeps sounded from the SUV's console.

"Son of a gun," Fleming said. The tank had been full when he got the car from the lot, but now the low fuel light was on. Fleming had been bone-weary when he picked up the car last night after three consecutive flights, starting from Punta Cana International Airport in the Dominican Republic, to JFK, and then back home to good old Detroit, a place he hadn't seen in years. But no amount of fatigue could keep Fleming from making the trek north even if it was just to pass by what he'd been fixated on for the past three decades.

The plan to return to Detroit was quickly set in motion just a week prior, when Fleming had called his old colleague Chip Haskell, to whom he'd paid five grand a year for the past thirty years to store Fleming's property. But even more so, the money was paid every fifth of the month, always on time, to ensure Haskell kept his mouth shut.

Back in the Dominican Republic, Fleming had gotten word that he might have a narrow window to return and make a quick grab, in and out, for what was rightfully his. Fleming didn't need to think twice about the opportunity. He wasn't a man who cooled his heels and waited for someone else to call the shots, but Haskell had insisted they wait until this morning to meet, and then they'd go to Haskell's hiding place to do the exchange. Fleming wasn't excited he had to wait an extra day to claim his property, or the fact that he had dropped a total of $150,000 to Haskell through the years, but in the scheme of things, the money was chump change.

Fleming searched for a gas station as the revitalized downtown core of Detroit slipped away. The glut of abandoned buildings and houses in the outlying neighborhoods surprised him, the Detroit of his youth now looking like a cesspool, just a bunch of turds circling around a just-cleaned, peroxided drain. But he felt no nostalgia. Fleming had long ago blocked out any memories of Michigan and what he left behind. Memories were dangerous, like live grenades if you picked one up. Fleming's lifelong mantra, which hung just below the surface of his cement shell, was *"If you don't think about the past, it's like it never happened."*

A tug of anticipation pulled in Fleming's gut as he eased the Explorer in front of a pump. Fleming pushed his designer shades farther up the bridge of his nose to conceal his bright, piercing blue eyes. He was in his sixties now and knew he no longer looked like his younger self, who once thought he'd own the city of Detroit one day. But with age, he had realized how to better not get his ass handed to him, so Fleming knew he'd have to be extra careful as not to be recognized.

Fleming plunged the nozzle into the tank and watched as a large, white SUV maneuvered a quick three-point turn and then a hurried reverse into the only available gas pump space left, which was right in front of him. The white SUV jerked to a stop, leaving just a few inches of space between its bumper and the Explorer's grille. Fleming wanted to give the pushy driver a dose of hell for boxing him in, but kept his mouth shut as a woman in a pastel lavender-and-turquoise paisley dress got out. Fleming stared anonymously through his dark glasses at the well-dressed woman's back. He could see the woman was trim and had long, thick, dark hair, which hung halfway down her back.

The gas pump pinged as the nozzle to the Explorer shut off, the tank now full. Fleming tucked the nozzle back in its cradle, feeling slightly disappointed that he wouldn't get the chance to see the woman's face. He grabbed his receipt and felt an annoying trickle of sweat ease down his temple. Without thinking, Fleming quickly removed his dark glasses so he could wipe it away.

As if on cue, the female in the paisley dress turned around. Fleming felt his breath catch as he saw her face, one that he could never forget despite the passage of time. She was a woman now, but Fleming knew the person standing just a few feet away from him was Julia Gooden, with the same high cheekbones, dark hair, and large blue eyes that he remembered from so long ago.

Fleming quickly turned away, pushed his dark glasses back on his face, and reached for the driver-side door.

But it was too late. Julia Gooden had seen him.

Fleming stared at Julia's reflection from the car door window for a second and watched as an expression of realization and surprise spread across her face. A haunted look seemed to pass over her eyes, but then it was gone as quickly as it came. Julia Gooden stuck her hands on her hips defiantly, and her eyes turned into accusatory slits.

"Hold on!" Julia called out as Fleming hurriedly got back in the Explorer and quickly snapped the locks in place.

He jammed the Explorer in reverse and hightailed it out of the parking lot just as Julia's car got sandwiched between a newly arrived RV and a small sports car, which had zipped in and had taken Fleming's place at the pump.

Fleming watched Julia from his rearview mirror as she took a picture of his vehicle with her phone and then scribbled something down in what looked like a skinny reporter's notebook, likely his license plate number, Fleming realized. He then watched Julia say something that he was pretty sure he could make out as: "You son of a bitch."

Fleming shook his head as his shitty karma began to hit him. Less than one day back in the city, Detroit was turning into a mother-freaking bad-luck charm. Kirk Fleming knew he'd have to rip off another license plate, but the bigger problem was that he'd just been made.

Despite the deep throb that began pulsating in his left temple from the fresh mess, Fleming found himself smiling. He watched Julia disappear in his mirror and allowed himself just one brief flicker of sentimentality before he went cold again.

"That's my girl," Julia's father said.

CHAPTER 4

Julia sat in her car across the street from the Gilbo Avenue crime scene and realized her hands were shaking after having to face down the one thing that terrified her most, not the criminals on her beat or even the people who had tried to kill her. Julia easily knew her greatest fear was the dark side of her childhood, something she had tried to beat back for good and thought she had succeeded in doing after working as hard as she could to create a stable life for herself and her sons.

The face of the man at the gas station kept coming back to her. Julia was certain the person she had seen was her father, Benjamin "Duke" Gooden Sr., who along with her mother, Marjorie, a drunk, had abandoned Julia and her older sister, Sarah, right after Ben disappeared. She and Sarah, who was fourteen at the time, had lived alone in their sorry excuse for a house without their parents until they couldn't stand being hungry anymore after all the food in the refrigerator and the pantry was gone. Julia closed her eyes at the sudden memory of their neighbor in Sparrow who had called social services after Julia and Sarah had shown up at her doorstep like frail, forgotten waifs, begging for food. After a week of being shuffled around in the family court system, Julia and Sarah had moved in with their aunt Carol, not a perfect situation, since Julia always felt like an inconvenience, but she had fared better than Sarah. Her sister had started getting into trouble and was eventually sent into the foster care system, the experience leaving Sarah not even close to ever being the same again and on a path that turned her into a shady hustler, just like their dad.

Julia slunk down in the seat, ashamed and disappointed in herself over her unexpected emotional reaction over seeing the man who abandoned her. She silently cursed herself for being so weak. Julia knew she wasn't that seven-year-old kid anymore who could be hurt or left behind. She looked down at her hands and tried to convince herself that she was a grown woman, a good mother, and a respected reporter. But after all these years, her father could still manipulate her feelings like she was still a powerless, unimportant child.

A cop car slowed as it cruised by Julia's SUV, but she looked away and instead stared into the field where the body of the now-deceased Angel Perez still likely lay. Right now, Julia couldn't concentrate on the story she needed to write as memories of her childhood came fast and quick, and there was nothing she could do to stop them.

"Where's Ben?" a seven-year-old Julia asked her parents, who were sitting around a cheap card table cov-

ered with a maroon vinyl tablecloth. A nearly empty bottle of gin sat between Marjorie Gooden and a strange man Duke had brought home.

"He's watching the New York Yankees game downstairs," Duke responded. Her father gave the stranger one of his big, dazzling smiles, and Julia noticed the familiar light that shone from Duke's eyes, as if something so special was about to happen, it had ignited a blazing fire inside him. Julia knew this look well. It meant Duke Gooden had a sucker in his crosshairs, and her father was about to pounce.

"Now, Jim," Duke addressed the stranger. "I don't think you realize what a genius I have on my hands. Tell me, Julia, what's the square root of twenty-five?"

Julia knew the answer was five. She had no idea what a square root was, but Duke had made her memorize the answer so she could perform like some sort of clever circus act in front of Duke's "guests." Julia's reward from Duke usually was a pack of bubble gum or a candy bar whenever she got the answer right. When she didn't, Duke never hit her, not even once, but his sulky silence or, worse, his crushing criticism that she'd let him down again were punishment enough.

"That's easy. The answer is five, Daddy."

"Smart girl," Jim answered. Julia could tell that even though the Jim stranger was sitting down, the man was short and pear-shaped like one of the Humpty Dumpty twins and had a tangle of dark, wiry hair on each knuckle. "She looks just like her mother, but she's got your eyes, Duke."

"Both my girls are stunners, but my youngest, my Julia, she's smart, too. Now come here, my little delight. Look inside the palm of my right hand. What do you see?"

"A quarter," Julia responded.

"Yes, a quarter. Now I want you to make a wish."

Julia closed her eyes and pretended to concentrate as hard as she could, just like her daddy had told her when they rehearsed. It was all part of the act.

"What's your wish?" her father asked.

"I'd like my quarter back," Julia recited.

As expected, the man her dad was trying to con—Jim with the hairy knuckles—started laughing.

Duke then handed the quarter over to his wife, Marjorie, and blew hard into his empty, closed fist.

"That's not much of a trick," Jim said.

"Trick's not done yet, my friend." Duke made a dramatic, sweeping motion with his arm, reached behind Julia's ear, and then extended his hand toward his would-be client. There, in Duke's open palm, was the original quarter.

Jim clapped his hands together and reached for the gin bottle. "Good trick."

Before Jim could grasp it, Marjorie quickly grabbed the bottle and poured the last few inches of booze into her glass, giving her houseguest a careless shrug.

Julia had always thought her mother was a beauty. Marjorie was in her thirties and had a figure a man would fight to the death for, Duke liked to say. Marjorie had thick, dark hair and an olive complexion from her Italian heritage, giving her an exotic look. But Julia had noticed her mother's face had started to change, and now often looked haggard and puffy, and her eyes took on a glazed, vacant expression every time she "overindulged." That's what Duke called it when her mother drank too much.

Duke hurried over to a cabinet in the kitchen to refuel his guest, but came up empty.

"Sorry about that, Jim. Tell you what. I'll run out and get another bottle for you. Never had a taste for liquor myself, but I don't have a problem with people who do," Duke said. He grabbed his coat, a suede jacket that Marjorie had scolded him for purchasing, since they couldn't afford to buy new winter jackets for their own three kids, yet Duke "had the balls" to blow money they could use to feed and clothe their kids on himself, Marjorie had yelled. But that was last year. Something had changed in her mother since, Julia had noticed, like the light had gone out in her eyes and she didn't even bother to fight for her kids anymore.

"Think a little harder about that real estate investment we talked about, Jim," Duke said. "All I need is ten thousand dollars down, and I guarantee I'll be able to turn that into a cool million in less than a year. Detroit is going to be a developer's paradise one day. Investing now in the future of the city is going to make us all rich. Now, Julia, be a good little delight and don't cause Jim or your mom any trouble while I'm gone. Not that she would. Julia acts more like an adult than one of those mouthy kids you see disrespecting their parents."

Julia watched as the front door closed. An uneasiness seemed to slither through her tummy as Marjorie stood up and walked past Julia, slipping her finger across her youngest daughter's shoulder as she went. Julia tried to grab her mother's hand and was able to *graze her wrist, causing Marjorie to stop for a second and turn around.*

"Make me a promise," Marjorie said to Julia.

"Okay," Julia said uneasily.

"Don't ever become a girl like me," Marjorie answered. Her dark eyes hung on Julia until she turned around and, in uneven steps, continued her way down the hallway toward her and Duke's bedroom.

"Wait, Mom," Julia called out.

"Just tell Julia if you need anything," Marjorie told the guest. "I'm going to lay down for a little while. What was your name again?"

"Jim. Jim Donnenfeld."

"Right, Mr. Donnenfeld. Duke will be back in two shakes," Marjorie said; the word "shakes" sounded more like "snakes" as the booze began to kick in.

Julia started to call out for her mother one more time, but the door to Duke and Marjorie's bedroom had already closed.

Now that she was alone with the stranger, Jim patted the seat next to him for Julia to sit.

The strange feeling in her stomach returned, and Julia instinctively ran away from the man her dad had brought home and downstairs to the basement to search for Ben. She flicked on the light, praying she'd see Ben, and heard the scuttle of cockroaches scurrying across the floor and over the near-empty pizza boxes that were tossed carelessly around the room. The Goodens' shabby black-and-white TV set, its rabbit ears taped together in Ben's jerry-rigged attempt to try and get a better signal, was off, which meant Ben wasn't downstairs anymore because the game was over.

Julia looked at the basement door to the backyard and thought about sneaking outside, but decided Ben was probably upstairs in the room they shared. Julia willed her footsteps to remain silent as not to draw attention to herself. But as soon as she reached the landing, Jim was waiting for her.

"Julia's your name, right? That's real pretty," Jim said.

"I'm looking for my brother," Julia stuttered.

"Is that your room? Why don't you show it to me?"

"My mom is going to be out in a second."

"No, she's not, honey. Your mom's out cold. I just checked," Jim said, leaning in close to Julia. She hunched her shoulders to try and make herself as small as possible, and she could feel Jim's breath against her cheek, smelling like garlic, cigarettes, and the sour mash of booze.

"Come on. Jim's not going to hurt you. We have to hurry before your daddy gets back."

Jim glided his hand to Julia's waist and then down the smooth line of her child's thigh, giving it a pat, while he steered Julia toward her bedroom.

"Get your hands off my sister!" Ben yelled as he appeared from the other end of the hallway and ran in Julia's direction. "You get away from Julia, or I'm calling the cops."

Jim dropped his stubby hand from Julia's waist and backed up a few paces.

"No need to be rude, boy. I was just trying to be nice. Your parents left me in charge. Your mom is sleeping and your dad went to the store," he said.

"I'm in charge. Now get out," Ben said. "You're a disgusting creep and don't think I won't tell the police

that. You come back here again, you'll regret it," Ben
called out as Jim the disgusting creep slowly backed
his way toward the front door. Ben was only nine, but
his fist shook in the air, and his cheeks were red and
shiny, like he was about to erupt.

"Your mom is a stinking drunk, and your dad is full
of shit," Jim countered. "Tell Duke the deal is off.
You've got some anger issues, boy."

The front door slammed shut, and Ben ran to the
window. He watched until Jim's car peeled out from its
place on the street and took off down the road.

"Are you okay? Did that guy do anything to you?"
Ben asked.

Julia felt a sharp pain move across her body as the
adrenaline began to pump through her as she let down
her guard, knowing that Ben had saved her.

"I didn't know where you were!" Julia cried.

"You're fine, kid," Ben said. He pulled Julia to his
thin chest and stroked the back of his little sister's hair.
"Daddy's got to stop bringing those losers around."

The front door swung open and Ben pushed Julia
behind him, expecting to see Jim after the man Duke
brought home came to the embarrassing realization
he'd been intimidated by a fourth grader.

But Duke stepped inside, instead, with a brown
paper bag in his left hand. He looked past his two
youngest children and offered up his widest smile to
the man he thought would still be sitting at the card
table.

"Where did my client go?" Duke asked.

"That man was about to do something really bad to
Julia, Daddy. I made him leave."

"You made him what?" Duke answered very slowly.

The shark smile had vanished and his lip curled back in disappointment as he looked down at his only son.

"Mom was passed out drunk again. That guy tried to get Julia to go into her bedroom alone with him. We should call the police."

Duke dropped the bottle in the brown paper bag down hard on the counter and raked his fingers through his sandy blond hair.

"Did Jim touch you, Julia?" Duke asked. He got down on his knees and took Julia's hand.

"He touched me right here," Julia said, and patted her thigh with her small hand. "He wanted me to go in my bedroom with him. Then Ben got here and started yelling at him. Ben made him leave."

"That guy was a loser, Daddy!" Ben fought back. "These people you keep bringing around the house, they're creeps. I don't want them around Julia anymore."

"You don't get to decide, Ben. This is my house."

"Until we get evicted or you go to jail again. If you won't take care of Julia, I will."

"I'm sorry about what happened, Julia. If I ever see Jim again, he'll be lucky if he can walk after I get through with him. Your brother did a good job looking out for you."

"I was just scared is all. Ben saved me. I'm fine now, Daddy," Julia answered.

"No, she's not. You hang out with creeps," Ben said.

"You need to learn about the world, son. There's good in bad people and bad in good people. You walk a fine line and take what you need from the bad ones and hope the small part of them that's good will keep you safe. But you don't count on it and you use your *smarts. Jim was a bad one. I know that now. I don't like most of the people I bring by here. I just play the game so we can all get ahead."*

"Your game stinks," Ben said. "Come on, Julia. Let's get out of here."

Ben led Julia outside, and the two sat on the front porch's warped step and stared silently at their dad's newly waxed Chrysler.

"Is Daddy going to call the police?" Julia asked.

"No way."

"Maybe we should tell someone else, like a teacher. They could help us," Julia said.

"Anyone who comes down from the school is going to call social services or the police," Ben said. "They'll see Daddy has a record, and if they show up and we're alone, or if Mom is passed out drunk, they'll put us all in foster care. They'll split us up and I won't be able to take care of you. I need to make sure we stick together."

"What are we going to do?" Julia asked.

"I'm not sure. But we're going to be all right. I don't know how, but we will."

Julia needed to find her center, so she reached into her bag and eased out her wallet, finding her safe place, two small pictures she carried with her always.

The first photo, now a small, weathered square, was Ben's fourth-grade school picture, the one police had used in his missing person's photo. In the picture, Ben's jet-black hair was shiny and his large, dark eyes turned up on the ends, just like their mother's had. Ben smiled with an air of confidence in the picture, even though he and the rest of the Gooden family were dirt-poor back then, despite Duke's big dreams. Julia felt her face flush in embarrassment as she recalled how everyone in Sparrow seemed to know her mom bought her and Ben the cheapest of cheap sneakers at the A&P grocery store when the Goodens could afford it.

The second photo was one she had taken of her two sons at the beginning of the summer during a getaway to Lake Huron. Logan was trying to smile in the photo, but every mother knows her child's true face. Julia recognized the trace of hurt still lingering in Logan's expression, even though Julia knew he was trying to be the good boy, and not show the hurt he was feeling inside over the loss of his father.

Most people thought Logan looked like Julia, but Julia knew her oldest son was a dead ringer for Ben. In contrast, her three-year-old son, Will, was blond and fair, taking after David. Julia allowed herself to feel the tender ache of residual memory of her and Ben as she looked on lovingly at the picture of her two boys. Logan had his arm around Will's waist in the photo, her oldest son already understanding his lifetime responsibility to watch out for his younger brother.

A fierce sense of protectiveness almost overwhelmed Julia as she took in the image of her little boys. In the past, Julia had fought to the death for her children, and she knew she'd do it again, over and over, as long as they would be safe. How Duke and Marjorie Gooden could carelessly abandon their own flesh and blood like they were worthless pieces of trash, especially after Ben was abducted, would never be anything Julia could ever understand, let alone forgive.

Julia slid the pictures back into her wallet and reached

for her tape recorder and old-school reporter's notebook. It was go time, whether she was ready or not.

The crime scene was cordoned off in a large, deep square. Julia had purposely parked on the other side of the large lot, away from the majority of the cop cars that were parked along Gilbo Avenue. She'd worked the crime beat long enough to know most of the players, but some of the newer cops who felt like they had something to prove would likely block her from entering the crime scene, while the veterans usually let her in, at least momentarily.

Dry weeds from a rainless summer scratched against Julia's calves as she picked her way under the yellow tape and followed what looked like a man-made path toward the far end of the lot, where Angel Perez's body likely lay.

Six cops stood in the near distance, a few were huddled over the body, and another small group was gathered around Chief John Linderman, who was impossible to miss with his bright red hair and physique that could intimidate Andre the Giant. Navarro was on the periphery of the group talking to a medical examiner from the coroner's office.

Linderman, still a street cop at heart, made Julia in an instant and signaled with a slight nod of his head for one of the officers in the huddle to go deal with her.

Linderman's pick, Navarro's partner, Detective Leroy Russell, approached Julia and greeted her by tapping a finger against his watch. Russell was in his early fifties and had worn a Mr. Clean buzz cut since Julia had first met Russell some twelve years earlier.

"I was wondering when you were going to show. I was given orders to keep the looky-loos and the press out, but Linderman says if you have a specific question, he'll talk to you, but you need to make it quick before the media vultures get here, you not included, of course."

"I appreciate it."

"You okay, Julia? You look kind of, what's the word my mom used to say? Peaked. That's it. Your kids all right?"

"Everyone is fine," Julia answered, and switched gears so Russell wouldn't pry any further. "Have I told you how happy I am that you're back at work?"

"I cut my medical leave short. I had no choice. Ray would have gotten his ass shot out on the street without me. How are you and my partner doing?"

"What do you mean?"

"Come on, Julia. I've known for a while. Ray didn't tell me, if that's what you're thinking. The guy is smiling all the time now, and he's usually a sullen, brooding bastard, even on his best days. The only time I've ever seen him this happy was when the two of you were first together when we were all kids. Okay, when you and Ray were kids."

"Ray and I are just friends."

"It's me you're talking to here."

"You're a bad liar, Russell. Did Navarro say something to you?"

"Ray didn't tell me. I swear. I saw you guys a couple of months ago outside of Ray's building after I'd gotten out of the hospital. I thought I'd surprise Ray and take him out to dinner for saving my life in the Packard Plant. I pulled up across the street from Ray's place just as the two of you came out. I saw Ray walk you to your car, and he didn't exactly give you a kiss like he'd give his cousin, if you know what I mean."

"Mouth shut on this, Russell. I'm asking you as a friend. My kids have been through a lot, and I don't want the word to get out before I tell them first."

"You got it. I'm happy for you guys."

"There's a dead man over there. Let's shelve the conversation about my personal life, okay?"

"Just trying to lighten the mood. Crime scenes are kind of a downer, in case you haven't noticed, and we're going to be here for a while."

"Do you have a profile on the killer yet?" Julia asked.

Russell looked over his shoulder at the chief.

"Let's walk and talk. Make it fast."

"I understand there have been other victims killed with a bow and arrow, but this is the first one in a long time. Is this a copycat, or do the police think the killer came out of hibernation?"

"We don't know for sure. Linderman says there were three people who died the same way, all male. The first body was found around thirty years ago."

"There was nothing about this in the press. I checked on the way over here. Not one story. Why is that?"

"I don't know. Ask Linderman. He was working patrol when the first body was found. Corporal Stanger jogged the chief's memory when we got the call about Perez's body. Same type of kill like the one he saw when he was starting out on patrol."

The two walked in silence as they approached the body of Angel Perez, who was lying on his back, facing the sky. Angel's eyes were open wide, as if still chronicling the horror of the last moments of his life. His hands were curled into clawlike fists and lay posed in a crisscross fashion over his stomach. A thick patch of dried vomit caked the right side of his face, and Angel's T-shirt was stained red, the darkest bloom coming from the area surrounding the left part of his chest.

"Run-DMC. They played the Palace last summer," Russell said.

Linderman shot his detective a look and then gave Julia a slight nod of recognition.

"Miss Gooden. You seem to be under the impression that you're an honorary member of the Detroit Police Department," Linderman said. The chief wore one of his trademark suits. This one was dark blue and was undoubtedly soaking up the scorching sun. But the elements didn't matter. Linderman always made it a point to dress the part of the boss, lest anyone forget.

"Not at all, sir. I'm just trying to figure out what happened to Mr. Perez," Julia answered.

"That's our job. You're not allowed here, Julia. You know that. But if you've got a question, ask it now," Linderman said, and motioned for Julia to follow him, away from his officers and the unobstructed view from Gilbo Avenue, in case another member of the press showed up and caught Linderman possibly giving the scoop to the competition.

"I understand this may be the work of a serial killer who's been dormant for a while. Is that right?" Julia asked.

"I'm not going to bother asking who your source is on this. But what I will ask is that you wait to write anything about a possible serial killer angle until after Councilman Sanchez's press conference."

"I can't do that, Chief."

"I'm not a fan of bargaining over a dead man, but I'll give you something if you hold off. Edgar is a mess about his nephew. Angel's girlfriend is pregnant, and that boy had a bright future ahead of him. He was about to graduate from community college next month, and then he was going to work for Edgar in City Hall. It's a damn tragedy for that family. I gave Edgar my word I'd try my best to keep the possible connection to the other victims away from the media until he had the chance to do the press conference. Edgar wants the killer found, no doubt, but he doesn't want the memory of his nephew to get lost in the 'serial killer on the loose again' headlines that you people are going to run."

"I don't want to disrespect the victim or his family, but you and I both know how this works. If I know something and don't write it, and I get beat by the competition, I'll have hell to pay. I need something more than that."

"You hold off until Edgar gets his chance to memorialize his nephew to the public, you'll be the one breaking the story. I'll make sure none of my guys leak it. You have my word. You can use me as an unnamed, high-ranking source in the department, and I'll fill in some of the blanks. Deal?"

"I'm trusting you that the story won't get out," Julia conceded. "What do you know about the killer?"

"Right now, we think it could be the same person who killed three other victims spanning over several decades. It was a good call by one of our corporals who put it together. Granted, it's been a long lapse between the last killing and Angel Perez, but I've seen almost every way a person can be murdered, and I can safely say a bow and arrow is not a typical way to kill someone as a preferred method."

"You think the person who did this is a hunter? There are plenty of people in Michigan who bow hunt."

"Whatever he is, he's an expert. To kill a person with an arrow and hit them in about exactly the same spot in the chest each time takes remarkable skill and practice. The big link will be what we find in Mr. Perez's toxicology report."

"Drugs?"

"Not that the victims took willingly. The other three victims all had traces of arsenic and Rohypnol in their systems."

"Rohypnol. That's better known as 'roofie,' right?"

"The one and only. The date rape drug."

"You think the victims met the killer in a bar?"

"I'm not sure with Mr. Perez. But it's highly unlikely with the other victims."

"When was the first man found?"

"Not a man. It was a teenage boy. Vietnamese kid. Back in the summer around thirty years ago, my partner and I were on patrol and took a call about a really foul smell coming from a Dumpster behind the old Tiger Stadium. We found the kid. He was maybe fourteen years old. We were never able to get an ID on him. We didn't have the missing persons' databases that we have today, but my partner and I searched everywhere. The Vietnamese community here is pretty tight, but no one knew the kid."

"So someone local is lying to cover it up, or the victim is from somewhere else."

"That was our theory back then. Two years after the Vietnamese kid, we found another body. This time the male was a little older, seventeen and small, like Perez and the first victim. His name was Jackie Morgan and he was a runaway. His mom was a crackhead and was too stoned to report her own son missing."

"You said there was a third victim."

"That's the first long break. Another victim was found in ninety-eight. Stephen Johnson. He was a male prostitute. His body was found dumped in an abandoned lot in Highland Park. Same cause of death, same type of vic, small guy, dark hair."

"The media never picked this up. Three killings, the victims murdered in a ceremonial style with a bow and arrow, and no word gets out to the public that there may be a serial killer on the loose in Detroit? If the victims were related to a city councilman or the CEO of Ford, is that the only way they'd be worth a story?"

"There was press coverage, but only news briefs that ran about the three victims. The chief at the time didn't want the bow-and-arrow information out there because he didn't want to give the killer any glory that might fuel him to kill again."

"I don't buy that. You need to let the public know."

"Nothing was covered up here by the department, and I don't want that angle coming out."

Julia didn't respond to the chief's veiled threat, because if she found out there was a cover-up in the department for any reason, she wouldn't hold back.

"Like you said, the time between when the male prostitute was killed and now Angel Perez, that's a long time," Julia said.

"Off the record, we're looking at guys who served lengthy sentences for other crimes who may have been popped loose recently."

"So the cops catch the killer for something else, the killings stop for all these years because he's in jail, and Angel Perez gets murdered because the guy is finally free to start up again?"

"It's a theory," Linderman said.

Navarro broke from the medical examiner and made a beeline in Julia's direction. Julia felt a small strum go off inside her, not because she was worried about dealing with Navarro in a professional setting. They'd worked together for years, both as a couple in the early days and then later as friends, and never had they once crossed a professional boundary. Julia's internal reaction over seeing Navarro was completely visceral. After more than twelve years of knowing him, Navarro still had a way of making Julia feel like a high-school girl head over heels with her first big crush.

"Hey, Julia. I need to break up your sidebar here with the chief," Navarro said. "Don't turn around, but I'm pretty sure I caught the reflection of someone across the street on the second floor of that blue house, the one directly across from us. I think the guy's got a camera."

"A photographer?" Julia asked. "He's not with me. If he snuck in there to get a shot of Angel Perez, you know my paper doesn't run pictures of dead bodies. Not in good taste."

"You and Russell checked that house when you were knocking on doors, talking to neighbors?" Linderman asked.

"Yeah. No one answered," Russell said as he sidled up to his partner. "The place is a dump and smells like cat piss. We figured it for abandoned. The guy snapping photos probably did, too, and found an opportunity to be an asshole."

"Circle the place from the back, get inside with Navarro, and see what you got. If it's a photographer trying to snap pictures of the body, don't let him leave without erasing the memory card on his camera," Linderman said.

"You think it could be the killer?" Julia asked.

"No. I doubt he'd be dumb enough to stick around and take pictures to chronicle his work with a swarm of cops around his kill," Linderman answered.

Navarro motioned for Russell and then the two got into their unmarked Crown Victoria, which Julia knew was a decoy move. She figured the partners would likely drive a couple of blocks until they were out of sight, and then backtrack by foot to the blue house, jump the fence to the rear yard, and then enter through a back window. She'd been on a few stakeouts with the duo to know their MO as well as she knew her own.

Julia started to come up with her next question for Linderman, but the sudden image of Duke's face staring back at her in the gas station stopped her cold.

("I'm trying to build something for this family and all you do is just tear it all down.")

"Is that it, Julia? You come up with anything else, call me or Navarro."

Julia scrambled to go back to her center, but her father had once again tripped her up. She cursed herself under her breath as Linderman walked away, and felt ashamed that she had broken a cardinal rule. When you're on the job, leave your personal business at home.

"Hey, man, don't touch the camera!"

The front door of the two-story blue house across the street banged open and a man with dark hair that fell to his shoulders and a tall, ropy build came out. Navarro was a half step behind him, carrying the photographer's camera in one hand and the collar of the photographer's shirt with the other, as Russell took up the rear.

As the man approached, Julia realized he wasn't a familiar face from the usual players in the local freelance photography pool, the majority of them former staff shooters at major daily metros who were now scrambling to make a living after getting laid off from the still-smarting newspaper industry.

Julia placed the photographer with the thick mane of dark hair for midthirties. He had large, brown eyes, an olive complexion, and full lips that almost looked like they would be better suited on the face of a woman.

"I didn't do anything wrong," the photographer protested, trying to grab his camera back from Navarro.

"Trespassing," Navarro said. "That's thirty days in jail."

"Come on, man," the photographer pleaded. He looked over at Julia and his eyes lit up, as if he were just handed a "get out of jail free" card before his slow walk to the electric chair. "That's Julia Gooden. I'm with her."

Navarro loosened his death grip and looked over at Julia for confirmation.

"Hold on a second," Julia said. "Did Fish send you here? The chief photographer?"

"I was told to get my ass down to Gilbo Avenue to

shoot the crime scene before the other media showed up if I wanted to get paid," the photographer answered.

"That sounds like Robert Fishman. I'm sorry, Navarro. He must be a freelancer who doesn't know the rules. Before you erase his memory card, let me talk to him first."

Julia ducked under the crime scene tape and crossed the street.

The photographer stuck out his hand for Julia to shake, but she stood firm with her hands at her sides.

"Don't leave me hanging with everyone watching," the man said. "My name is Phoenix, and you're a legend."

"And you're obviously new and just screwed up royally. It's hard enough to get cops to trust you, but they're never going to trust you now."

"I was just trying to get the shot."

"Of a bloodied-up dead man with vomit stuck to the side of his face?" Julia asked. "I have no problem with you doing whatever it takes to get the picture, but that's not a picture the paper would run. Grab a couple of shots of the perimeter of the crime scene, the cops, Linderman, but no dead bodies. We're not *TMZ*."

Phoenix gave Julia a charming but jaded smile. He grabbed Julia's hand, and before she could pull away, he gave it a soft kiss.

"It's great to finally meet you," Phoenix said. "I've seen your picture in the paper."

"Hey, pretty boy. You can kiss Julia's hand, but don't bother trying to kiss her ass," Russell said. "She'll likely cover for you if you've got an assignment with her paper, regardless of your low-life, scumbag move back there."

"I'll tell you this just once, and after that I won't have your back. But don't pull stunts like this again. Find some better pictures if you don't get kicked out first," Julia said.

"You snuck into the crime scene and saw the body. What's the difference?" Phoenix asked.

"I look at the body, and it makes me work harder to tell his story and find out what happened."

"The pure of heart. I heard that about you."

"There's a press conference in a few hours. Every media outlet will be there. These things are staged, but check with Fish to see what he wants. I'd say take a few pictures there, but track down Angel's family first, see if you can get some old photographs of him and take some pictures of the family if they let you. But don't be a jerk about it. Grieving people are a lot more willing to share if you're compassionate."

"Let me shadow you, and I'll buy you lunch later. What do you say? I could use some tips from a pro," Phoenix said. He inched closer to Julia, invading her personal space, and she backed away.

"I've got somewhere to go right now. Give me your number. If I find out anything, I'll give you a call."

"You're not going to the press conference?" Phoenix asked.

"I'm going to see if Virginia can put the city reporter on it."

"A big story like this and you're not going to chase it down?" Phoenix asked.

"Like I said, I've got something to take care of," Julia answered.

"I hope we'll work together again. Can I walk you to your car?" he asked.

"No, I'm good. Navarro, you got a second?"

Navarro tossed the camera over to Russell.

"You know the drill," Navarro told his partner as he stared down Phoenix.

"I swear. I won't give the paper the pictures of the dead guy. Please, man, just give me my camera back. I'm sorry and it won't happen again, I swear."

Russell looked over at Navarro, who shrugged, and Russell handed Phoenix his camera back.

Navarro then escorted Julia back to her car, and the pair walked in a comfortable silence until they were out of earshot from anyone else.

"Mr. Charming back there. Phoenix, last name unknown, the hand kisser. Next thing you know, he'll be throwing his coat over a puddle so your feet won't get wet. I love it when guys hit on you in front of me, and I can't do anything about it," Navarro said.

"He wasn't hitting on me. He was just trying to get in my good graces so you wouldn't pulverize his camera."

"You're living in denial, baby. You're leaving pretty quick. Are you going to try and track down Angel Perez's girlfriend? Her name is Sophie, and she shared an apartment with Angel over in Dearborn. Twelve weeks pregnant. You'll likely not get much from her. The poor thing is a mess. But she's at Sanchez's house. The whole family is there. I'm sure he's expecting you to at least call."

"I'm going to write up what I have from Linderman and then hand the story off for now."

"You've never passed on a story, especially a big one."

"I'll come back to it. I have something I have to take

care of this afternoon, and I need you to do me a favor."

"Anything," Navarro promised, his deep-set hazel eyes stayed on Julia and she knew he meant it.

"I know you're wrapped up in the Angel Perez case, but if you get a break, I need you to run a name for me."

"Is this for a story?"

"No. It's personal."

"Who am I tracking?"

"Benjamin Gooden Sr. He used to go by Duke."

"Your dad? You never wanted me to help you look for your parents before."

"I know, but I'm sure I just saw him at a gas station. He's older now, but I know it was him. I haven't seen him in thirty years, but I'll never forget his face. The bastard looked right at me, and I could tell he knew who I was. And then he took off like a bat out of hell."

"Listen, if the guy you just saw was your father, don't let him get to you. A man abandons his kids and never looks back, especially after his son goes missing, he's not worth looking for. Your sister, Sarah, and your dad, those aren't people you want in your life. We're happy, Julia. I've finally got you back. I'll stick by you no matter what you decide, but I know what this does to you. You get down deep in a dark rabbit hole when you start digging around about your past, and sometimes I'm afraid you're not going to come back out."

"I'll be okay."

"I'll be sure you are. But if that was your dad, he just rejected you again by pretending he didn't know you."

"I don't want anything from him. I just want to know. Seeing him made it real."

"Okay. If you want me to run the trace, you know I'll do it."

Navarro opened the door of Julia's SUV and she slid into the driver seat.

"Where are you going?" Navarro asked.

"To Sparrow."

"There's nothing but bad memories for you there."

"I haven't been to Sparrow in a long time. I can't tell you why, but I feel like I need to go back there now."

"I'll run Duke's name and call you later. I'd kiss you goodbye if I could."

Instead, Navarro discreetly rapped his fist against his heart. As he walked away, Julia put the SUV into drive and took one last look at the crime scene. A new batch of police officers and a TV news van had arrived. Phoenix snapped a frame of Julia's car as she drove by and then he flashed her a thumbs-up sign.

Julia thought about what she had lost in Sparrow when she was seven years old, making her too distracted to notice the beige car parked three blocks away pull out from the curb and hang back far enough so Julia would-n't notice she was being followed.

Jameson, the tail for Duke Gooden's youngest kid, waited in his Band-Aid–colored sedan on the corner of Mt. Olivet Street and Gilbo Avenue and crushed out his cigarette when his target, Julia Gooden, unexpectedly walked away from the crime scene with a big cop. Jameson didn't mind the stakeouts too much. He liked watching the swish of the paisley fabric from Julia's dress seal against her hips when she walked, but he preferred his women with more meat on their bones. A grade-A ass was something you could hold on to in bed, not something you could barely find when you're reaching down to get a firm hold of the thing you were riding.

Jameson was parked one street over from Gilbo, on the other side of a large playground that gave him a perfect view of Julia and her SUV. After his new boss got a recent and solid tip that Duke Gooden was actually alive and hadn't died in the fire the big Indian set thirty years earlier, Jameson was assigned to watch Duke's youngest daughter. Jameson had his doubts, but he wasn't paid to give his opinions, so he kept his mouth shut when his new boss said he had intelligence that Duke Gooden was back on his old home turf of Detroit. Jameson's job was to keep a tail on Julia in the event that she could lead them to Duke, but more important, to what Duke Gooden stole three decades earlier.

Jameson counted to thirty and spun out a perfect trail of smoke rings from his mouth as he watched Julia get in her car and drive away from the big cop. Jameson gave her just enough time to get a small lead so she wouldn't notice him drop in line a few cars behind her.

Jameson reached for his phone and speed-dialed the last number that called him.

"The funeral just ended. What do you got?"

"She's moving," Jameson answered. "You said she'd be at the crime scene for a while, but it's only been, like, twenty minutes. What do you want me to do?"

"What do you think? Follow her."

"You think Duke's really alive?" Jameson asked.

"I bugged the phones. I'm sure he's the guy who called Chip Haskell."

"The Gooden chick just got on the highway going north."

"She's going to Sparrow. I knew it. She's probably going to meet Duke there. Now listen. If Duke shows up, keep him alive until I get there. Don't kill him. We need to find out where he hid it."

"What about the daughter?"

"You need me to draw you a map? If she doesn't lead you to Duke, bring her here. If Julia doesn't give up where Duke is, then we kill her."

CHAPTER 5

Julia finished writing her part of the Angel Perez story from her car and e-mailed it to her city editor, letting Virginia know she would need to get the city beat reporter to cover Edgar Sanchez's press conference, and she'd pick the story up after that. Two minutes after hitting the send button, Julia ignored two back-to-back calls from Virginia, obviously wanting a better explanation on why Julia wouldn't be there to cover it herself.

Julia sat in her SUV, which was now parked across from her childhood home in Sparrow, the town that had taken so much from her, and she wondered why the memory of a bad man and the sins done in his prime had prompted her to return.

"I'm not a kid anymore," Julia whispered as she took in her childhood home, one of the many that she had lived in after Duke had gotten the Gooden family evicted a half-dozen times for not being able to pay the rent. But this was the last place where they were all together, and the last place she had seen her brother.

The house was much smaller than Julia had remembered, but it still looked shabby. The home from her childhood was an old, run-down ranch, with peeling blue paint and an unkempt yard now thick with weeds, meaning it was likely unoccupied, or whoever lived there was as careless and neglectful as Duke and Marjorie Gooden had been.

The Gooden family had moved to the house in Sparrow's Limetown neighborhood, the poor part of town, four months before Ben's abduction. But Julia and Ben had thought the dumpy little house was a palace, because they had spent the previous weeks living in Duke's Chrysler after getting evicted from a cramped one-bedroom apartment.

Julia tried to get herself to start the car so she could get the hell out of there, the flight instinct kicking in as she realized she needed to leave Sparrow immediately. But she couldn't. As she slipped down the dark rabbit hole of memories that Navarro had warned her about, Julia knew Ben wouldn't be there to pick up the pieces this time.

"Come on, kid. Get up. I made something for you."

Julia shot up from the thin mattress of her cot and looked up to see Ben holding a small brown paper bag that he had decorated with crescent moons and stars with a purple crayon. Purple was her favorite color.

"Happy seventh birthday, Julia. It's not much, but I hope you'll like it."

Julia tore the tape away from the top of the bag and dug her hand inside, pulling out an incredible stash of loot for a Gooden: a pack of Bubble Yum bubble gum, a Little Debbie Cinnamon Streusel Cake, and a silver dime-store bracelet with a charm of a little boy and girl holding hands.

"Oh, my gosh, Ben. Thank you!" Julia cried, and threw her arms around Ben's neck.

"You don't think the bracelet is corny?"

"No, I love it!"

"They have other bracelets you might like better. I got it at Peterson's. Mr. Cole gave me ten dollars after I weeded his backyard. I told him I was going to buy you a birthday present with the money, and he drove me to Peterson's to pick it up. The other bracelets, they had flowers and hearts for charms. Girl stuff you might like better. But Mr. Peterson said if I was going to use all the money I earned on a present for my sister, then the charm with the boy and girl would be better because it would remind you that you've got a brother who puts you first. You sure you like it?"

"Yes. It's perfect. I love it," Julia said. She held the bracelet in her hand and stared down at the charm in wonder. Birthday surprises were rare in the Gooden family, and Julia squeezed her eyes tight, wishing this moment would never end.

Ben then eased a ten-dollar bill out of his pocket and gave Julia a wink.

"I got it from my paper route," he said.

"Ten dollars. Can I touch it?" Julia asked.

Ben let out a deep belly laugh. "Tell you what. You can hold on to it for me. Come on, let's go get breakfast. I got a big day planned for us."

Julia followed her brother out to the kitchen with the bracelet still safely in the palm of one hand and the ten-dollar bill tucked tightly in her other. She smiled to herself as she realized it was going to be a great birthday, probably the best one she'd ever had.

Duke stood in the center of the kitchen, wearing a long-sleeved, button-down, light blue dress shirt that just covered the bottom of his white underwear, as he worked an iron carefully over a pair of dark blue dress pants.

"Damn it. I've got a spot on these. Marjorie, didn't you take my pants to the Laundromat, like I asked? You know I have a big meeting today in Detroit."

Julia waited for a response, but when there was none, she figured her mother must still be sleeping.

"I swear, I've got to do everything in this house," Duke muttered, and began to run a hand towel under the cold tap of the sink. "Good thing it's going to stop."

"Dad, it's Julia's birthday," Ben said.

"Oh right. Happy birthday, my little delight," Duke said. He gave Julia a quick smile and then turned back to the ironing board as he scrubbed the wet cloth over the stain in his trousers. "Listen, son, do you have a couple of dollars you could lend your old man from your paper route? I need enough gas money to make it to Detroit. You lend me ten bucks, I'll pay you twenty when I get back. This meeting I have is going to be huge. It's going to be Easy Street from here on out for the Gooden family. The man I'm meeting with is going to change our lives."

"Sorry. But I don't have any money," Ben lied.

Duke pulled his pants on and tucked the shirttails inside.

"What do you say, birthday girl? How does your old man look?" Duke asked.

Julia couldn't help but smile at her father, who re-

minded her of the grown-up actor Paul Newman. Duke had taken Julia and Ben to see his movie The Sting *at a place that showed old movies. Julia had sat on Duke's lap, not understanding the movie at all, and had buried her face against her dad's shoulder during the violent scenes. After the show let out, Duke proclaimed it was, without a doubt, "the finest cinema I have ever seen."*

"You look handsome, Daddy. Like a movie star."

Duke smiled his dazzling smile and bent down so he was at eye level with Julia.

"Tell you what. I'm going to take you out for a big dinner tonight when I get home. But your daddy needs enough money to get to a very big meeting with a very important man. Could you do your daddy a big favor?"

"Sure," Julia promised.

"You're friends with that family next door. What's that girl's name?"

"Melinda?"

"Right, that kid. Go next door and ask her if she'd loan you ten dollars. Tell her you need it to buy your mom a present, and you'll pay her back."

"That's a lie," Julia said.

Duke flashed Julia another big smile and reached for her hand, but Julia snatched it back and hid both her hands behind her back.

"What you got there that you're trying so hard to hide from me?"

Julia opened her mouth to answer, when the sound of her mother retching in the bathroom stopped her cold.

Duke's mouth turned into a disappointed line. "Your mother overindulged again. That kind of behavior could make a man want to stay away for good."

"I'll go help her," Ben said, and launched into his usual routine. He grabbed a Styrofoam cup and filled it with water from the tap and shook out three Bayer aspirins from a jumbo bottle and headed down the hall.

"Is she all right?" Julia asked.

"Fine. She's just under a lot of stress, but our money situation is getting ready to change. Have you ever dreamed of being rich?" Duke asked.

"I don't really know. I'd just like to have enough money so we can stay in one place for a while."

"Never settle, young lady. Money is the key to happiness. You can have love, but if you don't have money to go along with it, then you'll never really be happy."

Julia's fourteen-year-old sister, Sarah, came into the kitchen, holding her nose. "Something's wrong with Mom. I just walked by the bathroom and it smells like something died in there when Ben cracked the door open."

"You know what's wrong with her. You still have any money left over from that modeling pageant you were in?" Duke asked. "I've got to get into the city."

"Spent," Sarah said. Sarah was tall and trim, with thick, blond hair and green eyes. Marjorie and Duke had pushed her into entering a local beauty pageant a month prior, where she came in second place, raking in a whopping thirty-dollar prize and free modeling lessons at Barbizon. "I used it to buy headshots. The photographer was going to give me a big discount if I let him take a couple of pictures without my shirt on, but the guy was a creep."

Sarah pulled out the last piece of Wonder Bread, scraped the mold off, and slathered a thin layer of mar-

garine over the top and then coated it with a package of brown sugar.

"Smart move. Make wise choices about your body, Sarah. You're a pretty girl and you're going to need that to marry a rich man one day. Julia, she's got the smarts in the family. We got some letter from the school saying she reads at the level of a sixth grader. Imagine being that smart," Duke said to Sarah. "Your sister is only six, but she's probably smarter than you. Don't worry about it, though. Some people are born with beauty and others are given brains. Julia, she's a rarity. She's got both."

"Seven, Daddy. I turned seven today. I'm not six anymore," Julia said.

"It doesn't matter how old you are. You're still an idiot baby," Sarah snapped, turning on Julia over Duke's hurtful comment.

"Don't talk that way about your siblings. You're going to need to step up when I'm gone."

"Where are you going, Daddy?" Julia asked, but Duke answered with just a wink.

Sarah stuck out her tongue at Duke, grabbed her coat, and headed out the front door.

"It's your sister's birthday," Duke called out to her.

"Happy birthday, idiot baby," Sarah said. When Duke turned his back away from Sarah, she shot him and Julia the finger and then shut the door behind her.

"Why's she so mean?" Julia asked. "She got mad at me for being in the bathroom too long and smacked me on the butt so hard, it left a big red handprint. I didn't tell Ben, because I knew he'd be so mad, I didn't know what he'd do to her."

"*Don't you worry about Sarah. She's just going through some growing pains that happen when you hit the teenage years. Now, my Julia, let me see your hand. I think I know what you're trying to hide from me.*"

Julia reluctantly gave her father the hand that held the bracelet Ben had given her.

"*My, my. That's a beauty. Let me put that on for you.*"

Duke clasped the cheap bracelet around Julia's wrist, and she was sure she had never seen anything quite as beautiful as she admired it.

"*Now, it was your other hand I was talking about.*"

Duke's eyes fell down to Julia's throat as she swallowed hard and her Adam's apple bobbed up and down, giving her nerves away.

"*No need to be scared around your daddy. Now come on. Do as you're told. Don't disappoint me, Julia. You know how much that hurts me.*"

Julia's eyes filled with tears as she slowly brought her right hand out from behind her back and Duke pulled it toward him.

"*I need to talk to Ben,*" Julia cried.

"*He's helping your mother. Now come on, open that hand up. Don't disobey me.*"

Julia's hand trembled as she opened up her small fist. The smile that spread across her father's face when he saw the ten-dollar bill made Julia feel sick to her stomach.

Duke carefully grabbed the money and slid it into his pants pocket.

"*Just as I thought. Birthday money. It's always the sweetest. Now, what's with the tears? I'll buy you the biggest steak dinner tonight when I get home later. I know that's your brother's money. He won't mind, and I'll triple his loan when I get home."*

Julia nodded, but she knew her dad was lying when he grabbed his old suitcase by the front door. She stood stalk still as Duke whistled some old Frank Sinatra song she'd heard him listen to on his record player. He picked up the car keys to his Chrysler, spun around, and gave Julia a big wink.

"See you soon. And happy birthday, kid."

Julia pounded her fist against her leg as the shame of what she did hit her. She wanted to run outside and beg Duke to give her Ben's hard-earned money back. But the Chrysler roared to life, and Duke navigated it out of the driveway until it disappeared down their road.

"Are you ready?" Ben asked.

Julia turned to see her brother, who was now in the kitchen unplugging the iron Duke had left on.

"You put the bracelet on. It looks nice. How come you look sad?"

"Something happened," Julia cried. She stared down at the floor, unable to face Ben. "Daddy took the ten dollars! It's my fault. I should have told him no, but he made me show him what was in my hand and then he took it. I'm sorry. I should have fought harder for you. You would have done that for me."

Ben's eyes closed into angry, determined slits and he shoved his hands into the pockets of his shorts.

"That jerk," Ben said, his voice suddenly sounding deeper and much older than his nine years.

"I ruined everything. It was going to be a special day."

"It's okay," Ben answered, softening his tone. "Come on. Mr. Cole said he could use his lawn mowed if I had time. I told him I was twelve so he wouldn't think I was too little to work hard, and he's got a push mower, so I'll be fine. We'll get the ten dollars back another way. Then we'll go down to the boardwalk and ride the bumper cars. Sound good?"

Ben's dark eyes now looked warm and hopeful, and the terrible feeling that Julia had carried that she had disappointed him eased.

"I promise. You'll still have a great day," Ben said.

Julia trailed her brother outside and watched as Ben picked up a rock and pelted it in the direction of their father's tire tracks in the gravel.

"How come you never give up?" Julia asked.

"What do you mean?"

"You act like everything is okay, when it's not."

Ben kept his gaze leveled at the flies buzzing around the mountain of discarded junk and garbage that had been piling up for weeks next to the fence on the side of their house.

"I have to. I can't give up," Ben answered.

"How come?" Julia asked.

"Because I've got you to take care of. Come on, let's go see if Mr. Cole is home."

Julia fell in place alongside Ben, her brother standing closest to the road to protect her from any passing cars, as they started the trek to their old neighbor's house three miles away. Julia didn't mind the walk, though, and heard herself sigh with contentment. Things were going to come right. Ben would make sure of it.

But Duke left the Gooden family for good that day.

And Ben was abducted a month later.

*   *   *

Julia got out of the car and tried to block out the Frank Sinatra song her father sang the day he abandoned the Gooden family, but it kept playing in a nonstop loop in her head. She walked along the broken path to the front door, wondering what in the hell she was doing, and rang the bell. When no one answered, she opened the gate to the fence that led to the backyard. Her heart beat triple time as she followed the route to the outside patio and the sliding glass screen door that led to the bedroom she had shared with Ben, the place she had last seen him after they fell asleep the night he was taken.

The flimsy metal screen in front of the glass door fell away in Julia's hand as she tried to open it, and she threw it on the yellowed grass. She wiped away a circle of dirt from the sliding glass door and tried to peer inside when she felt something small and solid shove itself into her lower back.

"You scream, I'll kill you."

A large hand spun Julia around and she looked way up to see a very pale, bald man with a tiny, thin nose. He had on a black suit and held his gun steady at her chest.

"Where is he?" the man demanded.

"Who are you talking about?"

"Your dad. Is he inside?"

"I have no idea. I haven't seen my father in years."

"I hate liars. You're meeting him here, aren't you?" the pale man asked. As he moved in closer, the air between them filled with the foul smell of dead cigarette smoke.

"My dad's an asshole," Julia answered. "I haven't

seen him in over thirty years. If you find out where he is, do me a favor and tell him to go to hell."

The pale man started to smile and then backhanded Julia across the face. "Let me ask again. Where's Duke?"

"Nobody hits me," Julia warned, and dove her hand inside her purse for the folding knife with the three-inch blade she always carried.

The pale man's free hand grabbed Julia roughly by the shoulder, and he pushed her in front of him, with the gun now wedged in the familiar place in the small of her back.

"Walk," he commanded.

"Who are you?" Julia asked.

"Not your place to ask questions, but you're right. Your dad is an asshole. You tell me where Duke hid it, and I won't have to take you to see my boss."

"Hid what?"

"Nice game, but it's getting old. People take what isn't theirs, then things get taken from them."

Julia tried to turn around, but the pale man shoved the gun in deeper into her flesh until it pressed hard against her kidney and she gasped. Julia stumbled forward toward the front of the house and a putty-colored sedan parked behind her car as the pale man pushed her forward.

"You should eat more. You're nice-looking, but men prefer their women with more curves. Doesn't matter, though, if you give good head. You up for that?"

"Go to hell."

"Your choice."

The pale man stuck his gun in his rear waistband and opened the trunk of his car. Inside was an overweight, older man with a bloodied letter "A" etched across his forehead. He lay hog-tied on a garbage bag that covered the floor and his eyes were shut tight. Julia assumed he was dead, until the man in the trunk let out a weak, begging moan from somewhere in the center of his chest.

"Jesus, what did you do to him?" Julia asked.

The sound of her voice made the man in the trunk pop open his eyes. The one that was still in the socket was bloodshot and brown and looked pleadingly up at Julia.

"Oh, my God! Hold on. The police are coming," Julia lied as her mind worked on how she could possibly save herself and the man in the trunk.

"No, they aren't. The big cop you were with is still back at the scene with the dead guy in the field," the pale man answered, and then looked on at the man in the trunk with bored annoyance. "Jesus, I thought you were dead already."

Julia turned away just in time as the pale man raised his gun toward the trunk and pulled the trigger. The pale man then slammed Julia against the car and pinned her in place with his hips.

"You aren't going to get away with this," Julia warned.

"Shut up," the pale man answered. The high-pitched wail of a car alarm sounded from a neighboring street and the pale man snapped his head in the direction of the noise, giving Julia the opening she needed. Julia reared up her strong runner's leg and slammed the man as hard as she could in the meaty part of his thigh.

Julia started to run, but the pale man yanked her back by the arm, and Julia froze when she felt the cool steel of his gun against her temple.

"Stupid bitch."

The front door of the house swung open and a male voice called out, "Hey, Jameson. Looking for me?"

The pale-faced man, Jameson, pivoted his gun toward the house and then started to duck behind his car, but he was too late. A shot rang out from the front porch, hitting Jameson squarely between his eyes.

Duke Gooden seemed to float as he moved quickly out the front door and up the path, his gun held steady in front of him as he coolly panned the scene.

Julia stood frozen as she looked back at Duke and worked her way through the initial shock that the father she hadn't seen in thirty years had just killed a man. Julia felt as if something had lodged in the center of her throat, making it almost impossible to breathe, as she took in the strange, yet hauntingly familiar person who had almost crushed her spirit as a child, but who had also just likely saved her life.

Duke was older now, but still handsome, a well-aged version of the younger, reckless father Julia remembered. Duke's hair was still thick, but now entirely white, and contrasted beautifully against his tan skin. Deep creases etched in a starburst pattern along the corners of his blue eyes, which had always reminded Julia of pieces of shimmering topaz, exquisite gems standing out against the ordinary.

Julia opened her mouth to begin a well-rehearsed, yet long-ago discarded, tirade against her father, where she would tell Duke to go to hell and to get out of her life. But instead, her plan for vindication was derailed by an unexpected memory from her past, a rare, happy moment between father and daughter that held her tight.

Julia could picture herself curled up by Duke's side on their worn plaid sofa as she read him a few pages from *The Adventures of Tom Sawyer.* Julia had carefully scanned the shelves of her elementary-school library for the book after Duke had mentioned the Mark Twain novel was his all-time favorite.

(*"You're a great little reader, Julia,"* Duke said. *"You keep reading the way you are, you're going to own the world one day. Mark my word."*)

Julia pushed away the forgotten memory as Duke Gooden shot her a quick, assessing glance. He then slid down, careful not to let his pants touch the ground, and lifted Jameson's gun and billfold from his body.

"You kept your cool. That's good," Duke said.

"We have to call the police. There's a dead man in the trunk. The guy you shot killed him," Julia said.

"No police. Don't say a word about this, Julia. Not a word," Duke said. He popped open the trunk and shook his head as he took in the sight of his dead friend inside.

"Damn it. They got to Chip. That freakin' Indian did it. Carved the first initial of his name in Chip's forehead, that sick bastard."

"Tell me what's going on," Julia demanded.

"I can't. You need to stay away from this," Duke warned. "There's only one story you tell, that I'm dead and the last time you saw me was thirty years ago when I took off. Don't trust anyone who comes out of the woodwork and starts asking questions about me. You let it leak that I'm alive or that you saw me today, you'll be killed. I'm not joking around, kid."

Jameson's phone began to ring in his suit coat pocket, prompting Duke to retrieve a pair of clear plastic gloves from a vinyl duffel bag, which lay by his side. Duke snapped the gloves over his hands and carefully retrieved the ringing phone, Duke's face remaining void of emotion as he looked down at the number.

"You need to get out of here. When they don't hear from Jameson, they'll be swarming this place."

"Who is Jameson? You have to tell me what's going on."

"Sorry, darlin'. I can't. You've only got a couple of minutes to get out of here. Do you have a gun?" Duke asked. He slid his hand down to his ankle and pulled out a second weapon and offered it to Julia.

"I don't want that, and I don't need your help. I learned how to take care of myself after you left."

"Your choice," Duke said, and slid the gun back in its place. He then picked up Jameson's body from underneath the armpits and began to drag him in the direction of the rear yard and the fence that led to a side street. "My car is around back. You won't see me again. Sorry about all this, kid."

"You're sorry? That's all you can say to me? You don't get to just walk away this time," Julia said.

Duke, still dragging the recently deceased Jameson across the length of the backyard, paused at the gate and offered Julia his killer smile, the one she could never fully forget, his blinding, glorious grin that could surely melt the Devil's own heart.

"See you around."

"No, you won't," Julia whispered, but Duke had already slipped through the gate.

Now alone and with her father's warning ringing in her head, Julia ran to her car as fast as she could. She got inside, hit the gas, and kept one eye locked on the rearview mirror until she reached the highway.

After thirty years of silence, Duke Gooden had returned to Julia's life and in a very violent way. As she reached for her phone to call Navarro, she thought about the saying that you could never go home again. At that moment, Julia realized she could go home. But if she dared, it would likely suck the everlasting life out of her.

CHAPTER 6

Julia kept the speedometer of her SUV locked at a heated ninety as she beat a fast track out of Sparrow and whatever fresh hell her father had dragged her into. She blew off I-75 toward Rochester Hills, desperate to get home, as the horror show of what had just transpired in Sparrow played out in her head. One thing Julia was sure of, she wasn't going to let herself be used as bait again for whatever mess Duke was in. But more so, she wasn't going to let her father's dangerous chaos trickle down to her children.

Julia eased off the gas when she neared Paint Creek Trail and what looked like a father and son riding their bikes along the side of the road. She used hands free to call her housekeeper and self-appointed den mother, Helen Jankowski, to be sure her boys were okay. Helen was a whippet-thin, older woman with a distinct Polish accent and the best pierogi recipe north of Detroit. Helen had moved in with Julia after Helen's husband, Alek, had died of a heart attack a few months earlier, causing Helen to christen Julia's house *"wdowa cen- tralny,"* or "widow central."

"Are the police there?" Julia asked as Helen answered. "I'm five minutes away."

"Yes. Two sheriff deputies. I just gave them cake."

"Thanks for the hospitality, but they don't need cake. They should be watching the house. Where are Logan and Will?"

"Here with me. I took Will to the zoo, and we picked up Logan from his morning camp and came home. They're safe, but with the police coming by here again, it worries the children, especially Logan."

"Today was just a precaution. I ran into a situation, and I reached out to Navarro. I needed to make sure you and the boys were okay. Everything is fine, though."

"Fine, right. The police show up here just to eat my cake. I don't think so. I'm not a foolish old woman. You tell me what happened," Helen insisted.

"Someone wanted to find a man I used to know. But he's gone now, so everyone is fine."

"You like this word 'fine.' You keep saying it so you'll believe it. Who is this man you speak of?"

"I can't tell you. I'm sorry."

"You keep chasing life like it's a mystery, then that's what it becomes."

"At least I've got you to keep me sane."

Julia hung up with Helen and thought about the pale man in the suit whom Duke had killed. Whoever Jameson was, he obviously wanted Julia to lead him to Duke. But Julia wondered why someone would want to use her as a bargaining chip to get to her dad, who was no more than a ghost of a painful memory in her life.

Being a reporter for fifteen years, Julia considered herself fairly skilled at tracking people, but she had never once tried to find her parents after they abandoned her and Sarah. When it came to Duke and Marjorie Gooden, Julia had long ago given up any thoughts of justice or vindication. All she wanted from her parents was for them to be gone for good.

As Julia pulled into her driveway, she noticed two things: the Oakland County Sheriff's Office cruiser was parked on the street out front; and the FOR SALE sign that had been a fixture on her front lawn for the past few months was missing.

Julia made her way inside, never happier to be home, dropped her bag by the front door, and beat a quick path to her kitchen.

Two sheriff deputies sat on stools next to the kitchen island. One was broad and middle-aged, with salt-and-pepper hair. His partner looked to be early twenties, with a lean build and a buzz cut, probably trying to look tough to make up for his inexperience. Both had plates of homemade honey cake, courtesy of Helen, who was wearing a bright red apron and topping off their coffee cups.

"You smell like cigarettes," Helen said to Julia. "Smoking can kill you."

"The cigarettes weren't mine, and the person who was smoking them doesn't have to worry about that anymore," Julia answered.

The older deputy stood up quickly from his stool, and Julia read his name tag, SCARBOROUGH.

"I appreciate you coming over," Julia said.

"We've been parked outside your house for the past half hour, and we didn't see anything suspicious. My partner talked to your neighbors. They said they hadn't noticed anything out of the ordinary going on. But we can stay awhile longer if you need us to," Scarborough said. "I wasn't one hundred percent clear on the situation. Detective Navarro didn't give specifics when he requested a unit over here."

Julia let the not-quite-asked question hang in the air. Duke Gooden was one of the last people on earth she was going to trust, but when someone warned her she could die if she told anyone what just went down in Sparrow, she took notice.

"Thank you for the offer to stay, but we're good. I appreciate you coming by," Julia said.

"Can I take a piece of this cake to go?" the younger deputy asked. "This is, like, the greatest thing I've ever eaten."

"It's Polish, that is why," Helen answered, and began to cut two more slices of cake for the deputies.

"Well, Julia Gooden. It's nice to finally meet you. I've been reading your stories for years," Scarborough said.

The younger deputy got up from his stool and looked at Julia for the first time with interest.

"Julia Gooden. No kidding. Now I know why your name sounded familiar. You were married to that D.A. guy, David something," the younger deputy said.

"Tanner. That's correct."

"Right. That story was all over the news."

Julia felt an uncomfortable prickle run through her, not wanting to rehash a dark and painful time for her and her boys, especially in what should be the sanctuary of her own home. Julia turned her back on the rookie and reached her hand out to the senior officer.

"Deputy Scarborough, thank you for coming by, but we're fine here."

Helen glowered at the younger officer, handed Scarborough his container of cake, and shoved the other one into the refrigerator.

"If anything else happens, feel free to give the substation a call and we'll send someone by," Scarborough said.

Julia walked the deputies to the door, and when she returned, Helen was pulling a plate of stuffed cabbage rolls out of the oven.

"That young cop eats my cake and then has the nerve to bring up hurts from your past. He's lucky I didn't dump this pan of *Golabki* in his lap," Helen said. "He tries to come back for the cake, and I will do it, I swear."

"I've got a pretty thick skin, Helen. But thanks for having my back."

Julia reached out and patted Helen's hand as a pair of fast-moving feet tore down the hallway. Julia looked in the direction of the sound to see her youngest son, Will, pounding toward her, full throttle. Julia almost lost her balance when Will threw his arms around her legs in his trademark fierce hug delivered with the force of a mini linebacker.

"You're stronger than a superhero," Julia said.

Julia picked Will up in her arms, realizing she needed his comfort probably more right now than he needed hers. Julia swung Will around in the air until he squealed for her to stop, and when she did, he squealed for her to do it again. Julia let herself get lost in the simple moment where everything was small, unburdened, and perfect. She buried her nose against the soft skin of her little boy's neck, making him laugh even harder, and felt the tight knot that had settled in her chest start to loosen just slightly.

"You, little sir, give the best hugs. It's just what your mom needed."

"The police came," Will said.

"I know. They were just checking on you while I was gone. That's all. Police officers are good guys."

"Helen took me to the zoo!" Will said, clearly more excited about the zoo than the police. "Show Mom. Show her the picture."

"That child is getting so big, and he refused to go in the stroller. I had to carry him back to the car because he was too tired to walk. Soon he will be carrying me around in a papoose," Helen said. She lifted a postcard from a bag with the Detroit Zoo logo on the front and handed it to Will, who grabbed it greedily and presented it to his mother like it was as wondrous to him as the keys to Disneyland.

"Is that a fox?" Julia asked.

"No. Red banda. Can I be him forever?" Will asked.

"He means 'red panda,'" Helen corrected.

"Can I be him forever?" Will asked again.

"Yes, forever," Julia said, and turned her attention to Helen. "Where's Logan?"

"He's been in his room since he got home from camp. He came out once to drill the police on why they were here. That child was relentless. Then he made Will go back into his room with him. The boy tries to protect his little brother."

"Damn it. Okay. Let me go talk to him."

Helen raised her eyebrows and tilted her head in

Will's direction, making Julia wonder who really was the head of the house these days.

"Sorry, Will. Mom said a word she shouldn't have."

Julia handed Will off to Helen and felt a pang of guilt as she approached Logan's room. She didn't want the police to cause him any more anxiety, but she needed, first and foremost, to be sure her family was safe.

Logan's door was closed tight, and Julia knocked while she opened it.

Logan was sitting cross-legged on his floor, drawing Pokémon characters, with his baseball bat from Little League next to him.

"Anyone home?" Julia asked. She took a quick pan of the room and noticed Logan's closet door was ajar, and the missing FOR SALE sign was poking out of it.

"I'm guessing that bat isn't for practice," Julia said, and sat down next to her son on the wooden floor.

"The police were here. The police only show up if something bad is happening."

"The police came by to talk to me about a story I'm working on," Julia said, her lie feeling like a sharp pin caught in her throat. "Nothing bad is going to happen. Not to you, not to your brother, not to Helen or anyone else close to us. Got it? I won't let it. I promise."

"Cross your heart, right?" Logan asked.

Julia drew an X over her heart with her index finger.

"How about we put the bat back in your closet. Do you have something in there you want to tell me about?" Julia asked.

A shot of red blossomed up Logan's neck as his head darted in the direction of the closet door and he realized his mistake.

"Nice job trying to hide the sign, but we journalists tend to pick up on things. What's going on?"

"I don't want anyone else living here. This is our house. If someone buys it, then I'll have to switch schools."

"I thought you wanted to switch schools."

"I did when I got in trouble, but I'm okay now."

"You sure?" Julia asked, remembering the call she got a few months earlier from the principal's office telling her that Logan had gotten into a fight with another boy at school.

"What happened, it wasn't my fault. That Luke kid said something really bad about Dad. I couldn't let him get away with it."

"What Luke did wasn't right. But if something like that happens again, use your smarts and your words, instead of your fists, or you tell a teacher. You don't get in a fight."

Four sharp knocks sounded on the door and Helen barged in without waiting to get official permission to enter.

"Your phone keeps ringing in your purse," Helen said.

"We'll talk more about this later," Julia said to Logan.

She gave Logan a quick kiss on the top of his head, dashed to her bag, which was still lying on the entryway table by the front door, and saw that she had missed calls from Navarro. Julia made her way outside to her front porch, away from inquisitive ears, and hit the call-back button.

"What did you find out?" Julia said when Navarro answered. No "hello" required.

"You guys all okay?" Navarro asked.

"Everybody is fine. The sheriff deputies just left."

"I would've preferred they stuck around until I got through my shift. The guy who tried to grab you, whoever he was working for could be coming back. Someone must have tailed you and thought you'd lead them to your father."

"Knowing Duke, he's long gone, and I can't help whoever is after him."

"They don't know that."

"Did you get any more on Jameson?" Julia asked.

"I just got off the phone with the Sparrow cops. They went to your old house and couldn't find a thing, not even a speck of blood."

"That's not possible. That Jameson person, his blood was all over the windshield of his car after my dad shot him. The car was a tan sedan and it was parked out front of the house. And there was a dead man inside the trunk. Duke referred to him as Chip."

"There wasn't a tan sedan anywhere near the property. The cops said they got to the house ten minutes after you called me."

"Then whoever Jameson was working for had a skilled cleanup crew on the ready. My dad took Jameson's body. He dragged it around the back of the house."

"Strange souvenir. Your dad either got rid of the car with the other dead guy in it or someone else did," Navarro said. "I did a trace on your dad. Here's the thing, and it doesn't make sense. There are zero public records on the guy in the past thirty years. No driver's license renewals, IRS records, job history, arrest records, nothing. The only hits I got happened before your brother was abducted. Duke had a couple of misdemeanors for writing bad checks and one for embezzlement. He had a grand-theft one too, but that got dropped. I'm not sure if you knew this already, but your dad served some time."

"I know. I was five. Ben told me Duke was on a business trip so I wouldn't be upset. But one of the kids on our school bus, his dad was a prison guard and knew that my dad was locked up. The kid told everybody on the bus ride home one day about my dad being a convict, and Ben punched him in the nose. We had to walk home the rest of the way because the bus driver kicked Ben off, and I wasn't going to stay on there without him."

"There's a note in your dad's file that he was affiliated with a man named Peter Jonti, a hood who served time at the same prison with Duke. Jonti was younger than your dad, but it looks like he was connected. I did a check, and Jonti got popped again recently, but he's out now and working at a sushi joint downtown on Fourteen Mile in Madison Heights."

Julia jotted the name of her father's former associate down in pen on the palm of her hand.

"I'll check him out," Julia said. "There's one thing that keeps coming back to me about what went down in Sparrow. Before Jameson died, he said Duke took something that didn't belong to him, and when that happened, things got taken from him. He could've meant Ben. I'm sure of it."

"Don't go looking for this Jonti guy until I finish my shift, and I'll come with you. Your father has been leaving a hell of a wake in his trail since he resurfaced in the last three hours, so I'd prefer you stay close."

"How are things going with the Angel Perez case?"

"I'm just leaving his apartment. I talked to the pregnant girlfriend who just came back here after leaving Councilman Sanchez's place. Poor kid. She said Angel was trying to scare up some day laborer work to pay for an upcoming doctor's appointment for her. Angel didn't tell her where he planned to go this morning to pick up work, but she clued us in on some usual spots he'd go when they were desperate for cash. The problem is, she wasn't big on specifics. She said he went to Lowe's, Home Depot, and Menards at locations in the suburbs when he couldn't find work where they lived in Dearborn. We've got some ground to cover. But at least he was wearing a distinctive piece of clothing."

"The Run-DMC shirt."

"Someone should remember him."

"Keep me posted. I've got to head down to the paper, and we'll catch up later."

"Be careful. And call me if you need anything. I'd feel better staying at your house until things settle down. I don't like the idea of you and your kids alone right now with what happened today."

"Thanks. Let me think about it, though. Logan is having a rough patch."

"You don't have to worry about me sneaking into your bedroom in the middle of the night. I can keep my hands to myself if I have to."

"I might be the one with the weaker flesh."

"There's absolutely nothing wrong with your flesh. Trust me on that. I love you, beautiful." Navarro hung up, not waiting for Julia to say it back. She'd often told Navarro she loved him, when they were first together, when she was twenty-five. She felt the same way now, and she was certain Navarro knew how she felt, but she hadn't been able to say it back to him just yet. It wasn't a matter of self-preservation or having the upper hand in the relationship. She just had far more than herself to worry about this time around.

Julia stared at the name she'd written down on her palm, did a quick Google search for an address, and headed out to track down Peter Jonti. Thirty years of never being able to find out what happened to her brother, if there was even a remote possibility Duke was involved—something the Sparrow cops had ruled out early on, since Duke had an airtight alibi—Julia wasn't going to wait another second to find out. And if Ben had been some kind of payback in lieu of Duke's personal pound of flesh for a long-ago transgression, Julia swore to herself that she'd make sure her dad would pay for what he'd done.

Sushi Z, where Peter Jonti worked, was located in a depressing, faux-brick strip mall. It was located between a bail bondsman's office and an adult-entertainment shop advertising some sort of LIQUIDATION SALE, EVERYTHING MUST GO.

A tiny bell sounded as Julia entered the sushi place, and four waving *maneki-neko* cat statues, which needed a good dusting, greeted her as she made her way to the hostess stand. A lone sushi chef behind the bar eyeballed Julia and then barked something to a dark-haired woman in a midnight-blue satin dress. Julia took a seat at the far end of the bar and ignored the only other patron, a biker-looking man, who appeared to have taken on the full-time job of staring at her.

The waitress came around the bar and handed Julia a menu, which had dried stains of what looked like soy sauce on the vinyl cover.

"You here for a late lunch?" the waitress asked in a sulky tone. "My shift ends in five minutes, so you need to order."

"No, I'm here to see Peter Jonti."

The waitress's impatient demeanor softened as she realized she could probably go home soon, after all. "I'll see if he's around. What's your name?"

"Julia Gooden. Tell Mr. Jonti he knew my father, Duke."

The waitress disappeared behind a door with an EMPLOYEES ONLY sign posted on its front. Julia watched a fly pick its way across a plastic California roll on display as the door to the back room opened back up in a hurry. A solidly built man in his fifties came out. He had dark, greased-back hair, which curled at his shoulders, and a gold chain around his neck. Peter wore a short-sleeved, white T-shirt that exposed a tattoo on his left upper arm of a ghoulish-looking, bald-headed figure that had its mouth wide open and its hands clasped to either side of its wan cheeks.

Peter gave Julia a friendly smile as he approached her. With every step, his cologne got stronger and stronger until Julia had to stop herself from wincing.

"Mr. Jonti. I believe you knew my father, Benjamin 'Duke' Gooden," Julia said, and eyed the tattoo again. "That image on your arm there. It's from the painting *The Scream,* right?"

"Yeah, but there's no good backstory about it. I was coming off a killer hangover at the time and the picture of the guy pretty much summed up how I was feeling when I saw it at the tattoo parlor," Peter said. "Sure, I knew your dad. What can I do for you?"

"I need information about Duke."

"You need information about your own father?"

"I don't know much about him. Duke took off when I was seven. I don't care what happened to him. But I believe whatever my father was mixed up in at the time you knew him could be connected to my brother's disappearance. My brother, Ben, was abducted when he was nine."

"I'd heard about what happened to Duke's boy. Your brother was never found?"

"No. It's a cold case."

"All right. I'm not sure how I can help you, but if you've got questions, shoot," Peter said, and led the way toward the door behind the sushi bar.

"I appreciate your time. First off . . . ," Julia started to say as the door closed behind them, but her words got lost as Peter shoved her against a wall and then started to pat her down with more expertise than a TSA handler.

"What the hell is this?" Julia demanded.

"Sorry," Peter said in a thoughtful tone. When the body search was done, Peter dumped out the contents of Julia's bag on the floor.

"Hey, what are you doing? I'm not carrying and I'm not wired," Julia said.

"That's what they all say." Peter combed through Julia's wallet and pulled out her license and her press pass, which he studied until he shoved both documents back inside Julia's purse.

"Well, you're definitely Duke's kid. Who are you working for?" Peter asked. He offered Julia a smile, but then pulled out a knife from his back pocket and snapped open the blade. "I liked your father, but if you're trying to set me up, I'm afraid I can't extend any favors to his daughter." Peter backed Julia up against the wall and ran the smooth side of the blade across her cheek. "Pretty girl. It would be a shame to have to carve you up."

"You try and cut me with that, you're done. The cops know I'm here," Julia bluffed. "And for the record, I'm not working for anybody, and I don't care what kind of front you're running. I'm trying to find out what happened to my brother."

Peter looked up at Julia's face and seemed to study her, unblinking, until he pulled away and slid his knife back in his pocket. "All right. I think you're being straight with me. We can talk in my office."

"Let me make one thing clear. If you ever pull a knife on me again, I'll make sure your so-called business and whatever you've got going on here is shut down."

"Aren't you Duke's little firecracker? Come on."

Peter led the way down a narrow hallway until he reached a door with a security pad mounted on the wall next to it. Peter then plugged in a series of numbers that deactivated the alarm and went inside. Julia followed him and did a quick assessment of the room, which consisted of a scuffed wooden desk, two folding chairs, and stacks of boxes that lined the walls.

Peter caught Julia studying the boxes and sat down on his desk, facing Julia with his arms crossed in front of his chest. "Mind your business, or I'll mind it for you."

"Like I said, I'm not interested in what kind of business you've got going on here. How do you know my father?"

Peter motioned for Julia to take a seat, but she kept standing. "Ancient history. It must have been my second lockup when I first met your dad. I was a kid, probably around twenty-five, when I met Duke. We were both serving time at Macomb Correctional Center. Your dad wasn't in there long, though. Just a couple of months, as I recall. Anyway, I was working a couple of guys in a card game. They caught on that I was conning them, and they were about to jump me. Your dad had a pal who was King Kong huge in there. Duke was always real good at making friends. Duke sicced his giant friend on the two guys and saved my ass. What else do you want to know?"

"My dad was working a job in Indiana when my brother went missing. It sounded legit, like maybe Duke was trying to go straight. He was working for a flooring company. His foreman gave my dad an airtight alibi the night Ben was abducted, and the St. Clair County Sheriff's Office cleared him as a suspect. I've worked with the deputy who was the lead investigator on my brother's case through the years, and I trust him."

"You trust the deputy, but you shouldn't trust your dad. The thing about Duke's alibi, it was fake. The man Duke was working for owned the foreman. That's how he got off," Peter said. "Your dad wasn't anywhere near Indianapolis at the time your brother went missing. He was here in Detroit. I saw him myself that day and later that night. Sounds like a bunch of people have been lying to you."

Julia tried to keep a straight face as a fresh burn of anger moved through her.

"What do you know about what happened to my brother?" Julia demanded.

"Not a thing. Duke told me about it after the fact."

"If you're lying to me, you'll regret it," Julia warned.

"Tough one, aren't you? But if you make a threat like that to me again, you won't be walking out of here."

"Who was my father working for? I need a name."

"Not coming from me. I'm trying to do business in this town again, and I don't want trouble."

"What kind of business did you and my father do together when you got out of prison?" Julia asked.

"Your dad was an excellent salesman. I located the product, he made the sales."

"Are we talking drugs?" Julia asked.

"No. Drugs are a dirty man's business. Your dad was working a real estate scam for a while, trying to sell bogus properties down by the Detroit RiverWalk before it was developed. He had a buddy who was a maintenance guy in one of the buildings down there. He'd give your dad the key after hours, and Duke would show these hapless idiots around the place, acting like he was a real estate agent or something. But that didn't go far, so he used his skills to help me unload some of my product, usually electronics, that I lifted from shipments down at the port."

"The man my father was working for who gave him the phony alibi, he was in on this with you?" Julia asked.

"No. He was involved in a different type of sales, you could say. You said Duke took off when you were a kid. You still must've been upset when you heard about the fire."

"I don't know what you're talking about."

"You know your parents are dead, right?"

"Sure," Julia lied, backtracking as not to show her hand again. An old, tucked away memory rushed back as Julia recalled a police officer coming to her aunt Carol's house when Julia and Sarah were living there after their parents took off. Her aunt had scooted the girls upstairs to talk to the officer, and when Julia came back down, the officer was gone, but her aunt was sitting at the center of the kitchen table, crying, likely over the news that her sister Marjorie's body had been found, Julia now realized. When Julia had asked what was wrong, her aunt had composed herself and promised everything was "Fine, just fine."

Julia tried to process the secret her aunt had kept to the grave as an unexpected image of her mother sparked through her mind: beautiful Marjorie Gooden, with her thick, black hair and lovely smile, which she had lost to booze. Julia looked away from Peter over the unexpected painful memory, but he seemed to sense a shift in her demeanor.

"Memories can be brutal. Especially if a good one surfaces about someone who's done you wrong. Lots of times, I've seen suckers go back to the people who've hurt them because they remember a single act of kindness, like an abused dog that runs away, but then returns home to the bastard that's been beating him, because the dog remembers the asshole petted him once. Still, whether you hated your dad or not, you must have been upset when you heard your parents died. There were rumors, though, lots of them, that

Duke got out and may still be alive. That's my theory. I think he's been running fast under the radar all these years. Did Duke ever try to contact you?"

"No. I haven't talked to my father since he walked out on me when I was seven. Tell me about the fire."

"I can tell you what I heard. A week after I got the news your brother was abducted, your dad fell completely out of sight. Two weeks later, a car registered to Duke was found burned to a crisp in an abandoned lot in the boonies, with two bodies inside. You hear things on the street. I had a real good source that said the cops couldn't get a positive ID on Duke, since all the teeth had been pulled out of the dead guy's mouth. But they found Duke's wallet, with just his license inside, a couple of feet away from the car. They were able to ID your mom, though. You want a drink? You look like you could use one."

Peter reached into one of his desk drawers and pulled out a bottle of scotch and two filmy tumbler glasses. He poured one to the fill line for himself and belted the contents back without waiting for Julia's response.

"You know, you don't look like your sister. What's her name again?" Peter asked.

"Sarah. You know her?"

"That's right. Sarah, the blonde. Tight little body like yours, but she's older, or looks that way. Booze and drugs will do that to you. I ran into her recently, and she started asking the same types of questions you did, but not about your brother. Seems like she wanted to find Duke to make him pay for running out on her. She seemed pissed when she found out he was dead."

"That sounds like Sarah. You saw her in Florida?"

"Florida? No, at the Renaissance House. I was locked up the last time for arms possession and intent to sell, but I was drunk when the cops did the sting. They added insult to injury, making me serve time and then having me go to AA meetings once a week when I got out."

"My sister is at the Renaissance House in Detroit?"

"That's the place. I tried to ask her out for a drink after the meeting, but she turned me down. Her loss. You know, I lent your dad something before he took off and he never returned it. Did Duke have a storage unit or anything where he stashed stuff?"

"A storage unit? We could barely afford rent. I can't imagine my father had the money to pay for something like that. At least he never mentioned it."

"Your father never tried to reach out to you after he took off?"

"No. And that was fine with me."

"Maybe now, but I doubt that's how you felt when you were a kid. Children always want to be with their parents, no matter how bad they treat them. Little girls look up to their daddies."

"My father was never my hero. Thank you for your help, Mr. Jonti. If you remember anything else about Duke, please give me a call," Julia said, and slid her business card across the desk.

Peter filled his glass halfway this time with scotch and raised the glass to Julia just as a fist banged against the office door.

"Peter," the waitress from earlier said in a panicked rush from the other side of the door. "There are two men out front with badges. They don't look like ordinary cops."

"Could be ATF. Damn it." Peter shoved the bottle of scotch and the glass back in the drawer and pulled a tan sports coat from the back of his chair. He threw the blazer on, which didn't help him look any more presentable than he did without it. His fingers beat a fast rhythm against the keypad to deactivate the alarm.

"Do yourself a favor," he told Julia. "Go out the back door and don't come back. But if the rumors are true that Duke is alive and he looks you up, you let me know. That bastard owes me."

CHAPTER 7

The Renaissance House was a prettied-up name for a not-so-pretty substance abuse center on East Jefferson Avenue in downtown Detroit. The facility was across from Erma Henderson Park and sandwiched in between a dumpy McDonald's and a cheap cell phone store, which displayed a female mannequin clad in green neon shorts and a matching tube top holding a fake bedazzled phone to her ear.

Julia was familiar with the Renaissance House from her beat. It was a no-frills, state-subsidized facility where people who were arrested for drug and alcohol charges wound up in a trade-off to expunge or lessen their charges if the judge laid that option on the table. For most addicts, it beat jail time.

At the entrance, Julia hesitated, second-guessing her decision to see Sarah, but, ultimately, there was no other choice but to confront the only accessible link to her past. Julia put her bullshit meter on high alert and went inside.

A female receptionist, who looked early twenties

with dyed blue hair and an elephant tattooed on her inner wrist, was engrossed in a self-help book. She sat behind a thick glass partition and didn't look up as Julia stood waiting to get her attention. Julia counted to ten and then knocked hard on the glass between them.

"I'm here to see Sarah Gooden," Julia said.

The receptionist came slightly to life and gave Julia a robotic stare.

"You have an appointment?"

"Sarah will see me. I'm her sister."

"I need to see your driver's license."

Julia dug through her purse and pushed her license through the partition.

The receptionist studied it for a few seconds and then took a slow walk to the copy machine.

"Sarah is in group right now," the receptionist said, and shoved Julia's license through the space between the glass when she was done.

"Tell her I'm here, please. It's important. She can miss a few minutes of her therapy session."

"Sarah isn't a patient. She's a group leader."

"A group leader," Julia repeated, feeling immediately sorry for anyone Sarah was trying to help.

"Come back in twenty."

"I can't. It's an emergency. This will only take a few minutes, I promise. Just tell her that I'm here."

The receptionist, who obviously had to cultivate a high-bullshit monitor herself to work in a place like this, studied Julia and then put her book down.

"Okay. I'll tell her."

The receptionist flashed an ID card in front of yet another locked door, which led her into the bowels of the place.

Julia's instinct was to get the hell out of there before she brought any more trouble on herself, and that's all Sarah had pretty much ever been to Julia: TROUBLE, with every letter uppercase and in screaming bold.

Sarah had gone into foster care as a teenager after their aunt Carol had taken the girls in when Duke and Marjorie had abandoned their daughters following Ben's abduction. Julia knew her aunt had no choice but to give Sarah up after she wound up in trouble with the law for shoplifting and drugs. The last straw was when Sarah stole money from their aunt Carol's wallet. Sarah's pattern with drugs and brushes with the law had continued long into adulthood. Sarah had continually declared her sobriety as an adult when all she was trying to do was hustle Julia for cash. After Logan was born, Sarah and her boyfriend had shown up at Julia's house carrying a stuffed teddy bear, in the guise of wanting to see the new baby, but as Sarah visited with Logan and Julia in the nursery, Sarah's boyfriend staked Julia's house and stole her credit card information and jewelry. When Julia had figured out what had happened after tens of thousands of dollars' worth of charges were racked up on her credit cards, Sarah threatened she would come after Logan if Julia went to the police.

Julia looked at the exit sign and knew seeing Sarah again went against any fiber of sanity and self-preservation she possessed, but Julia resigned herself that if she was going to find out anything more about Duke that could possibly lead her to Ben, she was going to have to work Sarah by playing nice, like the times when she was civil to a source she detested deep down in order to get a story.

The door to the facility buzzed open and a much healthier-looking Sarah than Julia remembered strode into the room. Sarah was seven years older than Julia, forty-four, and attractive, still with her lean build. Julia gave her a quick assessment and had to admit Sarah looked good. Sarah's once waist-long, blond hair was cut into a professional-looking, shoulder-length bob, and she'd lost her previous trademark low-cut, tight outfits that screamed for attention. Instead, she wore a pair of flowing tan pants, flat sandals, and a sleeveless, loose white top, which was closed at the neck.

"Look, if this is about me being back in Detroit, you don't have to worry or file a restraining order. I've been back in the city for over a year, and see . . . no trouble to you," Sarah said, and held her hands wide, in an "I'm innocent" gesture. "I'd give you the line about how I changed my life and I'm clean and sober, but you've heard it before, and it was always a lie. I was a piece of shit and treated you worse than one. I'm clean now, but I'm not going to make you try and believe me."

"You're like a counselor here?"

"A group leader, and a good one."

Julia made herself hold her tongue, because she really wanted to tell Sarah she probably cleaned herself up to look like a rehabilitated, model citizen so she could scam some vulnerable men in the Renaissance House and help them part with their money.

"You want your cop buddies to come by and talk to me to be sure I'm not going to come knocking on your door, feel free. You know where I work, obviously. I've got to go back to group."

"Hold on. I'm not here to drill you about why

you're back in Detroit. As long as you leave my kids and me alone, I don't care."

"Then why are you here?"

"I need to talk to you about Duke and Ben."

"I guess pigs really do fly," Sarah said. "Ginny, ask Bud to take over for me."

The blue-haired receptionist, Ginny, who was now back at her desk in the reception area, nodded and picked up the phone.

Sarah pulled her employee badge out from her pocket and flashed it in front of the security sensor. "Follow me," she told Julia.

Julia trailed her sister down a long, sterile corridor, passing about a half-dozen meeting rooms and a depressing-looking cafeteria, until they reached the back of the building, where Sarah flashed her badge once more and led Julia outside to a rear alley.

Sarah dug into her pocket, pulled out a Marlboro Lights cigarette, and took a long drag after she lit up.

"My only vice these days. I quit booze and drugs a year ago. Believe it or not, it doesn't matter. But I can't give up the cigarettes, and I can't smoke inside. It's not the usual PC 'secondhand smoke kills' bullshit. Someone came up with the brilliant idea that if addicts or former addicts smoked, the smell alone would be so overpowering, everyone would be shooting up in the hallway within minutes of their first puff. Never your problem, though, Miss Squeaky Clean."

Sarah propped herself up against the alleyway wall of the treatment center, took in another long drag, and looked at Julia with a cool shell of suspicion. "You got my attention, little sis. What do you want to know?"

Julia reached into her bag and pulled out a hundred-dollar bill. "As long as you're telling me the truth, I'll pay you for information."

Sarah thumped her hand with the cigarette against her chest in mock pain. "You think I'm still a whore for cash. That hurts. I don't want your money. You want answers, I'll tell you what I can."

"I think Duke may have been involved in Ben's kidnapping. Maybe not directly, but whatever he was up to, I think he might know who took Ben."

"No shit," Sarah said. "Duke was a player, but he was small-time."

"Do you remember anything about Duke or our mom or anyone who might have come over to the house in Sparrow that made you think twice? Maybe someone said something, or Ben told you something?"

"Ben was your angel, not mine. We didn't talk much. I wasn't the best sister, even back then. Things were bad. It was every man for himself."

"Did anything happen the night Ben was abducted that you didn't tell the police?"

"I don't know. It was a long time ago. I don't think about when we were kids anymore," Sarah said, her voice sounding hard like rough grit being run through a blender.

"I think you do. The addicts I meet on my beat, I always know that somewhere, deep down, there's a memory of something good, something hopeful, that got lost or taken from them. They hit the bottle or take drugs to get a momentary reprieve from the memories, but what they long for, what hurts them the most, comes out even more crystal clear in the moments that they're using. Remember our place in Sparrow, after Mom and Dad took off, and it was only us after Ben was taken? You let me sleep in your room because I was afraid. Our last food in the pantry . . ."

"A tin of Dinty Moore Beef Stew," Sarah said. "That crap makes me want to puke if I see it in a store now."

"You let me have it. It had been a month since our parents took off, and you tried to hold it together, convincing me they were coming back."

Julia held Sarah's gaze, but felt dirty for trying to play up to her sister. But, she realized she had no other choice.

"Life's a bitch. We survived, though," Sarah said. "But foster care wasn't a good place to be if you were a pretty teenage girl. I got pregnant once from one of the foster fathers. I never told you that."

"I'm sorry. I didn't know. I sent you letters up until I went to college. You never responded."

"I was still pissed at you. It's a whole lot easier to blame other people for the shit storm you created for yourself. The foster dad, he had three biological kids and always acted like he was a saint around them and his wife. He drove me to an abortion clinic and left me there to take care of the 'mistake.' Gave me twenty dollars to take a cab home. I took care of it, and then ran away. Two stints in juvie later for stealing food and the rest is history. But I'm turning it around now. You end up where you end up. My actions were my fault for stealing from Aunt Carol. But you didn't need to rat on me and tell her I stole money from her purse. Everything changed for me after that."

"I was seven. I told our aunt because she thought I took the money, and I wanted to do the right thing. I would've never told her if I'd known she was going to kick you out. I get it. You don't want my money, but you want me to feel bad. You want someone to blame for your mistakes. Well, meeting you here, this is one of mine."

Julia started to walk down the alleyway toward the street, when Sarah called her back.

"The night Ben was taken, I heard something. Our parents' room was on the other end of the house from yours and Ben's. I don't know if you remember."

"I remember every inch of that place."

"You and Ben probably didn't hear, but since my room was right next to our parents', I did. I heard something, quiet and low, like someone being slapped by something sharp like a belt, and then I heard crying, until it just stopped. Duke never hit our mom, but I figured it was the other way around, that she had gotten shit-faced and hauled off and punched Duke. I thought at the time she was pissed because he'd finally come home after being gone for so long. There was a bathroom that connected my room to theirs. I got out of bed and went in there. I hid behind the bathroom door and looked through the crack into their bedroom. And then I saw it all going down."

"Goddamn it, Sarah, if you're making something up . . ."

"I'm not. I saw Mom sitting in a chair. She was slumped over, and there was this giant man standing over her who had a long, black braid that went down to his waist. I knew Mom was drunk, and he kept hitting her across the face with his belt, like he was trying to get her to sober up. Then he shoved his hand over her mouth so if she cried, no one would hear her. I was scared out of my mind. I thought I was a tough kid, but it was like my legs turned to jelly. I ran into the backyard and hid behind a tree. I stayed there for a while."

"I woke up that night in the closet in my bedroom. When I didn't find Ben, I ran into your room and you were there in your bed, not outside. Your story isn't lining up."

"After an hour, I came back in the house. The man was gone, and Mom was passed out in bed. I didn't go and check on you guys. I should have."

"If this is true, why didn't you tell the police?"

"I was scared. I figured it might have been a man Mom picked up in a bar. I saw her leave that night around nine. She took the remainder of the money Duke had wired, to buy booze, instead of food for us, and she was already half-cocked when she left. I didn't know what to do."

"What did this man say? Did you see his face?"

"I didn't hear anything, and I only saw his back. He was huge, I remember that. And the braid. There was one other thing, though. He put something on the dresser next to Mom's bed. It was a piece of paper, I think."

Julia stared through Sarah and instead saw the police officer who had questioned her in the station the night Ben was taken.

"Do you think anyone had been in the room with your mom? Like a stranger she might have met while she was out?" the officer asked Julia.

"I don't know. I didn't see anyone in her room after I woke up. I remember . . . Wait. There was something I saw on her nightstand. I don't think I'd ever seen it before," Julia said. "It was like a picture or something. Somebody drew it. It scared me."

"Tell me what it was."

"I didn't like it. It was like a giant bird with wings, but it had legs like a man and red glowing eyes, but the eyes weren't right. They weren't in the bird's head. They were drawn in where a person's chest would be."

"The man. Did he look like he was American Indian?" Julia asked. "The police found an Indian arrowhead under Ben's bed."

"I don't know. Like I said, I never saw his face. So what's your plan? Are you going to question every Native American male in the state? For all we know, the guy in the room was having rough sex with Mom. The guy was a freak and left behind some weird picture he drew of some Indian-bird thing."

"The man and what you saw scared you so much, you ran outside and never told anyone about it, not even the police. If it's true, you might have been able to save Ben."

"I know," Sarah said. She stared down at the pavement and refused to meet Julia's gaze.

Julia fought a primal urge to run up to Sarah and make her pay for what she didn't do, but she coiled her right hand, instead, into a tight fist and kept it at her side.

"You have a chance to make it right now."

"What do you want from me?" Sarah asked.

"Information. Did you ever try and find our parents?"

Sarah pulled out cigarette number three since they made their way into the alleyway, lit it, and closed her eyes as she inhaled deeply.

"You bet I did. I wasn't looking for some kumbaya, let's hold hands around the campfire moment. I wanted to track them down so they would pay for what they did to me."

"That doesn't sound very twelve-step."

"This wasn't during one of my wannabe sober periods. Anyway, I remembered a guy Duke brought over a couple of times to the apartment we used to live in above Lingo's Market before we got evicted. Remember that dump? That was before we moved into the Sparrow house. There were more cockroaches than floor in that place."

"Who's the guy?"

"His name is Mike Ballentine. This was ten years ago, so I'm not sure if he's even around anymore. Ballentine lived in a dumpy trailer in Metro Commons, off Van Born. He was good-looking for an older guy. So I get to his trailer and Ballentine starts telling me how Duke had gotten mixed up with some bad people who put a hit out on him. Ballentine was pretty sure Duke had screwed the people over in a business deal. He said Duke and Mom came over once, and Duke begged him for help, but Ballentine sent them away. Ballentine never saw Duke or Mom again. Then he tells me, he heard our parents were killed, so I washed my hands of it. I had sex with the guy before I left, and he gave me fifty bucks. Not one of my finer days. I figured he'd tell me more if I screwed him."

"You got a number for Ballentine?"

"Are you kidding? This was ten years ago. With all the shit I used to do, you're lucky I have any memories at all."

"If you think of anything, let me know. Here's my

cell phone number," Julia said, and handed Sarah one of her cards. "Why'd you come back to Detroit anyway?"

"I had nowhere else to go. I was down in Tampa with my boyfriend, when I had to look way up to see rock bottom."

"Steve?"

"Steve Beckerus, the one and only. We made some good money together. I'd pick up a guy in a bar, the guy would take me home, and then Steve would show up like the jealous boyfriend, beat the shit out of the guy, and then take his money. Old tricks, they used to work for us. But down in Florida, Steve got heavy on the junk."

"Heroin?"

"You got it. He got messy and went to jail again, ten years this time for robbery and aggravated assault. So I'm all alone. I wake up one morning, hungover to beat the band, and I realize I'm lying under a park bench with my panties at my ankles. My bag was gone, my money was gone. I was such a mess, I couldn't even hustle anymore. I went to a treatment place down in Florida for a few weeks, swore I'd make it this time, but I fell off again. I took a bus back home. You were right about what you said before, about addicts going back to that one shining moment. Our past, it was a mess, though, right? But that time when we were all together in the early days, when I was growing up in Sparrow, that's all I ever had. I felt like if I could just get it back for a minute, like if I could just reach out and touch it with my hand, a good memory, it would be all I needed to get clean. I'm doing okay now, though. Nine months and sixteen days clean and sober. That's a record for me."

"Congratulations," Julia said, not believing it.

"It is. I'm a good group leader in there," Sarah said, and thumbed her finger toward the center. "I'm not lying to you. I relate to addicts, and I know when they're lying. Maybe that's my only gift, knowing when people are feeding me a line of bull. That's why I think you're not telling me something. I know damn well you'd never show up here to talk to me unless you were desperate or you found out something new."

"You're wrong," Julia answered, surprised over Sarah's sober clarity and dead-on deduction. "I'm still trying to find out what happened to Ben. That will never stop. Do you need any money?"

"Nah," Sarah said, and snuffed out the scant remains of her cigarette butt against the side of the building. "This is where I'm supposed to give you a hug, or invite you to get a coffee, and we say fake things about how we're going to get together, but we both know it'll never happen. Wouldn't it be nice if we could just pretend and be normal that way?"

Julia stared back at her sister, and the hard mask that Sarah had worn since Julia could remember seemed to slip just slightly, and Julia thought for a split second that Sarah was about to cry. Instead, Sarah twisted her mouth up in a jaded smile and gave Julia a reticent nod. "Just playing with you. We're way, way past that, aren't we?"

"You have my number if you remember anything else. Good luck, Sarah. I hope things come around for you this time."

Julia made her way out of the alley to her car and was surprised when she realized she truly meant it.

CHAPTER 8

The big Indian, Ahote, wiped the mud off his boots that he had carefully placed beside the door of his work trailer. He rinsed his hands in the tiny kitchen's rusty sink and went to his workplace. In the center of a small table was a cheap bowl from the Dollar Store filled with a few inches of water. In the center of the bowl was a large bullfrog. Its face was bright green, while the rest of its body looked more like brown-and-murky camouflage coating its pimply ridges.

Ahote raised both his hands up over his head, closed his eyes, and let out a deep shudder. When he had hunted with his grandfather and father in the same woods where he found the three-pound whopper of a bullfrog, the elder male Indian statesmen had told Ahote to respect all of nature and its occupants. If you didn't, they warned, you would bring bad luck to yourself and to generations to come.

Ahote picked the remaining skin away from his raw thumb as he recalled how his father had made him stay alone in the woods for a day and a night when he was fifteen. That was his punishment after his father had caught him trying to light a stray dog on fire. His dad had discovered Ahote in the back of their property and set the terrified animal free. Animals, nature, and the world they lived in were all part of the earth and heaven, and each was equal to man and must be treated with reverence and respect, his father had reminded him in a shamed, disgusted tone.

Ahote wiped away the slick perspiration beginning to form on his brow as he recalled the fear that he was sure would paralyze him as he ran through the woods the night of his penance, all the while trying to evade the evil spirits in the woods that were rumored to hunt down lost souls and eat them.

Ahote dipped his mammoth hand into the bowl, causing the bullfrog to clumsily wobble backward in an attempt to evade its captor. Ahote smiled and stroked the bullfrog's back in a slow movement, starting from its head and going down the length of its back. The frog closed its eyes, as if it enjoyed the unexpected affection.

Ahote then grabbed the frog out of the bowl, held it high over his head until the frog's body skimmed the ceiling, and stared into the creature's eyes. Ahote chanted his own made-up language, which he had created in the woods that night so long ago, one he hid from his family and one that only he understood. *"Beh San! De Na Ma Ta Son!"*

He stroked the frog one more time, and the big Indian was sure he saw the frog begin to smile. He moved one hand swiftly behind his back, pulled out a knife, and plunged the blade into the frog's center mass, gutting it in a fast, straight slice. Ahote then expertly extracted its heart. He dropped the frog's body back into the bowl and held the still-beating heart in his hand for a second, until he put it in his mouth and swallowed, feeling the small thing beating, *tick-tock-tick,* inside his throat until it went all the way down.

Ahote closed his eyes, remembering how his grandfather had told him as a child that frogs represented healing, ancient wisdom, and transformation, so now that power was part of him. Ahote sighed deeply, as he understood he would have to be quiet for another long spell. For now, this type of sacrament and self-evolution would have to do.

The power from the dead creature's soul seemed to ignite through Ahote's body. He went over to a small locked cabinet, opened it, and pulled out a shoe box of carefully arranged pictures, catalogued by date. He labored over each photo of the men and boys propped against trees. The pictures captured the light draining from their eyes and fueled Ahote's spirit as his victims died.

The first photo that Ahote pulled out with his thick fingers dated back nearly forty years, the big Indian's first kill, when he was just nineteen. The deceased was a transient male who was too easy to hunt because he was as high as a kite and wouldn't give chase. Not a worthy trophy and a mistake, and one Ahote regretted. He breathed out hard, trying to expel the remnants of the man's spirit that he believed still weakened him and caused illness, and hurried the picture back in its place.

The fifth picture in the careful row of his collection was of a Vietnamese teenager, the kill almost ruined by the Duke Gooden man his old boss Max had hired.

Ahote was sure the boy possessed the essence of the dragon, which held the four-prong power of clouds, rain, thunder, and lightning. As that boy died, Ahote felt an electrical current surge through him as the teenager's spirit entered him, and Ahote's body had convulsed in a series of rhythmic shock waves.

Ahote closed his eyes, and his fingers instinctively went to the back of the pack to the special one.

"Sae tong! Lo tenen son!" Ahote whispered, speaking his own language as he pulled out the photo that he studied every night.

This picture was different from the rest, and it always had been. The photo was of the Ben boy. The child wasn't propped against a tree, but wedged in the corner of his old van, the one that was used when Ahote snatched Ben from the house in Sparrow. The child was young and should have been afraid, but in the photo, his spirit and expression were angry and defiant. Ahote had taken the picture seconds after he had pulled the Ben boy back in the van when the child had tried to escape.

"Where were the others, boy?" Ahote asked. "There was supposed to be a girl at your house, too. A little sister."

"I don't have a sister. It's just me," Ben lied.

"What are you hiding in your hand, boy?" Ahote asked.

"Nothing," Ben answered.

"Give it here," Ahote said.

Ben stretched his hand out and opened his palm, where he revealed Julia's birthday charm bracelet, which he had snatched up after it had fallen off his sleeping sister while he hurried her inside the closet before Ahote came into their room.

"You said there's no girl in the house. That's a girl's bracelet," Ahote said.

"A girl at school gave it to me," Ben lied again. "She likes me. My dad is a cop and he's going to kill you when he finds out what you did."

Ahote opened up his big mouth and laughed. He reached his hand out to pat Ben's, but the boy snapped his hand back before Ahote could reach him.

"You lie like your father. And you'll pay like he will, too," the big Indian said.

The door of the trailer swung open and slammed against the aluminum siding as Ahote hurried to hide his photographs. He looked up to see his new boss entering inside, with the same look of revulsion and disappointment the big Indian's father had worn when Ahote was a young man.

"Was this you?" the boss yelled. He thrust his cell phone in front of Ahote's face. On the screen was a story from a local Detroit newspaper about the brutal murder of Angel Perez.

"I promised I'd stop. And I did for a long time," Ahote tried to explain. "I was careful. I always am. He was a nobody, a day laborer, probably an illegal that couldn't be tracked. No one cared about him."

"That's where you're wrong, idiot. The kid you killed was the nephew of a city councilman. Duke Gooden's daughter wrote the article, as if what you did wasn't bad enough. I warned you, Ahote. You had some good years, but you failed your job with Chip Haskell. You went too far with him. You torture someone, you pull back so they can give you what you want, before you go at it again."

"He was close to telling me, but he had a heart attack or something."

"You carved his friggin' eye out. You want to cut his ear off, okay. Guy would've likely bled out from the eye thing, if he hadn't had the heart attack first."

"It won't happen again."

"It better not. I hear you've done some real good work through the years. Chip Haskell's body is still in the trunk of Jameson's car. Haskell was shot in the head. You know anything about that?"

"No. Jameson took Haskell after I had my round with him. Jameson must've shot him. Jameson worked with me for a long time. It sounds like his style."

"You need to get rid of the body and the car. Don't do anything weird with the body, like I know you're going to want to do. Be clean about it and just bury it in the woods. Are we clear?"

"Yes."

"We've got more problems. Jameson's gone."

"What do you mean?" Ahote asked.

"When I showed up at the Sparrow place, Jameson wasn't there, but his car was. Either Duke got him, or his kid did."

"The reporter woman?"

"Another problem. She had the local sheriffs at her house earlier, and I hear there's a guy in the Detroit PD who's watching over her like a hawk."

"Do we have another back door to get to Duke?" Ahote asked.

"Duke's got another daughter, Sarah. We thought she was still in Florida, but turns out she's working at a rehab facility downtown. Julia just met with her. Sarah's got a record. Not close to being the con that Duke is though. It takes a master's hand to make people believe that you've been dead for the past thirty years."

"I started the fire."

"Well, you should've stuck around to be sure they both burned. This whole Gooden situation is your fault. The night you snatched the boy, you should've checked the house better and taken the other kids, at least the Julia girl. You threaten to hurt a little girl, it has a deeper impact on a man."

"I went back and looked. There was nobody else in the house besides the mother. I had to hurry."

"You keep screwing up, Ahote, I don't know."

"What do you want me to do?"

"Curb your twisted bow-and-arrow killing shit and bring me Julia or Sarah Gooden by tomorrow. One of those girls knows where Duke is. And your pet in the bowl there, it looks like it's got some problems."

CHAPTER 9

Julia ran the four blocks from the Renaissance House to her paper, and then sprinted up the six flights of stairs until she reached the newsroom. She hurried to her desk, which was positioned on the far side of the newsroom next to the now-vacant, recently laid-off business editor's desk, and was greeted by a large yellow Post-it note from her city editor, Virginia, that read, *GET IN MY OFFICE. NOW.*

Julia shoved the note into her wastebasket and looked up the contact information for Mike Ballentine on her computer. A quick search showed three Mike Ballentines listed in the Greater Detroit area. By process of elimination by age, Julia found a Mike Stavros Ballentine, sixty-five, who lived in a different trailer park, Red Run in Madison Heights this time, as opposed to the one Sarah had first found him in during their visit with benefits ten years earlier.

Ballentine answered on the third ring in an annoyed, drowsy tone, like Julia had woken him up, even though it was late afternoon.

"Mr. Ballentine. You used to know my father, Duke Gooden. I'm his daughter Julia. I'm a reporter. I'm not writing a story about Duke, but I'm trying to find out some information about my dad that may link to my brother, Ben."

"How do I know you're Duke's kid?"

"You had sex with my sister, Sarah, when she came to talk to you about Duke ten years ago. Does that work?"

Ballentine let out a dry hack on the other end of the line.

"Duke never mentioned you," Ballentine answered.

"No surprise. Duke had three kids, Sarah, Ben, and me. I'm guessing you only knew about Sarah from her visit. My dad brought plenty of people over to our house in Sparrow, but I don't remember you."

"No. We'd usually meet at my house in LaSalle Gardens back then."

"LaSalle Gardens. Did you live in a yellow duplex?" Julia asked.

"That's right. How'd you know?"

"There was a time when my family lived in Duke's Chrysler. I remember he left us in the car for hours in front of your place a couple of times for some big meeting he said he had."

"Jesus. I didn't know Duke had his kids out there. What do you want to know about Duke? An FBI agent, Terry something or other, came by a couple of weeks ago asking about your dad. The agent showed back up here again yesterday. I can tell you what I told him."

"The FBI is looking for Duke?"

"Duke was part of a case the agent was working. That's all he'd say."

"How did you know my father?"

"Duke had oversized dreams, but not the means to make them real. We had worked a couple of cons together, small stuff. Fake real estate deals, passing bad checks. One time, Duke and I were having coffee at a sandwich shop, and I bumped into a guy I knew, but made a big point to avoid at all costs. Duke could smell money on him and threw him that killer smile of his. Duke could turn that smile on and make a person feel like they were the only ones that mattered in the entire universe. He had a skill that way."

"I remember. Sort of like a snake that hypnotizes a mouse just before it swallows him whole."

"The guy we ran into that day, he was a businessman, if you could call him that. He picked up something in Duke that he liked right away, and the two started talking, like I wasn't even there. By this time, I had somewhere to be. I'd heard there was a shipment of electronics that was going to be delivered at the port, and I had partnered with a worker there to benefit our mutual interests. He had the product, I had the customers. When I left Duke, he was still talking it up with the guy."

"The man you're talking about, was his name Peter Jonti?"

"Never heard of him."

"Jonti knew my dad and it sounds like you two were in the same line of business," Julia said.

"Then I would've definitely known him, but like I said, I've never heard of the guy."

"What was the other man's name, the one in the sandwich shop?"

"Max Mueller. I just read his obituary online in the *Free Press.*"

"Who is he?"

"No way. Like I told the federal agent, you can figure that out on your own. I don't want anything coming back to me. You look the Mueller family up on your own. Don't you dare mention my name or that we talked."

"Do you know what happened to Duke?"

Julia listened in as it sounded like Ballentine was hocking up a phlegm ball.

"You don't know?" Ballentine asked.

"I'd heard my parents died in a fire."

"That's right. The day before I got the news that your parents were dead, Duke shows up at my door with Marjorie. She had always been a fine-looking woman, but the booze made her sloppy. But this night, she was stone-cold sober. I hear someone pounding on my door real hard, and it's Duke. Your dad, he always liked to look sharp, even if his clothes were from Goodwill. But this time when he showed up at my house, he was all spiffed up, wearing a real suit that fit. The guy had friggin' cuff links on. He looked good, but it was the first time I'd seen him nervous. I mean that cool, relaxed thing he always had going was completely gone. Duke was scared shitless. He asked me if I'd be willing to stash something for him, and he'd pay me to do it if I kept my mouth shut. Five grand a year. Can you imagine? But I didn't want to risk it."

"Did he tell you what he wanted you to keep for him?"

"No. I liked your dad, and the five grand was real

tempting, but I knew what Max Mueller was up to. He had two businesses. Neither of them was good, but one was downright evil. I like money, but not at that price."

"What can you tell me about Max Mueller?"

"Nothing if I want to live."

"You said Max is dead. Why should you be worried about talking about him?"

"Max's got a bunch of goons and a son who might be running things now. The kid's name is Liam. I don't know if he followed in his old man's footsteps or if someone else is heading the Mueller show. For all I know, the business got parceled out to Max's competition at a price before he died or if there's a power struggle going on. Listen, I've told you all I can. You need anything else, don't call me. Do me a favor, though. Tell your sister Sarah I said 'hey.' "

Julia hung up and made another phone call, ignoring an incoming call from Virginia, and hoped one of her ace-in-the hole sources, Tyce Jones, would answer.

Tyce was an up-and-coming Detroit music producer after his previous life as a drug dealer put him in a wheelchair, although Julia was never quite convinced that Tyce was completely out of the life.

"Julia Gooden, damn, girl. I thought you'd died. I personally saved your ass a couple of months ago, and you only came to see me one time since. You use a man for his connections, a brother has to start thinking it's a one-way street."

"Nice to talk to you, too, Tyce."

"How's Helen since her old man died? I sent flowers to his funeral and she sent me a real nice thank-you card. A man doesn't forget something like that, appreciation. Do you know what that word means?"

"I do. And since I helped incarcerate the man who put you in your wheelchair, I'm thinking that we're even."

"Big Nicky Conti. All right. You laid your case and we're square. What do you need?"

"Information about a man who just died. His name is Max Mueller."

Julia could hear Tyce groan. "I'm not talking to you about this shit over the phone. You want to drill me for what I know, you know where my place of business is."

"Okay. I need a few minutes to wrap something up."

"Come by in an hour. You're not the only one who's busy," Tyce said, and hung up the phone.

Julia was about to launch into an online search for Max Mueller, when a tall, redheaded woman, with her arms folded across her chest, rapped hard on Julia's desk with her knuckles.

"So nice of you to join us. Can I have a word if you can fit me into your schedule?"

Virginia made her way to her office, and Julia followed, all the while working up a strategy on what she could tell Virginia to buy some time. Julia knew Virginia respected her, and Julia felt the same way about her city editor.

Virginia had worked her way up from general assignment reporter to covering county government, where she nailed the Wayne County treasurer for her coverage on how he skimmed three million dollars to finance his second home and mistress. Virginia's series on the treasurer landed her the coveted investigative reporting slot, which she had held until she took a management job as a way to avoid an early buyout, like many other fiftysomething veterans in the newsroom had taken under duress. The two women would never call themselves friends, but they both had a mutual admiration for each other's work.

Virginia shut her office door and pulled the shades.

"What are you doing, Julia? This is a big story, the biggest one in a long time, and you're dumping it off on the Detroit reporter. We both know Tom lost his fire years ago. Between us, he's next on the chopping block, and rumor has it he's short-listed for a public relations flacking gig with DTE Energy. I hope to God he gets it, because I'm getting an ulcer from having to lay off people I used to go out for drinks with after deadline."

"I'm sorry, Virg. But on the Perez murder, I got you information no other news organization had on the serial killer and bow-and-arrow angle."

"I know. Thank God for your sources. CNN picked it up and they're citing us. That was good work. But I don't get what you're doing now, passing the story off to the B Team. I had to pretend that I had a great reason why I sent Tom to the press conference when Edgar Sanchez called me and wanted to know why you weren't there."

"Sorry to put you on the spot like that. Edgar is a good man, and that's horrible what happened to his nephew. I promise, I'll help Tom fill in the blanks if he can be the point person on the Angel Perez coverage for now. I'm looking into something else. I need some time to work on it. A few days are all I'm asking."

"I don't like this. What's the story?"

"I'm sorry. I can't tell you right now. Something heated up on a prominent cold case. It could be huge."

"I don't like betting on a horse when I don't know its odds. The Angel Perez story is big right now."

"I understand. But I also know that you've been in my shoes, and you've had to sit on a big story until you could get more information to back it up," Julia said, and then she played her next card. "I don't want to get pushed to write what I have now, because I'll run the risk of my sources clamming up and the competition getting it before we do."

"Fine. I'll keep Tom on the Perez murder for now, with the understanding that you'll give us twice-daily updates on what the cops tell you. Tom isn't even close to being as connected as you are with the Detroit PD. You know I'm doing you a big favor here."

"I appreciate it."

"You still like being out there?"

"You mean reporting? I do. Journalists go into this thinking we can make a difference, but we rarely do. But on those few occasions, it makes it all worth it."

"What I wouldn't do some days to be back on the beat instead of worrying about ad sales or how many stories we should let online readers access before we put up a pay wall. But the money is better in management. Between us, there's talk about the metro editor leaving to take a job at the *Globe*. I'm the obvious successor. You'd be a great city editor. I could put a word in for you if it works out."

"Thanks. But sitting behind a desk all day would kill me. I need to be out on the street. Did things work out with the freelance photographer Fish used for the Angel Perez story?"

"I think so. Fish showed us the photos his freelancer took during the press conference, and he got a couple of old family photos of Angel at his prom, one with his pregnant girlfriend, and one with his uncle Edgar. Fish showed us the pictures at the three o'clock editorial meeting. They looked good. The photographer must have made some inroads with the family, which helps. You never know when you work with freelancers, but they are cheaper than full-time employees, who need benefits."

"Have you ever turned into a bean counter."

"A good one, too. Call me at five and give me a briefing on what the cops tell you. I'm trusting you on the Angel Perez story and on the article you're working on. We've got at least one dead body in the Angel Perez story. Possibly three more. How many bodies do you have in your mystery article? None?"

"At least two that I know of," Julia answered.

"Okay. Sounds promising."

Julia left a message for Navarro to see if he could run a background check on Max Mueller after coming up with scant information on her father's old associate through an online search and the paper's own database. All Julia could find was that the man Duke had been affiliated with at the time of Ben's disappearance owned a company called Mueller's Antiques and Fine Goods, in the Greater Detroit area, and it specialized in consignment sales of jewelry, vintage books, and various objects of fine art. The only news story Julia could find about Max Mueller wasn't crime-related, as she had expected, but was on the obituary page. In addition to his business, the obituary said he was the son of immigrant parents from Germany who settled in Detroit after World War II, and that Max was a patron of the arts, specifically the Detroit Opera House and the Detroit Institute of Arts.

Julia closed out of her computer, feeling frustrated over her lackluster search, and decided to go to Tyce's place, even if it was early.

Julia took the stairway again, down this time, and came out in the lobby. She made her way toward the revolving glass door just as the photographer she had seen earlier, Phoenix, came through it into the building.

Phoenix moved his camera bag to his hip and flashed Julia a peace sign.

"Julia Gooden. My lucky day. I was hoping I'd run into you back here. I wanted to thank you for your advice earlier and for keeping me from getting kicked out of the Angel Perez crime scene. I owe you big-time."

"You don't owe me anything, and nice work. I heard the pictures you got from Angel Perez's family were good."

Phoenix's smile widened even further, and he started to walk backward to keep pace with Julia's forward motion toward the street.

"You could trip doing that. And good luck trying to make it through the revolving door in reverse," Julia said.

"I was going to drop off a memory card with some photos to Fish, but it can wait. How about I buy you a drink as a thanks?"

"I appreciate the offer, but I have somewhere I need to be."

"Okay, then. How about five minutes for coffee? I wanted to run something by you on the Angel Perez case. Fish wants me to shoot other assignments connected to the murder story if they come up, and I could use your thoughts on an idea I had."

Julia looked at her watch. She didn't want to slow down, but she could afford five minutes to help out a fellow journalist, who was trying to get his foot in the door.

"Okay. There's a bagel shop at the end of the block. Let's swing by there and we can talk for a minute. A minute is about all the time that I've got."

"Then a minute is all the time I need. How did you wind up as a reporter?" Phoenix asked as he shoved his way into the narrow revolving glass door slot with Julia.

"You have an issue with personal space, don't you?" Julia asked.

"I figure if I don't have much time to talk to you, I need to make the most of it."

"Some breathing room. Please," Julia said.

The two made it out to the street and Phoenix moved to the opposite side of the sidewalk and away from Julia.

"Is that better? I can yell louder if you can't hear me," Phoenix called out as a passing businessman carrying a briefcase shot the photographer an odd look.

"Very funny."

Phoenix sidled up to Julia again and kept her fast-moving pace.

"You didn't answer my question. How come you became a journalist?" he asked.

"I got a full scholarship to Syracuse University, and they had a great J school. But I guess the real reason is that I like to help people find answers that they're looking for, especially if they've undergone a tragedy in their life. I'm not a big fan of personal questions. What did you want to ask me about the Angel Perez case?"

Phoenix held the door to the bagel shop open and spread his other hand in a sweeping gesture for Julia to enter.

"I'm going to start calling you Dudley Do-Right," Julia said. She took a seat on a stool next to a high counter that faced the street.

A waiter appeared, and Phoenix ordered a coffee and a bagel and Julia ordered a bottle of water.

"You're a cheap date," Phoenix said.

"This isn't a date."

"That big cop who walked you to your car at the crime scene, are you seeing him?"

"And the five minutes I said I could spare just ticked down to two."

"Okay. So I heard you were the one who dug up that bow-and-arrow angle on the killer. I was going to pitch this to Fish, but I wanted to see what you thought first. What if I called some local bow-and-arrow hunters in the area and took some pictures of them out on the hunt? I could shoot inside some hunting shops that sell the gear, too. What do you think?"

"Maybe an interesting sidebar story, if Tom worked with you on a short piece about how hard it is to kill a human being with that kind of weapon. What I would do, and I'm sure Tom is working on this, is I'd start digging around the other victims who were killed the same way. Unless there's anything new on the investigation, that's the angle I'd take. You could also go to the Home Depot and Lowe's to interview day laborers to see if they saw Angel. Best time to go would be first thing in the morning when they're trying to get work. Be sure you work with Tom."

"See, I knew I needed to talk to you. I'm good at taking pictures, but I'm still green. Photography is a second career for me. I was an art teacher before this. After ten years, I realized I couldn't handle teenage angst anymore."

"High school, then."

"In Grand Rapids. I went back to school at Wayne State, got my photography degree, and then realized pretty quick that the photojournalism career I had dreamed of was going to be harder to break into than I thought. You have family here?"

Julia looked at her watch and started to stand. "Thanks for the water. I'm going to take it on the road."

"You really don't like personal questions, do you?"

"I have no problem with questions. I just prefer asking them. And besides my kids, I don't have any family here."

"You're an orphan?" Phoenix asked.

"Something like that. What's your last name? You never told me. I only know you as Phoenix."

"Pontiac. Phoenix Pontiac. Oh shit," Phoenix said, and pointed his finger toward the glass window in front of them and the street. "I'm about to get a ticket. I parked illegally in the red unloading zone, and there's a cop up the block who's starting to give out tickets. I'll be right back."

Phoenix ran out of the bagel shop, giving Julia her cue to cut and run. Julia put down five dollars for her water, which hadn't arrived yet, when she noticed Phoenix left his camera and camera bag behind on the counter. It was a Nikon D800, an expensive piece of equipment that Julia realized if he purchased it new, would cost him several thousand dollars. Julia realized if she left now, she'd still have a few minutes to wait around for Tyce. She sighed, anxious to get moving, but she also knew the right thing to do, and she didn't want Phoenix's camera, which doubled as his livelihood, to get stolen. She watched as Phoenix got into his car, a Subaru, and squeezed his way into traffic, maneuvering his way several cars ahead of the cop car before it reached him and turned the corner. She sighed, sat back down on her stool, and picked up the camera. Julia wasn't much of a shooter, but she was curious to see what pictures Phoenix had taken for the Angel Perez story and began scrolling through his recent shots.

The most recent picture was of Julia and Chief Linderman talking at the crime scene. The photo had been taken at a distance, and Julia realized Phoenix must have shot it while hiding out in the house across the street. Julia began to skim through the other photos and felt an icy prickle go down her back when she saw herself in each subsequent frame, going about her daily activities over the last few days, running along the Detroit RiverWalk, outside of Navarro's apartment, and giving Logan a hug as she picked him up from summer camp.

"Who are you, asshole?" Julia asked.

Julia popped out the camera's memory card, shoved it in her bag, and hurried out of the bagel shop to her car. She started up the engine and called Fish's number at the newspaper.

"Photo desk," Fish answered.

"It's Julia. There's a guy who's doing freelance work for you. Phoenix Pontiac. I met him at the Angel Perez crime scene. Something's not right. What do you know about him?"

"Nothing."

"You have to know something. You hired him. He used to be a high school art teacher and got his degree at Wayne State."

"I don't know what you're talking about. Damon Crandall shot the Perez story. He was at Edgar San-chez's press conference. Damon did a good job. He met with the family and warmed them up. I'll use him again. He got a bunch of family photos of the victim."

"What does Damon look like? The man I met at the crime scene has shoulder-length dark hair and an olive complexion."

"Not my guy. Damon is bald and black. Whoever claimed he was one of my guys is a liar."

CHAPTER 10

Julia parked her car outside of Hello Records on Bagley Street and made her way to Tyce Jones's studio, which encompassed a three-story brick building that had been newly renovated, thanks to a grant from the city of Detroit. The elected officials had obviously forgiven or turned a blind eye to the reputation of its former drug-dealing prodigal son. Julia knocked four times on the front door, and Tyce's Rasta security guard opened up, shielding the interior with his mammoth body as if Julia could somehow squeeze by or outmuscle the mountain that stood before her.

"I'm here to see Tyce. I have an appointment. I'm Julia Gooden."

"Let me see your ID."

"You know who I am. Come on," Julia said.

"You carrying?" he asked.

"No. I don't own a gun and I haven't bought one since I saw you a couple of months ago."

Tyce's guard gave Julia a suspicious once-over, and then slammed the door in Julia's face, a greeting Julia was starting to get used to from him. She waited for five minutes until the door opened and the very large man reappeared.

"Dude, you treat my guests this way?" Tyce Jones called out from behind the big Rasta. The security guard moved out of the way, and Julia could see her source whiz down a ramp in his wheelchair in her direction.

"Julia's a VIP. Don't act like you don't know who she is. Julia's on the approved list. So stand the hell back."

"People change," the Rasta answered. "Just because she was on your side before doesn't mean she won't turn on you. Let me pat her down first."

"Like hell you will. This is the house that Tyce built," Tyce said and turned to Julia. "Please excuse my cousin."

"You're related?" Julia asked.

"My mother's from Jamaica. You know that."

Three years earlier, Tyce Jones had been gunned down in a territory dispute, and Julia had visited him in the hospital, where she had met Tyce's mother. Tyce had become a close source for Julia on the beat, and although she surely didn't condone his line of work at the time, he usually provided her with valuable information when it came to the goings-on of the street.

Tyce Jones made his right hand into the shape of a gun and blew on his index finger, giving Julia a wink. He had on a yellow L.A. Lakers jersey, which contrasted against his dark skin, and a purple baseball cap, which was turned backward on his head. He wore a pair of white gleaming Versace Medusa high-top sneakers on feet that no longer worked, and in his lap was a pile of demo tapes.

"You come empty-handed," he said.

"I didn't have time to run home to get you eats from Helen."

"You keep losing points with me, Gooden. But you're still in the safe zone, for now anyway. Follow me. I want you to hear something."

Julia tailed Tyce up a wheelchair ramp to the second floor of his building, to his recording studio, where a young, skinny teenager, with almost-white blond hair and a streak of freckles over each cheek, was belting out in a perfect falsetto "Ave Maria." Next to him was a shy-looking black teenage boy, who had his eyes closed tightly as he listened to the music.

"Last time I was here, you were mixing rap and opera," Julia answered. "That young man has a beautiful voice."

"I'm still looking for the right mix, things need to juxtapose, you know? That's right, 'juxtapose,' Gooden. I know your mind is working, like how does this fool know that big, fancy word. But I did not become the man I am today without being close to brilliant. Now watch, wait, and listen. That white boy singing now, I handpicked him from St. Aloysius Parish. The other kid, man, you should hear him sing. He's about to go to town on 'Go Tell It on the Mountain' in a minute and you gonna melt. That was my all-time favorite gospel song when my mamma used to take me to church. I found that boy at my grandma's place of worship at Second Baptist. Makes the goose bumps bust out on me just about everywhere I can feel these days."

"So you're doing gospel music now."

"Not just gospel. Gospel mixed up with speed metal, kind of like a heaven-and-hell matchup in the big ring. It's going to be off the chain. Already picked out my suit for the MTV Music Awards. You could be my date," Tyce said, and gave Julia a wink. "Don't worry. You booked with a guy now, I'll take Helen. I'm just playing with you. Gooden, you've got one serious look on your face that won't let go. You want to talk business. I gotcha."

Tyce led the way up the ramp until they reached the third floor, where his office was located. The space was filled with giant white leather couches and Tyce's bright red desk, which stood in the middle of the room. Big and gaudy, Tyce Jones's style.

Tyce pulled out a cigar, removed the cellophane, and stuck it in his mouth.

"Don't worry. I won't light it 'til you leave. What you need to know, reporter girl?"

"I need to know everything about a man named Max Mueller. He died recently. I don't know much about him besides I heard he was running a couple illegal side businesses."

"You always come to me about the bad dogs. The worst ones in the pack. Granted, what big daddy Max was up to, in the early days, that was way before my time on the streets. But that Max dude was a trip. The guy went to the opera, wore these little square-framed glasses, and walked with a cane. Not because he needed to, but because he thought it made him look dignified. That's what I heard anyway."

"You ever meet Max Mueller?"

"No, but he had a reputation. As a businessman

through the years, I needed to know what was happening on the streets and people like to talk," Tyce said.

"Max had some kind of antique store?"

"That's right. In the front room anyway. I heard he had a private collection of stolen stuff worth a lot of money, old books, sculptures, paintings, jewelry, that kind of shit. Not my style, but it could make you some bank if you're into that kind of thing."

"So he stole high-end items."

"Yeah, and other things too."

"Like what?"

"People. That's what I heard anyway. Max had a pretty decent-sized human-trafficking ring back twenty, thirty years ago, right here in our 'God bless America' of Detroit. But I'm pretty sure he hung up that end of his business a while back. Too risky. The Feds were close to busting him."

"Human trafficking?" The word came out of Julia's mouth like a stutter, something she hadn't done since she was a child, right after Ben was taken. "Are we talking kids here?"

"I don't know the specifics about the freaky deaky's business. All I heard was that Max, he made his cash on his human-trafficking shit, and that helped him bankroll his art. I heard the guy was nutty for weird collectibles. Paintings, rare books, sculptures, and some odd-ass crap that only crazy people would want. Torture shit from like a thousand years ago or something."

"Tell me more about Max's human-trafficking business," Julia said. She hid her hands underneath her legs on the seat so Tyce wouldn't see that she was trembling. Julia had pushed away the darkest folds of her imagination that taunted her with scenarios of what really happened to her brother, but if he had been sold as a nine-year-old boy for God knows what, Julia wasn't sure if she'd be able to face that truth.

"I think it was a domestic setup. Max would prey on illegals or the people on the fringe or young runaways, then he'd sell them to a third-party source for some kind of indentured-servitude shit. Don't know who Max was working with on the back end, though. But like I said, he stopped all that probably twenty years back. The consignment joint he owned may still be around. He had a kid. Maybe he's still running it."

"Liam."

"Right. Liam Mueller. We don't run in the same circles, but the guy is weird, just like his dad was. All this Julia Gooden shakedown on the Muellers, is this for some kind of story you're working?"

"It's personal. You ever hear of a man named Phoenix Pontiac?"

"No, but that would be a damn fine name for a recording artist. You going to try and find Max's kid?"

"That's my next stop."

"What you really want with him?"

"Between us."

"Always, you know that. I got you covered."

"My brother disappeared when we were kids. My dad worked with some shady figures at the time, and I believe whoever my dad was tangled up with is connected to my brother's abduction. I believe my dad was working for Max."

"Damn, Gooden. You keep your personal life on a tight leash. If you're looking into the Muellers and the other dudes your dad messed with, then take Animal

with you. You call me when you need backup and he'll
be there."

"'Animal' is the name of your cousin?"

"His nickname. Animal's real name is Rupert."

"Thanks for the offer, but I work alone."

"I'll have Animal follow you, then. Where you going next?"

"Birmingham, to Mueller's Antiques and Fine
Goods."

"Fine, then Animal is your shadow. You don't come
out of the building within five, ten, my man gets you
out. Like I said, the Muellers and I don't play in the
same pen, but I know the old dude's rep. I'm not sure if
the kid took over his dad's bad ways, but you know the
platitude 'The apple doesn't fall far from the tree.'"

"Platitude?" Julia asked.

"I live my life to blow your mind."

"Thanks for your help, Tyce. I'll tell Helen you said
'hello.'"

Julia got up and Tyce scooted his wheelchair from
behind his desk and opened the door. "I'll give you a
personal escort out, reporter girl. I want to show you
something before you leave."

Tyce zipped down the wheelchair ramp ahead of
Julia, but instead of heading to the Bagley Street entrance, Tyce led Julia toward the back of his building
and to a room with a bank of windows overlooking a
fairly decent-sized backyard for a property within the
city limits. The yard was filled with man-made bee-
hives, and what looked to be hundreds of honeybees
lazily hovering around each one. A giant man wearing
protective covering on his head and body held his arms
out at his sides as the bees circled around him.

"Check this out," Tyce said. He wheeled over to a table that was stacked with jars of honey. Tyce handed one to Julia and she read the label DETROIT HONEYBEEZ. On the back of the plastic jar was a large label that said, *Made in Detroit, Baby.*

"So you're into the honey-making business now, too?" Julia asked.

"People are suckers by nature. They can't help themselves. They just love themselves an underdog. Since the city's bankruptcy shit and the auto industry tanking, Detroit is making its way back, and people want to be part of it. I'm living the American dream, mamma. I just got my first order from Costco. The mayor's office just gave me another loan for fifty thousand to start work on a manufacturing plant in some old-ass building where they used to make windshield wipers for Ford."

"Congratulations. I never saw you as a beekeeper, but if that's your calling, I'm happy for you," Julia said.

"I don't give a shit about bees. That's Animal's thing. I just want to make money."

"That's your cousin out there?" Julia asked.

"He loves that stuff. I'll tell him to follow you to the Muellers'."

"Thanks, but I'm good," Julia said.

"They say cats got nine lives. I'm not sure about people. But I know I'm down to my last one," Tyce said. "But, you, Gooden, you keep poking around bad stuff, you may be down to your last one, too. Watch your ass. You change your mind about my cousin having your back, you call me."

Tyce escorted Julia to the front door and reached for his gun in his rear waistband before he opened it.

"I didn't realize the music and honey business were that dangerous," Julia said.

"I still got a lot of enemies from the old days."

"Are you still dealing?" Julia asked.

Tyce flashed Julia a smile and handed her a jar of Detroit HoneyBeez.

"Like I said, Gooden, I like money."

The door closed behind her, and Julia hurried toward her car as her cell phone buzzed in her purse. She looked over her shoulder, considering her ambush up in Sparrow, and answered.

"You okay?" Navarro asked. "I've been working the Angel Perez case, but I got your message about Max Mueller. I've got the lowdown on him."

"I just got it myself. I'm going over to his family's consignment place right now. I found a listing for it in Birmingham."

"Wait for me. Russell and I can meet you when we're done with our shift."

"No time. I need you to run another name for me if you would, please. Phoenix Pontiac."

"The photographer?"

"I ran into him at the paper and found a string of pictures he took of me on his camera."

"I knew that guy liked you."

"No, these were personal shots. They looked like surveillance pictures. Whoever Phoenix Pontiac really is, he's been following me and knows my patterns. He had pictures of me leaving my house and your place, and there was also a shot of me running at the River-

Walk. I called Fish, and he said he'd never heard of Phoenix Pontiac before."

"You think he's a stalker?" Navarro asked.

"I doubt it. I'd never met him until I ran into him at the crime scene. I realize you're swamped with the Angel Perez case, but if you have time later, let me know what you can find out."

"You know I will."

"I was talking to a source, and he told me Max Mueller was running a human-trafficking ring at the time Ben disappeared. And my dad knew Max. I found out Duke was working for him. What if Mueller is the one who kidnapped Ben and then sold him?"

"Don't go from zero to sixty on this just yet. I found out Mueller was never arrested, but the cops were looking at him at the time. I've got a copy of Mueller's file and Ben's original one from when we ran Will's missing person's case when we were looking to see if there was a connection. I'll bring both of them by and we can go through them at your house tonight. I'm staying over, on your couch, with my eyes on the front door, until things settle down. No debate. The sheriff's substation's guys who were at your house have been monitoring your neighborhood. Everything is quiet."

"I appreciate the offer, but I don't know how Logan is going to feel about you staying over. He was rattled when the sheriffs came by."

"Maybe I can talk to him. Let him know that I'm just making sure everything is okay for a few days."

"Are you kidding me? Logan will eat you alive. He's one shrewd kid. He'll drill you every way since Tuesday to find out why you're really there. I'll handle it."

"Russell and I should be done in about an hour. Meet us at the station and then we'll take a ride to Mueller's store together."

"Sure."

"I wish I could believe you, beautiful."

Julia hung up the phone, and as she started the car, she felt the familiar sickening ache in her gut about her brother. She was ready to pull out into the street when she noticed a small envelope tucked under the windshield wiper on the passenger side of her vehicle.

She figured it was a promotional flyer, but then realized it was a white, letter-sized envelope, not a typical marketing piece. She stopped the car, pulled the envelope open, and found a note.

> *Julia,*
> *He'd want you to have this. I need a chance*
> *to explain.*
> *Phoenix*

Julia reached farther into the envelope until her hand felt a small metal chain. She tipped the envelope up and the object inside fell into the palm of her hand.

"Oh, my God," Julia whispered as she stared down at the bracelet, now long-tarnished but with the boy-and-girl charm still intact. Julia felt outside of her body as she looked down at her hand and the bracelet Ben had given to her on her seventh birthday.

CHAPTER 11

Mueller's Antiques and Fine Goods was located on a tony side street in downtown Birmingham, an upscale suburb of Detroit that was half an hour away from the city. Julia pressed the charm bracelet in her hand as tightly as she could as she made a fast path up the sidewalk toward the business. After an unsuccessful Google search on her phone for a Phoenix Pontiac in the Greater Detroit area, and the principal of the Grand Rapids high school's confirmation that no such person had ever worked as an art teacher there, Julia was growing increasingly desperate to find whatever answers she could about Ben and her father's connection to his disappearance, something that Julia was certain of now.

The consignment store was in a stately brick building. Its first front window showcased a stand of jewelry, mainly watches and rings. The second window featured two large jade elephant sculptures and a painting of what appeared to be Lake Michigan, circa the turn of the century, as a female sunbather in a midcalf, short-sleeved dress, bloomers, and a bonnet walked barefoot along the shore. Julia tried the door of the shop, but it was locked. She took a quick pan of her watch and saw that it was quarter after six, which meant the antique store was likely closed for the day.

A chest-high wooden fence hand-painted to replicate a Claude Monet water lily painting wrapped around either side of the store. Julia studied the fence as she hid her purse behind a bush. Realizing she had no other options, Julia pulled off her heels and lifted herself up and over the fence, cursing under her breath as the hem of her dress snagged on a post.

Julia unhooked her dress from the fence and then dropped down on the other side. She did a quick assessment of the scene and saw a small Victorian-style yellow cottage in the rear of the property. Julia hurried barefoot down a brick path to the small building, which looked to be dark inside. Julia knocked on the front door, waited ten seconds, and then put her hand on the doorknob when no one answered, ready to break into the place if she had to.

"I'll take it you don't have an appointment. Usually our clients are wearing shoes when they visit. I wouldn't suggest trying to open that door. If you do, an alarm will go off," a voice from behind her called out.

Julia turned quickly to see a tall, wiry man with reddish-brown hair and small, round glasses perched on a long and slender nose. The man was standing on the back steps of the antique store and politely extended his hand. Julia estimated he was probably in his midforties.

"I'm sorry, have we met before? I'm Liam Mueller, the owner. Are you a garden-variety thief, a collector, or are you actually here to buy something? We don't sell shoes, though, I'm afraid."

"None of the above. Your father knew my dad, Duke Gooden. They were in business together. The problem is, I can't figure out which part of your father's business my dad was involved in."

"I'm sorry?"

"I believe you know exactly what I'm talking about. Was it antique sales or people sales? Human trafficking is a cruel, cruel business."

"Ms. Gooden, I'm sure you're unaware that my father just passed. I can't imagine anyone, even someone as brash and as rude as you appear to be, could speak ill of the dead."

"I know your father ran a human-trafficking business. How did you know my last name?"

"You told me your father's last name was Gooden, and you aren't wearing a wedding ring, so I assumed. What's your first name?"

"Julia. I'm Julia Gooden. I want to know about your father."

Liam Mueller took his glasses off and rubbed his eyes as though he were tired. "You want to know about Max? My father loved art more than anything else, including his wives and children. Truth be told, he wasn't a very good man. I'm guessing you already know most fathers aren't. But your accusations about Max are wrong. Come on, let's go inside."

Julia looked over her shoulder at the fence and thought about what she had left on the other side, not her shoes, but her handbag with the three-inch knife.

"Are you coming or not? I'm willing to talk to you,

instead of calling the police, but I'm not going to stand here all night."

Julia made her choice and followed Liam into the cottage, which felt as cool as an icebox and smelled like oranges and flowers. The place was sparse on furniture, except for a bar stool next to a small desk, with a purple orchid plant on top. What it lacked in furniture, it made up for in artwork. Paintings filled almost every space of the walls and a single, strange-looking sculpture, which looked like a bent cane, was encased in glass by the front door.

Liam looked out the window dreamily and his eyes hooded down halfway. "I see you noticed the cane in the glass display box when you walked in. It's a black coral walking stick. If you look closely, and I'm guessing you didn't because you're clearly not a collector, you can see that the cane is shaped in a sharp curve, like a bent snake. I believe that in art, without pain, there can be no beauty. Take the master Vincent van Gogh, who cut off his ear. The artist sees the beauty so closely, there must be suffering and torment to balance the ecstasy. Art is rapture and pain intertwined. Only those who truly see can understand."

"I didn't come to talk about the finer points of philosophy and art."

Liam walked over to the sculpture and rapped his fingers gently on the top of the glass. "My father beat me with that cane, whenever he felt like it when I was a child. After my father died, I discovered two pieces of the cane broken in half that he kept on his dresser. He'd saved them like a trophy. I had the cane repurposed so it could be whole again. Do you know how hard you would have to hit someone for a carved piece of black coral to snap in two?"

"I'm not your therapist, Mr. Mueller."

"But you're a journalist. I recognize your name from the news. Journalists are paid to hear the stories and the sufferings of others. I invite you in, but you won't indulge me?"

"I know plenty of people like you. They think they're smarter than the whole world, and they spin their smoke and mirrors to distract from the truth. That's what you're trying to do here, or to gain my sympathy. Say whatever you want, Mr. Mueller. But understand that no matter what happened to you, or what kind of monster your father was behind closed doors when he got home, it won't influence me."

Mueller closed his eyes while his fingers played a slow beat against the glass container.

"I was ten, sleeping in my bed when Max got home from the opera. It was *Madama Butterfly* at the Detroit Opera House. The *Free Press* panned the performance, and my father agreed. I woke up to Max standing over my bed with this look of rage on his face. Then he started beating me with the cane. He was a slight man, but when he was angry, he seemed to possess the wrath of an Old Testament God. Max shattered both my wrists and knocked out two of my teeth. The next morning, after the nanny called my father's private doctor to stitch me up, I came down to the breakfast table. My father asked me how my eggs tasted. So as you can see, Ms. Gooden, Max was cruel. Coming here and throwing insults about him is quite tame in comparison to what I've thought about the man myself. Considering the circumstances, I couldn't be happier that he's dead. Lung cancer. It was slow, painful, and well-deserved."

"Did Max ever mention Duke Gooden or a boy named Ben?"

Liam outstretched his hand and tapped it gingerly against Julia's. "I remember your father. Benjamin Senior, I think his name was. That's what my father called him. The name Duke seemed so low-class. I met him once or twice. He worked for my father only for a short time, maybe less than six months. My father had to fire him. Benjamin Senior worked for Max as a driver, I believe."

"A driver, like a personal chauffeur?"

"Max saw great promise in your father. That was a tremendous compliment. My father didn't see promise in anyone, including myself. But your father—Max took him in, almost as an apprentice, and let him live in the carriage house in our Grosse Pointe property. But something soured between our fathers. I'm not sure what, but I believe it had to do with Duke's drinking."

"My father didn't drink."

"We all block away memories that are the hardest. I clearly remember Max telling the family over dinner one night that Duke had shown up to work that day barely able to stand. He was supposed to pick up a shipment for my father, and Max had to send him home."

"A shipment of what? People?"

Liam's top lip curved into a nasty smile. "I had heard those rumors through the years, but they simply weren't true and were created by a rival company in Chicago. My father was independently wealthy from his own father, who brought millions of dollars' worth of paintings here from Germany after World War II. Max didn't need more money, and he never would have done anything as dirty as what you're implying, not because he was a good man, but because he would have felt that kind of thing, selling people, was beneath him."

"You're saying my father was a drunk?"

"Max told me the last time he saw Duke, he was slurring his words and could barely stand up. That was right before Duke got in a car accident. He hit a utility pole, as I recall, and his car burst into flames on impact. A terrible way to die. But, hopefully, the end was quick. There were rumors, though, that Duke escaped and fled the country, since he wanted to run out on a debt. Is that true?"

"My father is dead."

"Is that so?" Liam said, and hit a buzzer behind his desk to unlock the front door.

Julia felt something squirm inside her as a giant man came inside and seemed to swallow the room as he approached.

"Ms. Gooden, this is Ahote. He is an old friend of my father's. He was just visiting me. Coming to pay his condolences."

Ahote positioned himself inches away from Julia and stared at her, as though he could read her thoughts. Julia kept his gaze and tried to hide the screaming memories of the picture of the strange bird she saw by her mother's bed the night Ben was taken, and Sarah's description of the giant man with the long braid down his back, who had interrogated their mother.

"You're in my personal space. Back up," Julia warned.

"I think the two of you know something about my brother, Ben, and you're going to tell me."

Ahote's voice was smooth and sounded deeper and more ominous than the Devil beckoning her inside the gates of hell. "'Ben.' I don't know anyone by that name. But it is true. All souls on this earth know each other."

Julia reached her fingers into the pocket of her dress. She clutched the bracelet Ben had given her, as the pain she had carried for the past thirty years pulsed up like a deadly wave, ready to drown her and anyone else in its path.

"We have another guest," Liam said in an emotionless tone. "Coming up the path."

Julia could feel Ahote's warm breath on her shoulder as she spun around toward the door to see another towering figure on the other side.

The buzzer to the cottage rang and Liam nodded at Ahote to answer it.

"We're closed. You're not supposed to be back here," Ahote said.

"The gate was unlocked," the man said, and pressed his badge up against the glass.

"Open the door," Liam directed, but Ahote stood motionless with his hands at his sides. "I said buzz the officer through. *Now.*"

The big Indian pounded out the security code on a keypad on the wall and let in Chief John Linderman. The chief of police brushed by Ahote, making sure the big Indian felt the weight of his chest as he went by him. Linderman did a quick pan of the room and then stood protectively next to Julia.

"Never really liked antiques and art much. The wife, though, makes me go to the Detroit Institute of Arts whenever there's a new opening."

"What are you doing here, Chief?" Julia asked.

"It was passed along by one of my men that you were coming here alone. Since my guy is still tied up at work, I promised him that I would stop by. I'm on my way to see my son. He lives in Birmingham, so I promised my officer that I'd check in. Is everything all right here?"

"No. I think these two men have information on a cold case they're refusing to divulge."

Linderman gave Liam and Ahote a stony look and pulled out his badge again. "I don't think we've met. I'm Detroit chief of police, John Linderman."

Liam Mueller held out his hand to shake, but Linderman stood stock-still, the weight and strength of the chief seeming to come off him in waves. A squeaky hum of rejection came from Liam's throat as he retracted his hand and put it inside the pocket of his pants.

"You might know a friend of mine, Harry Hall. He's the chief of the Birmingham Police. Let me give him a call. I'm sure he'd be more than happy to swing by," Linderman said.

"No need for concern, Mr. Linderman. Mueller's Antiques and Fine Goods has been in business for fifty years here in Birmingham. We're a respected part of the community. And I certainly don't have any information about a missing child. You know, at one point, my father, Max, had thought about opening a second gallery in downtown Detroit, but he felt it would have lessened our family's stock, so we've stayed with our kind here."

"I'm very familiar with Max and the filth he used to run, so don't bother to try and play uptown with me," Linderman said. He moved his suit coat slightly away from his torso in a play so Liam and Ahote could see his gun in his shoulder holster. "Julia, are you ready to go?"

"We were just starting here."

"We're all through. Let me walk you to your car," Linderman said, not giving Julia an inch to disagree in his tone.

Julia felt her face burn with anger as Linderman escorted her out of the cottage and then through the now-open fence, where her shoes and bag still waited for her tucked behind a bush.

"What do you think you were doing back there?" Linderman asked. "Navarro wouldn't tell me what was going on, but he said he was worried about you coming up here alone and that the Muellers might be after you. If this is for a story you're working, that's reckless, and don't plan on me playing babysitter again. I've got Angel Perez's killer still on the loose, and the only reason I came here is because I was on the way to see my son. You got lucky."

"I didn't come here for a story. It's personal. Liam Mueller knows what happened to Ben. I'm sure of it now. You heard him back there. I mentioned my brother, but I never said anything about him being abducted. Liam knew. You need to go back in there and arrest him. If it's out of your jurisdiction, call your friend."

Linderman put a calming hand on Julia's shoulder. Julia almost smiled at him for his kindness, but quickly looked away when she realized the chief was looking back at her with pity. Julia had known Linderman for twelve years, ever since she started at the paper covering the crime beat. While she had at first labeled Linderman "the Red Devil" around the newsroom for his initial cold reception to her, including his refusal to ever let Julia interview him directly in the early days, the two had built a mutual respect for one another through the years. Linderman had also been a steady rock for Julia during Will's abduction case, when the police, at first, were certain Will's disappearance was linked to Ben's.

"Max Mueller was an evil man. I heard stories about him when I was first on patrol. I knew Sex Crimes and Robbery were trying to nail him at the time, and the Feds were looking at him, too. Max was either the luckiest man alive or had friends in high places. I don't know anything about Liam, but why do you think the Mueller family had anything to do with your brother's disappearance?"

"My dad used to work for Max."

Linderman raised his giant eyebrows in surprise. "That was never brought up in your brother's case."

"I just found out."

"You need to slow down and think things through before you get yourself into something you won't be able to get out of. Let the authorities handle it."

"You wouldn't understand," Julia said.

"Maybe not, but I do know something about loss. It can eat you alive and make you stretch the limits of what you think you'd be brave enough or foolish enough to do to try and get back what you had. My son who lives here in Birmingham, his name is Joseph. He had a heart transplant when he was ten. Before that, my boy was the star of his Little League team, a natural athlete if I've ever seen one. One day, Joseph's up at bat, and, my God, could this kid swing. My wife and I were in the stands, and we see him up there at home plate, with his blue uniform on, kind of swaying. I figured he was getting ready for the pitch, but then he collapses. I convinced my wife it was just from the heat while we were in the ambulance, but after the tests, we found out."

"I didn't know. I'm so sorry," Julia said. "But he's okay now."

"Through the grace of God. My wife, Trish, pretty much lived in the hospital with Joseph while we waited for a donor. Every night, I'd go home and pray, begging God to save my boy. After three months, we benefited from another family's loss. A twelve-year-old got killed while riding his bike on his paper route. I remember, during those times, I would've done anything to save my boy. We were lucky. Our story had a happy ending. But I know your story didn't."

"Ben's story has no ending. I appreciate you showing up here to check up on me on behalf of Navarro, and I'm happy that your son is okay, but in all due respect, our stories aren't the same."

"Understood," Linderman said, and opened the driver-side door to Julia's SUV.

Julia got inside and looked back at the gallery, wishing she could firebomb the place.

"Do me a favor, Julia. I'm not sure about Liam Mueller, but I know his father was bad news, although there was never enough evidence to nail him. Don't come back here again unless you have help. You have a charming way about yourself that pisses people off."

"No guarantees, sir."

"In that case, dinner at my son's isn't until seven thirty. Consider me your escort."

"That's so not necessary. Go to your kid's house. I'll head home."

"Mind your speed. I'll be behind you."

Linderman pulled his aviator sunglasses from his suit coat and slid them up the bridge of his nose as he got into his car. Julia's gaze hung once more on the Muellers' store, and as if Linderman realized her intent, he pulled up closely behind Julia and flashed his lights.

"Fine," Julia said to herself, and put her SUV into drive.

Liam Mueller removed the square-shaped glasses from his face and rubbed his eyes as he sighed deeply.

"You . . . did . . . not . . . do . . . your . . . job," Liam said in a slow, halting warning.

"Everything changed when the cop showed up," Ahote said.

"My father's sins come back to haunt me. You have a pickup soon," Liam said.

Liam turned his back on Ahote, reset the alarm to the cottage, and then studied a security camera to monitor the activity on the street. When he saw the police chief and Duke Gooden's daughter drive away, Liam reached for a remote control on his desk and pressed a button that activated the shades. Once the room was secure and there was no visibility to the place from outside, he pointed his finger at a large red-and-black oriental rug that covered the dark cherrywood floor and cleared his throat.

"Open it," Liam said.

Ahote bent down and grabbed the corner of the rug between his big hands and pulled, revealing a trapdoor underneath. Once the door was visible, Ahote looked back at Liam.

"Go on now. You know what to do. I don't know why my father kept you on so long."

Ahote muttered something in a language Liam had never heard before. Ahote then pulled a leather strap that was connected to the trapdoor and opened it.

Liam pushed his way ahead of Ahote and peered down below, clapping his hands, which activated the lighting system in the hidden lower level. Once the two men were downstairs, Liam did a slow inspection of his stolen collection, a seventeenth-century Vermeer, an Edgar Degas, and a Jackson Pollock, the latter not usually appealing to Liam's particular taste, but he believed a collection needed juxtaposition of pieces to make it truly complete. Liam's eyes moved between a Gustav Klimt and a Renoir before he reached for a secure phone to call an old friend of his father's, and now his own unwanted and inherited colleague.

When Louis Lemming answered, the younger Mueller felt relieved that the man on the other end of the phone was in St. Louis and not Detroit.

"Julia Gooden was just here, Duke's daughter," Liam said.

"That's friggin' luck. She came on her own?" Lemming asked.

Liam could picture the older man's flabby gut pouring out of his thousand-dollar suit and the hideous black mole on the side of his nose.

"Yes, but then a policeman showed up. Actually, it was the police chief from Detroit."

"So," Lemming answered.

"I don't want any trouble. I was thinking, until this whole situation is figured out, I want to unload some of my father's paintings."

"Not my problem," Lemming answered.

"It is your problem," Liam said. "You and my father got me into this mess, and you'll get me out."

"There's a lot of money on the line, asshole. Everyone sits tight until Duke is brought in. Max was the boss, but now we're equal. You don't own me. The police chief coming to your store is not a problem. Not finding Duke is."

"Once we find him, I wash my hands of this," Liam said.

"You knew what your dad was doing back in the day."

"I was a kid," Liam whined.

"But you're not anymore. You get your shit together. It would be a shame if the cops found out what your daddy used to do, and how you helped him when you got older. Hundreds of people, kids, runaways. It's amazing what a healthy young person is worth."

"I wasn't involved in that part of the business," Liam said.

"You bought your stupid art through the money your dad earned that way. That ties you to it. Max and I had a real good business once. But now that he's gone, we're in it together."

Liam hung up the phone and handed Ahote a piece of paper with an address on it.

"You're heading back to the city," Liam said. "You have work to do tonight."

True to his word, Linderman kept a steady one-car space behind Julia during the twenty-minute drive. As Julia pulled into her neighborhood, Linderman flashed his lights again, and she pulled her SUV over to the side of the road. Linderman stopped alongside Julia and opened his passenger-side window.

"I meant what I said before. If you have new information on your brother's case, work with us or the St. Clair's sheriff's department. The crime wasn't in our jurisdiction, but I'd be happy to lend a hand."

Linderman's window closed and Julia watched as the chief pulled out of the neighborhood and headed back toward the highway.

Julia contemplated going back to the consignment store as she fingered the charm bracelet in her hand, but she knew Navarro and her children would likely be waiting for her. Julia drove through her neighborhood until she reached her house, but Helen's car was gone, which meant she probably got tired of waiting for Julia to come home and took Logan and Will out for dinner. Navarro's Chevy Tahoe wasn't in the driveway either, but a Subaru was parked out front, with a man sitting inside.

Julia jammed her car into park and stormed toward the waiting vehicle.

"Who the hell are you?" Julia demanded.

Phoenix Pontiac raised his hand up in a surrendering gesture. "I'm sorry I wasn't playing straight with you before. Your brother Ben, I knew him."

"Where did you get that bracelet? Goddamn it, get out of the car," Julia said, and grabbed the driver-side door.

Phoenix's eyes darted in the rearview mirror as Navarro's Tahoe turned the corner to the street four blocks away.

"We were both kidnapped by the same people, but I got away. I'll be in touch," Phoenix said. He hit the gas and pulled away from the curb.

Julia tore off her shoes and sprinted after the Subaru, her bare feet pounding down on the concrete as she desperately tried to chase down her past.

A sudden, piercing image of Ben, his suntanned, lean arms and legs running ahead of her as the two ran down the Sparrow boardwalk on their last day together, blinded Julia for a second, but she caught herself right before she stumbled.

(*"I promise I won't ever let anything bad happen to you. Not ever."*)

The jagged concrete tore up Julia's bare feet, but she pushed herself harder, faster, than she had ever run before in her entire life. She felt a screaming pain in her hamstring, but pushed through it as she caught up to the Subaru and pounded her fist against the car's trunk.

Phoenix caught Julia in the rearview mirror and his eyes widened in surprise.

"Stop!" Julia called out.

The Subaru made a squealing sound as Phoenix floored the engine.

"Can't let you go," Julia panted as she tore across the street and down the sidewalk in the direction of the car.

Julia was sure she could catch up if she just ran faster, when the passenger door of a VW Bug parked on the sidewalk opened directly in her path. Julia lunged to the right to avoid slamming directly into the metal door at high speed, but lost her footing. Julia skidded across the gravel and screamed in defeat as Phoenix Pontiac's car disappeared from her sight.

CHAPTER 12

Duke Gooden used his high-powered binoculars that made the Renaissance House lobby look so close, it was as if he could reach out and touch the blue-haired bangs of its receptionist. Duke was in position next to a bank of windows on the second floor of an unrented former office space, which was directly across the street from the substance abuse center. Duke's eyes ticked to the street, where he had seen a car circle the block several times, always slowing down in front of the Renaissance House. Duke settled on the fact that the occupants of the car, a dark blue sedan with tinted windows, were his former boss's men. He watched as their vehicle pulled into a parking spot ten places behind the Renaissance House and had stayed there, without the driver getting out, for the past hour.

Sarah's car, a run-down Toyota, was on the sixth floor of a parking lot adjacent to where the blue sedan had parked. Duke had noticed the Toyota needed a paint job, badly, when he had stuck a tracker under the car when Julia had been visiting her earlier, a fortuitous two-for-one opportunity, since he was able to put trackers under both of his daughters' vehicles.

His tail wasn't to keep them safe. Julia and Sarah were adults now, unlike Ben who was just a kid when everything came crashing down, but his daughters could take care of themselves. It wasn't his job to protect the girls from the people of his past who were fools to believe Duke would fall to sentimentality after thirty years and want to catch up with his seed when they realized he wasn't dead.

The fact that the blue sedan was waiting for Sarah meant one thing: They hadn't found it yet, and Chip hadn't given up the location where Duke had stashed his prize so long ago, despite Chip having to pay a hideous price for his silence.

Duke started to close up shop, satisfied now with the current situation. It was time to get what was rightfully his. He felt the anticipation of excitement start to move through him, but Duke knew he had to play it cool. Out of habit, he scanned the scene one last time.

The inner door to the lobby of the Renaissance House opened and Sarah appeared. She chatted with the blue-haired receptionist, leaving Duke to wonder why a woman would do that, making herself purposely unattractive, by coloring her hair such a hideous shade.

Duke gave the scene one more go and pivoted so he was in view of the blue sedan.

"Come to Papa, baby. Which grizzled asshole is still working for your lousy organization?" Duke asked as the driver-side window of the sedan began to crack open.

A brown arm inched its way out the window and threw a cigarette on the curb. Duke made a tighter focus of the man and caught the familiar giant with the scar he had carved into the big Indian's face thirty years earlier.

Duke watched on as Ahote got out of the car and pulled a Detroit Tiger hat down low to shield his face.

"Ah, shit on a sundae," Duke said.

Duke noticed Ahote was wearing a long, beige, cloth coat, even though it was easily one hundred degrees outside, leaving Duke to quickly deduce that Ahote likely was hiding a weapon or something worse inside of it, which he planned to use on Sarah.

An unfamiliar feeling moved through Duke, a paternal worry, ringing like a sonic boom inside him as he watched Ahote duck across the street and make his way inside the parking garage, where Sarah's vehicle awaited her.

Duke dropped the binoculars down to his side, and an old memory he had long buried worked its way back.

"You want to talk to your boy, Duke?" the man on the phone asked.

"Put Ben on. Now!" Duke answered.

"You know, your son, he's a strong kid. And he's smart. He hasn't asked for you once. Only his kid sister. Julia, right? He begged us to leave her alone when we found out you had more than one. We make the deal tonight, or we kill your boy. And your doll baby girl is next. Ahote is hungry to start hunting again."

Duke closed his eyes to block the memory. He had tried to make it right, and if it were all going down now, instead of when he was young and inexperienced, he would be able to stop it.

Sarah moved toward the front door of the Renaissance House as Duke looked at her from across the street. All that he had fixated on for the past three decades was still in his grasp, if he played it right. Every nerve of his being told him to get out and not look back, to just get in his car and pick up what was his.

"Good-bye, kid," Duke said. He took one last look at his eldest child and a strange knot built up in his chest as he realized Sarah looked a lot like him.

"Damn it." Duke grabbed his burner phone, the one he picked up at the 7-Eleven, and dialed.

"Renaissance House."

"I need to talk to Sarah Gooden. Now."

"She's gone for the day."

"No, she's not. She's in your lobby and she's expecting my phone call. Put her on."

Duke could see the receptionist put the phone on hold and motion to Sarah.

Duke had never tried to find out what had happened to his kids. With Ben, he'd likely never know, but his girls, he could have, but he knew all too well that sentimentality made you weak. That was tripping him up now. After being sidelined with Chip, Duke had done some research on his girls over the past few hours. He had discovered Julia had done well for herself, despite the loser assistant D.A. she had married, but Sarah had a record, and Duke knew she liked money. Duke worked his con in his head and waited for Sarah to pick up the phone.

"Who is this?" Sarah asked.

"Your lucky day. Your friend down in Florida sent me up here with some money for you."

"Bullshit. The only thing my friend down in Florida would hand deliver me is a pipe bomb if he could."

"I wouldn't know about that. I have five thousand dollars in cash that I'm supposed to give you. Something about a deal you were working in Tampa," Duke bluffed, piecing together what he had read about Sarah earlier that morning.

"Where can we meet?" Sarah asked.

"There's a back alley to your building. Whatever you do, don't go out the front. Give me five minutes, turn around slowly like nothing's going on, and meet me out back."

"Sounds like a setup."

"It's your money to lose."

"All right. Five minutes. You don't have the money or you try anything, I'm packing."

Duke put on his dark glasses, hung up the phone, and walked quickly to his own car parked behind the building. He backtracked south, out of sight from the blue sedan, and came around the Spring Street alleyway, where Sarah was waiting for him with her arms folded across her chest.

Duke stopped the car next to Sarah and rolled down the passenger-side window.

"Get in. Now."

"Like hell I am. Let me see the money. Better yet. Get out of the car. I don't like what's going on here."

"We don't have much time," Duke said.

"Really? I've got all the time in the world."

Duke sighed, got out of the car, and moved quickly toward Sarah.

"Nice suit. If your clothes match the money you're carrying, then we're good. But explain one thing to me, why did Steve send me the cash? I figured he'd keep it for himself until he got out of jail," Sarah said.

Duke lowered his sunglasses and grabbed Sarah's hand.

"You're in trouble. Get in the car. There's no money."

She started to reach into her bag for her gun, when she took a good look at Duke for the first time and her hand froze midair.

"Dad?"

"That's right," her father said, and pulled his gun out from behind his waist. "Now get in the car."

"I don't care if you shoot me, I'm not going anywhere with you."

Duke saw the punch coming, but it was remarkably fast and powerful for a woman of Sarah's size. He moved away from her swing in time, but it still caught him on the side of his cheek.

"You don't like me, fine. But there's an evil guy with some torture tools stashed in his coat, and he's waiting for you by your car to take a ride with him. Come on, Sarah, you're going to pray that you're going to die by the time he's through with you. I've seen him work before."

"How do I know you're not lying?" Sarah asked.

"You don't," Duke answered, and opened the passenger door of his SUV.

"There's no money?" Sarah asked.

"Not a cent. Not now anyway."

Sarah stared at Duke, and then climbed inside her father's car.

"I must be a sucker to believe you," Sarah said.

"I'm the sucker," Duke said. "Hand me your purse."

"Screw you," Sarah answered.

"If you'd like me to hand deliver you back to your car and the guy who's about to go medieval on you, I'd be pleased to accommodate," Duke said. He reached down and quickly grabbed Sarah's bag before she could stop him. He carefully took out a black snubnose Smith & Wesson, a snakeskin silver wallet, and a bottle of pills.

"Thought you were clean," Duke said.

"Read the label. They're prescription. For my anxiety that all started because of you, asshole."

Duke took a quick look at the label on the bottle: XANAX.

"As if you have the balls to judge me," Sarah said.

"You have a record."

"So do you," Sarah said. She tried to grab the contents of her purse back, but Duke was too fast.

"You and your sister close?" Duke asked.

"Me and Julia? Yeah, I go over to her house every Sunday for dinner."

"Really?" Duke asked. "I don't see that somehow."

"I'm joking. Julia was always better than me, even when she was a kid. You knew it, too."

"But Julia was here earlier. You two must have some kind of relationship going."

Sarah tried to snag her pack of cigarettes from her purse, but Duke chucked them far into the recesses of the backseat.

"Not in my car you don't."

"You touch my cigarettes again, I won't hold off on my punch next time," Sarah said. "Julia just came here to get information. She doesn't like me. I tried to screw her too many times. You know how that is, right?"

"I don't hang around long enough to let people's sentiments about me sink in."

"Where are you taking me?"

"To a safe place."

"Why should I believe you?"

"Because you don't have much of a choice," Duke said.

"Julia thinks you had something to do with Ben's kidnapping. Is that true?"

Duke looked into his rearview mirror and at the parking garage disappearing behind him, where Ahote likely was lying in wait for Sarah.

"That's right. I did."

CHAPTER 13

A stream of ice-cold water blasted against the gash in Julia's hand. Julia cursed under her breath over her failure to catch up to Phoenix Pontiac and her subsequent swan dive onto the concrete to avoid slamming into the car door that had opened out of nowhere in her path.

Julia's entire family was crammed into her bathroom, while Navarro stood in the hallway, barking orders on his cell phone as he demanded to know why no one on patrol had been able to locate the Subaru yet.

Julia sat on a stool in front of the sink as Helen held Julia's hand under the water to try and clean out the dirt and gravel that had embedded into a nasty cut that ran the length of Julia's palm.

Will looked away from Julia's bloody wound, covered his face with his hands, and started to bawl his eyes out in a quiet, but unrelenting, wail.

"Mom's okay, sweetheart," Julia promised. She grabbed Will with her uninjured hand and pulled him close, while trying not to wince as Helen turned the faucet off and used a pair of tweezers to extract with a not-so-forgiving touch the leftover debris that the water didn't remove.

"Don't cry," Logan said, and put his arm on his brother's shoulder. "Mom just hurt her hand is all, but she'll be okay."

"You need stitches," Helen said. "Sit still and stop wiggling. It wouldn't kill you to be still for a minute. It's after hours, so I'm taking you to urgent care."

"I don't have time for a doctor. I just need a Band-Aid."

"If your cut isn't bad, how come Uncle Ray won't look at it?" Logan asked.

"He's on the phone," Julia said.

"Please. He shoots people, but can't handle seeing a little blood from his lady friend," Helen said.

"I'm not scared of blood," Logan said, and shot a suspicious look in Navarro's direction. "If you don't get all the dirt out, you can get an infection."

Logan reached up in the medicine cabinet and pulled out a tube of Neosporin. He squeezed some out on the palm of his hand and began to dab it on his mother's wound.

"Thank you, Logan. That's just what I needed. Since we're all here, I wanted to tell you, Uncle Ray is going to spend the night."

"You're having a sleepover?" Logan asked.

"No, nothing like that. I'm working on a story and Uncle Ray is going to help me. It's going to take a while, so he's going to sleep on the sofa," Julia said, feeling bad that she was lying to her family, but she couldn't tell them about her earlier encounter in Sparrow and that Navarro was staying at the house to ensure nothing would happen.

"Mr. Raymond is too big to sleep on the couch," Helen said.

"He'll be fine," Julia answered.

"Maybe I should sleep in your room tonight, to be sure you're okay," Logan said.

"Too many worrywarts in this house over a tiny cut. Everyone is going to sleep in their own room tonight, and it's probably time for little boys to go to bed."

"It's summer and it's only eight thirty," Logan said. "Could we have a few more minutes?"

"Okay, fifteen minutes, though. That's it," Julia said.

"Did you eat?" Helen asked.

"I'll open a can of soup," Julia answered.

"A can of soup? Not in this house," Helen snipped. "You should change. And a shower would help. I don't think even a cat would drag you in, the way you look right now."

"Thanks for the compliment," Julia answered.

"Mom looks beautiful," Logan said. "Will, do you want to watch something on TV?"

Logan's attention perked Will up immediately, cementing Julia's theory that Logan was trying to be the man of the house. Despite the fact Julia didn't want her eldest son to feel like he had to carry that burden, it was working in everyone's favor for now. Will stopped crying and looked up at his older brother with rapt admiration.

"Come on then," Helen said. "Follow me. If everyone is good, there may be ice cream."

Julia watched as her family left and felt a familiar melancholy settle around her, now that she was left alone with her memories that had intensified since she saw Duke. Julia turned the shower on and allowed herself the luxury of feeling the hot water soothe her. Julia looked at the water circling the drain and thought about the charm bracelet Ben had given her on her seventh birthday. The morning after Ben went missing, Julia had returned from a marathon session at the police station, where she had been questioned all night. Tough work for a seven-year-old. Julia had returned home exhausted, but knew before she could let herself fall asleep, she'd need to find the bracelet that she had discovered missing from its usual place on her wrist when she woke up in the closet that night and couldn't find Ben.

Back then, Julia had somehow believed if she could just find the charm bracelet, Ben would come home. But Julia had searched the entire house all morning, and her precious gift with the boy-and-girl charm had vanished along with her brother.

Julia put the water on the coldest setting and made herself stand under the freezing spray for a minute, her usual habit, as the cold seemed to awaken her senses until she granted herself a reprieve and got out shivering. Julia towel-dried her dark hair, and as she dressed, she stared vacantly at her reflection in the mirror, wondering what Ben would have looked like as an adult. She had never told anyone, not even Navarro, but she still searched strangers' faces, hoping—against the most impossible of hopes—that one could belong to her grown-up brother. She knew the improbability of that happening, but she had never been able to stop herself from holding on to a sliver of the fairy-tale ending she knew rarely, if ever, happened in the real world.

Julia opened the top drawer of her bedroom dresser and lifted out a small envelope, where she had tucked the bracelet when she got home. She turned the scenario over in her head, wondering how Phoenix Pontiac could have wound up with something so precious that had once belonged to her and if anything he had told her was the truth.

Julia pulled out the other items in the envelope, the only physical connections that were left between her and Ben, and scattered them across her bed. She ran her fingers gingerly across the New York Yankees pendant Ben had worked so hard to buy after mowing lawns the summer before he vanished. She then lined up four Polaroid pictures that were taken of her and Ben by a man who'd been following them on their last afternoon together on the Sparrow boardwalk. The photos might have been strange things to hold on to, since they had previously been evidence in a criminal investigation, but since they were the only photographs she had of her brother, despite the circumstance of how they were shot, Julia had to keep them.

Julia took in the image of the last Polaroid, one that she had looked at hundreds of times, but each time she looked at it afresh, it stopped her cold. The picture was of her and Ben, their backs to the camera. Julia wore a thin jumper and looked up toward her brother, who was holding her hand, as the two neared the entrance of Funland, a seaside amusement park in their hometown. Julia wondered if the survivors, the "lucky" ones who were left behind, felt like she did, that time was forever frozen back to the moments before their lives blew up into a million stinging pieces that could kill you if you held on to them too tight.

Julia tucked the items back inside the envelope as the sound of laughing little boys made its way down the hallway from the living room. Julia followed in the direction of the noise to find Navarro now off the phone and with Will sitting high up on his shoulders.

"Be careful," Julia warned.

"There's no way I'm letting this kid fall," Navarro answered.

"It doesn't matter, Mr. Navarro," Logan said. "Will could still hit his head on the ceiling."

"Sorry, I guess the ride's over," Navarro told Will. He gently lowered Will to the floor and turned to Logan. "What's with this 'Mr. Navarro' stuff? I thought I was 'Uncle Ray'?"

"You're not really my uncle."

"That's true, but I've known you since birth, so I think I've earned uncle status, but you can call me whatever you want."

Helen put down two plates of pierogies on the kitchen counter, along with her stuffed cabbage rolls, for Julia and Navarro, and a bowl of ice cream each for Logan and Will.

Logan took a stool next to his mother and studied Navarro like a cop trying to figure out the true motive of a perp. "How come you don't have kids?" Logan asked.

"I never got married," Navarro answered.

"Why is that?" Logan asked.

"The girl I loved married someone else."

"Do you have a girlfriend now?" Logan asked.

"I do."

Logan's eyes seemed to relax from inquisitor mode, the answer apparently satisfying him, and he dug into his bowl of vanilla ice cream.

"Your parents like her?" Logan asked.

"My mom died when I was eleven," Navarro said.

"Enough with the questions, Logan," Julia said, trying to keep the conversation far away from Navarro's childhood, which was as turbulent as her own. Navarro's dad had strangled Navarro's mother to death as an eleven-year-old Navarro watched on as he hid under the kitchen table.

"Is your dad still alive?" Logan asked, ignoring his mother's request.

"He's in prison," Navarro answered. "I haven't seen him since I was a kid. My nana, my grandmother, she raised me."

"Your dad is in prison?" Logan asked.

"This isn't a good conversation for children," Helen said. "Prisons, dead mothers. Next you'll be showing the boy your gun."

"Your dad must've done something pretty bad to go to prison. Are you ashamed of him?" Logan asked.

"I don't spend much time thinking about my father."

Julia shot Navarro a silent, pleading look, and he seemed to get the message.

"So you're in camp?" Navarro asked.

"Yeah, it's okay. I have to go because my mom works. Do you really have a gun on you?" Logan asked. "Why do you need a gun in our house, unless something bad is going on?"

"Nothing bad is going on," Julia said.

"No one tells me what's really happening, because I'm a kid, but I've seen bad things, and I'm not afraid."

"I know," Navarro answered. "What you did to try and save your mother and brother back at your old lake house a couple of years ago, that was brave. People always think they'd know what to do in a dangerous situation, even cops. But when they're really in it, most people run away from the danger, instead of running right toward it."

"That's it. Time for bed," Julia said.

"Can Uncle Ray take me?" Logan asked. "I want to ask him something."

"It's Uncle Ray again. That was quick," Helen said. "Nice way to butter up the child. I must learn your techniques, I think."

Julia looked over to Navarro and he nodded his consent.

"Fine by me, as long as it's a Mom-approved question. Got it, little man?" Julia asked.

"Sure," Logan answered.

"Okay, my friends, pajamas, toothbrushing, and bed. Mom has a lot of work to do tonight," Julia said.

Julia shoveled down three bites from her plate of pierogi and stuffed cabbage, kissed Logan on his forehead, and scooped up Will, carrying him in her arms until they reached his bedroom. She changed him into his Superman pajamas and brushed his white-blond hair with her fingers as she thought about her childhood home in Sparrow and the first seven years of her life spent with Duke and Marjorie Gooden. Julia squeezed her little boy's hand in hers, and prayed that despite the fact she was not always the perfect mother, at least her sons felt safe and loved.

"Are you okay, Mamma?" Will asked. "You look kind of sad."

"Just the opposite. I was just thinking how happy you make me."

Julia gave her youngest son one more kiss and left his door ajar, a habit she always did at night so she'd be sure to hear Will if he woke up.

The kitchen was now empty and Julia made her way to the living room, where Navarro had set up a row of files that were spread across the coffee table.

"How did it go with Logan?" Julia asked.

"I tried to steer him clear of any talk about guns, incarcerated parents, or dead mothers. But I could tell he wanted to talk to me about my dad."

"He's having his own dad issues right now."

"Sorry if I talked out of turn earlier," Navarro said. "I love kids, but I'm not around them enough to know how to put on a filter."

"Don't worry about it. It was probably the highlight of Logan's night," Julia answered. "Any word on Phoenix Pontiac?"

"We haven't found Phoenix or his car yet, but I just got a call from the station. There's a Phoenix Pontiac in the system, if it's our same guy. He was busted a couple of times for drugs, possession, and attempt to sell. There's also a conviction for aggravated assault. The guy's a real winner. I brought along your brother's file. I realize you probably know it better than anyone, but it's there if you want to take a look."

Julia took in the files spread across her coffee table and picked up a three-inch-thick folder with her brother's name scrolled across the top: *Benjamin Michael Gooden Jr.* Julia sat down on her sofa and opened it, the contents of an unsolved case that consumed her life whittled down to a mere folder.

The first document was Ben's missing person's photo, followed by the initial police report. Julia's eyes skimmed through the pages and the familiar information. Ben had been abducted on Labor Day in the room he shared with Julia at their Sparrow home. Police were called at approximately 12:30 AM by Julia after she woke up in the closet of their room and discovered her brother was missing. The first officers at the scene found a sliding glass door to the bedroom open and an Indian arrowhead was found underneath Ben's bed.

"There was a man I saw today at Liam Mueller's place. He was creepy, a giant Indian man named Ahote, with a big scar carved down his face. Sarah remembered seeing a man in my mother's room earlier that night and she thought he was interrogating my mother. It's got to be the same person."

"Did you get his last name?"

"No. But there can't be that many Ahotes around in the Greater Detroit area."

"Did your mother ever say anything about being assaulted?" Navarro asked.

"I'm not following."

"I talked to the sheriff up in St. Clair this afternoon who ran your brother's initial case."

"Sheriff Leidy."

"He and his partner had their suspicions that your mother might have been roughed up that night, but she denied it. Your mom was drunk, and she had some swelling around her face and a cut on her forehead. She told Leidy she had fallen down."

"So Sarah was telling the truth."

"Leidy said when your mom sobered up, she seemed scared. He believed your mom might know more about what happened to your brother than she was letting on, but he said she completely clammed up. Leidy looked into whether your mother and father were involved, but your dad had an alibi."

"The alibi was fake. Peter Jonti told me," Julia said.

"I told you not to meet with him alone."

"You were working. Jonti said Duke's boss paid off the foreman to cover for my dad. Duke was working for Max, so Max fixed the deal."

"Why would Mueller do that if he was involved in Ben's kidnapping?" Navarro asked.

"Maybe he needed my dad accessible and not in prison."

"We need to bring your dad in," Navarro said.

"Good luck with that. I'm sure he's long gone. We're close this time, Ray. I feel it. When we find the person who took Ben, I need to be sure I'm alone with him first."

"What do you plan to do? Get your payback before law enforcement shows up? That makes you as low as the criminals. You know that."

"I've never killed anyone before, not directly anyway."

"Keep it that way. Taking another man's life, even if he's a scumbag, is not something you get over easily," Navarro said.

"Things are getting messy for me again. I don't want to drag you into it. If you need to step back and take a break from us until I can figure everything out, I understand."

"Not a chance. I'm not going anywhere," Navarro

said. "When the world got too heavy for us when we were living together, remember what we used to do?"

"Not with kids in the house, pal."

"I'm not talking about that, although, believe me, I'd love to. Come on, Gooden, do you still know how to dance?"

"We're dealing with a serious situation here. You're crazy," Julia said.

"You know I am. Dance with me," Navarro said. He swayed his hips back and forth and clapped his hands in perfect rhythm to a silent beat.

"It's been a while."

"You know how to move with me. Come here, baby."

"You're trying to distract me and make me feel better," Julia said.

"Who me? It's purely selfish. I just like watching you move, Gooden," Navarro said.

Navarro reached out for Julia and pulled her into him. He put his left hand on the back of her shoulder and held her right hand in his own as his feet began to move to the rhythm playing in his head.

"We haven't danced since we were kids," Julia said.

"We're still kids. David didn't dance with you?"

"Never. I'm pretty sure he thought it was undignified."

"Undignified? Please. But you won't catch me speaking ill of the dead. Now follow my lead. Remember this salsa move I taught you? Move your right foot, back, together, forward. That's it. Just relax. Back, together, forward. Quick, slow, quick. Quick, slow, quick. Beautiful. See you didn't forget."

"We don't have any music," Julia said.

"Sure we do."

Navarro pulled Julia against his chest, pressed his lips against Julia's ear, and began to sing in Spanish in a low, raspy whisper.

"That's beautiful. What's the song?" Julia asked.

"You talk too much, when you should be dancing. But I know you're not going to stop asking. It's a Marc Anthony song, *'Valió La Pena.'* I love Latin music. My mom would play it on a little radio in our kitchen, and she would dance with me when she was getting ready for work."

"I love when you speak Spanish."

"Mmm, I know you do. Can't help myself. Spanish father, Mexican mother. Now that I've got you in the mood, let's see if you remember how to do a turn."

Navarro raised Julia's hand up and guided her under his arm. She heard herself laugh as she spun, but when she came out of the turn, she could see something shift in Navarro's face.

"What's wrong?" Julia asked.

"I heard something. A car door close outside."

"I have neighbors."

"I didn't hear a car start or see lights pass by the window."

"I'll go out and check," Julia said.

"Like hell you will. Stay here," Navarro said, and moved to the front door, where he shifted the curtain back a centimeter.

"There's someone outside. They're heading around the back of the house. Call for backup, but stay here," Navarro said.

Navarro shot out the front door and Julia hurriedly called 911. Julia slipped outside just as Navarro disappeared around the corner of her house. She followed his path and began to sprint, when she heard something fall against her fence and then what sounded like a struggle. Julia held her breath as a gun went off, and she raced around the corner to see Navarro straddling a man who was wearing a suit and lying facedown next to her garbage cans.

"Police!" Navarro yelled. Navarro twisted the man's hands behind his back and then patted him down, pulling out a gun from his rear waistband. "Who are you working for, asshole?"

"I'm on the job. Get the hell off me," the man said. "My ID is in my front pocket."

"Don't move," Navarro said. He reached into the man's pocket and pulled out an FBI badge.

"Agent Terry McKenzie. That's my name, but people call me Agent Kenny. Can you get the hell off me? Freaking Detroit PD."

Navarro held on to the FBI agent's gun, but let him get to his feet. "What are you doing here?" Navarro asked.

"I'm trying to find Duke Gooden. Hello, Julia. Nice to see you again."

Standing in front of Julia was the man from the sushi place, Peter Jonti.

"Sorry about pulling a knife on you earlier. I have some questions you're going to need to answer. I need to find your father. He's a dangerous fugitive and it's in your best interest to help me before Duke Gooden gets you killed."

CHAPTER 14

Julia sat alone in an interview room at the Detroit Police Department and gave an angry wave at the glass, knowing the FBI agent who posed as her father's ex–business partner was likely on the other side of the two-way mirror, watching her. Julia felt like a fuming hornet trapped under a glass dome. She had refused to let the agent, Kenny, talk to her inside her house, since her boys were there, but she had finally agreed to talk to the agent without the presence of an attorney if they found a neutral ground. So the Detroit PD was the compromise.

The interview room door opened and Navarro came in, looking equally pissed off, with a bottle of water for Julia. Still standing, he leaned toward her and said quietly, "Figure out how you want to play this. I know you don't want to talk to the agent, but you need to decide whether you want to tell him about your dad as leverage."

"Leverage for what?" Julia asked.

"To get information about Ben, if he has it. If they're

looking this hard into your dad that they're willing to go undercover to find him, they may have information about your brother."

"This is bullshit. If the FBI wanted to talk to me about my father, they should've played it straight."

The interview room door opened and Agent Kenny strode inside, giving Julia a hard-set grin. He'd cleaned up since she had seen him at Sushi Z. Agent Kenny was wearing a dark suit and his hair was buzzed short, instead of his slicked-back, curled-at-the-shoulder look he had previously worn.

"No heavy cologne or gold chain this time. You disappoint me," Julia said. She reached into her purse and pulled out a tape recorder.

"Whatever we discuss here, I'm recording it. I may turn it into an article, depending on what line of bull you tell me. I've already put a call into the paper," Julia bluffed. "Let me know when you're ready and I'll press play."

Kenny reached for the tape recorder, but Julia pulled it out of his reach.

"Are you going to leave out the part where you lied about your father?" Kenny said.

"I don't know what you're talking about. You misrepresented yourself, pulled a knife on me, and then stalked my house while my kids were inside sleeping. Not to mention the fact that a rogue shot went off, which could have easily gone into one of their bedrooms and killed them."

"I wasn't there to hurt your kids. And the gun went off because your buddy there tackled me from behind."

"You're lucky Navarro got to you before I did," Julia said. "I don't like being bait."

"Your alias was in Duke Gooden's file," Navarro said. "How did that get in there?"

"It was a plant," Kenny said. "We got intelligence that Duke Gooden was alive and back in Detroit. We needed a way to get to him."

"Your intelligence is lousy then. If you knew anything, you wouldn't have bothered trying to find a back door through me, because I haven't talked to my father since he walked out on me when I was seven."

"Is that right?" Kenny asked.

"Everything you told me when we were at the restaurant about my father's alibi and the fire, were those all lies?"

"No, those were true from what we've been able to piece together about your father. I tried to get information from your sister, Sarah, as well, but she was as equally tight-lipped as you."

"If you'd been honest about who you were, Sarah wouldn't have talked to you regardless, but why me?"

"Family allegiance. If I came to you as a federal agent looking to find your dad, you'd protect him. If I came to you as a former business associate, you'd be more inclined to talk."

"You clearly need to do your homework better. I had no close ties to my father and wouldn't have looked him up even if he were still alive."

"I don't think you're telling me the truth, Ms. Gooden. We believe a certain Jonathan Jameson, who was one of Max Mueller's former guys, was recently murdered. Do you know anything about this?"

Agent Kenny slid what looked like a surveillance shot across the table toward Julia and she made herself play cool as she easily recognized the man her father shot in Sparrow, but there was no way she'd tip her hand. Julia didn't trust Duke, but she also didn't trust the FBI agent either.

"I've never seen him before. And I'd definitely remember a face like that."

"Yeah, that's a face a blind mother wouldn't even love," Navarro said. "Why are you bothering to question Julia? You should've brought Max's son in, instead."

"We don't have enough on him yet," Kenny said. "This is where you can help us."

"You set Julia up. You could've gotten her killed."

"If she got killed, it wouldn't have been on our end. I just needed Julia to find me, like I was told by one of you guys that she would, and I'm assuming you were the leak," Kenny said. He looked between Navarro and Julia and gave a knowing, snide smile. "Posing as a former colleague of her dad's, we figured we'd have a better chance."

The interview room door swung open and Chief Linderman came inside, still wearing his dark suit from the morning. Somehow it didn't have a wrinkle on it.

"What's going on here, Chief?" Navarro asked.

"We're assisting our partners in the FBI to locate a fugitive."

"You knew about this?" Julia asked Linderman.

"I'm sorry I couldn't have been more forthcoming with you, Julia, especially since it involves one of your family members, but I had no choice. The order came down from above me and my hands were tied. I also know how important it is for you to find out what happened to your brother. I've been keeping a personal eye on you to be sure you were safe."

"That's why you showed up at Liam Mueller's gallery," Julia said.

"You're wrong. Julia hasn't been safe," Navarro said. "The agent over here pulled a knife on her when he was undercover and was skulking around her house tonight with a gun. I was there and thought he was an intruder. I tackled him, and when I did, his gun discharged. The shot just missed hitting the house, and Julia's kids were inside."

"You did what?" Linderman said to Kenny.

"It was part of the investigation," Kenny said. "Your detective here screwed up."

"I try and extend the courtesy of helping out our federal law enforcement officers, but when a citizen's safety is compromised, that's where I draw the line," Linderman said. "We're not the B team. I help you, you don't mess with one of my own."

"She's a reporter, not a cop," Kenny said.

"Julia has worked with me and my department for years, and she's viewed as a trusted and respected journalist around here. And I consider her a personal friend. You come to my precinct and debase one of my detectives and a newspaper reporter in excellent standing with this department, any help I've been willing to extend against my better judgment is over. I don't care what kind of personal flack I get in return. My department is currently knee-deep in a PR shit storm involving a possible serial killer whose latest victim just happens to be the nephew of a prominent Hispanic city councilman. Did I mention the killer is offing people with a bow and arrow? So if you want to talk, you better make it quick, because I'm extremely close to changing my mind."

"Let's all lower the hostility level, and we can work together for everyone's best interest," Kenny said. "All right, now that the proper introductions have been made, I'll tell you what I can. I work for the FBI's art crime division. We haven't been around that long, but in the last twelve years, we've recovered about one hundred fifty million dollars' worth of stolen art."

"Art crime?" Navarro asked. "You need a gun for that?"

"Art and cultural property crime are huge," Kenny said. "It's the third highest-grossing criminal trade in the past forty years. Weapons and drugs are the only other crimes that are bigger. Toughest job I've ever had with the Bureau. Art sales are usually unregulated. No transaction records. And there's no law that mandates art sales have to be publically recorded. We've had some big busts, too. We recovered Rembrandt's self-portrait in a joint Copenhagen sting, and a Francisco de Goya painting that was stolen while it was making the move from the Toledo Museum of Art to the Guggenheim in New York."

"You had that tattoo of the painting *The Scream* when I saw you at the sushi restaurant," Julia said.

"Bingo. You do this kind of job for long enough, you get to appreciate the talent of the master artists. We have lots of old cases we're still working, including artwork that was stolen after World War II. And then there's the five hundred million dollars' worth of paintings that were lifted from the Isabella Stewart Gardner Museum in Boston back in the early nineties. In that one, a security guard buzzed in two guys pretending to be cops. The ass wipes stole a bunch of paintings, including a Rembrandt and a Vermeer dating back to the 1600s."

"How does Duke figure into this?" Julia asked.

"Max Mueller's family, they were originally from Germany," Kenny said. "His father is believed to have stolen at least thirty paintings that belonged to Jews heading off to concentration camps during the 1940s. When Max's dad, Otto, came to this country, he took all the stolen artwork with him. And he sold his collection off before he got caught. Being exposed to all that art growing up is how Max got his first taste."

"Max inherited his father's penchant for being a criminal," Julia said.

"You're catching on. Your father was working for Max as a courier thirty years back. Duke picked up something for Mueller in St. Louis, and two days later, what was believed to be Duke's remains, and your mother's, too, were found in a burned-out car in the city of Hamtramck."

"Did the Wayne County sheriff ID the bodies?" Navarro asked.

"Marjorie's, yes. We couldn't match dental records for Duke because the teeth were pulled out."

"Torture?" Navarro asked.

"Possibly, but I'm not convinced the other body in the car was Duke. There was a possible sighting of Duke in Central America two weeks ago. We believe he either stole a painting we're trying to recover or knows where it is," Kenny said.

"What kind of painting is it that has the FBI so interested?" Navarro asked.

"I can't tell you specifics. We originally thought

Max Mueller still had it, but we raided his place ten years ago. Max was a smarmy little asshole and a weird guy. While we were raiding his warehouse, he just stood there smiling at us with this creepy, bent cane of his that looked like a snake. The raid was a bust, though. We couldn't find the picture, or any ones of much lesser value that we believe Max owned."

"What makes you believe Duke has whatever you're looking for?" Julia asked.

"There was chatter about the painting when it first went missing thirty years ago, but nothing since, meaning no one was trying to sell it. But a week ago, a fake collector, one of our undercover guys, got a bite from a man named Kirk Fleming. We're looking into whether Fleming is actually Duke or Liam Mueller. Max Mueller died recently, and the timing of the painting coming back on the underground black market is too coincidental to be ignored."

Kenny reached into a manila envelope under his arm and slid another picture in Julia's direction. The agent tapped his index finger against a picture of a well-dressed man who had thick, silver hair and a pair of dark glasses shielding his eyes as he got into a vehicle.

"That man is known these days as Roberto Sanchez, better known as Rickie Samuels back here in the States. Rickie used to work with Max until he set up his own business running weapons. He went south of the border to get away from the heat the Feds were lighting up under him. If the sighting is true and your father is still alive, we believe Duke may have hooked up with Rickie."

"I don't care about my father or a painting or if Duke is dead or alive. The only thing I care about is my brother and what happened to him."

"Sorry, but that's not my case. I do art crime, not kidnapping," Kenny said.

"You forgot human trafficking," Julia said. "You don't help me, I won't help you."

"Contact the St. Clair County Sheriff's Office. They ran your brother's case."

"That's fine," Julia said, standing up. "I can get my own information without you."

"We're not done yet," Kenny said. "You think you're in charge, and that you're the smartest person in the room. But you've done a pretty shitty job of figuring out what happened to your brother. Ben Gooden's case has been cold for what? Going thirty-plus years now? You really know how to get to the bottom of a story, Ms. Gooden. I always hated journalists."

"Let me ask you something. When we were at the sushi place, was everything you told me about my dad true?" Julia asked.

"Unlike you, I don't lie," Kenny said.

"This, coming from an agent who pretended he knew my dad to get me to talk. I've never once misrepresented myself with you. But if I were keeping a scorecard based on our meeting in the restaurant, I'd say I got way more information from you on the case than you got from me. Have a nice evening, Agent McKenzie. I'm going home to my family," Julia said.

Julia headed to the door with Kenny in pursuit, but Navarro blocked his way.

*   *   *

In the hallway, Julia pulled out her cell phone and called Helen, who answered on the first ring.

"How are Logan and Will?" Julia asked.

"Logan refuses to go back to sleep. He insisted on having Will come in his room and he has his baseball bat next to the bed. At least Will is sleeping, but I have a feeling Logan is going to be staying up all night."

"Okay. I'm leaving the station now. Tell Logan everything is fine."

"Since no one in this house believes that, except for maybe Will, because he's too young to know better, I'll pass on delivering the message."

"I'm sorry, Helen. I truly am."

"No need to say sorry. Before I met you, I used to watch *Sons of Anarchy* to get my thrills. But now I have you. If you don't get shot, I'll have a piece of honey cake waiting for you when you get home."

Julia hung up with Helen and headed to Navarro's office, where his partner, Russell, sat.

"Late night for you," Julia said.

"Finishing up some paperwork on the Angel Perez case. We may have a lead. A guy, another Hispanic day laborer, says he saw Angel get into an older-model white van this morning at the Home Depot over in Dearborn. He didn't get a look at the driver or a plate. But I've got this."

Russell pulled up a website called SecurityVideo-Watch.com. He reached in his shirt pocket for his reading glasses and slid them up the bridge of his nose. Russell inserted a username and password, and what looked like security footage outside a gas station appeared live on the screen.

"This is from a Chevron station across the street

from the Home Depot. Let me see if I can figure this out," Russell said.

"Let me help," Julia said. She moved next to Russell and pointed at his computer screen. "Okay, it looks like the dates of the surveillance footage are on the left of the screen. When did the day laborer say he saw the van?"

"Right before the store opened, so around six AM."

Julia grabbed the computer mouse from Russell's confused hand and clicked on an icon on the left of the page.

"This goes by the hour, so let's start at five AM."

Julia hit the fast-forward button and paused it at the 5:45 time when Russell grabbed her hand. "That's Angel Perez's car. A red Honda Prelude."

Julia froze the image on the screen and focused in on the fuzzy image of the driver.

"He's alone," Julia said. "Poor kid."

Julia hit the fast-forward button again and quickly hit stop when the nose of an older-model white van appeared on the screen. "Okay, that's it," Julia said. "The time is five fifty-five AM."

Russell hovered over her and put his hand on Julia's shoulder. "I love it when things turn out to be easy. Let's see if we can get a shot of the license plate."

Julia hit the play button again, but the image on the screen disappeared and turned to static.

"You've got to be kidding me," Russell said.

"Hold on. It could be just a glitch. Let's see if it comes back up," Julia answered.

The static played in the background until the security camera footage came back on at 6:15 AM.

"Shit," Russell said. "The guy from the Chevron

station, he told me he just upgraded to this new surveillance system and it's supposed to be top of the
line."

"He's got to have an original copy," Julia said. "Keep
me posted, all right?"

Russell groaned and took a long swig from his coffee cup. "I better tell the boss. Are you heading out?"

"Yes. Please tell Navarro I had to get home to check
on my kids. I think he may be tied up with the chief."

Julia grabbed her bag as she headed down the hallway toward the precinct's entrance to the street, and
she wondered what kind of strange path her father
must have followed that led him from small-time hustler to a fugitive wanted by the FBI.

Julia made it as far as the interview room door just
as Navarro came out.

"That Agent Kenny is a piece of work. He started
pumping me on whether you'd let anything slip about
your dad. Linderman wants me to talk to him about the
Angel Perez case. So I'm going to be hung up here for
a bit. Russell has a bite on a video we picked up from a
gas station across from the Home Depot we think
Angel Perez was at, so maybe we'll be able to get the
license plate on the van."

"You might want to talk to Russell about that. Con-
veniently, the tape cut out just as the van came into the
picture. I'm going to leave. Logan is still up and isn't
going to sleep anytime soon since Agent McKenzie's
gun unloaded."

"Be careful. Call me if anything happens. I'll see
you back at your place."

*   *   *

The muggy July Michigan night clung to Julia like a sticky veil as she walked out of the police station and made her way back to her SUV and the parking lot down the block.

Julia nodded as she passed Tom, a homeless man she had known for years and who looked like a long-faded hippie. Tom was sitting, cross-legged, on an old blanket that was neatly lined with his belongings, a dirty camouflage-green backpack, a beyond-worn copy of Jack Kerouac's *On the Road,* a half-dozen crystals, and a cardboard sign with a message written in red marker: WILL ENLIGHTEN FOR FOOD.

"How are you doing, Tom?" Julia asked, and handed him a five-dollar bill and a granola bar, which she had fished out of her purse.

"Thanks, Julia, my lady," Tom said. "May I offer you something for your kind contribution?"

"No need, but thank you."

Tom stroked his fingers through his long, white beard and looked back at Julia. "Most people don't even look at me, but you always treat me like a human being. Since you're always so nice, let me offer you a tip. Some street philosophy. It's a nice night, but be careful of the birds."

"We have a bird problem in Detroit?" Julia asked.

"The last few nights, you bet," Tom said, his eyes bulged and his right hand shot up and pointed to the sky. "No one else has been able to see them but me, but I bet if anyone else can, it would be you."

"Thanks for the warning. I'll be sure to duck if I get bombarded by a flock of pigeons."

"Not pigeons. Big red blackbirds that look like they'd fall right out of the sky. Never seen ones like that before. Be careful, Miss Julia. I saw a UFO last night. You look up at the sky just at the right time from this spot, you wouldn't believe the things you can see. You should join me here sometime."

"Thanks for the offer. Have a good night, Tom."

Julia checked her watch and hurried through the open, one-story parking lot. Out of a new habit, when she reached her car, Julia scanned her windshield for any potential notes, but found none. She leaned against the hood of her SUV and felt like the tight control she had spent a lifetime trying to perfect in order to protect herself was becoming horribly undone.

She made her way to the driver-side door of her SUV, where a white envelope was waiting for her, taped to the window.

"This is not a goddamn scavenger hunt," Julia said as she snatched the envelope open and found her second note from Phoenix Pontiac.

Julia,
    Go to the Verve Bar on Kirby Street. You bring the cops, I'm out of there before your foot hits the curb.
    Your brother Ben called me. He's still alive.

CHAPTER 15

Julia snagged a parking spot across the street from the Verve, a club that three years earlier had been one of downtown Detroit's main hot spots, but had since lost its prime status to a newer generation of bars that had sprung up throughout the city following the recent push for a renaissance of the downtown core.

Despite falling from its original A-list mantle, the Verve still had a large crowd for a Friday night. The club was dark as Julia walked inside, except for the bar that ran the length of the main floor and was lit up in neon blue. Julia could hear a muted thump of music coming from downstairs as Pitbull's "Fireball" made its way up to the main entrance of the club.

A muscular, bald woman, with biceps that rivaled Navarro's, held up her hand as Julia tried to shove her way through the crowd to find Phoenix.

"Ten-dollar cover for the bar," the female bouncer said. "The D Dance Club is in the basement. That's an extra ten."

"I'm here to meet someone," Julia yelled over the

din, and handed the female bouncer a fifty-dollar bill. "You can keep the change if you can help me find him."

"It's Friday night. The place is packed. And I don't get paid for helping people find their hookups."

"It's not like that. I'm a reporter. I'm looking into a missing person's case, a nine-year-old boy who was kidnapped."

The female bouncer's eyes shifted to the line forming behind Julia. She then gestured with her hand for Julia to pass the rope and enter the club.

"Okay. Who's the guy you're trying to find?"

"He's about five-ten and trim, with shoulder-length dark hair, a full mouth, and brown eyes," Julia said. "He looks sort of delicate. I'm pretty sure you could take him in a fight."

The female bouncer cracked the slightest smile. "I think I know who you're talking about. A real pretty boy, if you like that type. He got here about twenty minutes ago. Just paid for upstairs, so he should be here somewhere."

"How many exits do you have in this place?" Julia asked.

"Just the front door and the two fire exits, one on this floor and one downstairs. To get to the dance club in the basement, your man would have to get by me first."

"Thanks. The person I'm looking for, his name is Phoenix Pontiac. If you see him trying to get out of here, stop him, and I'll give you another fifty."

"If this guy snatched a kid, you don't have to pay me a thing. I'd be happy to hurt him, no charge. I'm Rita."

"Nice to meet you, Rita. I'm Julia Gooden." She reached out for the bouncer's hand and shook it. "I won't forget this."

Julia pushed her way through the bar and scanned the crowd on the first floor of the club, her eyes ticking off the faces of each person she saw. She did a sweep of the patrons milling around the bar and then stared down the people who were drinking in one of the club's eight electric-blue leather booths. When she reached the end of the bar and couldn't find Phoenix, Julia began to worry that he had set her up. She grabbed her cell phone, ready to call Navarro, when she was almost struck in the back by the men's-room door.

"Sorry. I didn't see you standing there," a man, who looked to be in his midthirties, said as he came out of the bathroom. He looked down at Julia's empty ring finger on her left hand and his eyes then made a slow crawl up to her face. "Let me make it up to you. You want a drink?"

"No. Was there a guy in the bathroom just now, with long, dark hair?" Julia asked.

"Yeah, he was in there," the man answered. "Is he your date?"

"No."

"Well, if you change your mind about the drink, I'm at the bar with some buddies."

"Not happening, but thanks."

Julia pushed open the men's-room door and spotted a squat, bald man, who looked like a banker in his black suit, finishing up at the urinal, but more important, Phoenix Pontiac was washing his hands at the sink.

"Hey, this is the men's room," the man at the urinal said as he zipped up. "Friggin' women always trying to come in here when the line to the ladies' is too long."

"I'm going to try and ask you this politely. Please leave," Julia said to the man.

"I'll leave when I'm done," the man answered.

"Fine, then. You've got ten seconds to get out of here. No need to wash your hands," Julia said, and gestured her head toward the door. "Now go."

"You're crazy," the man in the suit said.

"Just when I have to be," Julia answered. She quickly eyed the four stalls to be sure they were empty and then locked the bathroom door after the banker hurried out.

"What is this?" Phoenix asked. "You want to talk, I'm not doing it here in the bathroom."

"I need to be sure you don't get away this time. What kind of game are you playing with me?"

"There's no game."

"Sure there is," Julia answered. "I'm just trying to figure out which one you're running. You lied to me once, pretending you were a photographer. That means everything else that comes out of your mouth is a lie. What's the deal with making me meet you in a bar?"

"It's a busy place. If you showed up here with the cops, it would be harder to make me if I needed to make a quick exit. I have an outstanding warrant in Michigan. I've been living in Chicago for the last few years, but I came here to take care of what I promised I'd do, so my ass is on the line."

"Is it a warrant for drugs or assault this time?"

Phoenix's large, doe-shaped eyes looked back at

Julia with surprise. "How do you know that? The cops already ran my name through the system?"

"I don't care about your legal troubles. Tell me what's going on. You said my brother is alive. If you're lying, I'll make you regret it."

"I'm telling you the truth. I swear. Your brother called me about two weeks ago. I have no idea how Ben found me. It freaked me out. At first, I thought it was the man who abducted me when I was a kid calling or someone else playing a sick joke. But then everything Ben said during the call, I knew it had to be him."

"Back up. What did Ben say?"

"He said I had to find you. That you're in danger and to stay away from a man named Duke."

"Let me see your phone," Julia said.

"I'd show you, but it wouldn't make a difference. The number Ben called me from, it came up as 'unknown.' I called AT&T to try and get an actual name or number, but they said they couldn't give it to me."

"Your story is bogus. If my brother were still alive, he would've contacted me directly, and he would've done it years ago."

"He told me you'd think that. But Ben said he could never reach out to you, no matter how much he wanted to, because it would've gotten you killed. I have a message I'm supposed to give you from Ben. He said to stay away from Duke, no matter what, that Duke is dangerous and was behind his abduction. Who is this 'Duke' person?"

"It doesn't matter. Why would Ben contact you?"

"I'm not sure. But I think he might not have had

anyone else from his past that he could reach out to here, and I owed him for what happened at the house."

"What house?" Julia asked.

"The house in the woods. We were both abducted and held there."

"Give me proof."

"I did. I gave you the bracelet. Ben gave it to you on your seventh birthday. Come on. Stop treating me like I'm a liar."

A pounding sounded from the other side of the men's-room door.

"It's occupied, and I'm going to be here for a while," Julia said, and then turned back to Phoenix, who was shifting nervously on his feet, back and forth, next to the hand dryer mounted on the wall. "Where was this place you're claiming my brother was?"

"I don't know. I was just a kid. But I heard some of the other people who were trapped there talking, and they said it was like a halfway house before we got moved. I wound up there because I made a big mistake. I was a foster kid. I was eight and had this crazy idea that I was going to find my birth mom. The system took me from her because she was on drugs. There was a park up from the apartment where I was living. My foster parents didn't care what I did, so I went there alone one day. I remember sitting on this swing, trying to figure out how I could get across town to where my mom lived. This man came up to me and asked if I wanted a ride. I thought it was my lucky day."

"I don't need to hear your personal story. When did you meet my brother?" Julia asked. She knew all too well that her brother was taken on Labor Day thirty years earlier, a date that was emblazoned in her mind, and expected to catch Phoenix in a lie.

"I can't remember exactly. It was late summer and school was about to start. Maybe late August. I was at the house in the woods for about a week before Ben got there. I don't know where the house was, but there was like thirty of us crammed in there on the first level of the place, and it was roasting hot. All the windows were boarded up. Some days, I felt like I was going to suffocate. They barely fed us. Ben, though, he told me we'd be okay. He was going to get us out of there. He was only a year older than me, but it was almost like he was an adult."

"What did my brother look like?"

"He had dark hair like you, but his eyes were brown, not blue. His eyes kind of turned up on the ends."

"You could've gotten all that from his missing person's flyer. It ran in the news. How did my brother get away?"

"I don't know. But I know he tried at least once. Ben promised me we would get out, but I couldn't see how. Everything was locked, the doors, the windows, the whole place was like living in a tight tin can. And there was always at least one guard watching us. Ben and I were the youngest and the only kids. It was mostly women there. They seemed a lot older, but the females were probably just teenagers or early twenties, tops. I knew the stories of most everyone there a little bit. The majority of the girls were runaways. The only other people there were a group of illegals, Mexicans, and a family from Vietnam."

"Good story, but I still don't believe it."

"Hold on. Ben talked about you all the time. He told me he had to find a way out so he could get back home to you. That's all he cared about. He was just this little kid in a shitty place, and he probably knew something worse was about to happen, but all he could do was focus on you. God, this shit still haunts my dreams. There was this weird man who would come by every morning, an old guy with a bent cane, and when he showed up, we were all terrified, because he'd point the end of the cane at the people he picked who were going to be moved out next."

"Was his name Max Mueller?"

"I don't know," Phoenix answered. "It could have been."

"You mentioned the guards. Was one of them a big man who looked like he was Native American?" Julia asked.

"I'm not sure. There were about six guards who watched us. They all seemed huge to me. One day, though, Ben had a plan. There was one big guy who was mostly in charge of watching us in the morning. He'd wait until the old guy with the cane picked his latest round, and the guard would take them out of the house through a garage. It was always locked. I can still hear the people crying when they got picked. When the morning guard would come back, he'd tell one of the girls he had his eye on that he'd make sure she wasn't sold if she'd do him a favor. Then he'd go into another room with his latest girl and would come back, like, fifteen minutes later."

"So if your story is true, Ben saw an opening?" Julia asked.

"That's right. He was a wicked smart kid. There was

a pretty good-sized laundry chute that went downstairs. The door to the downstairs was always locked, but Ben thought he could fit down the chute. I was smaller than him, so he wanted me to go first, but I was too scared. I helped him, though. I gave Ben a hand up and he was able to lift himself into the hole. He got stuck at one point, and I was really scared, but he made it through, all the way to the bottom. I listened to him the whole way. All I could hear was him breathing at first, but then I heard Ben land, real soft, down on the other side. A couple of minutes later, the guard came back in with the girl, and it didn't take him long to figure out one of us was missing. He threw me against the wall and started hitting me. He knew Ben and I talked, and he started beating me."

Phoenix looked away from Julia and cast his eyes down to the floor.

"You told the guard my brother escaped," Julia said.

"You have to understand. I was just a kid, and I didn't have a choice. I prayed so hard that Ben would make it out, because I knew he'd bring help. But then, about twenty minutes later, the guard hauled Ben back inside. Your brother was kicking and screaming like a wild animal. Ben got locked in a room until the guy with the cane came back, and the guard asked him what he wanted to do with Ben. The guy with the cane, the one who was calling the shots, said to give him to the head of his security, that he didn't want to deal with Ben anymore and his supplier wouldn't want a kid that was going to be that much trouble. I never saw Ben again after that. I'll be honest with you. I thought they'd killed him. I couldn't believe it when Ben called me."

"Why do you believe the person who called you was my brother?"

"Don't make me for stupid. I've served some time and you have to know when people are lying. Otherwise you won't survive in there. I didn't believe the caller at first, but then Ben started talking about the house and the laundry chute. He knew too many details to be conning me."

"So you're such a Good Samaritan, you found me out of the kindness of your heart. I'm not stupid either," Julia said.

"I'm not going to bullshit you. I did owe Ben for turning him in to the guard, but Ben offered to pay me ten grand to find you and to give you the message."

"If Ben had a computer, it would be pretty much impossible for him not to find me himself. You do a Google search of my name, you'll find my byline."

"That's how I found you. I was following you for Ben, to be sure you weren't with Duke. I sent Ben some pictures."

"I saw the photos on your camera."

"Look, ten grand is a lot of money for me, but I didn't want to get killed for it. Ben said there were bad people who were going to come after you, now that this guy Duke was coming back to Detroit. I tracked you until I felt it was safe to contact you, but then I got made at the crime scene."

"Nice story you came up with there," Julia said.

"I scrambled for that. I had a camera in my hand, so it seemed logical."

"You're a hell of an actor," Julia said.

A series of hard, persistent knocks pounded on the other side of the bathroom door again.

"Hurry up, I've really got to go," the male voice from earlier called out.

"I'm not done yet," Julia called out. "Come back later or use the ladies' room."

"This is bullshit. I'm finding the owner," the man said.

"Knock yourself out," Julia said. She looked back at Phoenix, who had his eyes glued on the lock of the bathroom door. "How did you get the bracelet?" Julia asked.

"Ben told me he grabbed it when he was taken from your house. He knew something bad was going down, and he hid you in the closet so you'd be safe. Ben said you were asleep and that the bracelet had fallen off your wrist while he was moving you in there. He still had it in his hand when he got abducted, so he held on to it. Right after he called me, Ben left the bracelet in my mailbox. I still couldn't believe it was him when he called, so Ben said he'd give me proof."

"Your story is thin, brother," Julia said, but inside, she couldn't explain away how Phoenix would have the bracelet. Julia felt a rush of excitement begin to move through her as she started to allow herself to believe the impossible: Ben was still alive. But she also knew she couldn't be conned by someone playing on her greatest vulnerability.

"What happened to you? If your story is true, were you sold?" Julia asked.

"I was real close. I got picked one day with about eight others. They got us all together and shoved us in a van. I heard the guards saying something about St. Louis. Something was going down between the two guards who were going to take us there. They started to get into it, yelling about one of the girls, and one of the guards threw a punch at the other guy. I was the last person in and was right by the door, and it was open, just a little bit. I was small. I slipped through and ran as fast as I could into the woods. I found a road and flagged down a truck. I told the guy who picked me up that I had run away, but wanted to go home now. He drove me back to Detroit."

"And you didn't go to the cops?"

"No way. I was too scared. I made it back to my foster family, but I didn't tell them what happened because I was terrified the people who took me would come back. When Ben called me, I didn't want to get involved in this shit again, but I needed the money. Look, I've done my part. I gave you the warning. But now I'm out of here."

Phoenix started to move toward the bathroom door, but Julia blocked his path.

"You need to come with me to the police. If the person who called you really is my brother, I'm going to find him, and you're going to help me."

"No cops. They find out who I am, I'll go back to jail. I can't do that," Phoenix said as he reached into the front pocket of his jeans and pulled out a small folding knife.

"Take it easy," Julia said. "Put the knife down. You're not going to get in trouble. You help me, it's going to look good to the cops. I can tell you want to do the right thing. I'm just going to reach in my bag and call someone I trust. He'll meet us here."

"Don't make me do this," Phoenix said. "I don't want to hurt you."

Julia dove her hand into her purse for her phone just

as Phoenix charged her. She tried to pivot her body away from the knife, but Phoenix let it slide from his hand as he drove his shoulder into her rib cage.

Julia gasped as she fell to the floor and watched helplessly as Phoenix scooped up his knife and ran the length of the room to the door.

She scrambled to her feet as Phoenix hit the light switch, causing the room to go black. Julia pounded forward in the darkness and in the direction she was sure the door was located, but realized she had miscalculated when a dim sliver of blue light appeared to her far left as Phoenix Pontiac made his escape.

A piercing sound blasted through the club as a shrill *whoop-whoop-whoop* of a fire alarm rang out in a repeated loop overhead.

"Fire alarm, everybody get the hell out," Julia heard the female bouncer, Rita, bark.

Julia ran out of the bathroom and searched wildly in both directions for Phoenix as the crowd of bar patrons swept her up in the wave of movement toward the front door.

Julia shoved her way forward until she reached the bouncer.

"Phoenix Pontiac, where is he?" Julia asked.

"I don't know. I've got bigger problems right now. We're over capacity by about sixty downstairs and the fire department is going to be rolling in any second. Look, I can't be sure, but I don't think I saw him go out front yet. Check the other exit. End of the bar, in the back. If your asshole pulled the fire alarm, tell him I'm going to hunt him down," Rita said, and then turned back to face the bar crowd. "Let's go, people. This is not a drill. Single file, or you'll get your butt kicked."

Julia looked to the rear of the bar and the red glow of the EXIT sign as she saw the back door open. She tried to push against the steady tide of patrons all moving in the opposite direction, and finally lifted herself up onto the bar to lose the crowd. Julia ran the length of the bar, dodging glasses and beer bottles, until she reached the end, where she jumped off and raced through the exit and out into the still-warm night. She heard a car door slam and sprinted as fast as she could, until she made it to the end of the alleyway to the street, where she caught a glimpse of Phoenix Pontiac's Subaru shooting up the road doing at least ninety, and then taking a fast corner before it disappeared from her sight.

CHAPTER 16

The man had been driving the desolate, dark back roads for what seemed like forever since he had exited the highway. It was just past midnight, about the same time he had almost hit the boy who had run out in the middle of the road, the child had been waving his hands wildly and blinking against the oncoming headlights thirty years earlier.

The driver slowed down when he thought he'd reached the spot where he had picked up the boy. He had heard the child fighting hard to catch his breath after he had opened the window to see if the boy was all right. The sight of the child, alone in the middle of the night, so small and terrified, had stunned him. But there had been a determination that seemed to emanate from the child that made him appear far older than his scant years.

The boy was dirty and barefoot and practically dove into the passenger seat after the man had opened the door for him.

("Go! Please, mister! Drive away, now!")

The man's car eased past the spot where the road forked. If he had gone to the left that night, instead of taking a right, which, after all, would have been the practical thing to do, since it would have cut his ride short by ten minutes, he would have never seen the child.

The man pulled the car over to the side of the road and got out, listening to the magnetic hum of hidden insects that sought refuge in the thickets of the deep woods that stretched for a good twenty miles in the rural area of Macomb County, an hour north of Detroit.

It had been a fluke that he had come across the boy. But he knew destiny sometimes had a much different calling card than the one you thought you picked for yourself.

"My God, are you okay, son?" he asked the child, who was trembling and had hunched down as low as he could in the seat.

The boy's face was filthy, caked with dirt and with smears that ran down the length of his cheeks that the man realized must have come from the child's tears.

"I'm okay now. Please. I need to get home to my sister. She's in danger. Can you help me?"

"You're safe. I promise. What's your name?"

"Ben. Ben Gooden."

The man looked up at the brilliant canvas of the country sky and the stars that shone like a million desperately hoped-for wishes and knew that real good men always did the right thing, no matter the personal cost.

CHAPTER 17

The red numbers of the digital clock shone harsh and glaring against Julia's still-dark bedroom like watchful eyes, reminding Julia she would never fall asleep. Six AM and there was no point trying to sleep anymore, especially since Julia had spent the majority of the previous late night into the wee hours of the fresh morning staring at her ceiling, trying to make sense of everything.

A pair of little boy's feet jammed against Julia's back and she looked over at Will, who was sprawled lengthwise across the bed and was snoring softly. Logan was manning the bottom of the bed, curled up in a ball, but with one arm dangled over the side. He was positioned even in sleep near his Little League baseball bat, which he had insisted on keeping near him despite Julia's promises that he and the rest of their family were safe. Julia closed her eyes as the feeling of overwhelming frustration engulfed her. She had been so close to something the night before, closer than she'd ever been, but she had ultimately failed in the worst possible way, by letting Phoenix Pontiac get away from her again.

Having nowhere else to go, she had returned home, where she'd found both little boys in her bed. Will was sleeping and Logan was standing guard by his brother. During the night, Julia's eyes had drifted down to her oldest son to see him returning her gaze, both mother and son consumed by worries that would not allow sleep to come for either of them.

Julia crept out of bed and made her way into the bathroom. She splashed cold water on her face and pulled on a pair of running shorts and a tank top. She tried to be quiet as she moved past Helen's bedroom and stopped when she reached the living room, expecting to see Navarro asleep on the couch, but he was in the kitchen already with a fresh pot of coffee.

"I figured you would've woken me up if the cops found Phoenix Pontiac," Julia said.

"You know I would have. I keep my promises," Navarro said. He poured coffee into a mug that read *World's Best Mom* on the front, with a picture of Logan and Will on the back, and placed it in front of Julia on the kitchen island. "I've got a meeting at the station later this morning on the Angel Perez case. Russell and I went back to the convenience store across from the Home Depot in Dearborn last night after you left, and the manager swore the security video he gave us with Angel and the white van was intact."

"The convenience store should have the original video or at least have it backed up somewhere," Julia said.

"Russell and I looked at their feed at the store last night, and it was the same thing. The manager is supposed to call the security surveillance company this morning to see if they can figure out what's going on," Navarro said. "You okay, Gooden?"

"What do you think?" Julia asked.

"Sometimes you don't like to hear what I've got to say, but at the risk of pissing you off, Phoenix Pontiac is conning you."

"You don't know that. They never found a body in my brother's case. That's the only way I'll ever be sure."

"You know how this works, as well as I do," Navarro said. "Most missing persons' cases, especially the ones involving kids, never get solved. And if they do, there's no happy ending. I don't want you to get hurt or have someone play you. If you were thinking clearly on this, you'd agree that Phoenix Pontiac's timing is suspicious at best."

"I am thinking clearly," Julia said.

"No, you're not. You're letting your emotions sweep you up in whatever bullshit spin he's reeling you into. Your dad shows up out of the blue and then Phoenix Pontiac mysteriously appears, claiming your brother is alive and gives you some cryptic warning to stay away from Duke. For all we know, maybe they're working together."

"That makes no sense. Phoenix told me Ben said to stay away from my dad."

"You've got a harder edge than most people I've ever known. That's what makes you such a good reporter. But you're losing it right now because you want to believe what Pontiac is saying is true."

"You think Ben is dead?"

"Don't make me say it, Julia."

"Ben was the only good thing I ever had growing up. He planted a seed in me, and without it, I'm not sure if I would've turned out okay. I probably would've ended up like Duke or Sarah. All these years that have gone by, I never forgot my brother or what he did for me. Time passes, and the hurt is always still there, but it gets a little easier. I'm happy now, and content for maybe the first time in my entire life, with you and the boys, and that's because I was starting to let myself move away from my past. Not that I'd ever give up trying to find out what happened to my brother, but I stopped letting his loss consume me. But now with Duke coming back and Phoenix Pontiac's claims, my brother's abduction is like a fresh wound all over again."

"You're going to be okay. But you need to do me one favor, though. God knows I'm not the one to be giving parenting advice, but I do know what it's like to be a scared kid. Until this situation with your dad is over with, I want to move you and the kids and Helen into a safe house or my place. I'm going to be wrapped up in the Angel Perez case and I'm not going to be able to be around all the time. It's not good for Logan to be sleeping with a baseball bat next to his bed."

"I know. I'll think about it," Julia said. She put her untouched coffee mug down on the counter and reached for a bottle of water in the refrigerator. "I'm going out for a run."

"Not a good idea," Navarro said. He looked down the hallway toward the still-closed bedroom doors and pulled Julia tightly against his body. She felt his hand move inside the fabric of her shirt and then slide across the length of her bare back. Her breath came fast as Navarro pinned her against the kitchen island with his hips and his mouth parted her own.

"You're killing me," Julia said after she made herself pull away. "In case you forgot, there are little boys in this house."

"Sorry. I wasn't being a gentleman, but the next time we're alone, you're in for a world of trouble."

"Can I quote you on that?"

"I will deliver, beautiful. That's a promise. Can I grab a shower? I'm meeting Russell for breakfast at the Downtown Café to talk about the Angel Perez case before we head to the station."

"Sure. Use the one in the hallway, next to the spare bedroom. Just lock the door so Helen won't surprise you by accident."

Julia watched Navarro go into the bathroom and waited until she heard the water running in the shower. She wrote a quick note for Helen and the boys, in case they got up before her run, and headed out the front door to her porch to stretch. Julia worked through her series of movements, wincing over the fresh bruise that Phoenix Pontiac had inflicted on her right rib cage after he tackled her. It wasn't that Julia liked running, something that was confirmed each time she started off on her usual predawn morning jog. It was the challenge of pushing herself harder than she thought she could, but more important, it was something she could control.

Julia felt her breath match pace with the rhythm of the pounding of her sneakers on the pavement and did a quick sweep of her surroundings as she turned the corner away from her house. A black Ford Taurus was parked on the far end of a neighboring street, not a car she had seen before along her usual route. She reached toward the security of her waist pack and patted her knife with the three-inch blade.

She ran to the opposite sidewalk, positioning herself farther away from the car. As she heard its ignition start, she looked over her shoulder to see the vehicle make a fast move toward her.

The driver-side window of the car opened and Agent Kenny raised a Styrofoam coffee cup in Julia's direction as the car kept pace next to her.

"Ms. Gooden, good morning. We got off to a bad start. I was hoping I could make it up to you. I've got an extra coffee. Starbucks' finest. A break from your morning running routine would do you good. You're thirty-seven and young enough now, but all the pounding on your joints, by the time you hit fifty, you'll wake up to the sound of your bones trying to pop their way back into place through battered, chewed-up cartilage. Ten miles again today?"

"I don't like being followed," Julia answered as she picked up her pace.

"The pretty boy you were trying to find in the bar last night, I figured it was a hookup behind your cop boyfriend's back, and you had to have him so badly, you screwed the long-haired boy in the men's room. Classy-looking women sometimes will surprise you, but we all have our needs. But by the way he hightailed it out of the place, I'd say it was something different. Who was the guy? Someone who works for your dad?"

"No. It's a story I'm working on, and I can't talk about it."

"Is that right? Phoenix Pontiac, age thirty-eight.

Originally from Livonia, unknown address in Chicago now. His mother was a drug addict, and he got shuttled through the foster care system."

Julia stopped and Agent Kenny's vehicle did as well. He got out of his car and handed Julia a coffee.

"No thanks."

"Suit yourself," Kenny said. He buffed the roof of his car with the sleeve of his jacket and sat down. "I've got plenty more to share about Pontiac, if you'd like."

Julia turned away so Agent Kenny wouldn't see the expression of want on her face.

"I'm sure I've got as much as you do," Julia said.

"Pontiac dropped out of high school when he was seventeen. Got busted a few times for drugs, crystal meth, and low-end weed and drug paraphernalia charges. Then he got arrested on a charge of aggravated assault. He served time, but when he got out, he got popped again for drugs, made bail, and skipped town. The past year, he's been living in Chicago, running clean for the most part. Now, let me ask you, why would a nice girl like you be hanging out with a guy like that?"

"Like I said, it's for a story."

"I don't like making deals, but I'm going to hunt down your dad. I know what's most precious to you. Your kids, right? I've got three of my own. I think it's safe to say, you and I are very different, but we're the same in that we'd do anything for our children. But what happened to your brother, you've never been able to get over that. Your brother and what happened to him hangs as precious to you as your own little boys. Thirty years not knowing, it's got to nearly kill a soul. You bring me Duke, I'll solve your mystery."

"I can't bring in a dead man."

"I've scratched your itch, Ms. Gooden, haven't I? You think about it. You know how to reach me. And if I were you, I wouldn't make it a habit of running alone these days."

Agent Kenny poured the remainder of his steaming coffee out onto the street and got back into his car. "I'd hate to see something happen to you. I'm no fan of reporters, but I figured you've suffered enough in your life after what happened to your brother and the scandal with your now-deceased husband."

"You don't scare me."

"Sure I do."

Julia pivoted and ran as fast as she could in the opposite direction as Kenny started up his car. Julia looked over her shoulder at the FBI agent's oncoming pursuit and made a quick right into a neighbor's yard, pushing through the fence and running the length of the backyard until she made it to the woods that ran parallel to her house.

The woods were lush and thick from the July Michigan heat, and Julia tried to outrun the mosquitoes and deerflies that hummed in her ears and circled her bare arms and legs as she passed, until she reached her own backyard. She looped past Logan and Will's tree house and reached her hand into her waist pack, where she pulled out her ringing phone, assuming it was Navarro giving her a ration of grief for going for a run alone.

Julia glanced at her phone screen and the unknown number. She made it a habit never to answer unfamiliar calls, figuring it was a marketer or a pissed-off source; but this time, she held the phone to her ear and hit the play button.

"Julia Gooden," she answered as she circled around the side of her house to the front door.

Ten seconds of silence followed and Julia was about to hang up, but then a man's voice came on the line.

"Julia? I . . . ," the man started, his voice thick with emotion. "Is this really you?"

"Yes, who is this?" Julia asked.

"It's me, Julia. Oh, my God, it's me. It's your brother, Ben."

CHAPTER 18

Julia leaned against the side of her house to support herself as the world seemed to move in fluid ripples all around her.

"Ben?" Julia asked.

"Yes. God, kid. Are you okay?"

Julia closed her eyes as tightly as she could and wrapped every part of her being around the voice. She felt a dizzying joy move through her as she pictured her first hero, always preserved in her mind as a feisty and perfect nine-year-old boy, assuring her they were going to be all right. Julia realized this could be the moment she had always dreamed of since she was seven, one that she believed could never really happen. Julia scrambled to come up with all the things she had promised she'd tell Ben if he ever came home, a boundless list of wishes, failures, hurts, and secret dreams that had accumulated in her life like a brimming sack of personal, heartfelt letters never sent. All of it, every second she had missed with her brother, wanted to burst out of her in an explosive release, but then a reasoning voice in the back of her head cried out a warning that there was no guarantee it was actually her brother who was calling.

"You're Ben?"

"Yes. I swear, baby sister. It's me."

"I've got two answers for you then, depending on who you really are. If this is you, I've missed you more than you could ever know, and I never, ever gave up trying to find you. But if this isn't my brother, whoever you are, if you're playing a game with me, I swear, I'll hunt you down and kill you."

Julia heard a warm, heartfelt laugh on the other end of the phone.

"You toughened up, I knew you would."

Julia tried to keep her hand from shaking as she held on to her phone for dear life. She reminded herself how many times people who talked a real good game on her beat were merely working a very well-rehearsed lie they had perfected so masterfully, oftentimes it had morphed in their minds to the God's honest truth.

"Right now, to me, all you are is a voice. If you're my brother, prove it."

"Good move. You don't believe everything people tell you. I taught you well. As for your request, it's an easy one. I've replayed every minute I spent with you in my mind at least a million times. Each night, before I fall asleep, I think of you and I remember our life in Sparrow. We were born into a crappy life, but I always tried so hard to make it good for you."

"Then answer my question."

"You're direct, too. I like it. Okay, little sis. Before bed, we used to talk about the New York Yankees."

"When my brother was abducted, there was a picture of me that ran in the local paper. I was sitting on the front step of our house in Sparrow, holding his New York Yankees ball. Nice try. Give me something else."

"My Julia is tough. Okay, on the last day we spent together, I took you to Funland, and I got you tickets to ride the carousel. I thought you'd be okay to go on alone, but you were scared. I felt really stupid because I was nine, and I thought it would be lame if anyone from school saw me on the merry-go-round, so I was going to make you go alone. But right before the ride started, I could see that you were about to cry. I jumped on so you'd be okay. You want another?"

"Please," Julia answered, but this time her voice gave way and she cursed herself as she heard it crack.

"You okay, Julia? This has got to be a lot for you. It is for me, too."

"I'm fine. Keep going."

"Right before we moved into the house in Sparrow, we all had to live in Dad's old Chrysler for a couple of weeks, and you'd sleep with your head against my shoulder. I made up a story about a magical wizard named Mr. Moto, and I'd tell it to you so you'd relax. That was the only way you'd fall asleep."

She covered the phone with her hand and started to sob; her deep, wracking cries felt like they would never end.

"I'm so sorry, Julia. Please believe me. I would've never made you suffer all this time, wondering what happened to me. But I didn't have a choice. I had to protect you. Staying away was the only way I could."

"If my brother were alive, nothing would have stopped him from coming home to me."

"I understand why you'd think that way, but it's not true. If the people who kidnapped me thought I was dead, they would've figured they already had their pound of flesh. But if they knew I was alive, they would've come after you."

"Why?"

"I have so many questions I want to ask you, too, but we need to make this quick. Do you know where Stinson Trail is?"

"Sure, but it's closed right now. I used to run up there. The city is doing some kind of construction to fix the trail."

"You can still access it, though. Meet me there in thirty minutes. Come alone, and I'll explain everything. Has Duke contacted you?"

Duke's name made Julia pause as she wondered if Ben would call him that instead of "Dad." Her thoughts flew back to Duke's warning when she saw him in Sparrow, confirming that no matter how much she wanted this to be true, she needed to play it safe until she could see if the person she was talking to really was her brother.

"My father is dead."

"Don't believe it. He's alive and dangerous. Duke was the reason I was abducted and I barely escaped. All these years, I tried to keep what he did away from you. But he has a mark on your head now."

"What do you mean?"

"Just meet me at Stinson Trail, and I'll tell you everything, I swear."

"Where do you want to meet?"

"So you know about the two parking lots? One is by the main entrance and the other one is by the lake.

There's a service road if you take the second exit to the lake. Follow the service road. Leave your car in the lot by the beginning of the trail. About a quarter mile down the trail, there's a playground. I'll be waiting there for you. You need to come alone. You'll do that for me, right?"

"I'm going to bring a friend of mine. He's a police officer and I trust him with my life."

"No. It has to just be you. This is important. Don't let me down. I love you, Julia. I'll be waiting for you."

"Why do I need to come alone?" Julia asked.

"Just trust me, kid. I swear, I'll explain everything when I see you."

"Okay. I'll be there and I'll come alone."

The phone went dead and Julia looked back at her house where the beautiful life that she tried so hard to build was waiting for her inside as her past and present collided head-on.

Julia reached into her waist pack for her car keys and got inside her SUV. She looked inside the window of her kitchen and saw Helen pouring two glasses of milk and putting them in front of her boys as Navarro was busy showing something to Logan on his phone.

Julia felt a strong tug go off inside her, and she instinctively wanted to go back to her family.

("I'll never leave you. Not in a million years.")

Julia put her key in the ignition as Ben's voice from long ago whispered its haunting promise in her head. She looked back at her family in the window one last time and hit the gas. If it was Ben waiting for her at the park, Julia owed him her life. If she was making a mistake, one way or another, at least she had to know.

When Julia reached the on-ramp to the highway, she called Navarro.

"Where are you? Helen is trying to teach me how to make pancakes for your boys and it's not going well," Navarro answered.

"Ben called me. I know it sounds crazy, but everything he said, I almost believe it's my brother. Jesus, Ray. Maybe he's still alive."

"Hold on," Navarro said. Julia heard muffled movement as if Navarro was putting his hand over his phone until he could get out of earshot from her children, and then came back on the line. "Are you in your car?"

"Yes. I'm about half an hour from Stinson Trail. That's where I'm supposed to meet the person who called me."

"Where on the trail?"

"The meet-up spot is a playground a quarter mile off the trail by the second parking lot. You can access it from the service road. If the caller is my brother, I need to meet him alone. That's what he said."

"Pull over. Don't go any farther. Not yet. You wait for me."

"Ben told me to come alone."

"And now you're referring to the caller as Ben. Why aren't you listening to your instincts? You're so much smarter than that. Someone is setting you up. It's a trap to get to Duke."

"I've thought of all that already. But there were some things the caller said that only Ben and I knew about."

"Are you sure?"

Julia replayed in her head her short conversation

with the person on the phone and started to second-guess herself.

"I'm pretty sure."

"I'm calling Russell. I don't think he left for the restaurant yet, where we're supposed to meet up. He lives near Stinson Trail. If you care about me at all, you won't go there alone. Shit, you're breaking up. Can you hear me?"

"Ray?" Julia answered. But the call had dropped.

Julia hung up the phone and pictured Logan and Will laughing in her kitchen earlier that morning, her two little boys huddled together over the kitchen island, a testament to the good life she now had and a reminder of the responsibility she owed to her children.

When she reached the sign to Stinson Trail, Julia's mind was made up. She pulled over and texted Navarro, letting him know she would wait for him or Russell in the parking lot. She wouldn't meet the caller, who claimed to be Ben, without them.

She veered her SUV onto the service road and noticed two orange construction cones that looked like they had previously blocked the main road but had been moved to the side to let cars through. Julia drove forward and then hooked her way onto the service road that flanked the jogging path, which she used to run before the parks-and-rec department had closed off the park and trail due to heavy flooding earlier that summer. Julia pulled into the empty parking lot and an uneasiness slithered around her and nestled uncomfortably around her shoulders as she realized she was completely and utterly alone without another soul in sight.

* * *

The park worker took a long swig from his Dunkin' Donuts coffee cup and reached in the store's white paper bag with its trademark orange-and-pink lettering for his bounty: a double-chocolate-dip donut, his first course before he started on the egg white flatbread, tasteless crap. But even if he took a couple of bites of it after his real breakfast, he could tell the wife that he had eaten what he promised her he would as he walked out the door of their aging 1960s ranch just a half hour earlier. Sharing a select, small portion of the truth was better than telling a complete lie, Roger Bellows thought, as he pulled his work van, with the CITY OF ROCHESTER HILLS PARKS DEPARTMENT logo keenly displayed on both sides of the vehicle, onto the service road and his latest mess.

The Stinson Park and Trail project had become a colossal pain in his ass. Roger was Second Supervisor Grade II for the department, and the maintenance and repair work was his cross to bear since the usually popular jogging spot, picnic area, and playground had gotten doused from an especially heavy rain in the early summer. But that wasn't the worst of it. The daily deluge that went on for a good week had caused a wild cascade of mud and dozens of downed trees that now littered the park.

Roger scooted the van to the right to miss colliding into a massive red oak tree, which looked like an abandoned fallen soldier as the once-eighty-foot beauty now lay on its side, halfway across the service road. Roger felt an annoyance prickle up his neck as he licked the remnants of the sticky donut off his fingers and thought about his useless brother-in-law, Tim, whose maintenance division was responsible for cleaning up the mess. But Tim and his crew were three weeks behind schedule, and Roger was catching hell for it, since his boss reamed him out on a daily basis that the parks were supposed to be up and ready for summer. Roger knew his brother-in-law's crew was intentionally working one speed, butt-ass slow, to finish the project. Roger knew a time clock for many regular Joes working for the city was both something to be dreaded, but also something to be milked.

"Who the hell moved the cones?" Roger asked aloud as he pulled into the entrance to the park and felt righteous indignation that someone had the balls to move certified parks department property from its proper place and could endanger the public.

Roger got out of the van and figured some kids looking for a place to drink or have sex moved the cones to find a secluded spot to get wasted or laid or both.

Roger whistled Whitesnake's "Here I Go Again" and started to move the orange cones back in place, when he noticed an older-model white van, with its nose jutting out from behind the restrooms. This was a violation on a grand twofer scale. No one was ever allowed to touch the cones, let alone drive inside the park, unless they carried a parks-and-rec badge, something Roger had proudly kept snapped to his front pants pocket since he started working the job after graduating from junior college fifteen years earlier.

Roger didn't bother with the cones yet, since he'd have to replace them after he got the van out, and instead made his way toward the restrooms and the illegally parked vehicle.

As he neared, he could see the van had an old, weathered white paint job and lacked side windows. The front license plate was caked in dirt, but he could make out its first three letters and could see from the SHOW ME STATE logo at the bottom that the van was from Missouri.

Roger approached the driver-side door, but moved around toward the back of the van when he heard the passenger door open and then slam shut.

Roger pushed back his shoulders as he rounded the back of the van and came face-to-face with a giant six-foot-six man with a nasty scar that looked like a crescent moon that started at the corner of his eye and trailed down in a rough semicircle until it reached the center of his left jawline.

Roger took a step back and pointed to his parks-and-rec badge clipped to his hip.

"You the guy who moved the orange cones?" Roger asked.

"I had to go to the bathroom," the giant man said. "I didn't realize that was a crime. I'll be on my way then."

"Hmmm-hmmm. I'm going to have to write up a report about this. Going to need your license and plate number," Roger said as he tried to sound tough. He turned around to head back to his van to get his clipboard, and thought about the two bites of chocolate donut waiting for him, when a thick arm latched around his chest and something razor-sharp that felt like a wire snapped around his throat.

Roger fumbled backward against the weight of the man who felt like a block of solid cement, and Roger's arms and legs paddled in the air as the wire got tighter. Roger heard a high-pitched wheeze come out of his mouth and felt a slick of wet coat the nape of his parks-and-rec shirt as the wire sliced through his skin.

The bright morning sunlight seemed to fade and felt cold as it touched his body as the big man gave one last mighty squeeze and Roger heard something pop in the center of his throat. Roger lolled on his back as his attacker released him, and he felt his body being dragged over to a tree, where the man propped him up against its trunk.

In his last fifteen seconds of his life, Roger watched as the big man snatched his parks-and-rec badge from the outside of Roger's pants pocket and then pulled out a small camera from his blue jeans. The big man waited a few seconds until it seemed as though he had caught his moment, like a true artist waiting to capture an image at the exact moment when the lighting was perfect, and snapped a picture just as Roger took his last breath.

Ahote looked down at the badge of the man he had just killed and then dragged the body over to the parks-and-rec van and dumped it in the rear of the vehicle.

The morning was not going at all how Ahote had planned, he realized. He sized up the city van and then got inside. He eased the driver seat back as far as it would go and felt a strange shudder move through him as a blue sedan circled the lot. The car had a single occupant inside, a man with dark hair, cut short, probably in his late thirties. The two made eye contact for a split second and a hollow hum reverberated through Ahote as the car shot out of the parking lot and shuttled down the service road until it was out of sight.

The big Indian closed his eyes, drinking in the spirit of the park worker, but felt cheated over the quickie. To take another soul, the devotion of the sacrifice took time, like the delicious tease of foreplay before the final act. But Ahote knew he was on the payroll of a new boss and time couldn't be wasted.

Ahote noticed a City of Rochester Hills Parks Department dark green hat on the passenger seat. He picked it up and put it on. The hat fit snugly on his large head, but it was a convincing prop, like his new decoy vehicle as he waited for the Julia woman.

Ahote's new boss was smarter than Max Mueller had been and installed a listening bug behind the dashboard of Julia's car. The bug was a stopgap until they could hack into her cell phone and also allowed them to listen into her side of the conversation with Navarro that morning, which tipped them off that she planned to go to the park alone.

Ahote looked out at the service road and thought about the hell he had caught for not picking up Julia's sister from the parking garage. He had waited for an hour, but she had been a no-show, and now the Sarah person was missing. Ahote realized he couldn't make another mistake this time. He had to deliver Julia or his hard-earned status as a "closer" would be lost forever.

Ahote pulled out a Camel cigarette from a pack inside his shirt pocket and wondered if Julia could satisfy the want that still ached in his chest from not being able to take her brother's soul, and he swore that one way or another, he would have hers. His large black eyes blinked heavily as a black Crown Victoria pulled into the lot, driven by a bald man wearing dark aviator sunglasses.

The morning was going to shit, he realized. The man in the Crown Vic was definitely not part of the plan.

Julia nearly jumped when her phone rang on her SUV's inner console and she hurried to answer it.

"Julia, it's Russell. Ray called me. I'm just pulling into the other side of the park by the pond."

"That's where I'm supposed to meet someone."

"Besides a city park van, there's no one here to meet. There was a sedan that pulled in for a second and then left right when I got into the lot. A guy younger than me with short, dark hair. He left too quickly for me to get the plate number, though. You want me to meet you?"

"Stay put. I'll drive over to you," Julia said.

Julia pulled back on the service road and made a loop around the trail. As she approached Russell's unmarked Crown Victoria, she saw the parks-and-rec vehicle and its driver, who looked like he was on a break and reading a magazine that was in front of his face.

Julia pulled up next to Russell so their cars were side by side and then texted Navarro to let him know that she had met up with his partner at the other end of the park.

"Lovely morning, Gooden. Did you bring coffee?" Russell called out from his passenger window. Julia smiled as she got out of her car and headed over to Russell just as the city van's engine roared to life. Julia turned her head in the direction of the van as a shot rang out from the van's direction and Russell's front window exploded.

"Shit, Julia, get down!" Russell called out. He scrambled over the broken glass on the seat and pulled himself out of the passenger-side door next to Julia.

Julia grabbed Russell's hand and the two dove for cover by the nose of Julia's vehicle, the farthest spot away from the open road and the oncoming van.

Russell held his gun between his hands and fired off a shot, but the van barreled toward them like a runaway freight train gone off the tracks.

The sound of an approaching vehicle's car horn let out three long and angry blasts as Julia realized someone else had entered the service road and was heading in their direction.

The city van screeched to a fast stop directly behind Julia's car, and Julia watched as Russell quickly ducked around the nose of her SUV and fired his weapon again.

Russell then dodged back behind Julia's vehicle for cover. "There's another car. It's not Ray. It's another SUV, a big black one with tinted windows. Looks like a Ford Explorer."

Julia froze as she heard a door of the city van open. She crouched low and looked under her car, where she spotted two large dirty work boots exiting the driver-side door of the parks-and-rec van and landing on the pavement.

A series of rapid-fire bursts of gunshots snapped off from the newly arrived Explorer, and Julia kept watch from under her car as the big work boots scrambled back inside the van.

"Stay down, Julia. The new company could be the guy in the van's backup."

Russell broke loose from the cover of Julia's SUV one more time and shot at the van as it started up and then tore down the service road toward the park exit.

Julia ducked her head up quickly to spot the Explorer spin out to a perfect stop and the driver-side window opened halfway.

Russell caught his breath and then positioned himself on the edge of Julia's SUV.

"Stay in your vehicle and put your hands where I can see them," Russell warned.

"Hold on, no one needs to get hurt here. Julia, you need to come with me. You got set up. It was a trap. I thought you were smarter than that."

Julia got up from her crouching position behind her own vehicle to see her father staring at her from inside the Explorer, all cool and relaxed after a gunfight, with his dark glasses on.

"Who the hell is this guy?" Russell asked.

"He's my dad," Julia said. She stood up with angry fists held at her side. "Duke, this police officer is a close friend. If you dare try and hurt him in any way, I swear, I'll spend every day of the rest of my life making you regret it."

"I have nothing but the gravest of respect for the police. I just came here for my daughter," Duke said. "But if I hadn't shown up when I did, I can guarantee your friend here wouldn't be alive right now, and you'd be locked up in the back of that van that just left with a monster. Get in the car. You want to know the truth? I'm the only one who can give it to you."

"You're a liar, and you're the person who tried to set me up. My father is a fugitive, Russell. He needs to be taken into custody," Julia said.

"You're really going to make me do this, aren't you? Okay. If that's what everyone wants, I'll come out of the car, nice and easy, no one gets hurt. Easy, easy," Duke said, his voice sounding smooth and warm.

Duke seemed to glide out of the car, all the while smiling at Russell, with his killer-watt, electric welcome.

"I'm unarmed, Officer. As you can see, I left my gun on the driver seat of my vehicle. So sorry about this mix-up. I can't tell you how glad I am to finally meet a friend of my daughter's, and thank you for looking out for her. I'm Duke Gooden," Julia's father said as he continued his dead-on, confident approach with his hands raised in a surrender gesture.

"What's going on here, Julia?" Russell asked. He shot Julia a quick look, giving Duke the fraction of a second that he needed. Duke grabbed Russell's gun hand and then spun him around, knocking his weapon from his hand. Duke then quickly attached a pair of handcuffs around Russell's wrists like a blink-and-you'll-miss-it Houdini trick.

"Sorry about this. I really am," Duke said as he secured Russell and the handcuffs to the Crown Victoria's side mirror. "I wasn't lying to you. I truly have nothing but the greatest of respect for law enforcement, as long as they're not looking for me."

"You son of a bitch," Julia said.

"That's me," Duke said as he pulled out a gun from the back of his suit jacket and pointed it at Julia. "If this is the only way you'll get in the car, then that's how we'll play it."

"I'm not leaving my friend."

Duke pressed a button on his phone and studied it. He then put his hand on Julia's back and pushed her toward his waiting vehicle.

"A Chevy Tahoe is heading this way, about three minutes out. It was parked at your house late last night and this morning, so I'm guessing it's another cop. Your friend here will be just fine."

"Russell, I'm sorry," Julia said.

Russell jerked his head around and tried to spy Julia.

"We're coming for you, Julia. Hang on. And we're coming for you, too," Russell said to Duke. "Father or not."

"I left you your gun. I know it's bad for cops if they lose their gun or their badge. Nice to meet you," Duke said as he opened the driver-side door of his car and shoved Julia inside.

Julia scrambled to the passenger side and tried the lock, but Duke was already inside and he snapped the locks in place.

"Are you going to kill me?" Julia asked.

"That's what you think? I'm taking you to a place where I'll be safe and we can talk. You help me and I'll help you. You want to know what happened to Ben? I'll tell you what I know, if you tell me what the cops have and what Liam Mueller told you when you met with him at his store."

"What is this all about?" Julia asked.

Duke Gooden pulled his sunglasses from his face

and laid them on the dashboard. He rubbed his eyes and looked tired for the first time since Julia had seen him.

"Thirty years ago, I screwed up."

"I don't want your apology for abandoning us."

"That's not it. I took something by accident. I was going to give it back, but then things spun out of control and it was too late, so I kept it."

"What did you do?"

Duke scratched at his wrist, and Julia noticed the raised pink scars on his flesh as the shirtsleeve of his baby-blue shirt retracted up his arm slightly.

"I took a painting. An original Vincent van Gogh. It's worth five million dollars. At least."

CHAPTER 19

Julia scrambled to come up with her flight strategy as her eyes darted to the locked passenger door of her father's car and then shot over to the steering wheel.

"Don't bother," Duke said, as if reading Julia's mind. "You try to run the car off the road, we'll both get killed. You've got two kids. Boys, right? That's your something to hold on to. They always say boys will do anything for their moms. But girls can be loyal to their daddies, too. Do you remember that game we used to play? I'd give you a quarter if you could answer a line we rehearsed and impress one of my clients."

"I was part of your show. Nice parenting, exploiting your own kid. You stole the van Gogh from Max Mueller?"

Duke turned toward Julia with a look of surprise.

"You know about Mueller? You're something, I'll give you that. Okay. Here's how we're going to play this. I'll tell you what you want to know if you follow a few simple rules. Rule number one, crouch down on the seat so your head is facing the floor."

"You don't want me to know where you're taking me," Julia said.

"Smart and pretty my girl is. If you'd followed my career path, I think you could've made some real good money. Down on the seat, like I told you."

The one-mile exit signs for I-75 North and South appeared on the horizon, and Julia tried to wait to give in to her father's directive until she could figure out which route he was going to take.

"You want to know what happened to your brother, this is the only way you'll ever know. You give me information, and I'll give you some. Down on the seat. *Now.*"

"I swear, I'm going to get you for this," Julia said as she folded her body and put her arms over her knees as she looked down at the gray car carpet. Julia's eyes flicked to her left and she saw her father's gun jutting out just slightly from the rear waistband of his pants.

Julia kept her eyes on her watch to try and figure out their location based on the time elapsed until she felt the Explorer decelerate. She shot a look at Duke, who pulled his cell phone from the dashboard and hit a number.

"Two minutes out. Open the garage like I told you. No, I didn't bring food. Set the alarm again as soon as we drive in. I mean the instant."

"Who's that?" Julia asked.

Duke ignored Julia as his eyes moved to the right and left of the road in a constant motion, and then swung over to the rearview mirror in a steady rhythm.

"Twenty seconds out. Count to twelve and then open

it," Duke said, and then paused a beat. "Because I said so."

Duke slid his dark glasses back on and sighed with annoyance. "God."

Julia started to get up in the seat, but Duke pushed her back down. "Not yet. I'll tell you when we're clear."

The Explorer barely slowed as Julia heard the sound of an industrial-sized door crank open. She looked up to see the top of the SUV barely clear the opening before it zoomed to a stop.

"Don't move. Not yet." Duke's eyes stayed riveted on the rearview mirror until Julia heard the sound of the metal door connect with concrete as it came to a stop. "Okay. Get up."

The muscles in Julia's back felt like twisted coiled springs as she stretched back into an upright position. She quickly scanned the scene and saw they were in a garage that had a wall of exposed red brick and a single door with a security keypad next to it.

"Let's go," Duke said.

Julia got out of the car and trailed her father to the door, where he hit a quick six-digit combination of numbers and an almost-inaudible beep sounded as a security system deactivated and the door opened, revealing Duke's accomplice. Julia felt like she got sucker punched in the gut when she instantly recognized the person on the other side of the door.

"What is this?" Julia asked. "You two are working together? I should've known. Two cons."

"No, Julia. I swear," Sarah said. "Duke showed up at my work out of the blue. He told me I was in danger and pulled a gun on me. He made me get into his car."

"Sounds familiar," Julia said.

"Enough talk. Let's go," Duke said. He motioned with his head for his daughters to walk in front of him as they entered the place.

Julia followed behind Sarah and could feel Duke right behind her. She tried not to fixate on the idea that she had a red bull's-eye target Duke had placed on the back of her head while he kept his finger on the trigger, ready to fire.

The trio climbed three flights of stairs until they reached the main floor, which looked like an urban loft. The majority of the walls were comprised of expensive-looking cork and the floors were a burgundy polished bamboo. The place looked expensive and modern, like one of the upscale models Julia had seen advertised as hip, new urban housing in downtown Detroit, built by developers to keep the yuppies in, instead of making a mass exodus to better zip codes. Julia took one more look around and saw that the ceilings had silver exposed ducts piping through the place and the kitchen's walls were made up of distressed red brick, enough details for the location to click.

"Nice place. From the distance we drove, we're somewhere in downtown Detroit. And by the look of this place, I'm betting we're in one of the new loft housing developments in the city, so either the Regis, the Hampshire, or D Street."

"Very good," Duke said. He took off his tie and rolled up both of his shirtsleeves.

Julia stared down at her father's exposed right arm, which was nettled with a nasty map of scarring that ran from his wrist up to his elbow.

"A man I work for hooked me up. I told him I was in a jam, and I'd make it up to him."

Julia walked over to a black curtain that covered a bank of floor-to-ceiling windows and tried to look outside, but Duke pulled her back.

"Sit down," Duke said, and pointed to a table in the corner of the kitchen. Duke stood as his daughters took a seat across from each other.

"I'm tired of you making the rules. I need to know if Ben is alive," Julia said.

Duke looked past his daughter at the black curtain and a veil seemed to pass over his face.

"I don't see how he could be," Duke said. "Tell me how you wound up in the park."

"How did you know I was there?" Julia asked.

"I put a tracker on your car. I needed to figure out the game Max Mueller's guys were playing. I knew they would start circling around you and Sarah to get to me."

"I got a call from someone who said he was Ben and I was supposed to come alone and to meet him at Stinson Trail."

"You fell for that?" Sarah asked.

"I'm not gullible, but the caller knew specific details of our lives that only Ben and I knew about."

Duke's eyes hung on Julia like a lock and wouldn't let go.

"When I got to the park, I saw another car leaving in a hurry. It was a blue sedan driven by a younger man, maybe late thirties, with dark hair. It fits Ben's age. But I don't buy for a minute that it was Ben. The guy in the car could've been a decoy or just a random person driving through the park. You let yourself get suckered," Duke said.

"All I know is that I need to figure this out, and

you're going to help me. Liam Mueller is after you, right?" Julia asked. "His father dies, and you think it's safe to finally come back to Detroit to pick up the van Gogh, but you set off some kind of trip wire that alerted Liam when you did."

"Good reasoning, except I'm not sure if Liam is calling the shots, now that Max is dead. There's another guy in St. Louis who could have taken over," Duke said. "The FBI talked to you. What did you tell them?"

"That you were a selfish man who abandoned his family. I also told the agent that to my knowledge, you were dead and that you never contacted me after you took off when I was seven."

"Good move. Thanks for that."

"I didn't do it for you. I lied to protect my family."

"Who's the agent?" Duke asked.

"Terry McKenzie."

"Never heard of him," Duke said.

"He goes by 'Agent Kenny.' He knows you're alive," Julia said. "Your version of twenty questions is over. I want answers now."

"You toughened up, didn't you, kid? I don't know everything, but I'll tell you what I can."

"Will it be the truth?" Julia asked.

Duke sat down in a chair at the head of the table and flashed his daughter his brilliant smile.

"The truth is simply a juxtaposition of facts and lies. One man's truth is another man's falsehood," Duke said as his eyes ticked back and forth between Julia and Sarah, the audience members for his show. "Some men are hardwired to be providers. They're born to be alpha dogs, taking care of the wife and kids, but I never liked being tied down. You hate me now. I get that. But you would've hated me a lot more if I stuck around. I would've been miserable, and eventually I would've died inside."

Duke jumped up from his seat and walked over to Julia. He got down on one knee so he was staring directly into her eyes. Julia wanted to look away, but felt a strange pull to Duke, as if he were luring her under his spell.

"It would've been terrible for you kids to live with me, a man depleted of his true nature. And I would've probably taken it out on you kids. I've seen men like that, weighed down by resentment that niggles underneath their skin like an eternal itch they can never scratch. What I did, it was the best for everyone," Duke said. He stood back to his full height and rapped his knuckles against the table. "The world is one incredible big top, something truly marvelous to behold. I'm an ambitious, glorious bastard who was never able to get away from the pull of the circus. And I have no regrets about that."

"You talk a steaming pile of shit," Sarah said. "You think what you did was best for everyone? What you did ruined me. Kids whose parents don't love them enough to take care of them get tossed around to people who don't really want them either, or what they do want from them kills the kids a little bit more, each time they take it away, until the last piece of hope they have gets dried up for good. And then the kid is all gone, but they still have to keep on living in their shitty life."

"Remember, I just saved both you girls," Duke said.

"You brought this to us, asshole," Sarah said.

"You want to lay into me, too, Julia? This is your chance," Duke said.

"What you did, taking that painting, that's why Ben was kidnapped? Why didn't you go to the police?" Julia lunged up from her seat, wanting to grab Duke by the neck and choke him, but she steadied herself, knowing she had to stay calm if she was going to get what she needed out of him.

"I never meant for anything to happen. If you want to call me a bad man, well, I guess I am. But bad men, we come in many varieties, but I'm not of that particular ilk. I'd never hurt a kid, let alone my own."

"I don't want to hear about you anymore," Julia said.

"Fine. You want the story, here it is. I met Max Mueller at a coffee shop outside the Detroit Institute of Arts about two weeks before I left Sparrow."

"You mean left your kids," Sarah said.

"A business associate I was with knew him," Duke continued. "Max was an odd little man, walked with this strange, bent black cane that he didn't need. The cane was just for show. Max and me, we hit it off. He needed a courier, and I knew he had a lot of cash, so I took the job. At first, it was easy pickups and drop-offs. I'd meet Max at his consignment store up in Birmingham and pick up a briefcase that was filled with cash. Max would give me an address and I'd drive there. Then I'd exchange the money for whatever it was Max was buying, mostly paintings and strange collectibles. That man had eclectic tastes that ran to the deviant. I almost quit when Max told me one lamp I picked up for him was made out of the skin of a concentration camp victim. Turned my stomach, but Max gave me a raise, so I stayed on. I realized pretty quick all the stuff Max was buying was hot, but it wasn't my business and he paid me well."

"That painting you stole, it cost me everything," Julia said. "Tell me the truth. And don't you dare lie to me. What happened?"

Duke's eyes formed into half slits as he looked back into the deep abyss of his sins. And for the very first time in a very long time, he told the truth.

Thirty-seven-year-old Duke Gooden eased the seat back of the leased deep-red Cadillac and heard his neck crack as he twisted it from side to side to get the blood flowing again after the eight-hour car ride from St. Louis back home to Detroit. The pickup had gone without a hitch. The man he met, Louis Lemming, escorted him in like a high roller into the back of his bar and into the black leather booth reserved for the VIPs. Louis and Duke smoked a Cuban cigar each, and Duke tried not to reveal his disgust when a girl, who was probably just a few years older than his fourteen-year-old daughter, Sarah, came into the back room to deliver the drinks wearing a face full of heavy makeup, a skimpy dress that barely hung past her thighs, and a worn look of a hard-lived life for a girl her age.

As Duke drove on through the early evening, he cringed as he remembered how Lemming had cocked his head toward the teenage girl and gave Duke a lewd smile. Duke figured Lemming to be about his age, but on appearance, they were quite different. Lemming was a fat man with a large, bulbous nose that was topped off with a dark mole on one side. He wore an expensive dark blue pin-striped suit, but everything about Lem-

ming screamed cheap to Duke, like Lemming grew up on rough streets where hardened single mothers living in trailers raised their kids on food stamps and government-issued cheese. No amount of spit or polish could remove the stain of dirty redneck from him.

Duke passed the Michigan/Ohio border and thought about his meeting with Lemming to pass the remainder of the drive.

"You like what you see?" Lemming asked Duke as he gave the underage girl a lecherous stare.

Duke politely declined the offer and reached around the briefcase, which was handcuffed to his wrist, for his wallet as he tipped the waitress a fifty because he felt sorry for her.

When Lemming slipped to his back office to pick up what Duke had come for, Max's latest painting or weird artifact he'd just purchased, Duke leaned into the teenage girl and gave her a piece of advice.

"Go home, young lady," Duke said. "You don't belong in a place like this."

The girl looked back at Duke and then turned her face away. "I wish I could."

Duke decided not to push the matter further and spotted Lemming coming out of the back room. Lemming gestured with his head toward the rear exit and the street and slipped out of the bar. Duke took his cue and picked up the briefcase gingerly, because it felt much heavier than the usual load, and made his way out to the street and his Cadillac. He laid the briefcase down on the seat, looking forward to the moment when he could untether the damn thing from his wrist, and

*pulled into the side street that led to a loading dock
and the back of the bar.*

*This wasn't the first time Duke had dealt with Lem-
ming. Lemming and Mueller had some sort of ongoing
business transactions that Duke wasn't fully primed
about, since he was relegated to just being the pickup/
drop-off guy. For now anyway, but Duke had big
dreams and he was sure if he stayed on with Max, they
would happen.*

*Duke was new, but still savvy enough not to trust
Lemming. As he looked at the broken beer bottles lying
underneath the loading dock, he quickly came up with
a strategy in his head if things went bad.*

*Duke exited the car with the briefcase and eyed
Lemming, who came out the rear exit empty-handed.*

"Give me the briefcase," Lemming said.

"No exchange until I see what my boss ordered."

*Lemming gave him a mean smile with small, square
teeth and ducked back behind the rear exit door. Duke
counted in his head to thirty when Lemming returned
with a long, narrow box.*

"That's it?" Duke asked.

*"Doesn't look like much, but it's a beauty. And it's
got a hidden surprise. How much cash you got in the
briefcase?"*

*Duke shrugged his shoulders because he truly didn't
know. Duke would've looked if he could have; in fact,
he was dying to, and would have likely been more than
tempted to lift some, but Max had specific rules. Duke
wasn't given the combination to the lock that opened
the briefcase. The way the deals went down, Duke delivered a briefcase full of cash handcuffed to his wrist
in exchange for whatever Max decided to buy on the*

black market. Once the deal was complete, Duke un-locked the handcuffs, and Lemming made a phone call directly to Max, who would give him the code to unlock the briefcase and access the cash.

Lemming began to snatch at the briefcase, which made the handcuffs cut into Duke's wrist. Duke started to reach in his pocket with his free hand for the straight-edge razor he kept as protection for moments like this one. A gun would've been better, but Duke was scared to death of the things.

"Now, now, Louis. We're all friends here," Duke said, and smiled so wide, he could feel the muscles in his face ache.

"Okay. Give me the briefcase," Lemming answered, and took a step back from Duke and the money.

Duke unclasped the handcuff from his wrist and then did the same for the twin metal snap that was still attached to the briefcase.

"All yours," Duke said. "Have a nice night."

Duke reached for the painting that was propped up against the wall next to the loading dock, when Lem-ming motioned for his bodyguard. "Not until I call your boss with the combination and I count the cash."

Lemming scooted back inside the club, and Duke looked up at the night sky and his breath caught as he saw a shooting star streak by.

"Did you see that?" Duke asked the bodyguard, who looked as engaged as a sack of dry cement. "Now that, my friend, is a sign of good luck."

Duke fiddled with the ruby gold pinky ring he had just bought, thanks to Mueller, and pulled into his stop before he met his boss. Chums was a dive bar on Eight Mile, where his buddy Rickie Samuels was waiting for him. Duke knew Mueller wanted this particular pickup right away, but Duke had promised Rickie he would celebrate one last drink with him before Rickie got the hell out of town, since the Feds were about a half a hair away from nailing him.

Duke banked the Caddie across the street from Chums and checked to be sure the trunk lock was secure, since that's where he had stashed the painting. Assured Max's latest purchase was safe, he headed into Chums, which sported a blinking yellow sign out front that read: BEER AND BURGERS SO GOOD, YOUR TONGUE WILL SLAP YOUR BRAIN.

Bob Seger's "Beautiful Loser" belted out from a tabletop jukebox in the corner of the bar as Duke walked in and assessed the scene. The crowd at Chums was sparse, filled with just a couple of guys, who likely just got off their shift. The only two patrons besides Rickie were playing pool in the back, and Duke gave them a nod when he entered, figuring them for honest working men in their faded jeans and blue-and-gray short-sleeved Ford uniform shirts they still had on.

Rickie was leaning up against the bar and was dressed like Duke, both in a suit and tie, despite the ninety-degree heat that still hung around long past sundown. Rickie was blond and tan, and looked genuinely glad to see Duke as he took a long drink from his bottle of Bud Light.

"Rickie, my man," Duke said, and held out his hand to shake his friend's. Rickie had worked for Max once, but had started his own offshoot business, mainly gun trafficking. This endeavor had created a profitable solo

business—so much so, the ATF was now on his tail, hence Rickie's decision to move his business elsewhere before he got snared and wound up with the fate of thirty to life.

Rickie nodded at the bartender, who was busy wiping a glass and watching the Tigers game.

"Whatever my buddy wants," Rickie told the bartender.

"Club soda, with a twist of lemon, please," Duke answered.

"That's a pansy drink," Rickie said.

"Never had a taste for liquor. A man needs to be in control of his surroundings before his surroundings get control of him."

"Duke Gooden, the resident philosopher. You know, I'm almost going to miss this place."

"You heading to Florida?" Duke asked. He knew one of Rickie's main distributors was in Miami, so it made sense.

"No. I've got to get out of the States. I'm going to the Dominican Republic, to start anyway. A man can get good and lost down there, and that's what I need right now. Why don't you come with me? You don't want to be hanging with Mueller much longer. He's a bad man. I generally don't have a problem with bad men, but working for him was the dirtiest job I ever had."

"Max isn't so terrible," Duke said, and took a drink from the club soda the bartender had just delivered. "You can't fault a man for buying what's stolen, if that's what he wants. Max likes art and strange collectibles. Doesn't seem that bad to me."

Rickie beckoned the bartender back with two fin-

gers and waited until the bartender reluctantly returned, with his eyes still fixed on the game.

"A shot of Jack. Make it two. Might as well go off in style," Rickie said. "You know, the thing about you, Duke, is that you have so much potential, but you're still green. If you think all Max is doing is stealing artwork, brother, you're in a world of denial. You want me to tell you what Max really does?"

"No. If Max is into something dirtier than stolen art, I'd rather not know about it. The pay is way too good to tempt me out of the job."

"Suit yourself. You got a contingency plan, though?" Rickie asked.

"For what?"

"A man like Max, he's likely going to get caught one day, and when he does, the cops are going to be coming for his whole operation, and that means you, too. That is, if Max doesn't try and pin the blame on you first. I've seen him do it before. I bolted before he could do it to me. A guy who used to work for Max when I was still with him is serving twenty, up in Marquette, because Max sold him out to the cops to save his own hide."

"Is that right?" Duke said, letting the weight of his friend's words sink in just below the surface.

Rickie stood up from the bar as he checked his watch. "I've got to catch a plane to Miami in an hour. I'm leaving you with a parting gift. I like your style, and you've got plenty of it, almost more than any other guy I know, but you're still wet behind the ears. You change your mind about working for me, here's the number where you can reach me. You give it out to anyone, I'll kill you," Rickie said, and gave Duke a piece of paper with a number scribbled across it. Rickie then reached down for a brown paper bag, which was wedged between his stool and the bar on the floor.

"I should be getting you a gift," Duke said as Rickie handed him the bag. Duke took a quick glance inside, not really sure what he was expecting to find. He raised one eyebrow when he saw a gun and a fake passport with Duke's picture on it and a name that didn't belong to him.

"Stash this somewhere, along with some cash if you have it. Sort of like an emergency-supply kit you stick in the back of your car. It'll come in handy if you ever need it."

"Hey, thanks. Why are you doing this?" Duke asked.

"Because I don't like Max, and I know how to spot talent, and you've got it. Call if you change your mind about working for me. You don't have kids or family, right? That always makes things a lot more difficult in this line of work."

Since he had left them behind two weeks earlier, Duke's three children and wife were getting smaller and smaller in his mind with each passing day.

"Not me. A family ties you down."

Rickie clapped Duke on the back of his shoulder. "Hope to see you again."

Duke watched Rickie leave out the front door. Duke then slipped down the hall that led to the bathrooms and the pay phone. He fished a quarter from his pocket, plugged it into the slot, and called his boss at the strange number Max told Duke to call if he didn't get back to the city until after seven.

A gruff male voice answered the phone when Duke

asked for Mueller, and Duke waited less than five seconds before he could hear Max snatch up the phone.

"Mr. Gooden, you're late. Where the hell are you?" Max said in a dry, nasally tone.

"Just got to the city. Bad traffic all the way from St. Louis to Detroit," Duke lied, not wanting to tell Max he stopped off at a bar with one of Max's former employees, instead of meeting up with him as soon as he got back to the city, like Duke had promised.

"You got the pickup from Lemming?" Max demanded.

"I did. I didn't look at it like we discussed, but Lemming promised it's what you ordered. You want me to meet you at your place in Birmingham or your other one in Detroit?" Duke asked.

"Neither. I have a shipment that needs to get moved tonight. I have a property up in Macomb County. Meet me there and come right away."

Duke rolled his eyes as he thought about how he was going to have to log on even more miles to Macomb, but took down the directions, which were more like following markers rather than regular routes or street signs once he got off I-94.

Duke left a five on the bar for the club soda and got back into the red Cadillac, the machine feeling big and important, just like Duke was starting to feel about himself. He hooked onto the freeway and thought that when Max paid him next, he'd do the right thing and wire more money to his wife. Duke thought his absence might actually be good for Marjorie as it could be the catalyst to make her finally sober up and take responsibility for the kids. That's what he'd do, send her a Western Union cash wire from time to time so she could buy the kids shoes and food and pay the rent.

Enough money to supply the sheer amount of family shit they seemed to always need. Duke ignored a voice in the back of his head reminding him the rent on their place in Sparrow hadn't been paid in two weeks, and his family would likely get evicted unless he did something.

Duke looked back at his new pinky ring and took the speedometer up to ninety, feeling the freedom and the immense possibilities of the wide-open road ahead of him. The clouds that had hung low on the night sky for most of the trip parted, and Duke felt like he had been hit with an epiphany into his very soul as he pictured his own father, Hunter Gooden, whom Duke had seen last when he was five. Hunter had shown up shit-faced to Duke's mother's house on Duke's birthday. Hunter's real family—his wife and four kids, who didn't know about Duke or Duke's mom—was tucked away safely in their nice home in the suburbs as Hunter presented Duke with a brand-new Huffy bike and then vanished for good from their lives. Duke didn't know what happened to his father or why he never claimed him as his own, but growing up a fatherless bastard made him strong and resourceful. Duke knew the sudden memory of his father meant that his own kids would turn out just fine without him, too, maybe even better than if he had stuck around.

Duke turned the radio on and let it run on high decibel until he pulled off the exit and followed Max's direction of markers, which led him through a desolate country back road that turned to dirt about a mile in. Duke wondered if he wrote down the directions wrong, when he saw a red balloon that was hung on an old fence post, the last marker Max had given him.

Duke pulled the car onto another dirt road, which was tightly nestled between two thick lines of trees. Duke didn't consider himself a man who got scared often, but something felt off in his gut as he saw two buildings in the distance: a large two-story home, which had all the windows boarded up, and a trailer, with a large van parked between them.

Duke tucked the Cadillac behind a row of trees before the property and killed the engine. He looked at the house in the distance and saw one of Max's guards, the big Indian, Ahote, whom he had met before, rocking on his heels back and forth next to the van as he pulled the rear door open.

The night country air was thick with mosquitoes as Duke swatted them away from his face. He moved on the inside of the tree line, holding his breath all the while as he approached the house. He wanted to get paid and didn't plan to screw over the boss, but Rickie's comments about how Max would likely turn on him stuck, and something deep in his core screamed a silent warning that he needed to check out the scene before he entered it.

A gunshot blasted from inside the house, and Duke instinctively hit the deck and made himself as flat to the earth as possible. He lay down on his stomach on a nest of pine needles and peered out at the scene from behind a tree.

The garage door of the house opened, and Duke watched as a group of people, maybe twelve or so, walked out, single file. Their arms were bound, and two large, armed men were yelling orders to the group. Duke strained his eyes as he tried to adjust them to the dark as he spotted Max walking out of the garage be-

hind the group, which consisted of mostly females who looked, on first blush, to be in their late teens to early twenties. The exception was a Vietnamese woman and a young Vietnamese boy, whom Duke pegged for sixteen or so, and likely the woman's son. The woman was screaming something in Vietnamese—which Duke couldn't understand—and her son was trying to calm her down.

Max Mueller, who was wearing a suit and hat and leaning on his bent black cane, walked over to the boy and his mother.

"You speak English, gook?" Max asked the woman. "If you do, then read my lips. Shut the hell up before my man Ahote here puts a bullet in your head."

"My mother doesn't speak English, but I do," the Vietnamese teenager said. "Go to hell."

Duke watched as the teenage boy spit directly in Max's face, and Max cursed as he pulled out a handkerchief to clean himself up.

"No one does that to me," Max yelled, and began to beat the Vietnamese boy across his legs and stomach with his cane.

The boy looked as though he were about to fall to his knees but righted himself as Max began to walk away. The teenager then charged Max while his mother began to scream in a nonstop, anguished wail.

Duke watched as Ahote snatched the slight teenager up under his arm like a small toy before the teen could reach Max.

"You can have him. He's too much trouble, and I don't want any push back from Lemming. Where the hell is Duke?" Max asked as his eyes looked out toward the dirt road.

"He called over an hour ago, so he should be here soon," Ahote answered.

"All right. Load them up in the van and send them to Lemming. Tell him for this batch, he gets me a price cut on my next purchase," Max said.

The Vietnamese mother continued to sob as she was forced into the van, along with the other women. Duke shivered as the door to the van slammed shut, and he now knew the real business his boss was running.

"When Duke shows up, tell him to meet me at the Brandeis Hotel over in St. Clair Shores. I have a dinner appointment and can't wait any longer. Have Duke call the restaurant when he gets there, but tell him to stay in the parking lot. I'll meet him outside. Tell him I'm cutting his pay by a grand this week for showing up late and making me wait around for him."

Max got into his car and drove away as Duke scrambled to come up with a plan. He watched as Ahote dragged the softly crying Vietnamese boy into the trailer, and Duke felt disgusted as he started to think what Ahote was going to do to him in there. Duke realized the right thing to do would be to call the police, but then his own ass would be in a sling.

He could just give Max the painting and be done with it, Duke realized. He could quit and maybe go back to Sparrow, but he knew, deep down, the homecoming wouldn't last. Duke swatted at his ear as an ant crawled across it, and Duke climbed back to his feet, deciding upon his plan. He'd leave the painting and call his boss tomorrow to tell him he'd quit. The money was the best he'd ever had, but there was a low even a man like him couldn't stoop to.

Duke started back to his car, when he heard a door

open. He looked toward the house, but realized the sound came from the trailer. Duke watched on as the Vietnamese boy staggered out, looking dazed and groggy. Duke noticed he wasn't wearing any shoes as Ahote pushed him outside.

Duke reached into his pocket and felt his straight-edge razor. His mind quickly raced back to the paper bag he had left on the passenger seat, with the gun that his friend Rickie had given him, but Duke knew he didn't know how to shoot and wasn't sure he'd be able to aim straight because his hands would be shaking so much, trying to hold the thing steady.

Duke looked at the Vietnamese boy, who looked utterly terrified, and thought about how brave the teenager was to go after Max.

Ahote ducked back into the trailer and returned with something in his hands. Duke couldn't at first process what Ahote was holding because it seemed so out of place, but then he felt a cool trickle of sweat slip down his temple as he realized it was a bow and arrow.

"I'll give you a five-minute lead. After that, we start the hunt," Ahote said to the Vietnamese boy.

Duke pulled his straight-edge razor out of his pocket and opened the blade. He'd never used it before and wasn't sure he could now. Duke tried to be as quiet as possible as he moved along the protection of the trees, still safely hidden as he neared the trailer.

A low-lying tree branch snapped across Duke's chest and he froze in his tracks.

Ahote's eyes darted in Duke's direction, and he began to move quickly toward Duke.

Duke swallowed hard as he tried to make himself invisible behind the trunk of a tree and willed his rapid breathing to quiet and not give him away. Duke realized he likely wouldn't be able to outrun Ahote, and he didn't want to get on the receiving end of the arrow. So hiding was the desperate man's option he was going to try first.

Duke took a quick glance at the trailer and saw the Vietnamese boy dash into the woods until he got so far in, it looked like the trees had swallowed the teen whole.

Duke held the open straight-edge razor in his hand, close to his body, and heard his heartbeat thud along with the slightest of footfalls as Ahote made his approach.

Looking up to the night sky, Duke said a prayer, promising he'd do right by his family if God just got him out of this jam.

A loud rustle of underbrush startled Duke, and he turned his head slightly to see two wild turkeys scurry out of a thicket of weeds, high grass, and brambles directly in Ahote's direction.

"Is that all you are," Ahote said to the large birds. "Still better to check."

Duke felt like his heart was going to explode as Ahote moved past him, and Duke's eyes hung on the big Indian's massive back as Ahote continued to move forward.

Duke began to slip to the other side of the tree just as Ahote stopped in his tracks.

Before Ahote could turn around, Duke lunged at him, waving the straight-edge razor wildly in his direction, fighting for his life like a madman, until Duke felt the sharp blade connect and slide into Ahote's skin by the corner of his right eye. Duke's hand came down as the razor ripped its way down the side of Ahote's face until it reached the cusp of his jawline.

Ahote looked stunned for a second and dropped his bow and arrow. He clutched his bleeding face and blinked heavily as he tried to wipe away the blood that had seeped into his eye.

Duke ran, faster than he ever had in his life, even faster than the time when he was chased by a former client wielding a baseball bat after the man had discovered Duke had fleeced him out of a grand.

The moist Michigan air seemed to split open as Duke raced through it, never once looking back, as he was sure Ahote was steps behind him.

Duke reached his car and threw himself inside. His hands shook as he started the engine and Ahote appeared in his headlights, looking like a bloody, hulking monster from a horror movie as Duke banged a hasty reverse.

Duke spun the car around and slammed the gas pedal as hard as he could, right before Ahote reached his driver-side door, his giant fingers inches away from latching onto the handle.

It wouldn't be until three days later when Duke would remember the painting he had left behind in the trunk.

CHAPTER 20

Duke surfaced up from the thirty-year-old story and moved to the refrigerator, where he poured himself a large glass of orange juice and drank it all in one fast, long drink.

"You had a five-million-dollar painting in the trunk of your car and you just forgot about it?" Sarah asked. "Who does that?"

"I didn't know what it was worth at first."

"Jesus, I need a drink," Sarah said.

"I was right. You stole Max's painting and he kidnapped Ben as payback. I swear, I could kill you," Julia said. She shot up from the table and slapped her father as hard as she could across his face.

Duke took a step back in surprise and opened up his hands, as if encouraging Julia to take another swing. "I deserve that from you. You were always Ben's girl. But understand one thing. I tried to stop it. I did. You made me go this far, so let me finish."

Julia turned her back to her father and wondered if she had the gumption to kill a man, because she was certain she never hated anyone as much as she hated her father, right now, for what he did. She saw one of Duke's guns lying on the kitchen counter; for a second, she could see herself picking up the gun and pointing it at the man responsible for Ben's abduction. Julia pried her eyes off the gun and realized her entire body was shaking with rage. "Tell the rest of the story, before I do something I regret."

"You want to be angry with me, that's fine, but you hold on to it, that hatred will eat you up from the inside out," Duke said. "I caught you looking at my gun. You're not a killer. Self-defense is one thing, but you're not wired to pull the trigger first. That's a stain that would never let you go. A man kills another man, he's never the same afterward. So, if it's all right with you, Julia, I'm going to keep going here before I get slapped again or shot."

"Just do it," Julia answered.

"Okay, then. After what happened back at Max's place up in Macomb County, I laid low for a few days at a motel in Livonia. I didn't know what to do, so I called a buddy I trusted, Chip Haskell."

"The man who was murdered in the car back in Sparrow," Julia said.

"That was him," Duke said, and paced back and forth across the length of the kitchen. "When I was in the motel in Livonia, I remembered the painting and thought I might need it as a bargaining chip with Max because of what I'd done to Ahote. But I wasn't going to offer it up right away. Chip agreed to stash the painting while I figured out my game plan. But then, everything changed, and I knew I was in the center of a major shit storm. Before I brought the picture to Chip,

I asked a guy who was in the know about art. He referred me to an appraiser, who'd just gotten out of jail for forging paintings and selling them off as originals. The guy almost blew a gasket when I showed him the picture I picked up from Lemming. He told me it was an original van Gogh, a painting that must have been part of some very private stash, because the appraiser-forger guy claimed he'd never seen it before. He gave me the five-million figure, and, I swear, I thought my head would pop off. I needed a backup plan, and the appraiser knew how to make forgeries, so I paid him to make me a copy. The guy was a tattoo artist. I picked up the forgery in the back room of his place, and, I swear, it looked identical to the original I got from Lemming. With everything coming to a head, I remembered what my buddy Rickie told me about having a contingency plan. I stashed the gun and passport Rickie left me, along with five thousand dollars, in a safe-deposit box. I called Max and I told him we'd do a trade, and that if he did anything to Ben, I'd kill him. And then your mother showed up while all this was going on. I remember looking through the peephole of the motel and couldn't believe she'd found me."

"Tell the rest of the story," Julia insisted.

"Okay. And it will be the God's honest truth," Duke said, and for one of the few times in his life, he really meant it.

Marjorie sat at the scuffed, fake wood table in the motel room and clutched her hands underneath her chin.

"How'd you find me?" Duke asked.

"I begged Mike Ballentine to tell me where you were. He only did it because he felt sorry for me, because he knew what happened to Ben. Ballentine loaned me enough money to take a Greyhound bus down here. You need to come home."

Duke took in his wife sitting across the table from him and noticed Marjorie's eyes were clear for the first time in about a year since she'd first started drinking. But they were now filled with the hangdog look of someone whose internal light was about to be snuffed out for good.

"Somebody took Ben. Jesus, Duke. The cops are looking to file child endangerment charges against me for being at a bar and leaving the kids alone the night he was snatched."

"You left the kids alone?" Duke asked.

"Oh please. As if you're a saint," Marjorie said. "I was so pissed at you for taking off, I went to Shanty's, to take the edge off. I told myself I was just going to have one drink, but I lost count. I started to black out at the bar around ten. I'm pretty sure I remember getting home and crawling into bed. Then someone started shaking me really hard. It was like I was in a tunnel. I could feel what was happening to me, but it was like a dream I couldn't wake up from. But then I got slapped across the face, and I came to. There was a man, a giant guy with a braid, standing over the bed. He hauled me over to a chair and made me sit down. The guy, he kept slapping me, asking me where you hid it. He said if I didn't tell him, he was going to make us all regret what you'd done."

"Did you see him take Ben?"

"No. I was really sick."

Marjorie looked down at her hands, and in the growing folds of evening that cast dark shadows in the sterile motel room, Duke realized his wife looked far older than her thirty-five years. A vision of Marjorie fifteen years earlier flashed across Duke's mind when he first spotted her in a coffee shop across from the art school she was attending. Duke couldn't take his eyes off the gorgeous Marjorie as she sat alone, sketching a picture of Renoir's On the Terrace, *which she was trying to copy from one of her art books.*

"Did the man who hit you assault you sexually?" Duke asked.

"No. I was drunk, but that's something I'd remember. I tried to make it to the bathroom, when he let me up from the chair, but I only made it as far as the bed. I was lying on my back and the guy came over and just stared at me. Then he leaned down so he was just a few inches away from my face. I thought he was going to snap my neck, but he made this weird sound, like he was inhaling over and over again. I wanted to run, but I was so drunk, I couldn't move. Then he stopped. The guy got up and grabbed a pad of paper and a pencil on my nightstand. He started talking in some weird gibberish and drew something on the pad. Then he left."

"You didn't follow him?" Duke answered.

"I spent the next half hour throwing up in the toilet. You took off on me, leaving me with this mess. Now I have two kids to look after, and the cops thinking I was involved in our boy's kidnapping. You need to come back to Sparrow with me. You don't get to run off now and leave me with the wake you left behind. I had a life before I met you. You stole everything from me, Duke, every last dream I ever had. You made this shitty life,

you don't get to leave me alone in it. You were never going to come back, were you?"

Duke reached across the table for his wife's hand. "You stopped drinking."

"I did."

"You look beautiful, just like when I first met you."

"Don't try and charm me. You weren't planning to come back to us, were you?"

"I sent you money. Who's staying with the girls?" Duke asked.

"Nobody. Sarah's fourteen. She can look after Julia. If you're so worried about them, go back and take care of them yourself. You're a hypocrite. Always were and always will be."

Duke stood up, fastened a set of gold cuff links to his shirt cuffs, and headed to the door.

"Where are you going?" Marjorie asked.

"To make a phone call," Duke said.

"You're coming back, right?"

"Sure."

Duke made his way to the pay phone next to the motel manager's office and stood underneath a NO VA-CANCY sign that flickered above him. He dropped a quarter into the slot and pressed his head against the side of the phone as his foot tapped a nervous rhythm on the pavement. The number he called was the same one Max had given him when he was picking up the van Gogh in St. Louis. If Max wasn't at his Macomb County property, Duke figured he'd try the numbers he had for him in Detroit and Birmingham.

"Who's this?" an unfamiliar male voice answered.

"Duke Gooden, put Max on now."

Duke's heart hit a strange, uneven rhythm as he waited a good five minutes until Max came on the line.

"I've got your boy, Duke. I've been staying up late at night debating whether I'm going to sell him to Lemming or watch him die."

"I've got what you want. Put my boy on the phone."

"Which outcome would you prefer for your child? You know what happens to the people I bring to Lemming. You want your boy to die right away or be exploited by adult men in St. Louis?"

"I'll give it to you. Put Ben on. Now!"

Duke waited another ten minutes when he heard a child breathing hard on the other end of the phone.

"Ben? Duke asked. "I'm going to get you out of there, son."

"Is Julia okay? If you don't give them back what you took, they're going to come after her, too. Give it back. Damn it, Daddy. Give it back!"

"Okay. Don't swear. Are you hurt? Did Max and his men do anything to you?"

"Nobody hurt me. I'm stuck in a house with a bunch of other . . ."

Duke felt his gut tangle into a nervous bunch as the phone was pulled away from his son.

"Your kid is alive. For now. You've got two hours. Give me the shipment from Lemming, or I'll take care of your boy one way or the other. You don't want to pick what happens to him, then I will. If I still don't have the van Gogh shipment after the situation with your boy is tidied up, I'll go after your little girl next. Julia's her name, right? That's really pretty," Max said.

"*You're not going to hurt any of my kids. This whole thing was a mistake, Max. That's all. I got a little spooked when I went to your place up in the country. I needed a few days to lay low and think. But I'm fine with the type of business you do,*" Duke lied.

"*You stole from me and sliced up my head of security. These things a man cannot forgive. One hour and fifty-five minutes now. You know that field next to the new Kmart being built by the airport?*"

"*Yeah, I know the place.*"

"*Show up with the shipment from Lemming. I'll bring your kid.*"

"*What if I call the cops?*"

Duke could hear Max let out a caustic laugh, which sounded like a rusty old razor.

"*You won't. You like yourself too much to do that. You're late or you show up empty-handed, you'll never see your kid again. Oh, and I did you a favor. I bought you an alibi.*"

"*An alibi for what?*"

"*Cops are asking around about your whereabouts at the time your boy went missing. You're no use to me in jail while they sort it out, so it was a necessity. A foreman in Indiana told the cops you were doing work for him that night.*"

"*Hold on,*" Duke started to say. But Max had already hung up.

Duke began to turn around, but stopped when he felt a hand latch around his arm.

"*What did you do, Duke?*" Marjorie said. "*What the hell did you do?*"

* * *

Duke felt his left eye twitch as he and Marjorie drove toward the location where he was supposed to meet Max. It was ten o'clock at night. The red Cadillac that once felt like he'd arrived now seemed more like a tomb containing two people who were desperate to claw and bite and scratch their way out of their situation. Duke slid the windows down on the passenger and driver side of the Cadillac and tried to come up with his game plan as he hit the five-mile mark to the meet-up place. Between Max Mueller and himself, Duke knew only one side was going to deliver a touchdown, and the other would likely end up dead. Duke needed to be sure he was the one who was going to come out a winner and get his kid home, with a five-million-dollar payoff on the side.

"When we get to the place, just lay down on the seat until I know we're clear. I'm supposed to meet a guy in the back of the building. I'll park out front first," Duke said. "You remember the plan?"

"You come around the side of the building, and if you raise just one finger, I drive as fast as I can. I pick you up and we get the hell out of here."

"If it's two fingers . . ."

"I pop the trunk and pull out the painting," Marjorie answered.

Duke nodded, knowing the signal meant that Ben wasn't with Max and Marjorie would hand Duke the forgery. Then Duke knew he would have to make the decision whether or not he'd be willing to call the cops to get his kid back. If Ben was with Max, and Max realized the painting was a fake, as much as Duke hated to do it, he'd have to hand the real van Gogh over. But Duke trusted his gut on this. His only bargaining chip was the painting, and if he gave it to Max and Ben wasn't with him, then he and his son would both be killed, or Ben would be sold off to Lemming. That's why Duke had stashed the real van Gogh with his buddy Chip, along with five thousand dollars up front to pay for his services. He and Marjorie had stopped by Ballentine's first to see if he'd store it for him, but Ballentine had refused.

"I don't like this one bit. I think we need to bring the police in. Who are these people?" Marjorie asked.

"Better you not know. They'll kill Ben if we call the cops." *This wasn't exactly a lie. It was something Duke truly believed, but he also didn't want to get arrested and serve more time than he'd ever dreamed of for inadvertently lifting a masterpiece.*

"You've got a gun, right?" Marjorie asked.

Duke swallowed and covered his throat with his right hand so his wife wouldn't see his nerves and his Adam's apple popping up and down in his neck like a spastic Ping-Pong ball.

"Not with me. I stashed it with a few other items I might need if things get sticky here."

"What good is a gun for protection if you're not carrying it?"

"I've got my charm, darlin'. I've got my charm," *Duke said.*

Duke turned off the exit toward the half-built Kmart building and shut the Cadillac's headlights off as he eased the car a mile down the empty two-lane road.

"I'm scared, Duke," *Marjorie said.*

"Me too. We'd both be fools if we weren't."

A streetlight cast a pale glow on the parking lot in front of the Kmart building. Duke swept his eyes across the space and felt a slight sense of relief that maybe his plan might work, when he saw the front lot was empty.

"Okay. I'm getting out. Slip into the driver seat, but hunch down so you won't be seen."

"How am I supposed to know when you come out to give me the signal?" Marjorie asked.

"Just duck low enough so you can see me without being conspicuous. If a car drives in, hit the deck, though. Got it?"

"If we get Ben back, what are we going to tell the cops? They're going to arrest me, I know it. Maybe it would be better . . . ," Marjorie started, but then cut herself off before she revealed her true thoughts.

Duke took a look at his wife and realized she was just as bad a person as he was, both of them more worried about their own asses before their son's welfare. But Duke hoped he could make it right before he took off again. He didn't need to be a good man. There's no way he'd ever attain that mantle. But he didn't want a kid to suffer from his mistake, especially his own blood.

A slick, wet sweat coated the back of Duke's collar, but he still put his suit coat on. Look sharp, feel sharp, and then people will respect you. And without a gun, which he was now regretting big-time as he exited the car and began to walk in forced, steady steps toward the side of the building, he knew he better look sharper than hell.

The mid-September night air had the first delicious cool snap that Duke used to love, a reminder that fall would soon be settling in. But tonight, the first fingers of autumn just felt like a cold glass of ice water being thrown in his face.

Duke turned the corner of the building and stuffed his right hand in his pants pocket, hoping like hell it looked like he was packing.

He hugged close to the side of the unfinished Kmart structure and practiced his speech in his mind, over and over, until he reached the end of the building. He peered around the side and spotted Max's car and another vehicle, a blue van, similar to the one he had seen at Max's remote property, but this time in a different color.

"I've got the picture, where's my boy?" Duke whispered, over and over, as he approached the cars. A set of high beams cut through the darkness and Duke covered his forehead with his left hand to try and see. Through the glare of the headlights, he caught the image of Max Mueller exiting his car. Max was wearing a tuxedo and leaned on his bent black cane.

"I used to like you, Duke. A lot. Where's the shipment from Lemming?"

Duke pressed his right hand forward in the lining of his pants pocket to try and emphasize the impression that he had a gun.

"I got it. Like I said before on the phone, this is a misunderstanding. Where's my kid?"

"In the van."

"Not good enough. I need to see him," Duke said.

Max offered a subtle nod of his head in the van's direction. Duke realized he wasn't breathing as he watched what looked like a young boy with dark hair climb up to the passenger seat from the back of the van. Duke squinted in the direction of the child, but with the distance, he couldn't pin the boy as being Ben.

Duke heard the sound of a door opening, and Ahote

appeared from behind the van. He looked enormous to Duke and even more menacing with the fresh pink scar that Duke had sliced in the shape of a crescent from his eye to his jawline.

Ahote mumbled something in a language Duke had never heard before. The big Indian's right hand turned into a menacing fist, and he raised it over his head like a deadly mallet.

"Settle down," Max told his employee. "You don't give me the shipment right now, Duke, I'll have Ahote bring your boy out here, and he'll snap his neck."

An old VW Bug darted into the rear parking lot, and Duke spun around to assess the new danger. He spotted two kids, teenagers, a boy and a girl, who probably figured they found a perfect place to make out. The VW's headlights shot across the van, and Duke quickly scanned the front seat of the van to get a better look at the child. The boy had dark hair, but he was smaller than Ben. The boy wore a Detroit Tigers hat and Duke realized someone had stuffed the boy's dark hair inside it, since a few long pieces that skimmed to the child's shoulders had come loose and framed the boy's face. Duke instantly knew this was a setup, since Ben never had hair that long a day in his life.

Duke felt a sick plummeting in his stomach as the VW made a quick reverse and hightailed it out of the parking lot.

"You've kept your end of the deal by bringing my boy here. Now let me keep mine. I'm going to get the package from Lemming. I've got a team with me, so don't try and do anything stupid," Duke bluffed. "Give me two minutes."

Duke didn't wait for a response, figuring it wouldn't

be one he wanted to hear, and tried to walk confidently back to the side of the building. As soon as he turned the corner, he began to sprint. At the halfway point, he desperately wished he had a walkie-talkie so he could warn Marjorie to start the car so they could make a quick escape. He had only three feet left until he reached the front parking lot, but then a giant hand yanked him backward so hard, Duke stumbled and smacked the side of his head against the concrete wall of the Kmart building.

Duke felt his body being spun around, and before he could get his bearings, a mammoth hand connected with his nose like a fast-swinging club.

Duke hit the ground and could feel the blood starting to pour from his nose as he dodged another punishing blow from Ahote's fist, which missed its original target of his eye, but landed against his ear, instead.

The now-terrible scene playing out around him seemed to melt like a Salvador Dalí painting as Duke tried to speak. His big mouth had usually been his secret weapon in the past to get him out of sticky situations, but it was silenced when Ahote's foot drove into his rib cage and Duke heard something inside his body snap, right before he lost consciousness.

Duke came to, coughing and trying not to choke. He instinctively started to reach for a glass of water on his nightstand, but realized he wasn't waking up from a horrible dream in his motel room. Instead, he was strapped into the Cadillac with Marjorie next to him. Duke looked down and saw that both of his wrists were duct-taped to the steering wheel.

Duke turned his face away from his wife and spit out what was thick and floating at the base of his throat as a stream of blood spewed out and splattered across the driver-side door.

He quickly looked around and realized the Cadillac was no longer in the back of the Kmart construction site by the airport, but instead was lying nosedown in a ditch.

"Jesus, what happened?" Duke asked. His words got lost as he saw Max standing on top of the embankment next to Ahote.

The window of the Cadillac was open just enough for Duke to hear their conversation.

"They're beautiful," Max said as he examined the contents inside the box. "Put these in my car, and then take care of them."

"Yes, sir," Ahote answered.

Duke looked down at his arm and saw that Marjorie was holding on to it for all she was worth. But most important, her hands weren't duct-taped together.

"I've got a straight-edge razor in my pocket. It'll cut the tape free. Get it out and cut me loose. Do it quick, and then run! Ahote didn't tape you?"

"I got worried when you were taking too long, so I got out of the car to find you. Ahote hit me and I pretended to pass out, so he just dumped me in the passenger seat and I played dead."

"Good move. Get the razor and hurry," Duke said in a rush.

Marjorie dove her hand into Duke's front pocket, extracted the razor, and opened the blade. Duke's eyes stayed fixed on the embankment where Ahote and Max had disappeared from view.

"Too slow! You've got to work faster. Ahote will be back," Duke urged.

"I'm trying. Damn it, I cut my finger," Marjorie cried as the razor's sharp edge nicked her thumb in her haste.

Marjorie worked the blade back and forth across the tape as Ahote reappeared at the top of the embankment with a sledgehammer.

"What's he going to do with that?" Marjorie asked.

"I'm hoping he's going to use it on the car, so it will look like we were in an accident, and not on us," Duke said. *"Come on, hurry before he gets here."*

Marjorie cut the last strand of the duct tape that held Duke's wrists bound to the steering wheel.

"I'm sorry. I truly am. You deserved better," Duke said, and took a quick look at his wife of fifteen years. *"Now get the hell out of this car and run as fast as you can."*

Marjorie reached for the door, but Ahote was already coming down the embankment.

"Change of plans. You'll never outrun him. Down on the seat, quick. Make him think you're still unconscious," Duke said. *"That's probably the only way you're going to get out of here alive."*

Ahote reached the car and took a look at Duke and then up to the night sky. Ahote raised the sledgehammer over his head and dropped it down, letting it connect with a thundering blow against the Cadillac's hood. He then landed two powerful strikes that took out the car's headlights and then moved over to the windshield in front of Duke.

Duke ducked his head down to protect his face just

as the windshield exploded, and he could feel slivers of glass embed in his scalp.

Ahote dropped the sledgehammer and opened what was left of the now-misshapen Cadillac's hood.

The open hood obscured Duke's view of Ahote, but Duke could hear something like water pouring over the engine.

"What's he doing?" Marjorie whispered.

Duke knew the answer immediately as the smell of gasoline registered in his brain. "He's going to light the car on fire. Shit, he's coming. Play dead."

The passenger-side door opened, and Ahote reached across a prone and falsely limp Marjorie to the ignition and started the engine. Duke held his wrists tightly together and prayed Ahote wouldn't notice that the duct tape was severed in the mess of broken glass that littered across his body, the dashboard, and the seat. Duke wasn't sure how he'd get out of this, but he realized he'd made one small step ahead when Ahote got out of the car and shut the passenger-side door. Ahote started to move back toward the engine, but stopped and walked over to Duke's window.

"You got a beef with me, fine, but my kid and my wife didn't do anything to you," Duke said.

Ahote stared at Duke, his almost-black eyes fixated on him without blinking. He then rapped his giant fist against the window and started to move back to the engine.

"That scar I put on your face, you'll never forget me every time you look at it," Duke called out.

Ahote dropped the hood down a few inches, knowingly being cruel, so Duke could watch the onset of his death, and the big Indian pulled out a matchbook. Duke *held his breath as he saw the orange glow of the match catching. Ahote waited as the lit match burned down to his finger and then jumped back as he threw it on the engine. Then Ahote bent down toward the ground and lit the grass on fire on the passenger side of the vehicle.*

Duke watched helplessly as a dance of flame licked across the engine in between the sliver of space between the hood and the engine.

"We've got to get out!" Marjorie cried in a desperate whisper.

"Wait until Ahote is out of sight. You can do it," Duke said.

Ahote ran up the embankment and away from the quickly spreading fire. The second he disappeared, Duke scrambled for the driver-side door and then yelled to his wife as he leapt from the burning car.

"Run! Get out of the car!"

Duke dove from the Cadillac and ran to the back of the vehicle for cover; all the while, he was looking back toward the top of the embankment. But Ahote hadn't stuck around. Duke tried to look through the window to the passenger seat, but in the growing smoke, he wasn't sure if Marjorie had gotten out. He looked back toward a field and every fiber of his being screamed at him to take off and never look back, but Duke made one loop around to be sure his wife had run like he'd told her. He coughed through the smoke and started to reach for her door, when an inferno blasted from the engine and the car engulfed in flames. Duke felt a searing heat that went hot to cold run down both his arms. The words "drop and roll," which he had learned in the third grade at St. Mary's Catholic

School in Detroit, popped into his mind, and Duke fell to the ground and looked on in shock as both his arms were fully on fire. Duke began to roll away from the car, over and over, across the ground and away from the Cadillac, which was now nearly invisible in a wall of flame.

Duke stared down at his hands, which were folded in front of him, as he sat between his daughters at the kitchen table.

"I met Ahote at Liam Mueller's place," Julia said. "He's working for him, now that his dad's out of the picture. You said Ahote had a bow and arrow to hunt that Vietnamese boy. A young man, his name was Angel Perez, was just murdered and his killer used a bow and arrow. The police chief told me there were other killings dating back thirty years that were done the same way. One of the first victims was a Vietnamese boy."

"Ahote killed that kid then. I'd hoped he got away."

"You need to go to the police and tell them about what you saw. Ahote is a serial killer," Julia said.

"Not my problem right now."

"He's going to kill again. If you won't do the right thing and tell the police, then I will. The cops are going to pick up Ahote."

"Good luck with that. Ahote has always lived under the radar."

"He knows what happened to Ben. I'm going to find him, whether you help me or not."

"If he doesn't find you first. Vegas odds, he was the one shooting at you in Stinson Trail."

"Who cares about these people? Did Mom get out alive?" Sarah asked.

"I don't see how. We were likely headed for a split, but that's not the ending I wanted for her," Duke said. "If she'd run like I told her to, I would've seen her in the field, but I didn't."

"Mom didn't get out. The police ID'ed her body," Julia said.

Duke looked away from his daughters and shook his head.

"You didn't call the police. You didn't go back for Ben," Julia said.

"No. That's true. I was in horrible pain, and the only thing I was thinking about was survival. I don't know what Max did with Ben, whether he killed him or sent him to Lemming. I needed to go to a hospital for the burns on my arms, but I called my friend Rickie and he said he'd take care of everything. I got my stash and got out of the country."

"How do I find Lemming?" Julia asked.

"You don't."

"You can make it easy and tell me, or I can find out myself. Either way, I'm going to track him and Ahote down."

Julia began to turn pieces of Duke's story over in her head. "There was a male body found in the burned-out car, along with Mom. Who was the man?"

"Like I said, Rickie took care of everything. He was a fixer, and I didn't ask questions. I figured he found another body to take my place. Max and his clan needed to believe I was dead, and Rickie made sure they did."

Duke reached into his suit coat jacket, which was

lying on a chair in the kitchen, and pulled out Julia's phone.

"What's your password? I need to be sure your phone is safe."

Julia reluctantly gave her father the information and watched as Duke studied her cell, his index finger swiping and tapping on the screen until he found what he was looking for.

"It hasn't been hacked. Now . . . who should I call?" Duke asked.

"What are you talking about?"

"I'm calling someone you trust to pick you up. Who is it?"

"Ray Navarro," Julia answered quickly without having to think about her response. "He's a cop."

"A cop? Great. I'll put the call on speaker for your convenience. But if you say a word about where you think you are, forget my offer to help you."

"Just make the call," Julia said.

Duke hit the number and Julia listened as it rang for less than a split second when Navarro picked up.

"Julia, Jesus, are you okay?" Navarro asked.

"Julia's fine. You'll get a call in a few minutes where you can pick her up. If you're smart, you'll have law enforcement keeping a twenty-four-hour watch on her kids."

"Already done. Put Julia on the line. Now."

Duke held the phone out in Julia's direction.

"I'm okay, Ray."

"You hear that? She's fine," Duke answered.

"You asshole. You're Julia's dad. She told me everything about you, how you ran off and left her when she was a kid."

"Asshole. Right, that would be me."

"Everyone is looking for you, the Feds, Max Mueller's old crew. Turn yourself in before you hurt any more people. If you do anything to Julia, I'll kill you."

Duke looked over at Julia and raised his eyebrows.

"You love my daughter, I'm guessing. Do you believe in irony, Mr. Navarro?"

"It's Detective Navarro, and I believe that men who abandon their families, and then pull innocent people into their messes and almost get them killed, should go to jail. Where did you take Julia?"

"You didn't answer my question. I'm a firm believer in irony. And the fact that I'm a wanted fugitive and my daughter is a crime reporter who's with a cop, that, my friend, is fate laughing directly in our faces. Julia is safe. She'll call you after I drop her off, and she'll let you know where you can pick her up."

"What did you steal from Max Mueller? We brought his son, Liam, in, figuring he grabbed Julia in the park, but Liam swears he doesn't know anything about any bad dealing you had with his father or what happened to Julia."

"A minute until you keep me on the phone long enough that you can figure out my location. Nice move about Liam, but you don't care about what I stole. You only care about my daughter. Thirty seconds."

"Hold on, I need to tell him about . . . ," Julia started, but Duke cut her off.

"Have a nice afternoon, Detective," Duke said, and ended the call.

"I needed to tell him about Ahote."

"You can do it later."

Duke started to stick Julia's cell phone into his pants

pocket, but it rang again. Duke hit the play button and answered. "You don't give up easily. I told you, Julia will call you when I drop her off. I'm turning the phone off now."

Duke started to move the phone away from his ear, but froze in place.

"Ben?" he asked. "No way. I don't know who you are, but . . ."

"Give me the phone. Give me the damn phone!" Julia answered, and tried to snatch the phone away from her father's hands, but he wouldn't let go. Julia latched onto it, and the two clung to the phone and listened in to the person on the other end claiming to be Ben.

"Who is this? You set me up at the park and almost got me killed," Julia said.

"I'm so sorry, Julia. I told you to come alone, but you didn't. I had to leave. I wish I could explain."

"Why don't you?" Julia asked.

"Everything Phoenix told you was true. I have to go back. They don't know I left. I can't stay here anymore, no matter how much I want to. My time is up. If I don't leave now, we'll both be killed. I love you, kid."

"I don't know who you are, but Ben is dead. You aren't my son," Duke said. "Stop trying to screw with Julia's head to get to me."

"Duke? Get away from him, Julia! I told you. He's going to get you killed. Everything he told you is a lie. Where are you? Tell me. Get away from Duke. Now!"

Duke pulled the cell phone away from Julia's hand and ended the call.

"What did you do?" Julia cried.

"I kept everyone from getting killed," Duke said, and pocketed Julia's phone. "I'm keeping this for a while."

"You can't do that."

"I'm going to track the number," Duke said.

"The cops already tried and they couldn't."

Duke looked at Julia and offered up his most blinding smile.

"You're playing with the big boys now, honey."

CHAPTER 21

Ahote looked down at the parks-and-rec employ-ee's body and breathed in deeply before he dumped it in the fresh hole he had just dug deep in the woods near his trailer in Macomb County. The property had once been a busy hub thirty years earlier when Max Mueller was alive and still carrying out his human-trafficking business. But now it was just Ahote out here these days, giving him enough reclusive freedom to do whatever he wanted. Well, almost anything, except for what he wanted the most. Ahote's gray T-shirt clung to his still strong as a slab of granite, almost-sixty-year-old body, and he sighed as he realized the parks-and-rec employee would have to satisfy him. For now.

A fat, brown worm poked its head out of the latest shovel of dirt, and then was tossed over the parks-and-rec worker's body as Ahote thought through his busy-work. Ahote realized his new boss wanted Duke Gooden, first and foremost, not the daughter Julia, but Ahote hoped that when it came down to it, he could get Julia alone to see if she carried the same spirit of her brother, who had eluded him so many years before. As for the Sarah woman, he was glad when she didn't show up in the parking lot, as they had thought she would. There was something off in Sarah's spirit that Ahote could detect merely from the photograph his new boss had shown him. The darkness of another being's soul intermingles with one's own if you take its life, like drops of thick mud that are mixed into a crystal clear glass of water.

Ahote finished burying the man and made his way back through the woods to his trailer, dragging the shovel behind him as he walked. The old scar on his face seemed to throb anew as if Duke Gooden had just carved it with that straight-edge razor he had sliced him with so many years before. The fresh pain from the old wound meant only one thing to Ahote: Duke was close. Duke and Ahote would be together again soon, and the circle would finally close.

The dense packing of trees cleared and Ahote slowed as he saw his new boss's car parked by his trailer. He knew he was in trouble for coming up empty-handed once again, not to mention the still-brewing situation of his killing the city councilman's nephew. Ahote knew he might run the risk of dying for his slips in judgment, but he refused to go down without a fight. Ahote pushed his shoulders back, grabbed the shovel in both hands, and held it in front of his body like a battering ram as he approached the vehicle.

Two car doors opened simultaneously, and Ahote watched as the boss and another man, whose face looked hard and angry, got out of the car.

"What the hell is this?" the new boss asked, and jerked his thumb toward the city parks-and-rec van.

"It was a decoy. The guy got in my way and started to cause me trouble in the park. I figured the city van would be better anyway."

"You idiot. You left your piece of shit vehicle behind at the crime scene. This is a big problem, Ahote. A *really* big problem. The cops matched your plate to surveillance footage from a convenience station that places you at the Home Depot where the city councilman's nephew was picked up."

"I thought the security video was taken care of," Ahote answered.

"That was only a temporary fix," the other man answered. He wiped his brow with his shirtsleeve and then turned his attention to the new boss. "Why am I here cleaning up your shit? I took care of Max when I had to, and, believe me, that was the last thing I ever wanted to do. Max promised me my debt was paid."

"Max is gone. There's a change of guard now. Your debt is paid when I tell you it is," the boss said. He reached inside his own jacket, pulled out his gun, and shoved the barrel against Ahote's temple. "What good are you still to me? Tell me, screwup."

"Give me another chance. I'll bring you Julia Gooden, and I'll hurt her real good. She'll give up her father. No one can get people to talk like I can."

The boss seemed to consider Ahote's proposition and then smiled.

"Bang, bang," the boss said as he put his gun away.

"Do you think Duke knows the truth about what was in the box that Lemming gave him?" the other man asked.

"I doubt it. He was only trying to unload the painting when he thought he was in the clear after Max died."

"What's the other thing worth?" Ahote asked.

"Fifty million. At least," the boss answered. "Bring me Julia Gooden if you can't bring me Duke first. The sister Sarah's in the wind. But be careful, idiot. Your van's plates trace to St. Louis. I've got a work-around, so you may be okay."

"You didn't say anything about the reporter," the other man said. "I don't have any problem with whatever you want to do with Duke, but she hasn't done anything."

"Tough guy loses his swagger about hurting a girl. Don't worry. You'll get your cut when this is taken care of."

"I don't care about the money."

"That's where you're wrong. Everybody cares about money and everyone has a price. Even you."

CHAPTER 22

Julia felt the muscles in her back tense as she sat folded on the seat of Duke's car with her head tucked down by her knees. She was about to protest being forced into this position for the past ten minutes, again, until Duke offered her a reprieve.

"Okay. You're good. You can sit up," Duke said.

Julia took a quick look at her surroundings and knew she was in downtown Detroit as Duke's car cruised along West Fort Street, which paralleled the Detroit River to the right.

"Tell me about this Phoenix Pontiac," Duke said.

"He claims Ben reached out to him. Phoenix had the charm bracelet Ben gave me."

"Your seventh birthday. I remember. I snatched ten dollars from you then and never paid you back. Birthday money," Duke said, and began to reach for his wallet.

"Are you serious? Don't insult me. Ten dollars doesn't mean much to me anymore, but it did back then. That was Ben's money. He worked so hard for it and you took it from me. Who does that to a kid?"

"Are you always so hard on everyone? I remember when you were a little girl, you were so sweet, like you thought the world was one big beautiful place and everybody was your friend."

Julia's instinctual response was to snap at Duke, but she stared out the window, instead, and watched silently as a sign for the Ambassador Bridge slipped by.

"You want to hate me forever for all the things I did, go ahead. But don't let the true part of who you are get ruined in the process, because it was real pretty, something beautiful inside you, girl. Don't let someone else's mistakes take that away from you."

Julia felt tears sting the corners of her eyes and hated herself for her vulnerability over hearing her father's words.

"You care about the cop?" Duke asked.

"Navarro? Yes, very much. I was married before, to an attorney. His name was David. I thought David was everything you weren't, but he tricked me. David was more like you than I realized. Navarro is a good man, the best I've ever known," Julia said. "So what's your next move? You're going to pick up your picture and take off?"

"The van Gogh is mine. No question about that. But before I leave this time, I'll make sure things are taken care of. What happened to Ben and your mom, I'm sorry for that. I ran away from it for a long time, but I know what I did now."

"So Duke Gooden has finally gained a conscience? I'm pretty sure I can see a pig flying over the Detroit River. What's your plan? Are you going to keep Sarah on lockdown and swoop in when one of your guys comes for me, Dad?"

Duke smiled at Julia, and this time, it wasn't the fake ear-to-ear grin, but rather one that looked relaxed and like he really meant it.

"What are you smiling about?" Julia asked.

"That's the first time you've called me 'Dad' since you were seven."

"Don't read too much into it. The van Gogh painting, you never told me about it. Is it a self-portrait?"

"No. It's pretty ordinary, in my opinion, nothing like that famous one van Gogh did, *The Starry Night*. The one I got is just a picture of some tree with purple flowers and a little girl sitting underneath it. You can't even see the kid's face."

"Something about this whole situation seems off to me. You said the van Gogh is worth five million dollars. That's a lot of money for someone like me, but for the people who are after you to go to such extremes to find you and the painting, it seems excessive. Maybe the painting is worth more than you think."

"No, I had it appraised, and I check all the time to see if it's gone up in value," Duke said.

"That's all Lemming gave you? Just the painting? When you told the story about Max Mueller looking at what was inside the box, you said he used the word 'they.' He said, 'They're beautiful.'"

"There was something else in the box with the van Gogh, but it was one of those stupid things Max liked to collect. It looked like junk to me, but I figured it might be worth a couple thousand bucks, so I held on to the original and had my forgery guy make a copy that I stuck in the box with the fake painting that

Mueller took. I figured Max might get suspicious if his shipment from Lemming wasn't intact."

"What else was in the box?" Julia asked.

"Some old, dusty notebook. A leather journal, as I recall. Its cover was cracked and it was filled with someone's handwriting that looked like gibberish. I didn't bother to get it appraised because, like I said, it looked like junk. When I dropped the painting off with Chip, I almost tossed the notebook in his garbage can, but at the last minute, I stuck it in with the picture."

"How did your forgery con make a copy of the journal?"

"He had a buddy who ran a printing press. Some lithography thing, I think it was. Anyway, the pages, the copies, looked like the original, with the weird handwriting, and he distressed the leather enough on the cover, so I guess it worked. Max bought it at first anyway. I would've loved to have seen the expression on his face when he found out the van Gogh that was in my trunk was a forgery."

"This notebook, do you think the writing in it could have been Danish?"

"Danish? How would I know? It's not like I speak the language. Spanish, yes. Danish, I haven't got a clue."

"I'd like to see it," Julia said. "Where did you stash it?"

"Nice try, but no," Duke answered as he took a quick turn into the Greyhound bus terminal. "Here's your stop."

"The bus station? That's the best you can do?"

"I like to travel. The open road, there's nothing better in the whole world. And there's nothing wrong with buses," Duke answered. He reached into his pocket and tossed Julia her phone. "I should have a trace on the number and more information on Phoenix Pontiac soon. I'll be in touch."

Julia got out of the car and watched as a line of people carrying backpacks and suitcases unloaded from a recently arrived bus. She felt frozen in time as she recalled the last time she saw her mother. It was at a bus station in Sparrow. Marjorie had handed Julia a Hershey bar right before she boarded the bus to find their father, the candy her final parting gift.

Julia's gaze locked onto a mother clutching the hand of a little girl as they walked into the terminal, and then she called Navarro.

"You just tell me where Julia is, and I'll see what I can work out with the Feds," Navarro answered on the first ring.

"Navarro, it's me. I'm at the Greyhound bus station on Howard Street."

"Are you hurt?" Navarro asked.

"No. I'm fine."

"I'm five minutes out."

"I've got some news on the Angel Perez case."

"So do I. Weird coincidence, too. The van we found at Stinson Trail, the plates match the ones in the video by the Home Depot where Angel Perez was picked up. Russell and I were able to get the video in its entirety from the convenience store, since they had it on backup. We tracked the owner of the plate to a company called American Adult Entertainment. The guy owns a bunch of strip clubs and dive bars in St. Louis. His name is . . ."

"Louis Lemming. He's connected to my dad."

"The Angel Perez murder has to do with your father?" Navarro asked. "You're kidding me."

"The van is owned by a man named Ahote, who I told you about. I'll explain when I see you."

Four PM, the city's rush hour was starting to heat up as Julia sat in the passenger seat of Navarro's Chevy Tahoe, having just debriefed him on her meeting with Duke and the recent call from the person claiming to be Ben.

"One thing I'm sure of in all this, my brother was either killed or wound up with Lemming," Julia said. "Are the St. Louis cops bringing Lemming in, since the van's plate was a match to him?"

"Lemming is claiming the van was stolen three days ago, but he didn't file a report about it going missing until this morning," Navarro said. "He claimed it was a company car."

"That's bullshit."

"I know, but he's got a good lawyer."

"Did you put an APB out on Ahote?"

"Already done. His full name is Ahote Chogan. No record, if you can believe it. We brought Liam Mueller in again, and he swears he hasn't seen Ahote in a couple of days. Russell told Agent Kenny that your father cuffed him to his car. Kenny knows for sure now that your dad is alive and that you left the park with Duke. You're going to have to talk to Kenny. No way around it. Kenny wants to arrest you for obstructing a federal investigation. I don't know why you're protecting your dad."

"I'm not. I need information from my dad to figure out what happened to Ben. I'm not trying to put you in a bad spot. I know I have to talk to Kenny, but I need to make two stops first."

"Really, Gooden? What are they?"

"The Detroit Institute of Arts and then your apartment. I've got clothes at your place, and I don't want to be hanging out in my shorts and tank top while I'm being interrogated. I'm betting we'll get some answers at the art museum. Ahote, my dad, Angel Perez. They're all connected."

"Why the DIA?"

"I think my dad picked up something, along with the stolen van Gogh, that could be at the heart of this. Five million dollars is a lot of money, but this deadly full-court press to find my dad, there's got to be more at stake than what we think."

"You're killing me, Gooden," Navarro said, and did a quick U-turn toward the DIA.

The Detroit Institute of Arts, on Woodward Avenue, was one of Julia's favorite places in the city. Scrappy Detroit's art museum boasted one of the top six art collections in the country, but Julia's personal favorite in the museum was Diego Rivera's *Detroit Industry,* a series of glorious frescoes that made up twenty-seven panels and was a tribute to the city's manufacturing base, including Ford Motor Company.

Julia knew the museum's current director, John Hastings, from a previous story she'd worked on and hoped he'd bite.

Navarro parked his car, and he and Julia made their way inside the museum. Navarro flashed his badge at a wide-eyed ticket taker and the two were ushered through, posthaste.

An attractive woman in her sixties, who was impeccably dressed, hurried up to them as Julia and Navarro passed the ticket booth.

"I'm Betsy Candler, the public relations director for the museum. Is there something I can help you with?"

"We need to talk to your director, John Hastings. Please tell him Julia Gooden is here to see him. I'm a newspaper reporter, and John helped me on a story a few years ago."

Betsy disappeared into the museum and returned a few minutes later with Hastings, who was about ten years older than Julia. He was trim, with blond hair and a matching, close-cropped beard.

"Julia Gooden, I remember you from the story you wrote about the attempted robbery here," Hastings said, and extended Julia his hand. "Thanks for not misquoting me. I would've preferred the incident not run in the press, because it could've made us look like we had lax security and we could've become a target, but you handled it well."

"Thank you. Sorry for my casual outfit," Julia said, pointing to her running gear. "But I have a few questions. Is there somewhere we can speak privately?"

Hastings's eyes hung on Navarro, who Julia knew emanated "cop" by just standing there, breathing.

"This is Ray Navarro. He's a friend of mine," Julia said. "We're working together on this."

"I'm a detective with the Detroit Police Department."

"Is there some situation I need to be privy of?" Hastings asked.

"Nothing that has to do with you or the DIA. We need background information on a possible stolen painting, and we're looking for an expert to fill in the details," Navarro said.

"Any information I provide, will it be part of an article or made public as part of a police investigation?" Hastings asked.

"No. Everything we talk about is off the record," Julia said.

"I'm not looking to jam you up. Like Julia said, we're just looking for your expertise to help out on a case," Navarro said.

"I have a few minutes before I have to go to another meeting, so if I can be a help, by all means," Hastings said, and led them to his office.

Hastings shut the door and took a seat behind his desk. "Please sit down. What's this about a stolen painting?"

"I need to know about any van Gogh paintings that were stolen around thirty years ago," Julia asked.

"Well, we have five van Goghs here, including his self-portrait," Hastings said. "Stolen van Goghs are not uncommon. Van Gogh's works are generally stolen the most frequently, because they're usually prominently displayed. At least thirteen of his paintings have been stolen and recovered, two of them twice. Another eighty-five works have been lost and are still missing, and three other paintings are still at large."

"Do you happen to know if one of the missing paintings is a picture of a tree with a little girl sitting underneath it?" Julia asked.

"No. I'm not familiar with that one. But you have to

be careful with forgeries or paintings cropping up with false claims that they were done by a master."

"What about a notebook van Gogh might have had, maybe a journal he kept? Do you know if one existed?" Julia asked.

Hastings's eyes seemed to shine as he answered. "Well, that would be something."

"What would it be worth?" Navarro asked.

"A Leonardo da Vinci notebook sold for over thirty million a few years ago. If a van Gogh journal really did exist, and it included his personal writings leading up to his mental break, I couldn't even estimate the worth. Maybe fifty million dollars, but I'm just guessing here. Some of his sketchbooks are in collections and then there are the letters he wrote to his brother, Theo, but a diary, that would be quite a find."

"You were a big help. Thank you," Julia said.

"If you think of anything else, give me a call," Navarro said, and handed Hastings his card.

Julia and Navarro made their way back to his Tahoe, and Navarro began to clip through city traffic en route to his apartment.

"That's what you think your dad stole from Max Mueller? A van Gogh notebook?" Navarro asked.

"Maybe. My dad said there was a notebook in the box that had the van Gogh painting he picked up from Lemming in St. Louis. Duke thought the notebook was some worthless collectible, but I'm betting you it was van Gogh's personal journal or maybe another master artist's. Five million dollars is a lot of money, if that's what the painting is worth. But this huge push to find Duke at all costs, it makes better sense to me that there's a bigger prize at stake."

"Van Gogh's the guy who went crazy and cut off his ear, right?"

"That's him. He killed himself when he was just thirty-seven. Van Gogh was a misunderstood genius and was considered a failure when he was alive. He didn't find success as an artist until after he died. The journal, if it's real and his, would be worth killing for in the wrong company."

"Last stop," Navarro said as he pulled into a spot on the street across from his high-rise.

"Thank you. I mean it, Navarro. I'd go to my house if it weren't forty minutes away. I know I've been asking a lot of favors lately, and I appreciate everything you've been doing for me."

"Thanks aren't necessary, but you need to talk to Kenny, that's all I ask. Let's go up," Navarro said.

Julia looked over her shoulder as she and Navarro walked toward his building, as she expected to see Agent Kenny lurking in the bushes, ready to arrest her. But the two made it safely into the high-rise complex and then took the elevator up to his floor.

Once inside his apartment, Navarro moved quickly to his kitchen and began discarding leftover Chinese food containers that lined a counter.

"Sorry for the mess. I usually keep a clean house."

"We used to live together. You can't lie to me," Julia said. "Mind if I change?"

"Not at all."

Julia's private time with Navarro, when they weren't working or she wasn't at home with her children, was a tight, limited window, but it had become frequent enough for her to stash a few changes of clothes in a drawer she claimed in Navarro's bedroom dresser.

Navarro's apartment was a typical one-bedroom, simple bachelor pad that had about as much workout equipment in his living room as furniture, but it did have a killer view of the Detroit River from the ceiling-to-floor windows in his living room. Julia took a quick pan of the cityscape and then made her way to Navarro's bedroom, where she noticed a recently placed framed photograph of the two of them on his nightstand.

Julia smiled over the gesture as Navarro followed her path to the bedroom. He stood in the doorway as his phone started to ring, and he looked down at the incoming call.

"Russell, what do you got?" Navarro said as he answered. He then sat down next to Julia on the bed and rested his hand on her thigh. "Okay. We need to bring back Liam Mueller again and squeeze him to find out where Ahote is. I don't give a shit what his lawyer says. Bring him in and keep him there."

Navarro filled Russell in on the possible stolen notebook angle and then ended the call.

"Ahote's last known address is on Frederick Street, near Trinity Cemetery. The landlord said she kicked him out five years ago for not paying rent. We'll drill Liam Mueller again to see if he'll give up Ahote. Your dad didn't tell you where he stashed the painting and notebook?"

"No. I'd tell you if I knew."

"You know I'm going to have to arrest Duke if I see him."

"I understand. He's a fugitive."

"And Kenny's going to arrest you if you don't tell him everything you know about your dad."

"I realize that."

Navarro began to rub his shoulder in the place where he was shot a few months prior at the Packard Plant. "I think you should get a lawyer."

"If I get arrested, I might be holed up for a while. No conjugal visits," Julia said. She turned around to face Navarro, who was still sitting on the bed, and straddled him with her hips. "Do we have a few minutes before we have to leave?"

Julia pulled her tank top over her head and threw it on the floor.

"I can make the sacrifice," Navarro answered.

Julia closed her eyes as she felt Navarro's tongue trace along her birthmark, a small mole just below her left breast. "Before we do this, I need to tell you something."

"You can tell me anything, baby."

"I love you, Ray. God, I do."

Julia stood in Navarro's bathroom and pulled her hair out of the makeshift bun she had put it in to keep her hair from getting wet. Julia looked on at Navarro, still in the shower, and wondered if it was okay for her to feel happy for a second while the world was spinning out of control all around her.

"You want to come back in and join me?" Navarro asked.

"Thanks, but I know how that's going to end up. That shower cost us an extra fifteen minutes."

"Shower sex is always challenging, but I think we've perfected it."

Julia shook her head at Ray and smiled. She

changed into her backup clothes, a pair of jeans, a short-sleeved, black T-shirt, and flat sandals.

"You're way overdressed, beautiful," Navarro said.

"I'm going to give Helen a call again. She said the boys felt like they are under house arrest, so I told her they could watch a movie on Netflix and order in some delivery pizza."

"Sounds like bribery to me."

"You've obviously never had kids. Bribery is sometimes a mother's best friend."

Julia left Navarro and went into his kitchen, where she had left her purse and cell phone. She was about to call Helen, but then her phone rang and an unknown caller's name flashed across the screen.

"Here we go again," Julia said as she answered.

"It's Duke. I got the location for where the call was placed by the guy claiming to be Ben. It's a residence over in Palmer Park. I scoped it out already. This Phoenix Pontiac character, does he have long, dark hair down to his shoulders, late thirties or so, and kind of a ropy build?"

"That's him," Julia answered.

"He's been in and out of the place for the past hour. He's there now. I guarantee this little weasel is working for Lemming or Liam Mueller. Are you in, or what?"

"I'm supposed to go down to the station with Navarro to talk to the FBI about you."

"If you hadn't told your cop friend at the park that I was your dad, you wouldn't be in this position. I told you not to say anything. Come on. This Pontiac guy, I guarantee he is the weak link. I find out who's running the show from him, then I take them out. And you get to find out whether the guy calling you pretending to be Ben is legit, or a fake, like I know he is. Sarah and I are outside your boyfriend's place. I'm leaving in two minutes. What do you say?"

Julia heard the shower still running and felt a pull in her gut as she could picture Ben as a little boy, trying to reassure her that everything was going to be all right. She thought about her life now with Navarro and her boys as it played another tug-of-war with the debt and never-ending love she had for her brother, who had never come home.

"Last chance. I need an answer," Duke said.

"I'm in. Let me just leave Ray a note. If I tell him about this, he'll never let me do it. Don't leave without me."

Julia pulled her reporter's old-school notebook and a pencil from her purse on the table. She tore out a sheet and hurriedly scribbled down a note before Navarro could come out of the shower and convince her not to go.

She put the note on the table and read it quickly.

Ray,

Duke just called. He has an address for Phoenix Pontiac. I'm going with my dad because I need to find out the truth. I know if I told you about this before I left, you wouldn't let me go. I don't trust Duke, and I know I may be setting myself up. But please understand, I don't feel like I have any other choice. I'm sorry, but I have to do this. I owe my brother. I'll be careful.

And I swear I'll talk to Kenny when I'm done.
I'll take full responsibility for this decision, as I
don't want anything to come back on you.
  I love you. With all my heart.
                    Julia

Julia grabbed her bag and headed toward the door, knowing she was caught up in a stranglehold. But she also knew she didn't have any other choice but to team up with the most unlikely allies she could ever pick in her entire life.

CHAPTER 23

The place where Duke had spotted Phoenix was a nice two-story, single-family brick home in the Palmer Park/University District in northwest Detroit. Julia rode in the backseat of Duke's vehicle, with Sarah sitting in the front. Duke took a slow cruise by the address and Julia noticed Phoenix's Subaru was parked in a carport next to the house.

"Nice place for a former con if it's his," Julia said. "Phoenix told me he lived in Chicago."

"This guy told you a lot of things," Duke said. "He's home. There's a light on in the front window and his car is outside. You got the stomach for this, Julia?"

"How come you didn't ask me?" Sarah said.

"I'm guessing you've ridden this bull at the rodeo more than once," Duke answered.

"I'm fine. I've been in worse situations," Julia said. "One thing I want to make clear, Pontiac has been giving me the runaround and I want answers. I don't know what your plan is, but I'm not going to get tangled up or be an accessory to a crime."

"You already are for not turning me in. Now here's the plan. Be quiet. Be smart, and if you get shot and you're not dead, haul your ass back to the car. I got a floor plan for the house," Duke said. "There's a basement we can access from a door in the back. We get inside, don't make a sound."

"Hold on. Phoenix may have company," Julia said as she looked through Duke's tinted windows and noticed a Ford Taurus pull across the street from Phoenix's house and come to a stop at the curb.

Duke continued driving, careful not to speed up or slow down, as a man in a suit got out of the vehicle.

"That's Agent Kenny," Julia said.

"The FBI guy who's after me?" Duke asked.

"That's him," Julia said.

Duke took a right at the cross street and started to speed up.

"What are you doing?" Julia asked.

"I'm not afraid of bad guys. But the FBI, that's a whole different story. Your guy's caught up with law enforcement, I'm out."

"Hold on. You can't just leave," Julia said.

"Watch me, darlin'."

Julia grabbed the door handle as Duke leaned even harder on the gas.

"Stop the damn car!" Julia cried.

Duke eyed Julia in the rearview mirror and reached for the automatic door locks, but Julia was too fast for him. She opened the door and was about to jump out, but Duke hit the brakes and steered his car over to the side of the residential street before she could.

"You're nuts," Duke said.

"Maybe so, but I'm not a coward," Julia said.

Julia didn't bother to look back at her father as she got out of the SUV and started to run toward an apartment complex that she figured she could use as cover until she figured out the rest of her plan to try and approach Phoenix's place without being seen.

"Hold on, Julia."

Julia turned to see Sarah get out of the car. "I'll go with you."

"Jesus Christ," Duke said. He reached behind him to the passenger seat and grabbed a duffel bag. "If you're both going to be this stupid, you better take this."

Sarah reached for the bag and looked inside. "Excellent."

Julia skirted behind the apartment complex, with Sarah trailing behind her. When she reached Phoenix's street, Julia crouched down by a row of parked cars until she came to the road that paralleled his. Julia found the house she was fairly certain backed up to Phoenix's, a brick duplex, and gestured with her head for Sarah to follow.

A man jogged by on the sidewalk and Julia smiled at him, like she was just another friendly neighbor taking an early-evening stroll.

As soon as the jogger turned the corner, Julia opened the latch of a metal gate on the side of the duplex, hoping the backyard would offer some access to Phoenix's place.

The old gate let out a sharp squeak as it swung open, and Julia froze when she saw a light flick on inside the right unit of the duplex next to her. Julia ducked down and away from a window along the side of the house and motioned for Sarah to do the same.

"Shit, the owner must have heard the gate," Sarah whispered.

Julia cast her gaze toward the backyard and to another short metal fence, which buffered Phoenix's place. Julia heard the sound of a front door open, and she bolted toward the rear yard, where she easily cleared the low fence and found shelter behind a tall pine tree in the corner of Phoenix's property. Julia looked back at Sarah, who was several steps behind her. Sarah dove to the pine tree just as the resident of the duplex—a plump woman wearing shorts, curlers, and a worn Michigan State T-shirt—turned the corner. The woman walked through the gate and made her way to the backyard. She stood for a minute, with her hands on her hips, and took a slow pan of the property.

"Stupid college kids," the woman said, and then turned around and headed back inside her home.

"Jesus. I got to quit the cigarettes. I barely made the fence," Sarah whispered.

"What's in the bag?" Julia asked.

"A few essentials."

Julia surveyed the back of the house and easily spotted the door Duke had mentioned.

"If the door's locked, any chance Duke left you something in that duffel bag?"

"He's got lock picks. I know how to use them. But since there are people inside, let's hope the door isn't locked."

"Why'd you come with me?" Julia asked.

"I figured you and me, we got left behind once already," Sarah said.

"I appreciate that, Sarah. I do."

"Are you kidding? No need to thank me. I miss this shit."

Julia lost her cover of the tree and kept expecting Agent Kenny to appear as she made her way to the rear of the house. She went down six cement stairs leading to a lower-level door and motioned to Sarah to follow.

As her fingers latched around the knob, Julia felt a prickle of electricity move down her arms as the door easily opened. She put her finger to her lips to remind Sarah to keep quiet and tried to walk silently into what appeared to be a fairly barren unfinished basement. There was just a washer and dryer, and a lack of the usual clutter of boxes and other unwanted junk that usually got stored in the catchall space of most houses.

The basement was dark and smelled like mildew and detergent. Julia took in her surroundings and spotted a sliver of light at the top of a short staircase, which she figured led to the main floor. Julia motioned with a flat palm for Sarah to stay where she was, and then slowly made her way up the stairs to the door. Julia was afraid that the sound of her racing heart would give her away as she reached the top step and looked down a hallway, where she spotted Phoenix Pontiac and Agent Kenny in what appeared to be a living room. Phoenix was sitting on a brown leather couch with his feet casually sprawled in front of him, while Agent Kenny paced back and forth across the length of an orange rug.

"This situation should have been resolved yesterday. Did he just leave?" Kenny asked.

"Twenty minutes ago. He had to get back."

"Call Julia Gooden again. The Detroit cop who's screwing her just showed up at the station alone, and said when he got to the meet-up spot where he was supposed to pick her up, she wasn't there. She's playing him, too, or he's lying to protect her."

A pang of guilt went off inside Julia for having put Navarro in a situation where he'd have to lie to cover for her.

"She's still with the dad," Phoenix said. "Let me try and call her."

Julia looked down at her pocket, where she placed her cell phone, and felt the phone buzz on silencer against her hip.

"No answer. I'll try her again later," Phoenix said.

"If anything changes, call me," Kenny said. He pulled a thick envelope out of his inner suit coat pocket and handed it to Phoenix. "No more money, though, until you deliver."

Phoenix walked Kenny to the door, and after the agent left, Phoenix returned to the living room and put on the Tigers game on a massive flat-screen TV.

Julia crept back down the basement stairs to Sarah. "Kenny just left."

Sarah reached into the duffel bag and pulled out a gun and a roll of duct tape. "You ready to get to work?" she asked.

"Just don't kill anyone. Pontiac has been playing me this whole time, but I don't want him dead," Julia said. "I'm serious, Sarah. Don't do anything stupid."

"I won't hurt him, but I'll scare him real good."

"Swear to me," Julia said.

"I've got an ex-boyfriend doing time for aggravated assault. The minor shit I did, I only served a couple of months each. I don't plan on going back to jail. Stop worrying so much. I got this covered."

A tug of worry went off inside Julia over her last-minute decision to pair up with her sister; but at this point, it was too late to turn back.

Julia led the way as the two went up the steps to the main floor. The ball game playing on the TV was turned up loud and the sound intermingled with The Killers' "Somebody Told Me" blasting on full decibel from Phoenix's phone.

Phoenix drummed his fingers on a large wooden coffee table to the beat as Sarah approached him from behind. She pushed past Julia and stuck the barrel of the gun against the back of Phoenix's neck.

"On your feet, asshole," Sarah said. "Get up slowly. You try to reach for anything, you're dead."

"Easy. Easy," Julia said, trying to keep the situation from spiraling out of control. "Listen to me, Phoenix, and no one needs to get hurt."

Phoenix Pontiac dropped the remote he was holding onto the leather sofa and raised his hands up by his head in a surrender gesture as he rose to his feet.

"You've been telling me a string of lies. Is Phoenix Pontiac really your name?" Julia asked. She walked in front of Phoenix; and Sarah stood behind, with the gun pressed against the back of his neck.

"This is a misunderstanding," Phoenix said. "I just called you."

"Right. A few minutes ago when Agent Kenny was still here."

Phoenix's dark eyes shifted away from Julia and flicked down to the floor as he tried to come up with his latest story.

"Let me explain."

"How much money did Kenny give you?" Julia asked. "Let me see the envelope."

"I don't know what you're talking about."

"You can't even lie worth a shit. Give Julia the envelope," Sarah said.

Phoenix reached into his pants pocket and handed the envelope to Julia. She looked inside and did a quick count. "There's probably five grand in here."

"Against the wall. Now," Sarah said to Phoenix. She trained the gun at his head and followed him until he reached it. "Turn around, place your hands on the wall, and spread your legs. You know how to assume the position, right?"

Phoenix looked over his shoulder pleadingly at Julia, but he followed Sarah's directive.

"Make sure he's not carrying," Sarah said.

Julia had never frisked anyone in her life, but she'd seen enough cops on her beat do it in real life, so she patted Phoenix down to be sure he didn't have a weapon. Julia moved her hands over Phoenix's body until she felt the shape of something hard between the back of his shirt and belt.

"Gun," Julia said.

Sarah snapped the tail of Phoenix's shirt up and carefully pulled out a revolver from his rear waistband.

"What do you want to do here, Julia?" Sarah asked.

"I want answers."

Sarah looked toward a small, round table in the kitchen and slapped Phoenix on the arm. "Here's what we're going to do. You're going to walk to that table and sit down. Then you're going to lay your hands flat down on the table."

"I'm not doing that," Phoenix said.

Sarah cuffed the butt of her gun against the side of Phoenix's temple.

"Hey, what are you doing?" Phoenix asked.

"Getting a liar to move."

Phoenix quickly made his way to the kitchen table and shot a look toward a cell phone that lay on the counter.

"Don't think about it. Like I said, hands, palms down," Sarah said, and tossed Julia the roll of duct tape from the bag. "Tape his hands to the table. Just the knuckles down to the wrists. Make sure you don't get his fingers."

"I don't like this," Julia said.

"It's that, or you hold the gun on him, and I'm betting you don't do guns. If this is going to turn out the way you want it to, then you need to trust me. The only way to beat the bad guys at their own game is to play dirtier than they do."

Julia thought about the charm bracelet Ben had given her, and how Pontiac had somehow hijacked her brother's memory and a precious moment they had shared, and she begrudgingly relented. She grabbed the roll of tape and began to tightly affix strips of it across the bottom of both of Phoenix's hands.

"No one gets hurt here, Sarah. I mean it," Julia said when she finished.

Sarah checked the tape when Julia was done and then grabbed the roll and taped Phoenix's feet to the front chair legs.

"You've got a captive audience. It's your show now. Ask him what you want," Sarah said.

Julia sat down at the table across from Phoenix and stared into his eyes, which darted back and forth between her and Sarah in a nervous tic.

"You lied about knowing my brother and him being alive, didn't you?" Julia asked.

"No. I'm in deep shit here, and if I tell you what I know, I'm going to be dead or Kenny is going to put me back in jail. Please. I didn't lie to you. You've got to believe me."

"Last chance. Is Ben alive, or was the whole story a lie you concocted with Kenny to get to me so I'd bring you to Duke?" Julia asked.

"I like you, Julia. I do. But I can't tell you anything more," Phoenix said.

Sarah made her way over to the kitchen and a row of light wood cabinets. She opened each one up and began to poke around inside. Sarah studied the contents of a bottom drawer next to the oven and stood back up with an ice pick clutched between her fingers.

"What's she going to do with that?" Phoenix asked.

Sarah bent down over the table with the ice pick and pointed with her other hand at Phoenix's fingers.

"Spread 'em. If I were you, I'd move my fingers as far apart as possible. The closer your fingers are together, there's more of a chance I'll cut you. We're going to go fast now. Ready?"

Julia was ready to tell Sarah not to do it, but her sister was already busy with the ice pick. Sarah's hand was a blur as she drove the pointed tip of the blade skillfully between the spaces of Phoenix's fingers.

"You're crazy. Stop her!" Phoenix begged Julia.

"Did you lie about my brother being alive?" Julia asked.

"No. But I can't tell you anything more," Phoenix said.

The steady *tap-tap-tap* rhythm of the ice pick broke its stride as Sarah slammed the blade down hard a whisper away from Phoenix's middle finger.

"Stop! Jesus," Phoenix cried.

Sarah ignored Phoenix's plea and continued her game, this time grazing the tip of the ice pick against his thumb, leaving a fresh hole in his flesh, which started to draw blood.

"Okay! Please. I'll tell you what you want to know. Just keep her away from me," Phoenix said in a shaking voice.

Julia pried the ice pick out of her sister's hand and then grabbed Sarah by the arm.

"No more," Julia warned.

Sarah took a seat across from Phoenix, looking almost sulky without her toy.

"Okay. This is the truth. I swear. My job was to get you to give up Duke to the FBI. I'm an informant for Kenny. I got popped on a drug deal. I was going to be facing some serious time. I was desperate and pulled out an old ace in the hole, thinking I might have something to use. I told the cops about the Mueller thing when I was a kid, about being abducted and held there and how Max was running a human-trafficking ring. I sat in my cell for three days after that, so I figured the cops weren't interested because it was so long ago and Max Mueller had just died, but then Agent Kenny showed up, asking me about some art stuff. I told him I didn't know anything about it, but I did tell him what happened at the house in the woods. Kenny kept going back to some old notebook he wanted to know about that belonged to some painter. After about an hour, he stood up to leave. That's when I mentioned Ben, and Kenny sat back down, looking all interested this time. I swear, everything I told you about meeting Ben in that house was true."

"Things in life don't fall into place that easily. You're telling me that Kenny shows up, offers you some kind of deal if you can get me to bring him my father, and then Ben comes out of the woodwork? You tried to play on my vulnerability. But you made a big mistake," Julia said.

"Okay, I know how crazy this sounds, but Ben was just here, I swear. I couldn't believe it was him, but it was. Kenny arranged everything. All I know is the FBI is protecting Ben, as long as he gives up information on your dad. Ben agreed to anything they asked, as long as you were protected. Ben's been in hiding, but he went to the FBI when Duke came back to Sparrow to get the painting and the notebook. Ben knew you'd be in danger if people found out your dad was alive. That's all I know. I swear. Kenny wouldn't give me any more details, only that Ben got away from Ahote in the woods one night when he was hunting him. Ben was able to get to the road and flag down a car that helped him. I don't know anything else. I swear."

"If my brother was just here, where is he now?"

"I don't know. I swear to God. He left with the agent when Kenny was here the first time, about an hour ago. I'm an outsider in all this. Kenny paid me to get to you so you'd bring him your dad. Everything I told you about meeting Ben in the house in the woods, that was all true. Agent Kenny is using me as much as he's trying to use you."

"Let him go," Julia said.

"What?" Sarah responded.

"This guy's nothing more than a jailhouse snitch. Everything that comes out of his mouth is going to be another lie. He's a waste of time."

"Let me have another round with him," Sarah said.

"It wouldn't make a difference. Give Agent Kenny a message for me," Julia said to Phoenix. "If he wants to play, he delivers up Ben. Otherwise, no deal."

CHAPTER 24

Liam Mueller stripped down to his underwear and changed his clothes in the five-million-dollar home he lived in near the Birmingham Country Club. He still felt dirty after being forced to sit in a hideous police station for three hours and then being brought back a second time when the Detroit police questioned him again, this time not about Julia Gooden and someone trying to kill her in Stinson Trail, but about Ahote.

Liam got into the shower and nearly rubbed his skin raw before he felt clean. He dressed and started to relax, only after he put on Beethoven's "Ode to Joy," his favorite piece of music ever since he was a child. Liam slipped on his Italian loafers and poured himself a snifter of Glenmorangie Signet scotch.

The warmth of the liquor settled nicely through his entire body after his first sip, and he sat down at the head of a long, formal dining table as he tried to push away the darkness that was settling in all around him. He started to feel easier and closed his eyes, when an image of his father Max's black cane coming down hard on him when he was a child caused Liam to bolt up from his seat. Liam took one more drink of the expensive scotch and then threw the rest of its contents and the crystal snifter as hard as he could against the dining room's fireplace. He walked toward the mess he had created and picked up a fresh piece of glass, pressing it into the palm of his hand until it slid through his flesh. Liam winced when the pain hit, but he continued on with his self-inflicted assault. After all, why did he deserve to treat himself well, when his own father had beaten him and treated him like garbage?

Liam looked down at his phone and saw his lawyer's number flash across the screen. He knew it would be just a matter of time before the police would bring him in again, and he would be forced to tell them about Ahote and his father Max's business, one that had brought them both works of art that were far too glorious to put into words. Liam knew he would have to tell the dirty little story in order to protect himself. A plea deal was better than life in prison.

He closed his eyes and thought about the van Gogh notebook, dreaming of what it would be like to hold it in his hands and then open the cover to find the master's innermost thoughts, which he didn't share with anyone else, before van Gogh lost his mind and took his own life.

Liam's security system sounded with one short beep, which echoed down the hallway in his direction, alerting him that someone was on his property. Liam pulled out his phone and looked at the image on the screen. It showed the view from his front door and the street and the two men who were getting out of a car.

They were coming for him, because they somehow knew he was going to turn.

Liam walked to his desk, an antique. His grandfather had taken the desk, along with the entire art collection, from a Jewish family, four children, a grandmother, and two adults, in Germany before they were sent to a concentration camp. Liam ran his fingers over the hand-carved wood, the antique desk a piece that had a sordid history, but one that was still so, so beautiful.

The alarm sounded again, one long beep this time, alerting Liam that the two men had just deactivated it. Liam reached into the drawer of the antique desk and pulled out a gun as the music played on triumphantly in the background.

Liam felt a bittersweet ache of unrequited lust over the notebook he would never get to see, and how it likely held the secrets of the artist, his brilliance and madness, and the doubtless haunted shadows that skirted through his mind before he completely lost it.

As the sound of footsteps approached down the hall, Liam closed his eyes, stuck the gun in his mouth, and pulled the trigger.

CHAPTER 25

Julia gave the cabdriver twenty dollars, since Sarah didn't have any money, as he let them off in front of the parking garage across from the Renaissance House.

"What level are you parked on?" Julia asked.

"The sixth floor."

"Let's take the stairs. The police are looking for Ahote, so I'm guessing he's going underground, but I'd rather not be fighting for my life and be boxed in with him in a tight space if he comes around, so no elevator."

Julia panned the first-floor stairwell, which smelled like urine, and started to run up the stairs.

"Slow down, you're going to kill me," Sarah said, panting from behind.

"You've got to push yourself," Julia said, not slowing her pace.

When they reached the sixth-floor stairwell, Sarah grabbed Julia's arm.

"Hold on. Just in case," Sarah said. She pulled out

Duke's gun from the duffel bag she had brought along and then covered the gun with the vinyl bag and held the gun close to her stomach.

Julia opened the door to the sixth-floor parking level and quickly scanned the space, but on first blush, it appeared to be empty of people. Julia followed Sarah until her sister stopped in front of a faded, old Nissan with a dent in the bumper.

"Hey, it's paid for," Sarah said as she moved toward the driver-side door.

"One second first," Julia said, and looked underneath the car. "Pop the trunk."

Julia did a quick inspection and saw nothing more than a spare tire and a carton of cigarettes.

"Thanks for the ride. I think we're good," Julia said.

Sarah unlocked the Nissan and the two sisters climbed inside.

"Why'd you let Phoenix go?" Sarah asked as she started the car.

"Because he's a jailhouse snitch, and he'll say anything to help himself. Everything he told me was a lie and a manipulation. No use wasting my time with him. People like that from my beat, they'll tell you anything you want to hear in order to get out of the trouble they're in."

"If Phoenix is a liar, how did he get your charm bracelet that Ben gave you?" Sarah asked.

"It was probably a replica. People can fake items, but they can't fake memories. Someone told him about how Ben gave me the bracelet for my birthday. I need to talk to Agent Kenny. He's the one pulling the strings."

The older Nissan almost stalled as it made its way

toward the exit, where Julia handed the attendant a credit card to pay for the two-day and overnight charge.

"You don't have to pay for everything. I'm trying to get on my feet," Sarah said. She hit the gas hard and maneuvered around the light, early-evening traffic until they reached the highway to Rochester Hills and Julia's house.

"This isn't the life I want anymore, you know?" Sarah asked. "Did you ever wonder what our lives would've been like if we had different parents?"

"Ben would still be here. I know that. I'll be honest with you. Through the years, I met a lot of people who had worse situations than we did. It wasn't good growing up, but I know it could've been worse."

"You were the lucky one, always were. A purebred. You stood out, even in the shit we were in when you were little. Me, I've never been lucky. Some people are born with a dark cloud over their head, like you're cursed even before you're born. People like me, we're the dregs, black dogs in the sun, mutts tied up and chained in the heat. You can't escape from who you really are."

"If you believe that, then you're destined to stay down. No one is lucky. You fight your way out of your situation. When you went into foster care and I was with Aunt Carol, I knew she didn't really want me. I know it was better than where you ended up, but growing up in a place where you're a nuisance, that didn't feel good. I held on to Ben and that got me through."

"I know you don't want to hear this, but I can't see any way that Ben's alive. That FBI protection claim Phoenix swore was true, that sounded like bullshit to me. You really think if Ben had been alive all this time, he wouldn't have come back for you?"

"If he thought it would protect me, yes."

Julia watched the city pass by and the sun made its last appearance of the day as it slowly slipped down on the horizon; the signs for Rochester Hills appeared against the backdrop of its glorious orange-and-yellow brilliant finale.

Julia navigated Sarah to her address and felt uncomfortable when Sarah turned the car off in front of Julia's house. Helen's old Volvo was parked in the driveway, and Julia knew Logan and Will would be inside.

"Thanks for the ride and for sticking around back there. I can't invite you in. My kids are home."

A flicker of hurt passed across Sarah's eyes for a second, but then it was gone. "Sure. I'm no good with kids anyway. It's lucky I never had one. The kid and me, we'd both be miserable."

"I'll see you around, Sarah," Julia said. She reached across the seat and was surprised when at the last second, she found herself squeezing Sarah's hand.

Julia got out of the car and watched until the old Nissan pulled out of sight. She then headed into her house, where Helen, who was wearing bright red lipstick and had her hair pulled away from her face, was forming dough into bow tie shapes on a cookie sheet.

"You're always cooking," Julia said.

"Just cookies this time. It is late," Helen scolded. "You said you'd be home an hour ago. I wait to make dinner. But maybe the new officer who just got here would like to stay. By the time I feed everyone, it will be after ten."

"Don't worry about dinner. We'll just get takeout," Julia said. "You look really pretty. I don't think I've ever seen you wear makeup."

"It's nothing really," Helen said, brushing off the compliment. "The new police officer who just came, he's a very interesting man. He hasn't been over here for a shift before. We had a nice talk."

"You like him?" Julia asked.

"No, of course not. That would be a disrespect to my Alek. I just enjoyed our conversation."

"What happened to Scarborough?"

"He was here earlier, but had another call about a robbery and had to leave, but the new officer arrived right after Scarborough left. The police, they've been keeping a good eye on us. The new officer, his name is Kirk Fleming, and he used to live in South America. Such stories he had."

Julia felt a warning bell go off inside her.

"Where are Logan and Will?" Julia snapped.

"They're outside with Officer Fleming. They're playing baseball."

Julia ran out of the house and to the back deck. She felt a black fury move through her as she spotted her father with her boys.

Duke had his suit coat slung over the bottom rung of Logan's tree house, and he was throwing a baseball in Logan's direction. Will clapped his hands as Logan's bat connected with the ball and it sailed across the yard until it hit the fence.

Julia raced across the yard, scooped Will up in her

arms, and then positioned her body between Logan and Duke.

"What are you doing in my house?" Julia demanded.

"Hey, Mom, what are you doing? I just hit a home run," Logan said. "This is Officer Fleming. He's really nice."

"Go inside and take your brother with you," Julia said to her son.

"He was playing with us," Logan answered. "He didn't do anything wrong."

"Logan, go in the house. Now!" Julia said.

Logan gave his mother a stunned, hurt look, which pierced Julia's heart. Julia knew she had startled him with her harsh tone, but she couldn't help it. After all Duke had done to her as a child, she knew deep down to her primal core that Duke should be nowhere near her children. She quickly put Will down and then walked both boys to the rear deck to their safe passage inside and as far away from Duke as possible.

"I'm sorry. I didn't mean to sound harsh," Julia said to Logan.

But it was too late. Logan had already started to cry. Julia reached for his hand, but Logan pulled it away and ran inside the house, with Will following closely behind him.

"Logan," Julia called out, but her oldest son had already closed the door.

"He'll get over it. He just sees you being mean and controlling, but I know you were trying to protect him from me. I see you didn't get jammed up with the FBI. How did it go with Phoenix?" Duke asked.

"Don't you dare come near my children ever again. I want you gone, out of my house."

"Your boys, they're nice kids. Logan's got a hell of a swing. When I first got here, I'll tell you the truth, I felt like I was seeing a ghost. Your oldest boy's a dead ringer for Ben. I've got good-looking grandsons."

"They don't belong to you. You can't try and interject yourself into my life like this, not with my children."

Julia heard the back door open and looked up to see Helen waving her hand to get Julia's attention.

"A woman named Sarah is here to see you. She said you left something in her car she wants to return. I'm going into town with Will to pick up dinner at the Silver Spoon. Logan is in his room and won't come out."

Julia shot Duke a look. "I'm not through with you yet."

Julia left Duke, who was whistling casually and throwing the baseball up in the air, and walked through her house to the front door, where she saw Sarah standing on the property's edge, just inside the fence line.

"Are you going to let her in?" Helen called from behind. Will was standing at Helen's side as the two headed out to pick up dinner. Julia gave Will a kiss on his forehead and waited until Helen and her son got inside the Volvo. She then went to greet her sister after her family was safely out of earshot.

"You came back?" Julia asked Sarah. "What's going on?"

"Cute kid you got. I'm not trying to crash your party. I just stopped by to give you your phone. It must've fallen out of your pocket when you were in my car earlier."

"Thanks," Julia said. "Duke showed up here unannounced. But he's about to leave."

A blue Crown Victoria turned the corner and parked at the end of Julia's street. Julia squinted against the light to see Chief Linderman get out of the vehicle and walk in Julia's direction. Julia felt a strange feeling move through her, as her first instinct was to go warn her father that the police were here.

Linderman had a look of concern etched across his face as he looked at Julia and then turned to assess Sarah, the unknown commodity in the equation.

"Are you a friend of Julia's?" he asked.

"Something like that," Sarah answered.

"I need you to give Julia and me a minute. Can you go in the house?" Linderman asked.

"Go ahead," Julia told her sister. "It's okay."

Sarah shrugged her shoulders and went inside. As soon as she passed through the entryway, Linderman reached for the front door and closed it tightly, so he and Julia were alone on the front porch.

"The FBI is two minutes out. They know your dad is here. They're going to arrest him. I'm not here to help your father, but I've known you for a lot of years and I'm doing you a tremendous favor. Are your kids home?"

"Only Logan," Julia answered.

"Get him out. And do it quick. Have him go out back. I don't want your boy in the cross fire if things go bad," Linderman said. "I have to leave before Kenny gets here. I'll catch hell if the FBI knows I tipped you off. But Agent Kenny gave me his word that he wasn't going to arrest you, as long as he got Duke. Still, be smart. Now get your son out of here before it's too late."

Linderman returned to his car, and Julia didn't wait to see him drive away.

She ran into the house and sprinted down the hallway to Logan's room. She threw the door open and looked on at Logan, who was sitting cross-legged on his bed, with his baseball bat at his feet.

"Listen, baby, you need to get out of the house right now. I can't explain, but I need you to get out as fast as you can. Do you still sneak into the Davises' backyard by jumping from the big tree, where your tree house is?"

"No, I don't do that anymore," Logan said.

"It's okay. Just do it. I need you to run. Now! Stay at the Davises' house and don't come back until I tell you it's all right."

"I knew it," Logan said as his eyes grew wide. "I'll stay here and take care of you."

"Not a chance. Let's go."

Logan snatched up his baseball bat, and Julia grabbed his hand as the two raced to the backyard.

Duke watched their fast approach with an expression of caution and let Logan's baseball slip from his fingers.

"What's going on?" Duke asked.

"I'll tell you in a minute," Julia answered.

Julia waited until Logan skimmed up to the top of the tree with his baseball bat still firmly clutched in one hand. Once he reached the branch he needed, Logan lay flat on the log, with his arms and legs wrapped around it, and crawled along the length of the thick branch until he made it past the fence line. Julia watched her son drop from the branch and then let herself breathe again when she heard her boy land safely on the other side of the fence.

"What the hell is going on?" Duke asked.

"The FBI. They're coming for you," Julia said as she turned toward her father. "They know you're here, and they're a minute away."

Duke's eyes quickly scanned for the best escape route as Agent Kenny appeared on the rear deck from inside the house.

"Back away from me, Julia. As far away as you can," Duke said.

"I'm impressed, Duke. I figured you'd use your daughter as a shield. A guy who left his kids and family and didn't do enough to save his own son after he was kidnapped, I'd say you've changed," Kenny said.

Duke's right hand began to dart behind his back as Kenny pulled out his gun and trained it at Duke.

"You're not going to kill me," Duke said, and gave Kenny his broadest smile. "You'll never know where the painting is."

"The painting?" Kenny said, and laughed. "It'd be a darn shame if one of your kids got caught up in the cross fire. I can't guarantee it won't happen."

"Are you armed, Julia? See, we don't know that. If you think a person may have a gun, you need to subdue them," another male voice called out from behind the other side of her house.

"I'm not armed," Julia said. She raised her hands up above her head and turned toward the man's voice as Phoenix Pontiac turned the corner with a gun pointed at her.

"These situations, they can spiral out of control in seconds. You think someone's got a gun and they're about to reach for it, you've got to shoot first," Phoenix said. "What's it going to be, Duke?"

"You're not an informant. What are you? FBI?" Julia asked.

"I'm your very own man of a thousand faces," Phoenix said. "Which one did you like the best? The photographer? The poor kid who was held captive with your brother? The informant? You're not that smart, after all. I found your weakness and you were so easy to work."

"You get one more warning, Duke. Put the gun down on the ground and back away from it, or I can't guarantee what will happen to your daughter," Kenny said.

"Just do it, Dad," Julia said.

Duke, his smile intact, looked at Kenny and slowly put his gun down on the ground.

Kenny moved quickly to Duke's side, slammed Duke against the fence, and patted him down. Once he was finished, he handcuffed Duke and spun him around. "We have a lot to talk about, Mr. Gooden, or would you prefer me to call you Kirk Fleming?"

"I want a lawyer," Duke said. "I got information you need, but I won't say a word unless I have an attorney present. And my daughters had nothing to do with this. Julia didn't know I was here. I just showed up and she told me to leave. I picked up both my kids so Liam Mueller wouldn't get them."

"Liam Mueller is dead. He killed himself about two hours ago. He must've known we were closing in. We recovered twenty stolen paintings already from a secret stash he had hidden at his consignment store in Birmingham. But not as big as what you took, Duke," Kenny said.

Agent Kenny pushed Duke forward toward the side

of Julia's house in the direction of the street. As Duke passed Julia, he leaned into her and said, "Be smart, like I know you are. Just tell them the truth."

"Shut up," Kenny said.

"The sister, the friggin' one who cut me earlier, I found her in the house and she was packing. I got her weapon and stuck her in my car," Phoenix said.

"Good. Take Julia, too. Both of them. I've got Duke."

Phoenix moved to Julia's side and stuck his gun in her back. "Ready, sweetheart?" Phoenix asked.

"You played me. You'll pay for this," Julia said as Phoenix led her through the side gate of her property and to his car, a black Ford sedan, which was parked across the street from Julia's house, instead of his former Subaru.

"Don't worry. Your boyfriend will be waiting for you downtown," Kenny said. "We have a pit stop to make first, up north in Macomb."

Julia watched as Agent Kenny put Duke in the back of his unmarked car and then he approached Phoenix. "Put her in the car. We need to talk for a second," Kenny told Phoenix.

Phoenix unlocked his car and pushed Julia inside, where Sarah was waiting and looked on anxiously at her sister.

"What the hell is going on?" Sarah asked. "That Pontiac guy is an agent?"

"I don't know. Something's not right. A cop wouldn't threaten to accidentally shoot me to get Duke to drop his gun."

Julia felt her phone buzzing on silencer in her pocket and remembered how she had stuck the phone there when Sarah had returned it when she came back to the house.

Julia shot a glance over to Kenny and Phoenix, who were standing facing their cars near her front porch. Julia turned away from the two men so they couldn't see her face and pulled her phone out and put it on speaker.

"Julia, what the hell? Where are you?" Navarro asked.

"I can only talk for a minute. Agent Kenny and Phoenix Pontiac just arrested Duke. He showed up at my house. Sarah and I are being taken in for questioning."

"You're in trouble. I tried to reach Kenny and my calls kept going to his voice mail. I called the FBI station down on Michigan Avenue to see if he was there. I told the receptionist who I was, and I was transferred to Kenny's supervisor. His supervisor wouldn't tell me much, only that Kenny is on administrative leave pending an internal investigation because of possible misconduct charges. Whatever Kenny is doing, he's acting alone."

"Kenny's dirty," Julia said.

"You need to get out of there."

"I'm locked in the back of Phoenix's car right now with Sarah. Max Mueller used to have an old place up in Macomb County. It's in the middle of nowhere. That's where he ran his old human-trafficking business. You should be able to find it if you check tax or property records. I don't know if that's where they're going to take us, but I know we aren't going to FBI headquarters, and Kenny said something about going to Macomb."

"I'm downtown at the station. I'm calling the sheriff's."

"Call Linderman, too. He was just here."

"I've got to hang up now. I'm going to get you out of this."

"He's coming, Julia. Hide the phone!" Sarah warned.

Julia ended the call with Navarro just as the car door opened behind her.

Julia tried to hide the phone, but Phoenix was already there with his hands on her shoulders as he pulled her out of the car.

"Give me your friggin' phone," Phoenix said, and grabbed it out of Julia's hands.

"You didn't frisk her, you idiot?" Kenny asked.

"Doesn't matter. The Gooden family is about to be terminated," Phoenix said.

CHAPTER 26

The plastic ties that Phoenix had attached to her and Sarah dug into Julia's wrists as she sat in the back-seat of the car with her sister. Phoenix hooked a right onto I-94 North and followed Agent Kenny's car that was taking the lead. As they entered Macomb County, Julia realized her hunch was likely right that they would take the Gooden family to the late Max Mueller's remote property.

Phoenix's dark eyes stayed on Julia in the rearview mirror before they looked back toward the road.

"You played me where I was most vulnerable," Julia said. "You son of a bitch."

"What's the saying? The heart wants what it wants? Not in a romantic sense for you, but you were so desperate to know what happened to your brother. And the thought that he might be alive? You ate that up. Kenny didn't think you'd fall for it. But I convinced him you would. I know you, Julia, what makes you tick, how you operate, and the one thing that would make you drop your guard."

"I should've killed you back at that house when I had a chance," Sarah said.

"Shut up," Phoenix answered. "You're going to pay for cutting me."

"You never knew my brother," Julia said.

"No, no, no. Don't get ahead of yourself. You're missing one piece of the puzzle. I did know Ben. I met him when he was in Ahote's trailer. All that time in that shitty little place, Ben had nothing to do but talk. And all he did was talk about you, stories about your life. That kid, when he said something, you believed it. He told me he was going to get out. He was determined, you know? A kid that little who was so driven to make sure his sister was going to be okay, that was something. He cared more about getting back to you than making sure he was going to live. Someone who loves you that much, it makes sense why you'd go blind if you thought he was alive after all these years."

"How did you get my charm bracelet?" Julia asked.

"Ben knew Ahote was about ready to hunt him, so he gave it to me to hold on to. He said if he didn't make it, he wanted me to give it to you one day. I liked your brother. I really did. Tough little kid. I held on to the bracelet, kind of like my own personal good-luck charm. Truth be told, I didn't want to give it to you, but I realized it was probably the only thing that would make you believe my story, once you caught me in the lie about being a photographer."

"Who called me pretending to be Ben?" Julia asked.

"Wasn't me. I paid a guy to do it. Matt, he's got crazy talent. My buddy, he's an actor, or at least he was until his drug problem got out of hand. I met him in prison and looked him up for the job. I gave him the background about you and Ben, and you were just so wanting to believe it was true. Kenny and I figured your cop boyfriend would try and protect you in all this, but Duke, that was a surprise."

"Who's involved in this? Just you and Kenny?" Julia asked.

"You ask a lot of questions. But fine. We got some more time to kill. Kenny's the alpha dog in this pack, the new boss after Max died. There were four players at first—me, Kenny, Liam Mueller, and Louis Lemming out in St. Louis. Fifty million dollars is a lot of money, but Kenny and I didn't want to split it four ways."

"The notebook was van Gogh's personal journal."

"That's right. I don't care about that kind of stuff, but it's worth a fortune. But like I said, splitting the pot wasn't something Kenny or I wanted to do. Kenny and Ahote went after Liam. Max's kid was only going to get a cut because of his dad, but Liam killed himself before they got to him. Big daddy Max had promised Lemming a cut when he was still alive. Kenny told him the deal was off after Max died, but Lemming swore he'd rat out Kenny to the FBI, so we had to cut him in. But Lemming is out of the picture now. We hired a guy to take him out. He shot Lemming in the back of the head at one of his clubs in St. Louis about an hour ago."

"How do you know Kenny?" Julia asked.

"Through a relative. Anything else?"

"Go to hell. Did Ahote kill my brother?" Julia asked.

"Ah, Julia. Always such a hard edge on you. Ask me nicely, and maybe I'll tell you. You've come this far, right? Don't you want to know? Say 'please.' "

Julia looked out the window at the dark night and the road passing by them and could picture Ben in her mind's eye as if he had never left her side.

"I'm not going to beg you for anything. You wouldn't tell me the truth anyway. My brother, when I was a kid, he told me to always fight back against the bullies. You don't have anything over my brother and me. And you never will."

"Pride is a wonderful thing. Until it keeps you from what you really want."

Phoenix's eyes stayed on Julia again in the rearview mirror, but then darted away as he pulled his vehicle off the main road directly behind Kenny's car. Julia tried to take in her surroundings in the dark of night and saw the dirt kicking up under Phoenix's tires as they traveled several miles into a deep thicket of woods cut only by a narrow road.

Sarah leaned in toward Julia and whispered in her ear, "What are we going to do?"

"Hey, cut the shit. No talking," Phoenix said.

The two-car caravan went another mile on the desolate offshoot until it dead-ended at a clearing. A two-story white house, with its windows boarded up, sat to the right of the property, and to the left was an old brown trailer.

Julia felt a cool horror run through her as she realized this was likely the same place where Ben was taken.

Phoenix pulled up next to Agent Kenny's car between the two structures and killed the engine. "Don't move and keep your mouths shut," Phoenix said as he got out of the car and then secured the locks to ensure Julia and Sarah were trapped inside.

The door of the old trailer opened and Ahote came out. Phoenix extended his hand to Ahote, who, instead, grabbed the younger man in a big bear hug.

Phoenix had left the driver-side window open a crack, and Julia could hear the conversation play out between the two men.

"The deal is done. We got Duke and had to pick up his daughters to close the loop. I'll take care of them. You ready to get to work?" Phoenix asked, and winked at Ahote.

"Always. Where's Duke?" Ahote said. His gaze trailed over to Phoenix's car, and when he caught a glimpse of Julia sitting in the backseat, he seemed to lose interest over the man he had been entrusted to snare. Ahote made a slow, almost-zombielike approach over to Julia's window. He bent down so his face was next to the glass and stared into Julia's eyes without blinking and then mumbled something incoherent.

Julia heard a car door slam and looked over to see Agent Kenny exiting his vehicle. He looked irritated as he strode over to his security man and grabbed Ahote upright by his arm.

"What the hell are you doing?" Kenny asked. "Duke's in the backseat of my car. Take him inside. Don't screw it up like you did with Chip Haskell. Torture Duke, but keep him alive until he tells you where the notebook is. I mean it, Ahote. You kill him, I'll kill you. I haven't waited this long and come this close for there to be any mistakes."

Ahote followed Kenny's cue and pulled Duke roughly out of the agent's car. Duke shot a look at his daughters and gave them a bright smile, like everything was going to be all right, but Julia could see the fear in her father's eyes and she was surprised at the odd sense of loyalty she felt toward the man who had abandoned her and dragged her into this situation.

"Something doesn't feel right," Sarah said to Julia. "I got a sense about these things."

Julia let Sarah's words sink in as she looked back at the men. Agent Kenny led the way to the house, with Ahote and Duke behind him in a straight line, with Phoenix the last man in the row. When Kenny reached the front steps of the house, Ahote shot a quick look back to Phoenix, who reciprocated with a subtle nod, which prompted Ahote to cup his hand over Duke's mouth and move off the path.

Now steps away from the front door, Agent Kenny, still with his back to the men, waved a hand over his head like a warning.

"You're done, Duke. Your choice. Give up the location of the notebook and painting, and you die easy. Otherwise, my man, Ahote, here is going to make you beg for him to kill you. You've seen Ahote's work before. Is that how you want to go down?"

Kenny reached in his pocket for the keys to the house and began to open the door.

"Think about it, Duke. Fifty million dollars makes a man hungry enough to do anything," Kenny said.

As the front door slowly edged its way open, Kenny started to turn around. Julia could catch just a glimpse of the FBI agent's face from the headlights of Phoenix's car. The agent's eyes looked dark and mean, but he had a look of eager anticipation for the prize that was never so closely in sight.

Kenny's expression slipped to surprise as he quickly reached inside his jacket for his weapon. But, Phoenix was already there, now three steps away, with his gun drawn and pointed at the agent.

Julia heard a shot ring out from Phoenix's weapon and watched on as Agent Kenny crumpled to the ground. The agent struggled to get up, but only managed to turn on his side. Kenny tried to go for his gun, but Phoenix quickly reached into the agent's coat and removed the weapon from Kenny's holster.

"You bastard," Kenny gasped as he looked up at Phoenix.

"You were right. Fifty million dollars would make a man hungry enough to do anything," Phoenix said.

Julia scrambled to come up with an escape plan as Phoenix coolly bent down over the FBI agent, whispered something in his ear, and then fired his gun one more time into the agent's chest at close range.

"Oh shit. The game is changing," Sarah said to Julia.

Ahote stepped over Kenny's body, which was now strewn across the front entryway of the house, and pulled a struggling Duke inside with him.

Julia felt like a trapped animal as Phoenix came back to the car, with a huge smile on his face.

"Come on. Get out," Phoenix said. He opened the back door of the car and reached in for Julia, whom he grabbed and nearly flung to the ground as he pulled her out of the vehicle. He then locked an arm around Julia's waist and pointed his gun at the backseat for Sarah.

"Move," Phoenix said.

Sarah slid out of the car, and Ahote appeared from the front door of the main house.

"Don't tell me there's a problem already," Phoenix said.

"Not a problem. I'm just getting started with Duke," Ahote said. He then looked down at the ground sheepishly as if he were a little boy asking a favor. "I'd like to take care of Julia. I get Duke to tell me where the notebook is, you save her for me."

Phoenix shot Ahote a patient glance and smiled. "Whatever you want, Uncle. Just do your job and be quick about it."

"You two freaks are related?" Sarah asked.

"That's right. Blood is loyal, baby. We had a plan to take out Kenny from the beginning."

Ahote looked on proudly at his nephew. "Phoenix Pontiac is a brave warrior."

"He's a piece of shit," Sarah said.

"Find out where the notebook is, and you can have whatever you want, old man," Phoenix said.

Ahote moved in heavy, lumbering steps back toward the house, but then he stopped and turned around to look at Julia.

"Your brother, he was a worthy opponent," Ahote told Julia. "I wonder if you will be, too."

A rage built inside Julia at Ahote's mention of her brother's name. Julia began to lunge toward Ahote, but Phoenix pulled her back.

"What did you do to my brother?" Julia screamed.

Ahote looked back at Julia and pointed his index finger in her direction. "It is not what I did. It is what I didn't do."

Ahote then turned back around and continued up the path. Within seconds after Ahote shut the door, Julia heard Duke moan in agony as Ahote began his work.

"Come on, girls, let's go," Phoenix said as he pushed the sisters in front of him toward the old trailer.

Once inside, Julia felt Phoenix's hands shove her forward into the dim, narrow trailer, which had a hospital-like, antiseptic smell. She turned around to face Phoenix, but felt his leg sweep under her feet before she could catch herself. As Julia fell to the floor, Phoenix kicked her hard in the rib cage. She began to move back to the wall to get away from him, but Phoenix abruptly stopped his assault and laughed.

"Funny how you wound up right in that spot. Go ahead. See what your brother did," Phoenix said, and gestured with his gun to what at first appeared to Julia to be tiny dark scuff marks on the border between the floor and the wall. Julia looked more closely and ran her fingers over the words: *Ben Gooden was here.*

"Ben and I spent some time in this dump. Ahote stuck me in the trailer with your brother while he did work for Max. What I told you about my mom, that was true. She was crazy, just like Ahote, but she took drugs to make it stop. The courts took me away from her. I didn't wind up in foster care like I said, but Ahote took me in."

"I don't care about your personal story," Julia said.

"You're a reporter. You care about everyone's personal story, no matter what you say," Phoenix said. "You know, Ahote had a thing he did before he hunted. If he had the victim for a couple of days, he'd starve them so they'd be weak when it came time for the hunt. I felt sorry for your brother, I did. I brought him a candy bar every time my uncle locked me in here with him. You see, I'm not all bad. If you got to know me, you'd like me, just like your brother did. That's why he gave me your charm bracelet. I think if we'd met under different circumstances, you and I would've been friends. Or at least we would've had sex."

"You're disgusting," Julia said.

Julia, still with her hands tied behind her back, worked to get to her feet as she heard Duke's screams echo from the main house. Julia closed her eyes, praying that her father would be all right, when the screaming stopped and was replaced by an even worse silence.

"Jesus. Why is Dad quiet? Why is he quiet?" Sarah cried out.

The door of the trailer opened and Ahote appeared with a bright spatter of blood on both of his hands. "It's done," Ahote said; his smile was cruel and wanting as he looked at Julia.

"Duke told you where the notebook is?"

"Yes," Ahote answered. He leaned into his nephew and whispered in his ear.

"Nice job. Did you kill him?" Phoenix asked.

"He's got to be dead. I get Julia now," Ahote said.

"Sure, old man. Whatever you want," Phoenix answered. "Just be sure Duke is dead and you can have her."

Phoenix flipped his shoulder-length hair to the side of his face and smiled at his uncle as the older man left the trailer and began his short trek to ensure he had indeed snuffed out another man's life.

Phoenix stood silently in the trailer's open doorway and looked out at his uncle. When Ahote made it halfway up the path, Phoenix slunk his body down low, like a panther, and swiftly pursued Ahote. When he was just a few feet away from his uncle, Phoenix stood to his full height, pointed his gun at Ahote, and pulled the trigger.

Ahote lurched forward as the bullet embedded in his lower abdomen. Julia was sure he would fall, but the giant merely stopped in his tracks when the bullet hit him and doubled over for a moment before righting himself. He then turned toward his nephew with a look of surprise and hurt etched on his face. Ahote, with his dingy white T-shirt now turning red with blood, took a quick glance back at the trailer and his promised treasure of Julia, and began to run at Phoenix for all he was worth.

"Sorry, old man," Phoenix said. Ahote somehow stayed on his feet as the first two shots from Phoenix hit his body, but the third one to his chest crippled the giant, and Ahote fell to his knees.

Ahote looked up at Phoenix and his thick, dry lips parted. "Why?" Ahote asked.

"Sorry. I really am. But fifty million dollars, Jesus. You sure Duke is dead?"

"Has to be."

Phoenix bent down, patted his uncle's hand, and then tipped the barrel of his gun into Ahote's ear and fired.

Julia watched the gruesome scene play out and then turned to her sister. "We've got to get out of here. When he comes back in the trailer, I'm going to try and distract him, and I want you to run."

"Phoenix has got a gun, and right now, we don't. And even if I can get away, how are you going to fight him with your hands tied?"

"I'll figure it out. This is our only chance," Julia said.

Phoenix made his way back into the trailer and looked over his shoulder at his uncle. "It's a shame. I mean the guy was weird, but he was still blood. Now, here's how we're going to play. My uncle taught me to hunt. I'm an expert tracker. I know every inch of these woods, every tree, every smell, every type of animal that lives here."

He leaned into Julia and put his face next to hers. Before she could move away, Phoenix inhaled deeply. "And now I know your scent, just like Ahote taught me. Everyone has a distinct scent that can be tracked through the thousands of other smells in the woods, if you own it. And now I own yours. Don't worry. I don't do the bow-and-arrow shit like Ahote. That's too crazy for me. I just hunt with a gun. I picked you first because you're special to me, Julia. Are you ready?"

Julia gave the slightest motion with her head to cue Sarah to run as the sound of a bird cawed out a dark warning just outside the trailer. As Phoenix turned his head toward the noise, Julia used the only thing she had and kicked Phoenix as hard as she could in his thigh.

"Run!" Julia yelled to her sister as Phoenix fell back. But instead of heading out the door, Sarah ran directly toward Phoenix who had recovered and was closing the space between himself and Julia.

Phoenix quickly pivoted and swung his gun in Sarah's direction. A shot rang out in the confines of the small trailer, sounding like a deafening thunderclap in Julia's ears. She looked toward her sister as Sarah flew back against the wall, and a growing splotch of red quickly spread across her lower thigh.

"You bitch," Phoenix said, his eyes looking crazed with rage in the dim light.

Before he could fire off another shot, Julia called out a distraction to get him away from Sarah. "I'm the one you want. Not her. If you want to hunt, let's go."

Phoenix hesitated in front of Sarah, but then dropped his gun to his side.

"How bad does it hurt?" he asked Sarah, and smiled.

She sat with her knees bent on the floor and trembled as she looked down at her leg, but she didn't give Phoenix the satisfaction of an answer.

"I'm ready. Come on," Julia said.

"I like your spirit, Julia. I know you're a runner, so let's even out the odds. I'm going to take your shoes off. Running barefoot in the woods, not easy, especially with your hands tied behind your back. That's fair, don't you think?"

Julia nodded at Sarah, silently trying to let her know everything was going to be all right, as Phoenix removed Julia's sandals and then pushed her toward the door.

Out in the stillness of the country night, Julia looked up, hoping for a clear sky and the bright canvas of stars that would help light her way, but instead, a thick blanket of clouds hung in their path. Julia shook her head to try and get a buzzing mosquito away from her face and then panned the dense woods that encircled the house and the trailer to try and figure out her best route.

Phoenix locked the door of the trailer behind him and looked Julia up and down.

"I tailed you during a few of your runs. You were

good, and I enjoyed every minute of it. But I know these woods better than anyone, even Ahote. I'd normally give you a five-minute lead, but because it's you and I can't let you get too far ahead, you'll only get two minutes, unless I decide I've been too charitable. You ready, babe? On your mark. Get set. Go!"

Julia sprinted around the back of the trailer away from Phoenix's line of vision. Her usual effortless rhythm felt awkward at first, since her hands were tied behind her. Julia's legs found their usual routine and she quickly found her pace as she skirted in the direction she thought would double back toward the circle of trees that surrounded the main house and, hopefully, in the opposite direction Phoenix would think she was going.

The muggy air seemed to explode around Julia as she ran. She pounded forward to a destination unknown as she dodged through a maze of knee-high grass that coated the ground in between a dense nest of birch, red oak, and black gum trees that seemed to be closing in all around her.

Julia heard her breath coming fast and quick as her bare feet beat a path through the underbrush. She bit her lip to stop herself from crying out in pain when her foot caught something jagged that sliced through her right heel, and she continued on deeper into the woods. She stopped abruptly when she came to a clearing and stayed behind a giant fir tree to keep from being seen. The forest seemed to be swallowing her alive as she looked behind her, swearing she could hear the almost-inaudible footfalls of Phoenix's deadly approach.

Her eyes quickly darted back to the clearing and she started running in its direction when she heard an eerie, high-pitched cry of a bird above her. Julia stopped just as she was about to leave the cover of the tree and looked up at the bird, a kind that she had never seen before. It was large and brilliant in its crimson display, with wings that seemed to glint gloriously in the inky blackness of the woods. Julia held her breath as the bird hovered over her and then made a quick and low flight to the right.

Julia took one more look at the clearing, and then instinctively followed the bird as it seemed to float along the top of the tree line. A mournful wail of a coyote called out in the distance, and Julia picked up her pace as low-slung tree branches cut her skin as she passed. Julia looked up at the sky toward the bird and felt a strange ache of worry when she saw that it was gone.

"Keep going," Julia whispered, and began to sprint when she heard the sound of a car driving by just beyond the tree line in front of her. Julia's feet were torn up and raw, but she pushed herself harder at the promise of a road and her escape. She stopped short, though, when she saw a high fence, twice her height, six feet in the distance.

"No," Julia said as she slowed her approach. She looked to the top of the fence and saw sharp spikes of barbed wire lacing across the top. The hope Julia had felt seconds ago mocked her like a bitter tease. With her hands still tied behind her back, Julia knew there was no way she could ever get over the fence.

Julia began to run, realizing that keeping still wasn't an option, when a voice called out from behind her.

"It's amazing. You took the exact same path your brother did that led him to the road. Max put the fence up after that," Phoenix said as he appeared from behind a tree. "Don't feel bad about losing. You did great, but there's no way you could've gotten out. The fence wraps the entire way around the property. Get down on your knees, Julia. I won."

"No," Julia said.

Phoenix raised his gun so it was pointed at Julia's head.

"My game. I said get down on your knees. You die the way I want you to."

Julia heard the sound of something moving in the brush and started to run as Phoenix turned his head in the direction of the sound.

"It's over. Drop your weapon."

Julia looked toward the familiar voice as Chief Linderman appeared with his gun drawn and pointed at Phoenix.

"I'm not going to tell you twice," Linderman said.

"I don't think so. They're all dead except for me now. But I know," Phoenix said.

"You've been warned. Drop your weapon or I'll shoot," Linderman said.

"You'd love that, wouldn't you? Then all your problems would be over," Phoenix said.

"What's he talking about, Chief?" Julia asked.

"Phoenix Pontiac is a liar. Everything that he's said to you has been a lie. He wasn't abducted, like he told you."

"How did you know that he said that to me?" Julia asked. She looked back at the man she'd known for twelve years and something raw and slippery felt like it was crawling through her belly.

"Navarro told me. Julia, come stand behind me."

"I wouldn't if I were you," Phoenix said, and then looked to Linderman. "Tell her. Tell her how long you've known Max, you elitist dick. Tell her how you first met Max when you worked patrol and how I met you when I was a kid when you started coming around here to get your payoffs."

"That's a lie. Don't believe him, Julia. You know I'd never do anything like that."

Phoenix tossed his long hair and gave Julia a cruel smile. "Tell her what you did, Chief. She's been wanting to know all this time. Someone should put her out of her misery."

A shot rang out and Julia looked on as a bullet pierced through Phoenix's left eye. The man who had pretended to be many different people to her fell to the ground as a flash of heat lightning lit up the night sky.

A second shot stung the air, hitting Linderman in his gun hand. Linderman's weapon fell to the ground as Duke appeared from behind a tree and scooped up Linderman's weapon.

Julia felt an ache of relief as she ran to her father's side. She wanted to touch Duke, to make sure he was real, since she had been certain Ahote had killed him.

"You okay?" Duke asked. He gave Julia a quick assessment and then turned her around and removed the plastic ties binding her wrists.

"Yes," Julia said. "Did you hear?"

"Everything," Duke answered.

She looked at Linderman, a man she had sometimes disagreed with through the years when she worked the crime beat, but still a man she had always respected. "What did Phoenix mean? You worked for Max?"

"No, he's a liar," Linderman said as he clutched his wounded hand.

"Tell the truth. Tell the damn truth!" Duke yelled and kept his gun trained at Linderman.

The strong, familiar mask that Julia had always seen Linderman wear slipped as the police chief looked at Julia pleadingly.

"What did you do, Chief?" Julia asked.

"I'm a good man. You know that. I kept an eye on you when I knew Agent Kenny and Phoenix were going to come after you. That's why I came to your house to warn you they were coming for Duke. I didn't want your boys to get hurt. You have to understand. I was in a bad situation at the time when I first met Max. My son, the one I told you about, he had been in the hospital for so long. On a cop's salary, the medical bills were strangling us. Our house was about to go into foreclosure and my wife was under so much stress. She was going to leave me unless I could figure out a situation to get us out of our mess. I needed money. Everything was falling apart. I did it for my family."

"You worked for Max then," Julia said.

"I met Mueller when I worked patrol. He needed an in with the police department. Max was picking up illegals and runaways in the city in the area I patrolled and he needed a cover. So I gave it to him."

"He paid you off. Jesus, Linderman," Julia said. "You knew what he was doing, and how Ahote was killing those young men."

"I had no other choice."

Something Phoenix said to Linderman clicked in place for Julia.

"Stand behind me, Julia," Duke told his daughter as he seemed to sense her mood shift. But Julia held her ground and stood alone in front of Linderman, with both her hands balled into tight fists.

"You know what happened to my brother, don't you? Tell me. Goddamn it, tell me!" Julia said.

Linderman swallowed hard and shifted his eyes down at the ground. "I couldn't believe it the first day you walked into the station and I heard what your name was. Julia Gooden, the sister of the missing boy. The other cops, they didn't know your backstory, not even Navarro back then, but I did. When we were working your son's abduction case and we had to start looking at Ben's cold case, I thought about coming forward. I swear, I did, because I like you, and I knew my detectives were on the wrong trail, thinking the two cases were linked."

"Did Ahote kill my brother?" Julia asked.

Linderman looked back at Julia, and in the indistinct shadows of the night, Julia thought the police chief was about to cry.

"I held this secret for thirty years. A man does what he has to do to be sure his family is protected," Linderman answered.

"On your knees with your hands behind your head," Duke said. "You tell me what happened to my boy or I pull the trigger."

Linderman kept his eyes on Julia as he acquiesced to Duke's command.

"I had just picked up a payment from Max at his property here. It made me sick what he was doing. Just sick. I was driving home, and for some reason, I took the longer route. There were no other cars on the road and I was thinking about my own boy when this kid, he runs into the middle of the road. The boy, he was waving his hands at me to stop. So I did. The little boy, he was barefoot and terrified, but he had a presence about him, like he was a lot older than he actually was. I felt so sorry for the kid."

"The boy was Ben," Julia said.

"He told me his name and what happened to him at Max's place. When Ben got in the car, I promised him that everything was going to be all right, but then, I knew he would go to the police and tell them about what Mueller had done and the business he was running there. Max would have dragged me down with him. I was stuck."

Linderman looked down at the ground and away from Julia as if finally staring down his long-ago but never forgotten sin.

"Everything's all right, son. What's your name?" Linderman asked as the boy got inside his car.

"Ben, Ben Gooden. We need to go to the police! I was kidnapped by a big guy named Ahote. He was going to kill me. They've got a bunch of other people trapped inside a house there in the woods. There's a man named Max Mueller, who runs the whole thing. You've got to speed up. The people who took me, they're going to go after my sister Julia if they know I got out."

Linderman's hands froze on the steering wheel as he looked back at the little dark-haired boy who was still trying to catch his breath. His thoughts then moved on to his own boy and his wife, who had stopped talking about divorce after Linderman was able to get their house out of foreclosure and move their son to a better hospital because of the hush money Mueller was paying him.

Linderman began to turn the car around, back in the direction of Mueller's property, when Ben grabbed the patrol officer's arm.

"Hey, what are you doing?" Ben asked. "You can't go back there. You're not a good guy, are you?"

"No, son. I'm not."

Linderman reached across to snap the locks in place, but Ben's hand was already on the door and he pushed it open.

"Stop!" Linderman called out as he slammed on the brakes, but Ben had already leapt from the car and was running to the cover of the tree line.

Linderman jerked his car to a stop and jumped out. He reached for his gun and figured a warning shot would stop the child, who was about to disappear into the woods.

Linderman fired and began to run in the direction of Ben, but then he stopped when he saw the small boy fall.

"Oh God," Linderman cried out. He ran to the boy's side and watched as Ben, who had been struck by the bullet in his chest, stared up at the night sky as he struggled to breathe.

"Please. My sister is Julia Gooden," Ben panted as his eyes began to fill with tears. "Make sure she's okay."

"Hold on, son," Linderman said. He reached for the boy's hand, but it was too late.

Ben's labored breath stopped and his nine-year-old,

dark brown eyes stayed fixed and unblinking as if they were taking in the stars and the vastness of the universe. A single tear slid down the dead child's cheek and Linderman stood and looked up at the same sky, knowing that he had lost his soul forever.

Julia began to shudder as if she had fallen beneath the ice and was plummeting down into frigid black water.

Linderman, Duke, and the woods seemed to fade away as the weight of what happened to her brother began to settle in—a truth she had desperately sought to uncover for the past thirty years—but one so cruel, now that it was revealed, Julia wasn't sure she could ever accept it.

Julia closed her eyes and pictured her beloved Ben, her first and forever hero, who had devoted his entire young life trying to always protect her, just a little boy who knew nothing but hardship, neglect, and poverty, but somehow had seemed to still see the goodness in the world and fought to the end for his little sister.

Julia let out an anguished cry as she imagined Ben's final moments spent alone and terrified in the dark woods and prayed his last thought wasn't that he failed her by not being able to find a way back home.

Julia looked back with primal rage at Linderman, the man who had taken everything away from her. The silver metal of Duke's gun seemed to glint in the moonlight, and Julia fixated on the weapon, almost able to feel the weight of it in her hands as she imagined holding it against Linderman's temple and pulling the trigger.

"You're okay, Julia," Duke said. He clasped Julia with a firm and steady hand and pulled her to him.

"Let me go!" Julia cried. She began to hit her father with her fists, not wanting to be touched or comforted; but the harder she fought, the harder Duke held on.

"It's going to be okay. It might not seem like it right now, but you're going to come out of this all right," Duke said. "Now you know what happened, and that's how you're going to heal."

"Daddy," Julia cried. She fell into her father and buried her face against his chest as she allowed herself to weep.

"I got you. You're safe," Duke promised.

Julia stayed in the protection of her father's embrace for a minute, but then pulled away as a sense of duty about what she had to do next beckoned her forward to a place she now knew she had to go. She owed Ben that much.

"Give me your gun," Julia said. "I need to make it right."

"Are you sure?" Duke asked.

"Yes."

Duke looked uncertain but handed Julia the weapon. She held the gun between her hands and pointed it at Linderman's head.

"You killed my brother," Julia cried.

"It was an accident," Linderman said. "I didn't mean for it to happen."

"Even if it was, you were going to take him back to Max Mueller and Ahote, and they would've killed him."

"I didn't have any other choice. It was the worst

thing I've ever done in my life. I regret what happened every day, but I didn't have any other way out."

"There's always a way out," Julia said. Her hands shook as she held the gun inches away from the back of Linderman's head and willed herself to pull the trigger. "Where's my brother's body?"

"I buried him in the woods, near where we are. There's a willow tree right around the bend from here. He's there."

Julia felt a hand on her arm as Duke gently grabbed hold of her.

"This isn't you. Give me the gun. You kill Linderman, you're no better than he is. Ben was right about you all along. You're worth a whole lot. I know he wouldn't want you to do this."

Julia wept silently as she handed the gun back to her father and then stepped away from Linderman as Duke took her place.

"You killed my boy," Duke said. "Julia isn't a killer, but I am."

"Go ahead. I deserve it," Linderman said.

Duke looked at the police chief, prone on his knees, and nodded his head. "A guy like you, a lifetime cop, the big dog now, a secret gets out about what you did, something so terrible, and no one, not even your own wife or boy, would forgive you. If I kill you, you get off easy. You go to jail, that's the one hell you'd never want to face."

"Kill me," Linderman begged. "Please."

"No. You pay the consequences for what you did," Duke said.

"Drop your weapon!"

Julia spun around to see Navarro coming out from the trees, with his gun pointed at Duke.

"No, Ray. It's not what it looks like," Julia said. "Linderman was mixed up with Max Mueller. The chief killed Ben."

Navarro's eyes darted back and forth from Julia to his boss.

"I swear, it's true," Julia said.

"Chief, what's going on here?" Navarro asked.

"It's just a mix-up," Linderman said.

"Linderman confessed. He did. Duke and I both heard it," Julia said. "Linderman was getting kickbacks from Mueller when he was on patrol because he needed the money, and he was covering for Mueller in the department."

Navarro worked his jaw as he looked down at his boss of sixteen years. "Is that true? You're dirty?"

"I want a lawyer," Linderman said.

"Drop your weapon and back away," Navarro told Duke.

Navarro then got Linderman to his feet and handcuffed him.

"I looked up to you like a father," Navarro said to Linderman. "If it's true, you're a disgrace."

Navarro then looked to Julia. "I have to arrest your father."

"I know," Julia answered. "My sister, Phoenix shot her. She's locked up in a trailer at the main property. She needs help."

"We already got her. Russell is with her and the paramedics should've already arrived," Navarro said. "Let's go, Duke. Over here by Linderman."

Julia heard the chorus of sirens whir by her on the other side of the fence.

"Just give us a minute. My daughter is shaken up and I need to talk to her alone," Duke said.

Navarro disarmed Duke and shook his head. "You want to do that, Julia?"

"It's fine. Duke saved me."

"I've got my eye on you. Don't do anything stupid, Duke."

"You have my word."

Duke grabbed Julia's hand and walked a few feet away from Linderman and Navarro.

"I was sure Ahote killed you," Julia said to her father.

"Five more minutes with him, I probably would've been dead." Duke's right arm shot across his torso and he winced in pain.

"You okay?"

"I need a doctor. But I'll be all right. Take this," Duke said, and handed Julia a piece of paper.

"What's this?" Julia asked.

"You did good, Julia. You know what happened to Ben now. Don't let it consume you. Find your brother and take him home. Give him a real burial. Then you move on. That's what you're going to do. That's what Ben would want for you, to have a good life and to let it go. That's what you do now. You move forward, okay?"

Julia looked ahead in the direction where Linderman said he had buried Ben's body. She turned back to her father to ask him to go there with her, but Duke had already slipped back into the woods and out of sight.

CHAPTER 27

Julia looked at the bouquet of flowers she bought for Sarah in the hospital gift shop and felt awkward over the gesture. But Julia knew, deep down, that despite what Sarah had done to her in the past, she needed to at least try to give her sister a second chance, especially in light of Sarah unexpectedly having Julia's back over the last few days. As she walked down the hallway to Sarah's room, Julia realized her natural instinct was not to put herself in vulnerability's way, but she also knew she needed to keep moving forward, taking the advice from another unlikely ally, Duke. If Sarah was really trying to turn her life around, Julia knew opening the door a crack to her was the right thing to do.

Julia hesitated outside of Sarah's door and thought about the events of the previous evening, Duke slipping out of her and Navarro's sight, followed by Julia being detained at the police station until the wee hours of the morning to give her version of the events that unfolded at the late Max Mueller's Macomb County property. And finally, the most beautiful reprieve, when she had come home and stood over her two little boys, both asleep in Logan's room.

Julia told herself to buck up, that she needed to give Sarah a second chance, and entered her sister's room. Her sister was sitting alone, with her right leg bandaged and above the bedsheet, and she was staring out the window.

"How's the view?" Julia asked, realizing she was glad she brought along the flowers, because she didn't see any other get-well tokens, not even a single card, in Sarah's room.

"Can you believe it? There's a friggin' cemetery outside. What kind of lunatic builds a hospital right next to a cemetery? Anyway I appreciate you coming by. And you brought flowers. How about that? Not sure if you'll find a place to put them with all the others," Sarah said.

"How's the leg?" Julia asked, and put the bouquet on Sarah's side table.

"With some physical therapy, it should be okay. I've been cold turkey without a cigarette for twelve hours now. It's killing me. The doctor wanted to put me on pain meds, but I told him no. That shit gets into your system, you just want more. It's too much of a temptation, and I really want to try and stay clean this time."

"Good for you. That takes guts," Julia said. "Have you been watching the news?"

"Never if I don't have to. Why?"

"We found out what happened to Ben. The Detroit Chief of Police confessed to Ben's murder. The chief's name is John Linderman, and I've known him for a long time. Linderman was tangled up with the Muellers.

Ahote kidnapped Ben as payback for Duke taking off with the van Goghs, but Ben was able to get away. Ben flagged down a car, and it was Linderman who picked him up. Linderman killed Ben when he realized Ben would tell the police what happened."

"A cop killed Ben? Jesus, that's crazy. The poor kid. I guess the only good thing is at least you finally know. They got a body?"

"Yes. The police found Ben's body buried underneath a willow tree on Mueller's property. Linderman put him there."

"This Linderman guy told the cops this?"

"He confessed to Duke and me first before the police got there. Duke's alive. He made it out somehow."

"I know. He banged on the trailer door and told me he called the cops and help would be there soon."

"Duke called the cops?" Julia asked.

"That's what he said," Sarah answered. "So you and Duke were alone with the police chief and you didn't kill him when he told you what he did to Ben?"

"I thought about it," Julia said. She looked through Sarah and instead could picture herself holding Duke's gun between her hands, pointing it at Linderman's head and the temptation that ran through every cell of her body to pull the trigger.

"You're not a killer. It's better you didn't," Sarah said.

"I'm going to do a service for Ben. Something small. I want to lay him to rest. I can wait until you get out of here. I'd like you to be there."

"Of course. You and Ben were close, me and Ben weren't."

"It doesn't matter. You're his sister. I've been thinking about something. How come you didn't run out of the trailer like we talked about after I went after Phoenix?"

"Because he was a nut, and I was pretty sure he was going to shoot you. Did the police get him?"

"Phoenix is dead, they all are. I was thinking, maybe after you get out of here, we could grab a coffee or something. I mean, if you want to," Julia said. "If you're busy, it's okay."

Sarah's face softened and Julia realized her sister was truly beautiful when she let down her guard.

"Yeah, I'd like that. I'll pay this time, okay?" Sarah said.

A tapping sounded on the door and Julia turned to see Navarro.

"Helen told me you'd be here," Navarro said.

"Sarah, this is Ray Navarro. He's a Detroit cop."

Sarah raised one eyebrow at Julia and her usual hard mask returned.

Julia picked up on Sarah's vibe and moved to Navarro's side.

"I don't think Ray's here on official business. He's my friend. I've known him for a long time," Julia said. "We're seeing each other."

"My sister is dating a cop. How about that," Sarah said. "Well, at least he's good-looking."

"I've heard a lot about you," Navarro said to Sarah.

"I bet you have."

"Julia, you got a second?" Navarro asked.

"Sure," Julia answered, and turned to her sister. "I should get going. You need someone to pick you up when you get out of here? I don't think you're going to be driving anytime soon."

"That would be great," Sarah said. She waited a beat until Julia started to head out of the room and then called out to her sister. "Hey. Thanks. You coming here and everything else, that was something."

"Call me when you know you're going to get out," Julia said.

Julia left Sarah and then followed Navarro into the hallway and toward the elevators. When they reached the visitors lounge, Navarro turned around, and his expression looked tight.

"You hear from your dad?" Navarro asked.

"No. I swear. If I did, I would tell you. You think I helped him get away? Is that what this is about?"

"You tell me," he answered.

"I didn't know Duke was going to make a run for it. Come on, Navarro. You know me. I would never lie to you. I might screw up, and I'm sorry about leaving you at your house when I met Duke and Sarah. I knew if I told you about it, you would've convinced me not to go. I wasn't choosing sides. But if I had to, I'd pick you. Always. But I felt like for the first time, I was close to finally finding out what happened to my brother. And we did."

"I didn't want you to get hurt. I knew you were being set up, and Duke and your sister have done a lot of damage to you in the past. I don't trust them."

"I'm sorry."

Navarro shook his head and reached out for Julia's hands, taking them in both his own.

"You don't need to apologize. I understand why you did it. But next time, how about you rely on me, instead of relatives who've served time?" Navarro said.

Julia finally smiled. "That's a deal."

"So you're friends with your sister again? What's up with that?"

"I know how it must look. She's had my back, though, over the last few days. Phoenix was coming after me in the trailer, back at Mueller's place, and she stopped him. We're going to have coffee when she gets out of the hospital. Baby steps. So we'll see. Is there anything new on Linderman?"

"He's still in jail. I'm not sure what kind of bail the judge is going to set. He confessed to deleting part of the video footage of Ahote's van outside of Home Depot. He was also Kenny's liaison to the police department and you, since Linderman knew Kenny was on leave from the Bureau. Linderman's attorney is claiming his client was blackmailed by Kenny and his crew. I'm sure I don't need to tell you, but the media is going nuts with the story."

"I know. I've been getting calls all morning from the press. The only one I called back was my editor, Virginia. I did an interview with Tom, the political reporter. Virginia is champing at the bit to get me to write a personal column about what happened with Ben and my search for him all these years, leading up to Linderman."

"Are you going to do it?" Navarro asked.

"I might. It's not a story I necessarily want to keep bottled up inside me anymore. If I didn't tell you yet, I'm very glad to see you," Julia said. She wrapped her arms around Navarro and hugged him as hard as she could.

As Julia embraced Navarro, she felt something tucked inside the pocket of her jeans press against her thigh and remembered the piece of paper Duke had handed her in the woods.

"Hold on," Julia said. She pulled away from Navarro and fished out a folded piece of white-lined paper from her pocket and read the few words that Duke had written: *1680 Baker Rd., L. Left of the cornfield. Behind tractor. 77.9.37.4.*

"What's that?" Navarro asked.

"Duke gave me this right before he ran off. I'm not sure, but I think it could be the place where he hid the van Goghs."

Navarro ran the 1680 Baker Road address, and found sixty hits in the state of Michigan, but the one in the city of Leonard, which he and Julia realized the *L* stood for, was their jackpot, especially after Navarro discovered the now-deceased Chip Haskell owned the property.

Leonard was an hour north of Detroit and about thirty minutes from the hospital. Julia watched the suburbs and the big-box stores slip by as she looked out the passenger window of Navarro's Chevy Tahoe as the two drove to the clandestine address Duke had left for her.

"How are you doing about everything with your brother?" Navarro asked.

"We found him. And I'm going to bring him home."

"I know you were hoping he was still alive. This isn't meant to be a consolation, but now you know."

"That's what everyone keeps saying."

Julia looked down at her hands and thought about

Ben with his crooked smile and his devotion to her until he took his last breath, and she started to cry.

"He'll always be with me. I need to keep moving forward with my life. Ben would want that."

Navarro squeezed Julia's hand and then turned off the highway toward Leonard. The bucolic route took them through rural landscapes until they reached the Baker Road address. Navarro killed the engine, and the two did a quick assessment of the property, which consisted of a worn two-story white house, which was badly in need of a paint job, an old barn, and about ten acres of a dried-up cornfield that was infested with angry, cawing crows.

"Your dad hid something worth fifty million dollars here?" Navarro asked. "This place is a dump."

"I'm pretty sure this is the spot. Let's go."

Julia and Navarro exited the Tahoe, and the two wove through a littered array of rusted car parts and a faded John Deere grain harvester as they beat a path to the cornfield.

"Is this the tractor?" Navarro asked as he gave the green harvester a quick once-over.

"You are a city boy. Follow me," Julia said. She led the way, taking a left at the cornfield, like the note implied, and then stopped next to a large, rusted-out tractor with its hood open.

"This is the place. We're looking for something behind the tractor," Julia said.

"There's nothing here, but dirt and a field," Navarro answered.

"It's here. It's got to be."

"Fine. You check around the tractor, and I'll take the

field. Catch up with me if you don't find anything here, and we'll search the field together," Navarro said.

Julia watched Navarro make his way to the field and then got down on her hands and knees and began to sweep her hand across the dry, loose dirt and patches of gnarled grass behind the tractor. She worked for five minutes until her hand hit something smooth and a glint of silver poked through the dirt.

"I think I got something," Julia called out to Navarro.

She quickly brushed the rest of the dirt away from the area as Navarro jogged over to her side.

Julia used her forearm to remove the rest of the dirt, exposing a large, round metal hatch with a handle on top.

"Got it!" Julia cried out. She reached for the handle, but Navarro pushed her hand away.

"God knows what's under here. Let me go first," he said.

Navarro opened the hatch, and the two peered down to see a set of stairs that began at the mouth of the cinderlike hole.

"I'm going down. Don't follow until I tell you it's clear," Navarro said.

Julia waited for about a minute when she saw a light turn on at the base of the hole and Navarro waving at her. "Come on down, but be careful. This place, it looks like a doomsday bunker or something."

Julia made her way down through the cylinder until she reached the bottom rung of the stairs and found herself in a fairly large room. One wall was lined with a pantry filled with dried and canned goods and cases of bottled water. Along another wall, there were enough weapons lined up neatly in a gun rack to arm a small battalion.

Navarro whistled as he surveyed the place. "At least he's got a bed in here. Who the hell was this guy?"

"Someone my dad knew," Julia said.

Navarro began searching the pantry, and Julia flipped over the mattress of a double bed in the far side of the room.

"Nothing here. You have anything?" Julia asked.

"If you're hungry, I've got about twenty cans of Spam," Navarro said. "Haskell probably has a hidey-hole somewhere."

Navarro bent down and began to rap his fist against the floor as Julia's eyes hung on a large, cheap-looking oil painting of a hunter with a gun in one hand and his trusty dog beside him as the two pursued a duck mid-flight trying to escape.

"Why would someone decorate a bunker? Could you help me get this down?" Julia asked. "It's too high for me."

Navarro grabbed the picture and removed it, revealing a large metal safe built into the wall and carefully hidden away from sight.

"A picture behind a picture," Navarro said as he studied the safe. "Shit, there's a lock. We don't have a combination."

"Maybe we do," Julia said. She reached for the piece of paper Duke had given her, still in her pocket, and read off the numbers written there: *77.9.37.4.*

Navarro tapped his finger in a steady rhythm as he entered the code.

Julia heard a click as the door of the safe creaked

open and watched as Navarro carefully reached his hand inside and then pulled out an old leather-bound journal, which was cracked and weathered, an almost-150-year-old artifact finally coming to the surface after being hidden by Duke for three decades. Julia took the journal from Navarro's hands and opened the cover as gingerly as she could. She scanned the contents of the journal, which were written in what Julia assumed was Dutch.

"I wonder what he wrote," Julia said. "If this is van Gogh's thoughts before or during the time he went mad, it would be fascinating to find out what was going on in his head."

"The painting is gone," Navarro said as he finished inspecting the contents of the safe. "Duke must've taken the painting and left the notebook, because he probably figured it wasn't worth anything. I found something else in the safe. Looks like Duke left it for you."

Navarro handed Julia a white envelope with her name written across it. Julia tore it open to find a hand-written note from Duke and a ten-dollar bill.

Julia felt Navarro move in behind her as she began to read.

Julia,

I figured you'd be able to find this place. You were always a smart kid.

You brought Ben home. Be proud of that. I know your brother is proud of you.

Here's the ten bucks I owe you from lifting your birthday money when you were seven. One day, I'll pay you interest on the loan.

Have a good life, kid. The cop you're seeing doesn't seem half bad, for a cop anyway. If he makes you happy, that's good.

I'll be keeping an eye on you.

Duke

"Your father is an interesting man. But if he shows up again, I'm sending his ass to jail," Navarro said.

"I realize that," Julia said. "You break the law, you pay the consequences."

"Come on, beautiful. We have a notebook to deliver to the Feds."

Two days after the stolen van Gogh journal was returned to the FBI's art crime division, Julia stood in Logan's room, adjusting the knot of a red tie around her older son's neck as Will, dressed in a dark blue suit, sat on his brother's bed and pumped his little feet back and forth against the footboard.

"You don't have to wear the tie, if you don't want to," Julia said. "But you look very handsome."

"It's okay," Logan answered. "I know you want me to look nice."

"There's something I need to say. I want to apologize."

"For what? You didn't do anything."

"Yes, I did. More than anything, I want you and Will to feel safe. I know you've been worried lately, and I didn't mean to put you in a bad situation. You're safe now. I promise. And I'll do everything in my power to always keep you and Will that way."

"I wish you would've let me stay with you instead

of making me jump over that stupid tree to the neighbors' house. I would've protected you."

"I know you would have. But right now, it's my job to look after you and your brother, not the other way around. I was thinking after my brother's service, the three of us could take a little trip."

"Are you going to invite Uncle Ray?" Logan asked.

"I wasn't planning on it," Julia said.

"It's okay if you do. You're dating him, right?"

Julia looked back at her son and tried not to let him know how caught off guard his spot-on deduction had made her.

"Why do you think that?" Julia asked.

"I can tell you like each other. He looks at you just like Dad did a long time ago, before things got weird between you guys."

"How would you feel if I was seeing Detective Navarro?" Julia asked.

Julia watched as her little boy cast a glimpse at a framed picture on his nightstand. The photo was a picture of Logan and David on the beach taken two years earlier, before their family began to unravel.

"It would be okay. He's nice to me and Will. You seem really happy when he's around," Logan said.

"You're right. I have started seeing Ray. And I like him very much. But no one is ever going to replace your dad to you," Julia said, and immediately felt lighter when the words came out, instead of hiding their relationship from her children any longer.

"It's probably good there's a cop around, because stuff always seems to keep happening. But I'll still take care of everybody."

"Of course you will. You're a brave boy," Julia said.

Will leapt off the bed, not to be outdone, and dashed down the hallway, returning thirty seconds later brandishing his Captain America shield.

"I have two brave boys."

Will darted around the room, battling imaginary enemies, while Julia sat down on the bed and Logan took a seat beside her.

"Your brother, he died when he was nine?" Logan asked.

"That's right."

"So he was about my age. Kids shouldn't die."

"No, they shouldn't."

Julia looked back at her oldest son, who struck a remarkable resemblance to her brother, and felt a bittersweet pain in her chest. Julia reached for Logan's hand and recalled how, growing up, Ben had seemed more like an adult to her. But now an adult herself, and knowing the truth about his death, Julia knew Ben was just a little boy when he died, scared and running alone in the woods, using his smarts to escape when grownups failed to protect him. When the always-scrappy little boy, who fought for everything with all his might, thought he found a way home to his sister, he wound up hitching a ride with a seemingly Good Samaritan, who was really the Devil and took Ben's life to hide his sins from coming to light.

"Are you all right?" Logan asked.

Julia let her guard down and let herself cry in front of her children, something she had never done before.

"I'm just feeling sad. I miss my brother. But I'm so lucky that I have you both. I know Ben would've loved you two very much."

A knock sounded at the door as Helen, who was

dressed in a prim, black jacket and long, black skirt, and with her hair wound up in a bun on top of her head, announced her arrival.

"Mr. Raymond is here," Helen said, and then gave Julia's outfit a once-over. "Your skirt is black, but your shirt is red. You wear red to a funeral?"

"It was Ben's favorite color."

Helen nodded at Julia as Navarro appeared behind her, no longer in his usual attire of jeans, short-sleeved T-shirts, and motorcycle boots. Instead, Navarro looked strikingly handsome to Julia in a black suit, a white shirt, and red tie.

"Everyone with the red. Hold on," Helen said. "I'll be right back."

"How are you doing, Julia?" Navarro asked.

"It's time to do this. I'm ready," Julia answered.

"I hear you're dating my mom," Logan said.

Navarro shot Julia a look and then turned his attention fully to Logan.

"We need to make sure she feels okay today," Logan answered.

"Absolutely," Navarro said.

Julia swallowed hard and grabbed Logan and Will's hands and headed to the front door, where Helen was waiting for them with a red scarf now tied around her neck.

"My mother would be appalled if she knew I wore red to a funeral. But for your brother, Miss Julia, I will make the sacrifice," Helen said.

"How about I drive?" Navarro asked Julia. "Everyone can fit in my car. Funerals are never easy. Driving is one less thing you'll have to worry about."

Julia nodded her agreement, and she and Helen got

the car seats from her SUV and put them in Navarro's Tahoe. Logan, Will, and Helen fit into the backseat, and Julia sat in the passenger seat in the front, turning the charm bracelet, over and over, in her hand.

The cemetery was just five miles from Julia's house, and when they arrived, a small crowd had already gathered. Julia wanted to keep the service intimate and was relieved when she saw the handful of familiar faces as they stood near the seats. Julia wanted the service to be held outside, instead of in the confines of a church, and had asked a Baptist source on her beat, Pastor Darren Johnson, to say a few words before Ben was finally laid to rest.

Julia spotted Russell first. He was walking next to Sarah, who was trying to navigate to a seat in the second row of chairs on her crutches. Julia then shook her head and smiled when she saw Tyce Jones sitting in the back row with a wall of gaudy red flowers he brought to pay respects to her brother, sitting next to his wheelchair.

Julia kept a tight hold of her boys' hands as the three found their places in the front row. As soon as Julia sat down, she turned around to Sarah, Helen, and Navarro, who had found seats in the second row directly behind her.

"You all belong up here with us," Julia said.

As her family and the people she loved most gathered around her, Julia looked on at the small casket that carried the bones of a boy who once ran down the boardwalk in front of her, constantly looking back over his shoulder to be sure Julia was still following behind him, her forever protector, who paid the ultimate price for the careless mistakes and cavalier dreams of their father.

But Julia didn't want to blame Duke anymore. She wanted to be free, and she knew holding on to that anger over her father's foolishness would chip away at her soul and the best parts of herself that Ben had created inside her.

As Pastor Johnson began speaking, Julia closed her eyes and remembered her brother's words. They sounded so real in her head, she felt if she opened her eyes, Ben would be right in front of her, still and forever nine years old.

("One day when I'm older, I'm going to be mayor of this town. And we'll be able to go anywhere we want, whenever we feel like it. The bad stuff that we're going through now, it's going to be just like a dream when we look back on it. You'll see. You and me, we're going to make it out okay.")

Julia opened her eyes and took in her little boys sitting beside her, sitting up proud and strong, and staring straight ahead at her brother's casket. She felt a mixture of sorrow and joy, a lugubrious beauty of pain and hope, combined with an appreciation of all that she had and all that she had lost.

Navarro reached for her hand, and Julia squeezed his tightly, knowing she had a circle of people around her that would never let her break.

She looked up at the sky and thought about how life could be incredibly cruel. But if you were lucky enough, if you had people who would love you and never let go, then maybe that alone would be enough to take away the darkness that would undoubtedly come, and the love that you share in this life would somehow make everything all right.

Julia ached for her brother, but she was sure of one thing. No matter what happened, no matter the ugliness or another man's greed, deceit, or sin, the good always had to win.

And it must triumph. Ben had taught her that.

Julia stood up as Ben's casket was ready to be placed in the earth. With her family and loved ones all gathered around her, Julia knew that she had finally done one thing, a good thing, that was important.

She had brought Ben home.

In this gritty, riveting new novel, Detroit reporter Julia Gooden tracks down a serial killer—only to realize she has become his obsession . . .

Crime writer Julia Gooden has just completed the most important story of her life—a book about her beloved brother's childhood abduction and how she found his killer after thirty years. But that hasn't taken her focus off her day job—especially with what looks to be a serial killer terrorizing the city. Female runners are being snatched off jogging trails then slaughtered in abandoned churches.

As Julia begins investigating with help from Detective Raymond Navarro, she realizes just how personal this case has become. The murders, planned and executed with uncanny precision, are of women who share traits with Julia. Now the murderer is contacting her directly, insisting things will get much worse unless Julia makes him famous through her writing.

But no matter how skillfully she plays along, her opponent's ultimate goal is clear. And only by unraveling the threads that link a killer's twisted mind to her own dark past can Julia prevent herself from becoming his final victim . . .

Please turn the page for an exciting sneak peek of Jane Haseldine's next Julia Gooden mystery

YOU FIT THE PATTERN

Coming soon wherever print and e-books are sold!

CHAPTER 1

Heather Burns coiled her perfectly highlighted blond hair into a tight bun and frowned as she gave her face a brutal inspection in the mirror of her parked yellow Range Rover.

Dissatisfied with her appearance, Heather pulled the skin back from the corners of her jawline and took in the wistful reminder of what she used to look like when age meant nothing because the onset of its ravages hadn't yet struck.

God, getting older really was the ultimate bitch, the thirty-nine-year-old thought, and scanned the empty parking lot of Mayberry State Park in Northville, a suburb of Detroit, where she and her teenage daughter, Carly, lived.

Heather gave up on her face momentarily and spun around to the backseat to make sure she remembered the four FIND YOUR NEW HOME HERE! signs dotted with cheerful red-house emojis for her nine AM open house, her day's next order of business after her early-morning run. Satisfied when she spotted the signs poking out from underneath her briefcase, Heather took to the rear-view mirror to resume her search for any new wrinkles.

She needed new headshots for her latest batch of business cards and beat her French-manicured finger-nails against the dashboard as she fretted over the stone-cold fact that a pretty face sold more houses and raked in bigger commissions. She had learned early on that looking good was a job requirement for a successful Realtor. And Heather had already bore catty witness to a younger crop of thinner and blonder girls already jockeying at her RE/MAX office for a chance to snag her clients.

Heather dug her hand deep inside her bag and re-trieved a business card her friend had given her over drinks at a downtown Detroit bar during a recent girls' night out. Heather studied the phone number on the card and recalled how her friend swore to her with the enthusiasm of an infomercial host that if Heather just made an appointment, she'd feel so much better about herself. Presto chango, renewed self-esteem courtesy of a couple syringes of Botox and assorted fillers stuck in her face.

Heather tossed the card back in her bag and decided she'd stick with her crow's-feet. At least for now.

The sharp bite of the early-October Michigan morn-ing hit Heather as she exited the Range Rover and she began to shiver. Heather worked through her usual se-ries of stretches and felt a renewed pang of guilt for giving Carly a new phone. Her daughter had ultimately worn her down, complaining about the sheer humilia-tion of being the only person in her group that had a flip phone. Carly had hammered home the injustice that even elementary-school kids had iPhones, and there she was, a ninth grader, forced to use a relic.

Carly was a good girl, a straight-A student, and a solid athlete who excelled on her county-rec baseball and soccer league teams, despite the grenade Heather's dad had thrown into their lives after he walked out on his family to take up with a pharmaceutical sales rep he met at his physician's practice. After her ex had bailed on his latest weekend with Carly, Heather had caved on the phone as some sort of half-baked consolation prize to make her daughter feel better.

She was sure her good girl would never abuse the privilege of the phone. But three weeks later, Heather soon learned that phones with cameras, where images could be quickly snapped and texted to boys or girls who fluidly changed their allegiance of friendship in a teenage hormonal nanosecond, were dangerous toys, not modern-day commodities for kids to communicate.

One stupid slip of judgment and the selfie of Carly in her underwear had spread like wildfire around the school. But Heather would make it right. She hated confrontation and usually choked under pressure, her voice melting into a quaking stutter when she had to face down a hostile encounter. But this was for her little girl, so Heather had made an appointment to talk to the principal after the open house.

Moms would go to any length for their kids.

A cool gust of wind sent the fall leaves scattering like a swirl of bright copper pennies across the ground. Heather ignored her chattering teeth and took a quick glance at her watch: 6:00 AM. Her Range Rover was still the only car in the parking lot. But Heather wasn't worried about running alone. The park was an old friend, one that she had discovered during her sophomore year of high school when she first ran track. A sad smile played on her lips as she recalled the state record she set senior year for the eight-hundred-meter race, a crowning residual jewel she sometimes pulled out as a reminder of a time when she believed the world was brimming with endless possibilities just waiting for her with a beckoning hand.

Glory days, baby.

Heather's feet found their pace as she started her run. She completed her first loop around the lake, the one-mile mark of her four-mile run, and pushed herself faster and harder for her second round.

Running for Heather was like meditation. Her mind was usually clear of any worries or regrets when she ran, and the sound of her sneakers slapping against the pavement was a soothing white noise, a temporary respite from memories of her last date with her ex-husband who announced over a plate of shared pasta puttanesca that he wanted a divorce.

She discovered later that his new lady was at the restaurant waiting for him, watching the scene unfold from a seat at the bar.

Heather felt the tears come, but she forced herself not to cry. She was fine. Just fine.

The sun crested its way up to the top of the tree line and Heather checked her watch again: 6:45. Time to head home for a quick shower and to make Carly lunch before she went to school. Heather slowed her pace to a fast walk and made her way back to the empty parking lot, where she spotted another vehicle cutting around the corner, breaking her solitude.

As the car got closer, Heather could see that it was an older-model tan Buick driven by a gray-haired woman, who gave Heather a quick, friendly wave with a mittened hand as she passed. The Buick stopped at the other end of the park by the duck pond, where Heather frequently saw a group of people from the senior center do tai chi.

Heather did her usual routine and headed to the public restroom before she left the park. She always downed a large bottle of water before she ran, so the women's room was her final stop before her twenty-minute car ride home.

The door to the women's room creaked as she opened it. Heather hurried inside, grabbed a handful of brown paper towels from a dispenser near the sink so she wouldn't have to touch the icky bathroom door handle, and entered the stall closest to the door.

Heather began to come up with her strategy on how she could steady her nerves during her meeting with Carly's principal, when the bathroom door opened, the rough *screak, screak, screak* of its hinges sounding like a rusty nail being dragged across the floor.

Plodding footsteps thumped past Heather and then a stall door banged shut on the far side of the room.

Heather flushed the toilet with the toe of her sneaker and approached the sink. She did a quick look in the mirror and saw the reflection of someone's feet planted underneath a stall. The wearer had on a set of black orthopedic shoes and tan pantyhose that poked out from the elastic bottom of a pair of gray sweatpants, the outfit likely belonging to the older lady in the Buick, Heather figured.

Heather finished washing her hands and decided to slip a note in Carly's lunch box before she left for work, letting her daughter know she loved her and that everything was going to be all right. Something along the lines of, "I know this all seems terrible now, but it will be okay. I promise."

"Oh no," a woman's voice creaked. Heather turned to see a roll of toilet paper drop onto the floor from inside the occupied stall and then make a slow crawl in her direction, the tissue unwinding in a wide strip until it abruptly stopped and landed on its side next to the garbage can.

Heather started to move to the door, thinking she had to hurry if she was going to get Carly to school on time, but stopped when she realized she needed to do the right thing.

"Are you okay?" Heather asked.

"Just old age," the woman answered with a dry laugh. "I have arthritis and my hands don't work as well as they used to. Can you hand me the roll if it's not a bother?"

"Sure," Heather said. Something in the woman's voice niggled in the back of Heather's head, but she quickly moved on to the upcoming open house, hoping to God she'd get some actual prospects instead of the neighborhood looky-loos who usually showed up.

She carefully picked up the toilet paper, thinking how gross the outer layer was, since it rolled its way across God knows what was teeming on the gray cement floor. She wound a few loops of tissue off until the spots of wetness and dirt were gone and then shoved the wad of soiled tissue into the garbage.

"Here you go," Heather said. She bent down and reached her hand up under the woman's stall.

"Thanks so much, Miss Burns."

The thin chime of a warning bell went off inside Heather over the sound of her name being spoken so intimately by the stranger.

Heather tried to quickly retract her arm from under the stall door, but the vise grip of an unseen hand latched itself around her wrist.

"Hey! What is this?" Heather cried out. "Let go!"

The lady was senile, she had to be, Heather reasoned as she fought to keep her balance from her crouched position and free her hand, figuring the old woman inside the stall would be no match for her. Heather reared backward to try and break away, but her arm was pulled forward with such force, Heather was sure it would rip out of the socket.

"Help! Please! Somebody help me!"

Heather felt a second hand wrap around her forearm and she pitched forward, slamming her face into the gray stall door.

A sharp pain pulsed like a jackhammer from her nose as Heather's thoughts screamed out to her, *Don't give up, can't give up!* She started to cry and wondered how this old woman could be so strong.

"Please, I have money in my car. And my credit cards. You can have them. Just let me go."

An unexpected surge of hope spread through Heather as her attacker released their grip and Heather's arm slipped free.

This was her chance. She knew she needed to run,

to get out of the confined space as fast as she could. But Heather Burns, the queen of choking under pressure, kept her title and froze in place as the stall door banged open.

Her attacker ran a large hand across their mouth, leaving a smeared trail of bright pink lipstick down their chin. Heather slowly crabbed her body toward the door and spotted the tendrils of a gray wig spilling out from a small trash can in the back of the stall.

Two minutes too late, Heather realized she made a critical mistake by ignoring the off-sound of the woman's voice as a tall, well-built man with sandy-blond, short-cropped hair and a smile so wide, it almost split his face, exited the stall and loomed over her.

"Don't fight," the man said. "It's going to be much easier if you just give up."

"Please, I'll give you my money. You can have everything. I swear."

"I don't want money," the man said. He pulled out a folding knife from underneath a bulky dark blue sweatshirt and snapped open its six-inch blade. "On your stomach. Now."

Heather felt a sickly panic move through her as she stared at the weapon, which had a green-fatigue, military-like handle and a black blade with an inch of serrated teeth by its base.

The man was going to rape her. She was sure of it. She closed her eyes and wondered if it would be better if he just killed her instead.

"On your stomach, I said."

Heather thought of her daughter, who would be waking up for school about now and wondering where her mother was. She mustered a reticent nod, knowing she needed to do anything to get back home, and flipped over on her stomach in a prone position.

She shook as she waited for the man to pull off her running shorts. But he reached for her hands instead, roughly pulling them behind her back and then binding her wrists together with something that felt to Heather like hard plastic that bit into her skin.

"Let's go," the man said, and pulled her up. "We're going to take a ride."

Heather had stopped trying to find the emergency release latch in the trunk of the Buick, where the man had stuffed her. After realizing the car was an older model and didn't have a release pull, she had resorted to pounding her feet against the top of the trunk in a futile effort to get it open.

During the beginning of what Heather thought was so far a thirty-minute ride, she could hear what she decided was city traffic. But for the past ten minutes, the honks and revved engines of aggressive Detroit commuters had ebbed and all Heather heard now was the Buick's wheels humming underneath her as she sat, crammed in a fetal position in complete blackness.

The Buick came to a sharp stop and Heather tried to scramble to come up with a flight plan. She cursed herself for not leaving Carly a note to tell her where she was jogging, so her daughter could call the police with a location when Heather didn't come home.

Daylight flooded the Buick as the trunk swung open, and Heather squinted to see her attacker looming over her.

"If you try to run, I'll kill you," her abductor said, and flashed his ugly black and camouflage-green knife from the pocket of his sweatshirt, as if Heather really needed a reminder.

Heather could smell the sour musk of the man's sweat not quite masked under his cologne when he pulled her out of the trunk. He wrapped his arm around her waist, and Heather felt the dampness of his sweatshirt on her back.

Heather took a quick mental snapshot of her unfamiliar surroundings to come up with an escape route if she could get away. The Buick was parked on a desolate side street next to an old brick church that looked like it was about to crumble. A sliver of the remote Detroit skyline was visible from the side of the church, which meant the man had likely driven them to one of the city's run-down, left-for-dead neighborhoods that skirted Detroit. What that meant to Heather was, the likelihood of anyone stumbling by to help her was going to be as likely as her winning the lottery or getting crowned Miss America.

"Move," the man whispered in her ear.

In lockstep, the two entered the abandoned church. The depressing, cavernous space was littered with a few ruined leftovers of the church's likely golden era when parishioners filled its now-gutted pews. A splintered, keyless organ lay hangdog on its side in the middle of the aisle, and what was left of a broken stained-glass image of Jesus on the cross framed the rear wall of the church.

Heather shivered when she reached the end of the aisle, where someone had tagged *I love weed* in black graffiti letters, and she turned slowly around. She did a quick mental picture of the man's face so she could describe him to the cops if she was able to get free, and was struck by the odd realization that the man who abducted her was good-looking.

"Please. I have a daughter."

"No, you don't. You have two sons."

"You're wrong! This is some kind of mistake."

"No mistake. But you're not right yet. I need to fix you."

The man pulled out his knife, reached behind Heather, and sliced apart the twist ties. He then dug into a green-fatigue duffel bag and pulled out a long, dark wig and a piece of blue clothing.

"Put these on."

"Jesus, what is this?" Heather cried.

The man looked through Heather as if she weren't there. "I'll dress you."

Heather screamed and her voice echoed through the lonely belly of the church, a haunted cry to no one, as the man carefully arranged the dark wig over her blond hair. He took his time and teased out a few long strands so they cascaded down to the tops of her breasts.

"Better. But still not right. Put the dress on."

"Will you let me go if I do?"

The man continued to look through Heather and slid his tongue over his lips.

Heather grabbed the dress from his hands. She'd play along. He had to be a freak is all. If she just did what she was told, maybe he'd let her go. If he was going to kill her, he would've done it by now, Heather convinced herself. She looked at the piece of clothing she was supposed to wear. It was a bright blue dress, which was sleeveless, with a scooped neck, a fitted high waist, and an A-line skirt.

"Take off your shorts and shirt. It needs to be perfect," the man said. He turned around as if to give Heather privacy so he wouldn't see her in her underwear.

"Don't look," Heather said. She undressed and then pulled the garment over her head. "Okay. It's on."

The man cocked his head to the side as he took in his creation. He rearranged a few locks of the long, dark wig so they framed Heather's face, and, seemingly pleased with himself, smiled.

"Size two. It fits you perfectly, just like I knew it would."

"You've been watching me?"

"I've seen you running. You fit the dress, just like I thought."

Heather shivered and tried to move backward and away from the man, but fumbled and tripped on a step that led up to the altar.

"She would've never done that," the man said. "Don't ruin it."

"Who are you talking about? I don't understand."

The man grabbed Heather by the waist and drew her against his chest. Unable to hold it together anymore, Heather sobbed as her attacker began to sway with her in his arms.

"'Hold me close and hold me fast . . . The magic spell you cast . . .'"

The man sang softly and tenderly in her ear. His voice hung on the last word, triggering a memory for Heather, something long ago and familiar. She worked it through her head, and caught an image of her eight-year-old self rummaging through the contents of her family's garage and discovering her mother's old jazz albums.

The name of the song and singer was on the tip of her memory when her attacker spun her around and then slit her throat in a single fast, deep cut.

Heather's hand shot up to her neck in surprise. She tried to stop the bleeding, but there was so much of it and the laser-sharp pain was such that she had never felt before.

A strange wheeze came from her throat, like a child blowing a whistle, and she collapsed in front of the altar. She stared up at the splintered image of Jesus in the stained glass and was no longer able to fight off the truth.

She was dying.

Something warm and wet trickled from Heather's mouth. She pictured Carly from a long-ago memory when her daughter was just two, her Carly laughing as her plump little legs poked out of a striped onesie, her little girl racing down the hallway of their house, with Heather trying to keep up from behind.

She tried to hang on to the image and block out the horror around her, but was still vaguely aware of her killer, huddled on the floor over a piece of paper, drawing while he hummed.

The man stood above her now, smiling and holding up the picture he had drawn, strange and intricate symbols in turquoise and red.

"Do you like it?" he asked, and beamed like he was showing her his masterpiece.

He then lifted up Heather's left hand, slipped something inside it, and folded her fingers closed against her palm.

Heather struggled to take her last breaths as the man brushed his lips against her ear.

"We are one and the same, my Julia," he whispered. "For now, write everything for me. Every single little detail."